ALEX OCKENDEN

All The Gods Are Dead

Book 1 in the Daughters Of Mercury Series

First published by Alex Ockenden 2025

Copyright © 2025 by Alex Ockenden

All rights reserved. No part of this publication may be reproduced, stored or transmitted in any form or by any means, electronic, mechanical, photocopying, recording, scanning, or otherwise without written permission from the publisher. It is illegal to copy this book, post it to a website, or distribute it by any other means without permission.

This novel is entirely a work of fiction. The names, characters and incidents portrayed in it are the work of the author's imagination. Any resemblance to actual persons, living or dead, events or localities is entirely coincidental.

Alex Ockenden asserts the moral right to be identified as the author of this work.

Designations used by companies to distinguish their products are often claimed as trademarks. All brand names and product names used in this book and on its cover are trade names, service marks, trademarks and registered trademarks of their respective owners. The publishers and the book are not associated with any product or vendor mentioned in this book. None of the companies referenced within the book have endorsed the book.

No Generative AI was used in any stage of the publication of this novel

First edition

ISBN: 978-1-9194544-0-5

Cover art by Yana Hu
Editing by Laë Proofreads

This book was professionally typeset on Reedsy.
Find out more at reedsy.com

To my Dad, who hates fantasy but loves Lord of the rings and Crime thrillers. Hopefully this will convert you

"Christianity was not meant to be a weapon or an argument or a show of force or a political tool."

Murray Pura

Contents

Preface

The story of 'All the Gods are Dead' is a heavy and emotional one. Whilst it a tale about solving a murder mystery, discovering a found family and the start of a budding romance. This story tackles some very strong themes.

This story contains:

Religious Trauma & Abuse
Religious Persecution
Themes of Religious Desconstruction
Themes of Mental Health issues such as Depression
Child Endangerment
Alcoholism
Gore
Violence
Acts of extreme violence
& Sexual Abuse (Mainly the effects of SA on the protagonist, no on page description)

Please take care of yourself and enjoy!

I

Family Matters

1

The Church of The Swordsworn

Nymeria was pleasantly surprised that she didn't burst into flames as she opened the rickety wooden gate. The wood groaned in protest as Nymeria hesitantly entered the church grounds. It was so strange, there was no celestial energy, not a single drop. She expected to feel some residual energy; traces of divine magic or the presence of an angel or god, but there was nothing at all. It had been five years since the gods disappeared; those who once actively communed with humans, humans who built their society around worshipping and appeasing them. Treating the fables told in The Codex, the Holy Book written by the gods and their angelic children, as sacred rites. But that was no more. It had started with silence. One day, no word came out of Elysium, the city of the divine and the home of gods and angels. No matter how hard people prayed, their once talkative gods had grown quiet. Then, the city of Elysium, in all its golden splendour, disappeared from the sky and left the continent in a persistent grey. The city, angels and gods had vanished five years ago and the world was worse off.

Nymeria's hand paused on the old wooden door, intricate iron carvings on the handle and frame. She made it past the gate but there was still a chance she would be scorned if she stepped foot in the church. If she was burnt then so be it, wouldn't be the worst pain she had felt. Her hands braced against the door and she pushed it open, the old wood crying as it opened. Nymeria's face scrunched, preparing for the worst as she stepped inside. She almost jumped out of her skin as her heeled boot clicked against the stone floor, the sound bouncing off the walls. But the worst never came. The only sound that greeted her was the heavy thud of the door behind her as she stood in the long abandoned church, the stale stench of dust and abandonment was suffocating.

Nymeria coughed, her heeled boots kicking up dust that must have been waiting years for someone to disrupt its patient slumber, her maroon waves bouncing with each step. She sat down in one of the pews, more dust wriggling into her lungs. Her eyes watered and she wiped them with the back of her gloved hands. Through blurry eyes she looked up to the stained glass window at the front: despite the missing panes and cracked glass, she could make out a helmeted man with two sets of celestial bird-like wings holding a flaming sword. Of course she had entered a church dedicated to the Swordsworn, Nymeria chuckled bitterly; that was just her luck. When she had searched this place online, it never mentioned which god this church had been dedicated to. If she had known it was one to the god of War, she would have stepped foot elsewhere. "Looks like no one has been taking care of you," she spoke to the stained glass window. "Your clergy seems to have left you. Just like Ghenna's parish has disbanded since you all left." Nymeria crossed her arms, gripping her forearms tightly.

"Sometimes, I wonder where you all went. Did Mel know? Did the Elysium Council know? Are they all wherever you are now?" she ranted in the empty church. Nymeria paused as if waiting for a reply, but all she got was the soft whistling of wind through the church. Her eyes flitted to the silver candle on the offering table below the stained glass window. Frankincense and sandalwood and what used to be a hunk of bread were now long rotted away. "Other times I don't care at all that you're all gone. I only regret that I wasn't there to see it myself. And the rest of the time I wish I went with you all." Nymeria sighed and slumped back against the church pew, a dark chuckle ripped from her and her dull golden brown eyes narrowed. "You were all more than happy to answer everyone else's prayers. Strike down the forces of the underworld, protect everyone all across the world." She slammed her hands onto the pew in front of her.

"Why couldn't you protect *me?!*"

But only a single caw answered her. Nymeria's eyes snapped up to the stained glass window. A one-eyed crow sat in one of the cracks of the glass. The crow stared and tilted its head; it felt like the stupid bird was mocking her. "Piss off," she spat and the bird cawed back at her as if it was saying *no, you piss off*. Nymeria growled. Stupid fucking bird, stupid fucking church and she was an idiot for coming here. There was a word she wanted to say, it was on the tip of her tongue, boiling just below the surface, but she couldn't say it. After everything that happened, it felt wrong to be angry at The Faith. Nymeria stood up, approaching the offering table. She grabbed the hunk of bread and hurled it at the crow, the bird flying away with an irate squawk.

The old church door heaved open and shut and Nymeria whirled around. She didn't think any clergy members still ran this place, not with how rundown it was. "I'm sorry. I can—" No one was there. "—Leave." A tense and heavy silence fell over and the air seemed charged in a way it hadn't been before. "Hello?" Nymeria called out but nothing replied. Her fists clenched. This was bad, she should have let Ortega know where she was going, he was finishing up a lead they had.

A creak from the pews right of her made Nymeria jump. She saw the shape of something disappear behind the pews—a long slimy tail. That was never good. "Show yourself," she demanded in a voice she hadn't used in years.

"Such a commanding tone for such a feeble creature," a slimy voice replied. It sounded as if a marsh could talk; filthy and sickening. Nymeria's nose crinkled, and a rancid smell filled her nose. It was almost sweet, but Nymeria knew to pick out the undercurrents of rot and iron. Demons always tried to disguise their stench with something familiar to humans. "I know your stench, daughter of Mercury," the demon hissed and Nymeria rolled her eyes.

"I'm afraid I don't remember you." She whirled around, hearing another creak, this time much closer. "But this is a holy place! You shouldn't be allowed in here!"

"For this to be a holy place, there would have to be any celestial or the Creator himself present. There are no gods left in this husk or either of our realms. You, daughter of Mercury, no longer count!" Nymeria felt a rush of air behind her, the stench growing stronger. Something sharp cut a few strands of her hair and she quickly sidestepped. The rancid demon crashed onto the floor in front of her, crushing a few pews under its vast size. Nymeria looked down at her hand where a few strands of maroon hair now lay.

She growled. "I didn't think I needed a haircut that badly."

The demon hissed at her and a burp followed. It was a blue-skinned newt-like creature covered in a thick sheen of slime, its pointed tail lashing behind it. If Nymeria had to guess, something as ugly as that would have to be a gluttony demon, from the third ring of Hell. It had been quite some time since she had seen one up close, even with the increased demon attacks in Ghenna city and across the continent. "Your scent is divine, Mercury, just like the Good Lady promised. Let me have just a taste." The Good Lady? Nymeria didn't know anyone by that moniker.

She swallowed thickly. "This won't end well for you, Hellspawn!" she shouted, her foot just barely moving as the demon lunged at her again. Nymeria threw herself to the side, wincing as her ribs collided with the cold stone floor. The demon went hurling into the offering table, smashing it to pieces. Nymeria scrambled to her feet, her heels thundering against the stone, the clicks sounding like small thunderclaps as she sprinted for the door.

The demon was hot on her heels, crashing into the church pews and destroying them under its lumbering weight, its tail darting out, barely grazing Nymeria's shin. She hissed, feeling the very slight sting of its sharpened point. In another life, Nymeria would have destroyed any vile demon that dared to touch her. The creature's tail would already be separated from its body and an arrow through its rotted mouth. But all she could do now was run.

The demon snarled and spat at her, globs of green saliva flying at her. She hated the fact she had to run, if this was five years ago, she would have slain the creature in a second. A clean cut down the middle would be all it took to get rid of this foul thing, and deep within her, she still had the yearning to do just that. But now she was unable to and that was more humiliating than anything. Nymeria felt the rush of air again and she hopped up just as the sharp tail went to sweep her off her feet. "I just want a bite! The Good Lady wants you alive after all," the demon snarled.

"You going to tell me who this Good Lady is?" she called back but his reply was the sound of clicking claws and belching rumble. Once she got in her car, she could run this stupid creature into the tarmac.

Her hands clenched around the door and she pulled it open as fast she could, the padding of the demon's feet getting closer and closer. Nymeria burst into the churchyard, her feet crunching under the gravel as she sprinted for the gate. If she could get to the car, then at least she could put a barrier between herself and it. Nymeria didn't see what happened to the church door but she could hear the splintering of wood and feel drops of slobber as it gained up on her.

"Shit, Shit, Shit, Shit!" she cursed as her shaking hands fumbled with the lock on the gate, barely making it through. She turned around, her head barely passing her shoulder as she felt a great weight pressing on her back. Nymeria threw her weight to her side, landing on her back, the demon on top of her. She kicked out, her foot connecting with its large jaw and sending it stumbling back. Nymeria felt a course of pain through her body, her blood boiling and all too familiar searing heat across the scars on her body. *Pull yourself together!* she scolded herself. Her teeth clenched and eyes narrowed as the curse surged through her. The demon righted itself, a much deeper growl emitting from its rancid jaws; it was no longer amused.

Nymeria ripped her jacket off and fumbled with the buttons on her shirt. Her greatest shame was also her final saving grace. If not, then she would be the meal of a lowly gluttony demon. What an embarrassing end for her. It charged at her, its jaw unhinging as its foul breath washed over her, its many teeth aiming straight for her face. She felt the chain-like scars on her body start to heat up and she winced in pain—it felt like she was being put into an oven. The light grew brighter and brighter. The demon paused, turned away and began to run. Its horrible gurgled screeching almost made her ears bleed. Nymeria shielded her eyes with her free arm, but she could feel the burning light dry them out like she was staring into the sun itself. The screeches of pain from the demon were deafening; like nails on a chalkboard.

It took a few seconds but when the light died down, Nymeria leaned up, steam radiating from her scarred torso as the light faded. The demon was gone. A thick coating of ash lay over her body and the putrid smell was slowly disappearing, being replaced by the stillness of the nighttime air.

"Gross," she mumbled and stood up, brushing as much of the ash as she could off herself, but the dark stains were smeared against her warm-toned skin. Nymeria fell back against the tarmac. The cool road was a nice relief as the heat left her body. The scars bore a curse, one where no physical harm could come to her but she could not cause harm to others. A protection she loathed. Just another thing forced onto her.

Nymeria stared up at the starry sky; she hadn't seen stars in so long. The pollution of Ghenna usually blotted them all out, but very vaguely she could make out the silver planet of Mercury, the planet associated with the SwordSworn. "Family matters huh? What a joke."

2

The Docks

Nymeria wasn't sure when she got in her car and drove back, but it had been late and the sun hadn't even poked over the horizon. She had been attacked many times, mostly by humans and the odd cursed variant. Each time, the scars would burn and shine their light. More annoyingly, each time she would need a new shirt. Nymeria blinked away, tangled knots of maroon hair obscuring her vision. Why was she awake? She wasn't supposed to be in the office today. Ortega said he had things handled with the lead.

Nymeria groaned into her pillow as her phone rang again, the culprit of her ruined slumber demanding her attention. Her hand slammed a few times against her bedside table until she managed to pick it up. "Hello?"

"Ny! I've been ringing for twenty minutes. I thought you finally kicked the bucket."

"Is that hope I hear?" Nymeria grumbled, her voice still thick with sleep.

"Not funny, Ny."

Nymeria sat up. Caliban Ortega usually didn't dismiss her banter like that. "What's going on?"

"We got a crime scene."

"What kind?"

"Triple homicide, exactly the same as the others, right on the docks. Our killer is getting confident. The police are already here but you know what they're like. I thought you would want dibs on it as well."

Nymeria's legs swung off the bed and onto the floor. "You got our disguises ready?"

"Of course I do. Who do you take me for?"

Nymeria chuckled. "Meet at the office in fifteen?"

"Yeah, will do. See you soon Boss."

What was supposed to be her day off was now another murder investigation. That would make this the fifth one this month alone. Something wasn't right in Ghenna. The city that had once been the closest to Elysium, nicknamed 'The last stop before the heavens', had become a crime hotspot ever since the gods disappeared. But even worse, Ghenna was now overrun with half-demons—they weren't content in the Hells, they just had to take more and come to the overland as well. As far as Nymeria knew, Ghenna was the only one of the six city states on the continent to have such a rampant half-demon problem.

Nymeria quickly dressed, pulling on her usual outfit: a white blouse and black trousers with a grey overcoat, along with some more practical dark combat boots and finishing up with black leather gloves.

Nymeria grabbed her brush and tore it through her hair. Truthfully, she didn't know why she decided to become a private investigator. She could have just laid low, become a secretary or a bartender, lived a normal job and had a normal human life. But that sounded so painfully boring and it made her stomach knot with shame. She used to be someone. Someone important, someone that mattered to people, now she was simply nothing and it made her stomach churn. Nymeria rushed to brush her teeth, barely cleaning them, and she grimaced as she looked at herself in the mirror. She looked how she felt: tired. She used to be so beautiful when she was younger. But now, she had a gap in her teeth and her nose was crooked; broken one too many times. Same as her smile. Nymeria spat the toothpaste out in the sink and made her way out of her bedroom, nearly tripping over a rogue takeaway box, her footsteps leaving dusty shoe prints. She needed to have a clean around her apartment. Then again, she had been telling herself that for the past six months. She just never had the energy to do it and no real reason to—she never had anyone over.

Nymeria slammed the door shut and fiddled with the keys, cursing as they got stuck in the lock. She twisted the knob a few times after pulling her keys out with a fair amount of effort. She also really needed to get that lock fixed and the last time she tried to fix it herself, the landlord had screamed at her... Ringing that stingy old man could be a weekend job. Right now, she had a crime scene to look at.

* * *

"You sure it was a triple?"

"Yes, I'm sure." Caliban sighed and she could practically hear his teeth grind together. Nymeria could feel the annoyance radiating off him and she heard him shift in the driver's seat. "That's a lot of cars for just a triple homicide." Only across the road from where they sat in Caliban's car was one ambulance, and a few meters up the road was another one. Even further up, several police cars blocked off the entrance to the docks. Blue and red lights danced around the road and entryway like a club. "We should make a move soon," Caliban prompted and she rolled her eyes.

"I'm aware," Nymeria said distractedly, gnawing on her lower lip.

"You're thinking, that's either very good or very bad."

"For you, me, or the person on the receiving end?"

Caliban chuckled. "All three." A small silence fell over the two and Nymeria turned to face him. She hated how he looked at her; worried about her. The All-seeing Private Eye had only two investigators; herself and Caliban. Nymeria had put out multiple ads, but no one ever came forward. She wasn't sure if it was because no one wanted to be a private investigator anymore—long hours and uncertain pay were big deterrents that Nymeria understood—or if it was the fact that they were afraid to go against the police force.

Caliban's fingers drummed against the wheel and Nymeria cringed. When Caliban did that, an uncomfortable question usually followed.

"So...what happened last weekend?"

Nymeria groaned, she was far too old to be lectured like this, and this wasn't the first time. "I had a bit to drink."

She heard Caliban grind his teeth again. "A bit? Nymeria I had to bail you out of jail. Again! This is the third time in six months." Caliban's voice was rising.

"And I didn't ask you too! It was just a misunderstanding—"

"Misunderstanding? Nymeria, the officers said you were yelling into the night sky and when one of them tried to restrain you, you kicked him."

"He was using unnecessary force."

Caliban hit his head against the headrest.

"You've got to be joking," he groaned, barely concealing his disbelief, and Nymeria kept her eyes focused on the dashboard in front of her.

"I never asked you to bail me out. I don't know how many times we have had this discussion, but we're not friends. We're never going to be friends. You don't need to keep doing these things," she said quickly. Nymeria didn't want a friend, she didn't need anyone anymore. Let alone someone who wouldn't even be able to understand what she had been through. Their lives were so different he would never understand her and Nymeria didn't want to understand him.

"You're damn lucky the police have other things to worry about right now. No surprise crime rates have shot up with all the half-demons around," Caliban said quietly and she could hear him swallow as if a lump was stuck in his throat.

The police force was a powerful one and they weren't afraid to use violence. Their main targets these days were the half-demons. She only had Caliban's word to go by, but since the fall of the gods, money had become the life force of this city and those half demons—who were never just content to stay in the Hells—didn't have any. Whilst she never met Mayor Zai Alighieri, she wasn't surprised that the former head of the Ghenna parish and mayor five years in a row was not a fan of the influx of half-demons into his city. They were just trying to spread more chaos and now had all the opportunity to—despite the previous occasional cracks in the wards every time a few demons or half demons would slip through and cause trouble because that's all they knew how to do. When the gods disappeared, the magical wards—large stone pillars with runes inscribed into them that kept the Underworld and each of Hell's layers separate from Elysium and Earth—fell too. Hundreds of half-demons fled to Earth, and she almost couldn't blame them. Almost. After all, anyone who got sent down there was there for a reason or they had escaped and come up to Earth. Ghenna was the closest city to a lot of these wards, so every half-demon fled here.

Caliban's eyes narrowed again. "Ny!"

"Yeah, yeah I'm with you. Let's go." Nymeria unbuckled her seat belt and got out of the car. The pair slipped around to the trunk and Caliban unlocked the boot. Reaching inside, he handed Nymeria a white crime scene examination suit. Her cute outfit was gonna go to waste. "We're forensics this time?" It would reduce the risk of them getting caught.

"The high-end disguises were out of stock," Caliban grumbled back at her and Nymeria begrudgingly chuckled, pulling the suit up and over her clothes. Tying her hair up in a ponytail, she laughed as Caliban struggled to get the suit over his bulky frame.

Caliban was a broad man with lightly tanned skin, light brown neck-length hair and a full beard and moustache. He was a resourceful man and had good connections—as he used to be a cop—but Caliban hated the corruption of the force and told Nymeria many stories over a few drinks, despite her instance of drinking by herself most nights. "You got something on your mind." Caliban said it like a fact more than a question.

"I'm fine, Ortega. I've got a lot of stuff to deal with in my apartment. Shitty landlords, you know the deal." Caliban would always offer to help, always be there, and whenever he got a little too close, she pulled back. She knew it wasn't fair to him, but she did it anyway.

"I can always swing by—" he offered.

Nymeria shook her head and grimaced. "I'll manage Nasir—"

They both fell silent.

"Been a while since you slipped up." Caliban's voice was quiet like his pride had been wounded.

"Yeah." Nymeria didn't bother to apologise, she knew she would do it again. She didn't want Caliban to see the state of her apartment. He would just insist on helping her more. Nymeria was fine on her own, she could and would manage by herself. Keeping people at arm's length was the safest option. The two suited up in silence, pulling the respiratory mask over their faces. Caliban gave her a small card—a picture of her on it with the name Maria Forester. "You're getting more creative." Nymeria chuckled.

"You said to be creative and I listened. You can never tell me I don't listen to you." Caliban chuckled back, his voice had a slight rasp.

"Alright, show time. You know the drill," Nymeria instructed. The plan for infiltrating a crime scene was simple; disguise, take photos, have a look around for anything the cops missed and then leave quietly. It worked forty-five percent of the time.

Nymeria and Caliban walked up to the crime scene. "Stop." An officer stood in front of them, barring the pair from passing the yellow tape. The light from the police cars made Nymeria squint. A few of the officers behind the tape turned to look at them. "Provide IDs, otherwise I can't let you guys through." The pair presented them, the policeman glancing from the IDs up to their faces and back down.

"Everything in order?" Caliban asked, pitching his voice up a few octaves. Nymeria's lips quirked up into a small smile. Smart move.

A dark gloom always seemed to hang over the rainy city, so it wasn't surprising when the officer got out his flashlight and beamed it over the fake cards.

"All clear," the Officer called out and held up the tape for the pair of them. Nymeria quickly ducked under, making her way to the crime scene.

"Thanks," they both said, Caliban getting the camera ready and walking into the crime scene itself. Nymeria leaned into Caliban. "He had me worried for a moment," she whispered and Caliban nodded.

"Agreed. Thought he had seen right through them—" They

both stopped as they looked out at the scene before them. The red and blue lights of the cop cars suddenly seemed a lot less oppressive than the red bloodied runes drawn into the ground. Runes that funnelled around the corner and to the pier itself.

It only got worse as Nymeria rounded the corner. She had seen many grizzly sights—murder scenes and battlefields alike—but this made her throat catch. The waves from the Northern Sea were crashing against the wooden pier and it would have been dangerously beautiful if not for the grim display. In front of her, on the tarmac just short of the pier, was one large circle which swooped down, almost looking like a lock, with several smaller circles inside. Between the circle rings were more of those runes in a language she didn't know. The circles were drawn in blood and in the centre, bottom of the rune and at the top, were three bodies. Each was naked and face down, their arms and legs pointed outward, their rib cages split through their backs like blooming flowers.

"What the fuck?" Caliban growled, slowly lifting his hands to take a photo. It felt like a violation to do so. They had been people with families, jobs, friends, maybe even lovers. Now all they would be remembered for was their death. Nymeria's hand hesitated. She hadn't realized she had instinctively gone to clasp her hands together in prayer. After everything that happened, her first instinct was to search the gods for help. It was pathetic; she wasn't a blinded little girl, she knew better now. But they didn't— these now dead on the ground may have once been people of the faith. She doubted who or whatever did this wouldn't have given them a proper send-off.

"May the Shepherd guide you safely to your final destination." She whispered the small prayer to the god of death and guide to the underworld.

"Didn't think you were the religious type," Caliban muttered as he walked behind her, snapping another photo of the killing scene.

"I'm not," she said quickly, forcing her hands by her sides. Nymeria approached the body closest to her, the one at the bottom of the large circle. She crouched down. She didn't want to touch it, getting her fingerprints on the corpse would lead to a whole new mess. She grabbed her torch and shone it inside the cavernous expanse of the back; the way the ribs were positioned, it almost looked like a hungry maw or an empty cage. But nothing was inside—nothing at all. No bones, no organs, no tissue. This person had been carved out like a jack-o-lantern. Nymeria grimaced, this was the first scene of these homicides she had been to, and she wondered if any of the cops on the first scene threw up. Nymeria was used to violence; she had grown up with it, raised to be a master of all forms of violence. But this wasn't a random act, this was meticulous. This had to be something else, but what for?

Nymeria stood up, taking a few steps back. This was a ritual of some sort; no one went to this much effort and displayed bodies like this just for artistic expression. But what had caused this? Her mind jumped to demonic. It made the most sense; only a demon would conduct something so foul, humans were too simple for this.

The slam of a car door caught Nymeria's attention and she turned back to the entrance. A dark-skinned man with a full grey beard and bulldog-like features crossed the tape without the guarding officer stopping him. Chief Morgan Cordero, the bane of Nymeria's existence but also a useful contact. If he found out that she and Caliban were at a crime scene, they could be arrested. Again.

Bang!

Nymeria jumped and whirled around. Caliban clambered up one of the shipping containers, the camera bouncing against his chest. A few officers were looking up at him as well, puzzled expressions on their faces. "Just getting a better vantage point," Caliban called, snapping a few photos, the officers shook their heads and went back to investigate. Nymeria chuckled nervously; she could feel the Chief's eyes burning into the back of her neck. Caliban clumsily clambered down, almost tripping over himself.

"Hey." Caliban landed a few meters away and stumbled closer, leaning in close. His breath tickled Nymeria's neck. "I saw a shipping container about twenty meters west of here. There was blood coming out of it."

"Fresh?"

"Didn't look like it. I can get more evidence, try and get friendly with a few of the officers if you wanna explore more."

Nymeria huffed. "Letting me do all the hard work huh?"

"No, you just have lighter feet and more skilled hands," he said gruffly and Nymeria nodded.

"I'll meet you back here in ten minutes. If I'm not back

don't—"

"I will. Someone has to keep you alive."

Nymeria laughed loudly, a few officers turned to look at her for a moment before resuming their duties. "Asshole," she whispered and quietly walked away, slipping between officers and over evidence markers.

* * *

The rows of shipping containers were a maze. Nymeria would have gotten lost if she didn't have a red taunting trail of blood to follow. It was like an enchanting voice, beckoning her deeper into the labyrinth. A caw broke Nymeria from her thoughts. She looked up, finding the one-eyed crow sitting on top of one of the shipping containers, looking down at her. "You again?" Seeing one one-eyed raven was rare, two was a coincidence. Nymeria stiffened. "Are you gonna cause me trouble?"

The crow tilted its head, *maybe*, it seemed to speak and Nymeria scoffed. Now she was talking to birds, she really had lost her mind. Her boots echoed ominously between the containers, passing by each locked door, however one was not closed, just slightly ajar. Nymeria paused and looked at the floor, the blood trail stopped at the unlocked container. The heavy door handle was open, pulled to look like it was closed. The crow landed on top of it, "Not a word," she scolded the crow. Both of her hands gripped the door and pulled. Nymeria grunted, feeling her muscles tense and already ache with the effort to pull it open. Five years ago, she would have wrenched it open easily with one arm. She had been in Ghenna for only two years, and she had become acutely aware of just how powerless she truly was.

After a few strenuous minutes and a small break, the door was opened and Nymeria gagged at the stench that hit her. She knew the stench of death well. She clicked the torch on and shone it inside the container. A naked man was face up, with multiple stab wounds in his chest and neck. "May the Shepherd guide you safely," she muttered. Just out of the range of her flashlight she saw a shadow of movement. Nymeria jerked the torch upward. "Hello?"

Shaking and whimpering in the corner and covered in dried blood was a child in a thin rag. Brown eyes peeked from behind thickly matted black hair. Nymeria only took a step forward and the child started screaming, small thin hands covering her face and striking outward. The sound was so broken and shrill that it made Nymeria cringe.

"Hey, hey! It's okay!" Nymeria froze, she needed this child to be quiet, the other officers would be with her soon. Nymeria ripped the hood off the white suit and pulled the face mask down. "Hi, hi, hi," she said quickly, the small child's screams turning into a whimper. "See? I'm not that scary now am I?" Nymeria soothed and the child hiccuped, round green eyes full of worry that made Nymeria's heart clench. Poor kid.

"Would you like to come outside? All those monsters are long gone." The child went to move but hesitated. "I took care of them myself," Nymeria quipped. "No trouble for me."

Nymeria's heart clenched. She remembered saying the same thing to her little nephews a lifetime ago. Slowly, the child got up. The thin rag was massive on her, and one step at a time, the girl took a few steps towards Nymeria until she stood before her. "See? Nothing bad here." Nymeria stepped out of the container. "Just follow me—"

"Freeze! Hands in the air!"

Nymeria did indeed freeze upon hearing the click of the safety being flicked off several pistols. Nymeria's hands rose into the air and the child hid behind her legs clinging tightly and screaming again. "Guns down! All of you! God damn it, Nymeria Mercury!" This was probably the only time she was grateful to hear the deep doom of Chief Morgan Cordero's voice.

3

A Mysterious Girl

Nymeria winced from the flash of the camera, her fingers tightening against the cuffs around her wrists. This wouldn't be the first time she was arrested by the Ghenna City Police Department—or GCPD— and this probably wouldn't be the last. Nymeria turned to the side and another photo was taken of her, the flash a lot less oppressive this time. One of the officers from the crime scene grabbed her upper arm, his grip firm. "Alright you have the right—"

"The right to remain silent whilst you put me in holding, I know. I'm aware by now," Nymeria snapped and the officer grumbled something under his breath. She didn't struggle as he led her towards the white brick holding cells; she was confident Ortega would bail her out soon enough. Caliban had managed to get away after she was caught, making a beeline for his car. Nymeria wasn't mad, he had all the crime scene photos, it was better for their investigation if he got away. At least their evidence wouldn't be destroyed.

The radio on the officer crackled and he paused, Nymeria stopping just before the open door of the cell. Nymeria stiffened, looking into the cold maw of the holding cell. "Come again, Sir?" the officer spoke into the radio. She hated enclosed spaces.

"Are you sure sir?"

For a moment, she felt very far away. She wasn't standing in front of a holding cell in Ghenna. She was somewhere else, far above, with iron chains around her arms and body, holding her limbs apart. The officer behind her groaned. "It's your lucky day Mercury, again. The Chief wants to speak to you in his office. Again" Nymeria blinked a few times as she was escorted away.

Nymeria released a breath she hadn't known she was holding. "Where are you taking me?" Her mind was a fog of the past and present; conflicting images trying to force their way forward. It was distracting.

"Chief's office. Pay attention, " the officer snarled, pushing Nymeria forward. Down a long hallway past other rooms, as they passed one, Nymeria caught a glimpse of the little girl from earlier, swatting and kicking her thin legs at a doctor. The two had been separated upon arriving at the police station. The girl had been screaming in protest. The noise still made her ears ring. What the hell had that child been through? The girl had been scared when Nymeria first approached but fine afterwards. She only started screaming when the other officers arrived and then when separated from her. The girl was being left alone with men. A child, especially a little girl, would only be afraid of an adult man for a few reasons and none of them were good. Nymeria felt bile rise in her throat. She didn't even want to think about it. For someone so young to have experienced such cruelty, it made something deep within her—within her spirit—scream in outrage.

The officer pushed her onward through a set of double doors and past a group of cubicles in the central offices. A few of the on-duty officers glared at her. "Evening," she said, sickeningly polite. A few shook their heads and even more muttered curses under their breath. Nymeria didn't care, she did more work for the city than most of them combined. They disliked her because, more often than not, she called them out of their complacency. Covering the cases they didn't want to because it meant more paperwork, or helping out the undesirables; sex workers and the homeless were her usual clients, almost always human. People who couldn't pay a lot but those who needed help the most. Nymeria had always been the one to roll up her sleeves and do the so-called dirty work.

The officer led her through a polished oak door and into a small office. Chief Morgan Cordero sat behind a varnished desk, a case file in his hand. His eyes flickered to Nymeria and a gruff sigh left him. "Sit down Mercury," he grumbled, tossing the file onto his desk. The officer behind her pulled the chair out and sat her down in it with a firm push on her shoulder.

"Your dog still needs training," Nymeria muttered.

"Don't start Mercury," Cordero warned, looking up at the officer behind her and jerking his head.

"You sure?"

"I don't pay you to question me, Oliver. Uncuff her." Cordero's eyes met Nymeria's. "She's a smart girl, she won't cause trouble whilst in here." Nymeria met his steely gaze with her own, not bothering to thank Officer Oliver as he uncuffed her.

"You've learnt not to test my patience, boy," Nymeria spat. "That's a smart decision."

Something unspoken passed between Cordero and Officer Oliver, and Nymeria heard the open and shut of the office door behind her. Cordero slumped back in his chair. "I'm trying to be patient with you, Mercury I really am. You're a good woman, and I do believe you got good intentions"

"But," Nymeria interrupted.

"But, you can't keep doing this vigilante nonsense. If you wanted to help people you—"

"You should have joined the force. We've had this conversation many times." Nymeria was bored to death of this back and forth.

"So why do you continuously try to undermine me?" Cordero spat. "Why are you so insistent on twisting the knife every time? This is strike two, next one I'll have to throw you in jail. No bail and you'll go to court." Cordero leaned closer. "Is that what you want Mercury?!"

Nymeria held his gaze, not looking away. "If you really thought you were doing a good job, I wouldn't be needed and people wouldn't come to me for help." Her voice was cool and calm but it burned under Cordero's skin; she could see it in his eyes.

He stood up, pacing behind his desk for a few moments. "I'm gonna have to fine you for this."

Nymeria groaned.

"I gave you a warning last time you tampered with my crime scene. This time you get a fine, next time you're gonna get jail time."

Nymeria ran a hand down her face. "How much?"

"Five hundred."

"Five hundred?!" That would cripple her financially.

"I can lower it down to three hundred if you answer my questions honestly."

Nymeria shook her head and kissed her teeth in annoyance. "Fine, go ahead."

"That girl from the docks. What did you say to her?"Cordero demanded, his gaze trying to burn through Nymeria but she was heatproof.

But she did blink, taken aback. "The girl?"

"Yes, the girl. She won't speak to any of my men."

"Yeah, that's the problem," she snarled. "They're men."

"Bullshit—"

"She was clearly trafficked from somewhere and had to endure only the gods know what else! If she's that afraid of men, it's for a damn good reason," Nymeria boomed. Cordero looked out of the window of his desk and she followed his gaze. Both then turned towards the room Nymeria had passed, where the girl had been held in.

"We haven't been able to get anything from her, she either won't talk or can't. She refuses to let anyone touch her and she won't cooperate," Cordero muttered.

"You don't have a children's crime specialist?" Cordero's silence answered Nymeria's question.

"If I take you to her, can you talk to her? Get some information. I'll let you use whatever you gather in your investigation and reduce your fine." Cordero was a hard ass, a stickler for tradition and rules but he wasn't entirely unreasonable.

Suddenly, the lights flickered, sparking on and off. Nymeria stood up and Cordero stormed to his office door, flinging it open. "The hells is going on?" All he got was mumbled confusion. But just as quickly as it started it stopped, the lights flickering back to normal.

"Have you paid the electric bill?" Nymeria muttered, her body tense, and Cordero shot her a look. *Shut up.* Feet thundered down the hall and the doctor that Nymeria saw with the girl skidded to a halt at the edge of the bullpen.

"Chief, it's the girl! She's gone."

"Gone?!" he shouted, the chief's face reddening as he stormed towards the doctor. Nymeria followed quietly behind. "What do you mean gone? How do you lose a child?"

"I was trying to calm her down! I turned my back for a few seconds at most. I was going to give her a sticker sheet, then the lights started flickering—" The three rounded the corner and the doctor held open the door, inside was an empty room.

"She just vanished into thin air." The Chief stormed inside, looking under chairs and the examination table. Nymeria had to hold back her laugh. Clever girl.

* * *

After a few harsh words between herself and Cordero, she reluctantly accepted the three hundred pound fine and was given back her phone and purse. But she now had to walk from central Ghenna to the east side, where her shitty apartment complex was and where her messy apartment lay waiting for her to clean. With the day she had, she no longer wanted to. All she wanted to do was eat some two-day-old leftovers and then go to a bar. A good glass of wine always took the edge off.

But she needed to keep the edge on for now. Nymeria had been aware of the clumsy footsteps following her for two streets. Whoever was following her was doing an awful job of it, she never quite saw who it was but it was clearly someone inexperienced; their footsteps were too loud and they were far too close. Nonetheless, Nymeria didn't like the idea of anyone following her, whether it was a potential client or one of Cordero's officers.

She darted into a dirty alley with a sharp turn and her shadower stuttered, freezing in place. Nymeria reached out, but when her hand went to grab a chest she was met only with the air. "What?" she whispered but a small whine made her look down. Standing before her was the girl, a wide grin on her face as she waved at Nymeria.

Nymeria pulled the girl into the alley, crouching down to be at eye level with her. "You! What are you doing here?" The girl made a whining noise, still smiling. The girl seemed all too proud of herself that she had managed to follow her. "How did you even escape the police station?" The girl didn't answer again. "Well?" The girl looked around and grabbed a pack of pens in an open bin. She wanted to write something, and Nymeria patted her pockets. She didn't have any paper on her. "Just write on my hand," Nymeria relented and the girl walked over again. Her hand barely wrapped around Nymeria's wrist as she scrawled something on the back of her hand.

After a few moments, Nymeria pulled her hand away and looked at the wiggly scrawl; *My name is Jeniveev.* "Genevieve. That's your name?" Nymeria asked and The girl—Genevieve nodded.

"Okay, can I call you Gen?"

She nodded.

"Why are you writing everything?" She asked and Gen scrawled on her hand again.

I can't speak.

Great, the only witness alive couldn't talk and seemed to have a strange fondness towards Nymeria. This case couldn't become even more of a shit show.

"Why did you run away from the police? They can help you, more than me." Nymeria really wanted to get rid of this kid.

No, they scary. You safe. You fought demons.

Nymeria groaned. Of course her white lie had come to bite her in the ass.

"Well, I can't help you." Nymeria stood up, pulling her hand away. "Your parents will be missing you." Gen's face scrunched up and she shook her head.

"They won't miss you?" Gen snatched Nymeria's other hand and scrawled onto it. Nymeria snatched her hand back.

They dead, just me. Nymeria groaned again, this was just getting better and better.

"Listen, I'm a very busy woman—" Nymeria turned her back to the child and she heard a small whir behind her and a rush of air. "So I can't be on babysitting duty..." Nymeria trailed off.

Gen was now in front of her without even moving. Behind the girl was a crack in the air itself, like a broken mirror. From the shattered shards, she could see the entrance to the alleyway and the cars passing by. Nymeria blinked owlishly and looked behind her, another opening was there and she saw both of their backs. "What the fuck?" Nymeria grabbed Gen and pulled her deeper into the alleyway, both the portals mending themselves back together.

"How are you doing that?!" Gen shrugged.

Nymeria focused for a few moments, she couldn't sense any divine energy on this child so she wasn't an angel and she didn't look like she had demon blood in her.

"Humans cannot use magic. It's forbidden, you know that, yes?" Gen nodded again. There was no way this partially illiterate child, no older than eight, made a demon pact.

The Destroyer, god of the Arcane, gave magic to humans, thousands of years ago; it had solely been possessed by angels, due to magic passing through blood. He gave humanity just a taste of it and it nearly destroyed them. It only took a few days for the ground to split and storms to rage, for the dead to rise and curses to be created, the first of their kind. He used his human army to storm the heavens, he took the form of a great black dragon and tried to bathe Elysium in fire, but was defeated by the Swordsworn. The Creator banished him below the earth and anyone who still aligned with him. That was how the Hells and demons were made and subsequently half-demons. It was also why magic was forbidden amongst humans.

Nymeria studied Gen intensely, if this girl couldn't even spell her name properly, there was no way she would be able to read and understand an illegal magical tome. "Do you know what will happen to you if you're discovered? You must not use it!" Nymeria hissed, shaking the girl again. Gen's bottom lip trembled and her eyes became watery. Nymeria felt something twitch in her heart and she stood up, letting go of her.

What was this child? Nymeria didn't know, but she did know this girl was powerful. Portaling was a rare and powerful ability and that made Gen valuable, and with how dangerous Ghenna was, it made Gen a target not just to the murderer on the loose—her original captor, assumedly—but also the authorities. If the GCPD caught wind of a rogue mage, they would lock her up or worse.

Nymeria had been so lost in thought she hadn't realised she had been walking away from the girl until she heard a gurgle behind her. Gen looked up at Nymeria expectantly. She knew what she had to do but she was not cut out to look after a child. "You can stay with me. For now."

Gen grinned and she rushed up, wrapping her arms around Nymeria's waist. "Yeah, yeah okay," Nymeria said, uncomfortable, trying to pry the child's hands off her. "Ground rules; we're not friends, you don't touch any documents in my flat and you don't use"—Nymeria gestured behind Gen—"the portals. Got it?"

Gen nodded eagerly.

"Come on then." Nymeria walked out onto the pavement and Gen followed after her, almost glued to her hip.

* * *

The sun had started to set when Nymeria opened the door to her apartment and she frowned when Gen immediately scrunched her nose. "Sorry, not all of us live lavishly," she grumbled and sniffed the air. Her apartment wasn't that smelly, right? Regardless, Nymeria pulled open the two small windows in the living room. Gen looked around the apartment, unsure of where to step. Nymeria walked over to the spare bedroom. "Uh, you can stay in here—" Nymeria paused as she pulled the door open and looked into the room. It was piled with clutter and dust. Nymeria closed the door. She really needed to clean. "You can sleep on the sofa tonight. I'll make sure you have a proper room tomorrow." Nymeria turned around but Gen was gone.

Nymeria kissed her teeth in annoyance. "Gen, what did I say twenty minutes ago about the portals?" She called out, walking to her bedroom and seeing nothing in there, she went to the kitchenette. Nymeria heard a creak from one of the bottom cabinets and leant over. Gen had wedged herself into one of the smaller cabinets. "What are you doing?" Gen looked up at her expectantly and Nymeria knew what she wanted. Nymeria grabbed the pad and pen on the kitchen table. She kept it there in case a revelation about a case hit her as she was eating. Passing them over, Nymeria watched Gen scribble something down and then show it to her.

I can sleep here. What kind of place had she lived in before where she thought it was normal to sleep somewhere like that?

"What? No, don't be stupid. I just need to clean. Come on." She reached her hand down and Gen grabbed her wrist. Nymeria led her to the sofa and sat her down, Gen sinking slightly into the cushions. "See, much better, huh?" Gen clutched the pen and pad to her. Nymeria got up and Gen squealed. "Hang on, I'll be back." Nymeria rummaged through her small wardrobe and brought out a thick fluffy brown blanket. It was one she used when it was winter; it wasn't ideal but should make for a decent duvet for a night. Nymeria walked back in and draped it over her, completely covering her.

"See? Isn't that nice?" Gen's hand touched the blanket and instantly recoiled before settling back on it. Odd. "Sorry, it's not a hotel but you're a tough kid. You can manage for a night right?" Nymeria joked, but Gen seemed so fascinated by the softness of it. "I'm sure I can find some pizza to cook for us." Gen's eyes lit up and she gasped.

"You like that?" Gen nodded eagerly.

Nymeria felt her lip twitch upward. "Alright. Just make sure to leave me a slice, okay?" Nymeria found a frozen cheese pizza and flicked on the small oven, shoving it inside. Gen must have figured out the TV as she heard the living room erupt with noise and she shook her head. She now had a child living with her for the foreseeable future and had restricted leads on this case. How could this day get any weirder? Speaking of, she should let Caliban know she was safe. She sent him a quick text *'I'm safe. They let me out with a fine. Lots to catch up on.'* As soon as she pressed send, an unknown number started calling her.

"Hello? You probably have the wrong number—"

"No I don't. I hope I didn't interrupt your conversation with your little friend. Perhaps discussing details on that case?" A woman's voice interrupted her. One Nymeria hadn't heard before.

"Who's this?"

"We've met before but that's irrelevant, we shall meet properly soon. The Draig brothers humbly request your presence tonight at The Greed club at 11 pm. Don't be late and don't squander this opportunity. We may be able to help your case." Whoever was on the other side hung up.

Nymeria placed her phone on the counter and leaned against it. This was bad, getting involved with the Draig brothers was asking for trouble. The half-demon brothers, had led hundreds of half-demons out of the Hells when the wards first crumbled. They practically ran Ghenna from the shadows, operating outside of the law, and now they wanted to meet with her. This was going to be an interesting meeting and hopefully a short one.

4

The Draig Brothers

Nymeria hadn't been to a club before. She had gone to many parties, but they were more high-tension, sophisticated affairs. But nothing like the loose, wild and sticky chaos of a club. She had been a busy girl in her early twenties and felt too old at twenty nine.

Nymeria glanced down at her cracked phone, the map app chiming: "You have arrived at your destination!" Nymeria looked up at the brick wall of the large building, a green neon sign on the side shone brightly, and the word 'Greed' was written in cursive. Nymeria inhaled, pulling her jacket tighter as she walked towards the entrance, past the humans lining up to enter. Most ignored her but a few gave her strange looks. Nymeria ignored their shouts as she cut in line.

The bouncer on duty was a man much taller than her and twice as broad. "Sorry darling, you're gonna need to go to the back," he said as she approached, a sleazy smile on his face that made Nymeria's stomach churn, but she held her tongue. She didn't want to piss off any powerful demons—half or full-blooded—and she was in their territory; she had to play smart, even if she didn't like playing these games at all. Rumour had it the Draig brothers could hear every whisper and see through every shadow, she wouldn't be surprised if they already knew she was here.

But that didn't mean she would let these demons hurt her. The metal of her pistol was cold and snug against her back, tucked into her waistband. It would be a last ditch effort for defence rather than going in on the attack, and if other rumours were to be believed, these brothers were bastards of the Destroyer himself. Caution was warranted. Nymeria forced a polite and sweet smile, like she was trying to score free drinks at a bar, something she had done quite a few times. "No, I'm not here for the club."

The bouncer raised a brow in confusion.

"I have a meeting with the Draig brothers."

The bouncer laughed, which turned into a coughing fit. "You and every other man and woman want a private audience with those two. Back of the line." His tone turned snippy at the end, and she guessed he must have had this conversation half a dozen times tonight.

"No, I'm serious. I had a phone call!" she bargained, digging her heels into the ground as the bouncer tried to push her away.

"I'm too tired for this shit," he grumbled and let her go. Grabbing a clipboard that was resting against the door of the club. "Alright then, name?" He sighed.

"Nymeria Mercury." The bouncer gave a half-arsed look over the list.

"Yeah no Ny—oh." Nymeria's lip twitched up into a smirk but she pushed it down.

"Sorry miss, you're on the list," the bouncer apologised, ushered the line back and opened the club door for her. She was bombarded by the smell of sweat and alcohol, and the loud music assaulted her ears. "You see that big man back there?" The bouncer pointed to the far corner of the club, across the sea of dancers—hired and clubbers. Against the back wall, another burly man stood next to a set of stairs going upward.

"That's Alfie. Head to him and tell him you have a meeting with the Draig's, he'll go through the same process here. You're on the list so you shouldn't face any issue."

Nymeria paused. "You're not going to pat me down?"

"Do you want me to?" He grinned.

"No, no, thanks." She rushed inside, the door closing behind her. Nymeria enjoyed bars, she liked the warm and more intimate atmosphere. She could not understand how anyone enjoyed this, everything was far too oppressive; the smells, the noise, it was almost deafening. She slipped through the crowd, bodies pressed against her and each other and she grimaced as she stepped on something sticky. She now had a newfound respect for bartenders, she definitely couldn't work in this atmosphere night after night dealing with the drunk and belligerent.

Nymeria found herself in front of the other bodyguard and she quickly patted her pockets down making sure nothing had been stolen. "I'm here to see the—" She paused, a soft stench of demon energy hitting her, and she felt a familiar heat course over her scars. She looked up at the man before her. His eyes were a very soft red—almost brown. A half-demon. The man quirked a brow at her hesitance and then scrunched his nose. Shit. "The Draig brothers. I'm here to see them," she continued. He nodded. Apart from his eyes, he looked entirely human. The demonic blood in him must have thinned out over generations, though it didn't matter how diluted it was, they were all the same; all half-demons and according to the decree of the Creator, the King of the gods and All-maker, they weren't supposed to be out of the Hells. But he was dead now and the rules of the Faith no longer applied. The thought made Nymeria's gut churn uncomfortably.

The Half-demon checked his clipboard. "Go ahead. Be on your best behaviour. Any funny business and you'll see yourself taken out back." Nymeria knew exactly why his tone had become more hostile and slightly shocked, he caught her scent as well.

"Thanks," she said gruffly and walked past him and up the stairs. She could have sworn she heard the beep of a radio. She reached behind her back as she ascended. The gun was a comforting presence. If she did get in a fight, it wouldn't protect her much, if at all, and her scars torching the place would cause even more of a scene. She was walking straight into the jaws of the beast, but she'd been promised a meeting. Nymeria almost laughed, she was trusting demons to keep their word? She had lost it.

Nymeria reached the top and was faced with a black wooden door. She pushed it open and took a step forward, her feet landing on wooden flooring. "Hell—" If Nymeria hadn't caught the flash of white, her face would have been caved in. A fist, crackling with white lightning was lodged in the wood of the door frame, a deep fractured cave in the wood. "What the fuck?!" she barked, immediately grabbing the pistol in her waistband. Her blood boiled and she felt her vision blur. No, not now. She was dead if she passed out here. She heard a crunch as the fist was freed from the door frame and she aimed the gun at the man in front of her. A hand bigger than her own wrapped around her wrist and pointed the gun upward, she pulled the trigger and the bullet landed in the ceiling, dust raining down upon both of them.

Nymeria felt herself back up and she was soon against the wall near the door, the fist from before sparking and crackling angrily at her hovered just over her face. "You should not be here," the man above her growled, his growl had a deep animalistic timber that rattled her chest. She finally locked eyes with her attacker. His hair was in a short wolf cut, half of his hair was black and the other half was white: It was impossible to tell if the white or black was his natural hair colour. His irises were a steely silver-white. Definitely a half-demon and a very powerful one. Nymeria glared up at him, twisting her wrist, the barrel of her pistol now resting against his temple. He growled again.

"What do you think is faster? Your fist or me pulling the

trigger?" Nymeria hissed. She felt sweat bead down her forehead and her hand was shaking. *Do not pass out*, she scolded herself.

"You talk very confidently for someone who's shaking." His voice was cold and calculating as if he was waiting to pick her apart. Nymeria swallowed thickly. A spark of lightning bounced from his fist and burnt her cheek, breaking the skin. Shit.

"You should know how foolish it is to walk into a demon's lair." His eyes darted down to the blood and his eyes widened a fraction. "Angel?"

Nymeria could see her golden blood stain the corner of her blouse. "I was invited here—"

"No, the private investigator was invited, not your kind. Did your masters send you here to smite us, loyal dog? Is their death all a ruse? That's cowardly even for your kind," Nymeria bristled and her finger twitched against the trigger. "Poor discipline," he critiqued.

"Poor discipline? You came at me swinging!" she snapped back.

"Halloran, let her go!" a voice said behind the man. He snarled and stepped back, flexing his fist.

"I knew the name Mercury rang a bell." Another man stepped through a door on the opposite side of what Nymeria could now make out to be a pretty lavish office. He sat behind a redwood desk, and in a grand leather black chair was a russet-haired man, half of his long hair tied back messily behind him. Just like Halloran, a few strands of his hair were white, but nowhere near as much as Halloran. Nymeria's eyes widened as she realised they had the same eyes. They were brothers. The Draig brothers.

"When I first had my crow start following you, I kept thinking, 'Mercury, Mercury, why does that name make me so angry.' And now I remember, upon seeing your lovely face." The Man leaned back in his chair and Nymeria took a few tentative steps forward. Upon closer inspection, he had a large scar that spanned his lower face; a crescent-shaped scar and from its middle, a deep line that cut across his nose and lips.

"Your theatrics better have a point, Arwen," Halloran said sharply and Arwen shot him an exasperated look.

"According to the Faith—well, the dead Faith, the gods have a planet associated with each and the Swordsworn is associated with Mercury. Each of the seven angelic houses are named after that planet, and thus so are their children." Arwen leaned forward. "Making you one of the Swordsworn's daughters and perhaps the last of your kind." He stood up, his white eyes locking on Nymeria. But they seemed a lot warmer than Halloran's, almost trusting.

"The Swordsworn only has—well had, two daughters, and you don't look much like a High Priestess," Halloran said, Nymeria prickled. She didn't want to be reminded of her sister, Melantha. "If you're expecting us to bow, General, we shall not," Halloran spat. Nymeria hated hearing her old title, it felt like rubbing salt on an open wound.

Arwen frowned and Nymeria cursed under her breath that she allowed the hurt to cross her expression. "No, you're not an angel any more." He clicked his tongue, a smirk crossing his face. "You're a fallen one, aren't you? That's why you're here and haven't disappeared with the rest of your kind."

"Does it matter what I am?"

Arwen laughed, the sound was soft despite how big and broad he was. "Yes, it does. How, in all the rings of the underworld, did the hunter of the damned and general of Elysium become a fallen?" Fallen angels were a disgrace, stripped of the magic and status for crimes and actions unimaginable and unforgivable. Nymeria still didn't know what her crime truly was. She just loved someone and spoke loudly, did that mean she deserved the scars that now ran across her body?

"I fell," she said pointedly. "I make a living as a private investigator, there's nothing more than that." She could feel both the brothers eye her suspiciously. Their caution was warranted. Nymeria turned to Halloran but spoke to Arwen: "Does your dog always bite first?"

She knew the answer; after all this wasn't the first time she and Halloran had met. She had conducted countless campaigns in the Hells as general. To protect humanity and the angels, demons needed to be kept in line. The former Prince of the Hells always fought her to a standstill, yet this was the first time either of them had seen the other out of armour. It was strange and far too human.

Halloran's eyes narrowed and he almost snarled. "More so than I," Arwen warned. "But I do bite as well. Hush those pretty lips and let me tell you about this job offer I have for you." A job? That was what the Draig brothers had called her in for?

"Everyone is talking about those murders; five in two months is a lot of work. Humans are blaming us. I think they're trying to blame us so they can drive us out. This is turning into a massive storm and soon it's gonna come to blows." Arwen ran a hand—marred by what seemed to be burn scars—down his face. "It's gonna result in a lot of human deaths and our kind being kicked out of the city."

Nymeria crossed her arms over her chest. "You think I'm not already trying to solve it?"

Arwen shook his head. "I never said you weren't. But I thought you could use an incentive."

"I don't work for other people," she argued back.

"I can give you financial backing. A few thousand upfront and another thousand once the job is done," Arwan bargained and Nymeria raised a brow, she was suddenly a lot more interested.

"And you're gonna trust me, an angel, to do this? I can still feel my blood call to smite you both here, and considering the warm reception I had, I still might." She couldn't, but they didn't know that.

"You could," Arwen said, his voice like honey. "You may be an angel and you may hate our kind for simply existing, but you do prioritise justice; real justice, above all else. Our people are getting blamed for something we haven't been doing." Arwen's eyes met Nymeria's. "From what my crow tells me, you don't like watching innocents be killed." Nymeria averted her eyes. "Whatever you did, you still want to protect them. There's a bit of good in you."

"Fuck you."

"Maybe later." Nymeria rolled her eyes and Halloran groaned. Arwen shook his head at his joke, but his face returned to being hard set. "The police aren't doing nearly enough. I think everyone knows they just want to pin this on my kind and call it a day. But you"—Nymeria met his eyes once again—"you care about justice."

Was she really that transparent?

"You make a lot of assumptions," Nymeria said quickly.

Arwen shrugged "I've seen the reports. You help those the police deem too much trouble. The undesirables, and there's nothing as undesirable as a half-demon," he joked, but there was the tiniest flicker of hurt in his eyes.

A tap at the window distracted all of them and Halloran opened it. The one-eyed crow flew in and landed on the floor.

"You sneaky shit," Nymeria hissed at the crow, but what she didn't expect was for a ball of shadow to consume it. When it cleared, a woman was in its place.

A dark-skinned woman with one eye covered by an eyepatch and long locs of rich black-brown hair. "It's very cold out there, Arwen. I've been tapping for ten minutes now."

Nymeria's attention zeroed in on the white fangs that poked from her lips every time she spoke. Her single eye was a bright red and her skin was dull. A cursed human. One cursed with vampirism.

"Sorry, but I have a guest." Arwen gestured to Nymeria.

The woman smiled at Nymeria. "Sorry for spying, but I think you understand the sentiment that orders are orders." The vampire smiled and Nymeria felt a hot flash of anger, she recognised that voice.

"You spoke to me on the phone." Nymeria tilted her head.

"Clever. I knew you would recognise me, you're not stupid. I'm Imani Sayyid." Her voice was polite but cautious. Imani sat on a long leather sofa along one of the walls as the attention turned back to herself and Arwen.

"I can give you resources and you have the brains and talent. It would be a perfect team-up. Besides, if you're worried about getting hurt"—Arwen gestured to Halloran—"I can even throw in a free bodyguard."

"Absolutely not," Halloran said quickly. Nymeria grimaced, Arwen did have a point. Caliban was a useful partner, but if he got attacked by whatever or whoever was doing these murders, they would need someone powerful. But anyone would be better than the man who almost caved her face in.

"Harlo, it's the most sensible option. Besides, it stops you from moping around the estate—"

"I do not mope."

"It would mean a lot to me," Arwen interrupted, poorly hiding a smile.

Halloran froze. An unspoken message passed between the two brothers. Halloran let out a growl of annoyance. "Fine."

Arwen grinned. "Wonderful. Now is Miss Mercury okay to address you as or would you prefer your ladyship?"

"Nymeria," she growled, her teeth grinding together. "Nymeria is fine." Arwen opened his mouth for another remark but Nymeria shot him another steely look that silenced him, he put his hands in the air defensively.

"Do we have a deal, Nymeria?" Arwan held his hand out and a thick tension fell over the room. For a moment the sounds of the club were entirely muted. She thought only full-blooded demons could make deals, but here Arwen was, smiling at her in that sickly sweet charismatic way. This was heresy and everything screamed at her to not do it. But what was more maddening was that she was going to accept.

Nymeria took his hand and shook, the sounds of the club returning. "Good. My brother will be over at your apartment tomorrow morning. I look forward to this deal."

5

The Shining Mayor

Nymeria was in a partial daze when she walked back from Greed to her apartment. It was a long walk but a sobering one. She made a deal with a half-demon to solve this case, and in return get financing and resources. If she was willing to partner up with them to get what she wanted, maybe she did deserve to be a fallen after all. She felt a part of her past shrieking and scolding her. *How could she? They were the enemy, the unworthy monsters who had been turned from the golden embrace of the gods!* In equal parts, Nymeria wanted to hold and strangle that part of her. But she pushed that old part of herself down and back where it belonged.

Nymeria stumbled into her apartment in the early hours of the morning. She heard a small yawn from the sofa and saw a tumble of dark hair peek over the cushions. She'd completely forgotten about Gen. She'd made sure the girl was comfortable and fed before she left but hadn't told her when she would be back.

"It's just me, Gen." The little girl made an excited noise.

A tired smile pulled at Nymeria's lips. "You go back to sleep."

Nymeria stumbled to her bed and fell face first, putting her dead phone on charge. But despite how tired she was, she couldn't stop her mind from racing, replaying all the little comments made by the Draig brothers and Imani and the unsettling feelings they stirred in her gut—ones she didn't want to think about. She desperately needed a drink.

Nymeria got up and passed Gen. The little girl peered up at her, her skin grimy with dirt and sweat; Gen needed a shower, it would be annoying to have to wash her sofa cushions. The two spent the rest of the night quietly padding around the apartment, Nymeria giving Gen a quick shower and one of her own shirts to change into, the shirt was so big it was like a dress on her. After that, Nymeria drank whatever beers she could find and started to clean the spare bedroom. Gen still needed somewhere to sleep after all.

Nymeria was surprised she hadn't woken Gen throughout the night. She wiped her brow and swayed on her feet slightly as the first rays of dawn peeked through the curtains. All the spare bedroom needed was a good vacuum and dust and it would be fine, suitable for a child living there temporarily.

Ping. Ping. Ping.

Who was texting her at this hour of the morning? Nymeria crept back to her room, passing the still sleeping Gen wrapped up in the blanket. Nymeria grabbed her phone from the nightstand, ripping the charging cable out. *Three missed calls and eight texts from Caliban.* This couldn't be good. She hit dial on his contact picture. She didn't feel bad about ringing him at this hour; he was usually an early bird. He picked up after one ring. "Hey Cal—"

"Thank god, I've been trying to get a hold of you all night."

"I can see that. Listen a lot has happened—"

"Just listen! You need to be ready to go in forty-five minutes. We may have something big." Nymeria straightened, quickly pulling a fresh set of clothes out of her wardrobe and changing whilst on the phone.

"Like a big breakthrough?"

"No. A letter came through to the offices yesterday. The mayor wants to talk." Ah, shit.

"You think he wants to hire us?"

"I don't think so, but maybe we can get his blessing? It will keep Cordero off our backs." That was a good point. But they couldn't show up with a half-demon in tow and she had no idea when Halloran would appear.

"Alright, but we're taking my car." Shit, what was she going to do with Gen? Knowing how she reacted to men, leaving her alone if Halloran turned up might cause the girl even more distress.

"You never offer to drive." Caliban scoffed.

"True, but I have a child I need to keep an eye on."

"What?!"

* * *

"So you've kidnapped this child?"

That was the third time Caliban had said that and it was grating on Nymeria's nerves. "No, I didn't say that. She found me and she won't leave me alone."

Gen giggled from the backseat of the car. Nymeria looked a mess but she tried to be somewhat presentable in her black shirt and jeans, her red jacket was draped over Gen along with the blanket to keep her warm.

"Why can't you leave her with someone more..." Caliban trailed off as Nymeria shot him a heated look. "Never mind."

"No, go on say it," she snapped. She saw Gen flinch from the corner of her vision.

"Someone more qualified," Caliban said quietly. Nymeria knew what he really intended to say; she was a mess. Caliban had seen her at worst. She tried to be better, but sometimes she could slip back. Maybe Caliban did have a point but Nymeria didn't want to hear it.

She heard a sniffle and she reached behind, giving Gen a reassuring pat on the knee. "Caliban can be a dick sometimes, ignore him," she said pointedly. He just sighed.

Nymeria drove around the corner. The large gated and fenced-off manor on the outskirts of the city belonged to Mayor and former Bishop, Zai Alighieri. Most had expected him to retire once the gods disappeared, but he had been running strong as mayor. A very faith-based campaign he had created, his determination to keep the Faith going made her heart swell happily but a small part of her stomach churn as well. She could admire his perseverance, it was a quality she admired in humans; their tenacity to keep going despite everything.

Nymeria parked the car. "We'll just be a few minutes okay? You stay here." Gen was looking up at her with big worried eyes that screamed, *don't go.* Nymeria's hand hesitated on the door handle and she sighed. This girl was going to be trouble. She left the car without looking back.

Nymeria and Caliban walked down the street. "Didn't think you had a motherly streak." Caliban teased.

"I don't. I'll hand her over to an orphanage as soon as this case is wrapped up."

Caliban frowned slightly. "So as soon as she stops being useful then?"

Nymeria was quiet for a few moments. "Yes." A hard and uncomfortable silence settled between them as they made their way to the manor gates.

A buzzer clicked on as they approached. "Nymeria Mercury and Caliban Ortega?" Caliban said and Nymeria shrugged. She didn't know if they should say their names or what they were doing here. The buzzer shut off and for a few moments, they were left in silence before the big iron gate slowly opened.

"Fancy," Caliban muttered and they were both let in.

It was a short walk to the front doors of the manor where they were greeted by the mayor himself with a large, manufactured smile on his face. He was younger than Nymeria expected him to be. He seemed to be in his early forties, but his hair still had its full colour; a bright blonde accompanied by piercing blue eyes.

"Investigators." He beamed and walked out to meet them,

shaking Caliban's hand first and then Nymeria's. "I've been meaning to have this meeting for a long time now but it seems whenever I try, something gets in the way." He chuckled and ushered the both of them inside.

The inside of the manor was bright and decorated, every inch gold and white: the colours of the Creator and the City of Elysium. Nymeria's eyes landed on a thick black book. It was leather bound; adorned with golden foil and a seven-eyed owl on the front. "Our family's Codex," Zai spoke up from behind her and Nymeria jumped. She hadn't even heard him move.

"You worship the Creator?" Each family had a Codex and whoever was on the front tended to be the god that family worshipped. The contents would all be the same however; a family tree page, retelling of legends and stories of the gods, sermons and prayers. Nymeria used to have one; but now it was on Elysium, if Elysium still existed.

"Myself and my family worship all the gods but the Creator is my favourite." Zai then paled slightly. "If that isn't blasphemous to say."

Nymeria chuckled. "I think they won't mind."

Zai smiled and gestured for them to follow, falling into step next to Caliban. "The work you do at your agency is truly good work." Caliban's agency? Nymeria gave Caliban a quizzical look and he looked back at her equally confused. "I'm not usually a fan of vigilantism, but you're doing it for the right reasons, to protect the right people!" Zai opened a set of double doors and walked into a grand office. He gestured for them both to sit in two chairs opposite the glass desk and the three of them sat down.

Zai's hand steepled together and he leaned his elbows on the glass desk. "And that's why you do what you do, correct? For the right people." Nymeria glanced at Caliban, he looked as uneasy as she felt.

"And what is the right person?" She felt Caliban tense beside her and a flicker of confusion washed over Zai's face.

"You're in charge?"

"I am, the business is in my name after all." Zai froze and he hesitated, his smile falling for a brief second before rising again. "I'm dreadfully sorry. I had assumed it had been in Mr Ortega's name."

"Wouldn't be the first time," she said sharply. It was almost funny. The loan she got to buy the office space was signed off by him. It almost felt like a slap in the face to all her hard work.

Zai chuckled nervously. "Do forgive me, I didn't mean any offence. Strong leading women are good in this day and age. As you both should know, the Codex says how women and men are equal." She held her tongue from a scathing remark about how he had still assumed she was not the one in charge.

A flicker of movement caught her eye. She turned towards the door and saw a young woman close the door and scurry off. She had heard Zai had a daughter: Eleanor, former priestess of the Ghenna clergy. Apparently, she used to sing at the cathedral when it was in use.

Nymeria turned back to fully face Zai and even from the

outer edges of the city, the cathedral loomed above all. Dull marble which had once been sparkling. It had long fallen into disrepair and was closed off to the public.

"So it should not be too surprising for a woman to be in charge of her own law enforcement business. That's what I'm doing, protecting all people," Nymeria said. The manufactured smile returned to him.

"I do not wish for us to get off on the wrong foot. After all, I hope to be collaborating with you more closely."

"You want to work with us?"

"Of course, I want to protect and nurture the humans of Ghenna, as I have for a decade. Chief Cordero is becoming sloppy in his work, hence why I turn to you. Solve this case and the rewards will be great."

Caliban leaned forward. "What kind of rewards?"

Zai smiled again, a more genuine smile this time. "All in due time. But I won't keep either of you any longer. I'm sure you're both very busy today." All three of them stood up and Caliban and Zai shook hands. But when Zai shook Nymeria's, his grip was tight and he pulled her in close. "We have to protect our own after all."

"Yes...of course," Nymeria said slowly, trying to keep her tone even. Zai led the pair out of his office and towards the front door.

"I do apologise for any offence caused. I must admit, seeing a more headstrong woman is...refreshing." At this point Nymeria was zoning him out. She had heard this talk a hundred times and she didn't need a pat on the back for taking initiative. As Zai ushered them out of the door, Nymeria looked up to the big banner staircase. Looking down at her was Eleanor, she couldn't be older than sixteen with brown-blonde hair in a braid and bright blue eyes.

"Thanks for your hospitality Mr Alighieri and I'm sorry about your wife. I hope she's found safely soon," Caliban said softly, but Zai was still smiling.

"As do I. Eleanor has been in a state since her disappearance. The two were always so close." Zai closed the door behind them, the two walked in silence until the iron gates shut behind them.

"Weird man," Nymeria muttered. "Losing the Faith has rattled a lot of people."

"Give him some credit. His wife has been missing for five months now," Caliban countered and Nymeria hummed in thought. "But we now have more of an incentive to solve this case soon. Getting the mayor's endorsement could set us up in the long run."

"True. Not like we have any other benefactors." Caliban sighed.

Nymeria's eyes widened. Shit, she had to tell Caliban about the deal she made with Arwen before Halloran arrived. "About that, I've found us a sponsor..." Her words trailed off as they approached the car.

Halloran was sitting on the hood, dressed in a button up black shirt with matching trousers and dress shoes. Now that he was in the sunlight, Nymeria could actually make out his figure clearly; Halloran had a more controlled strength in his body; he was muscular but lither than Arwen, like that of a dancer. Hardly a typical fighter, he looked almost too pretty.

"Trying to run away already?" Halloran said dismissively, a spark of white flashing from his finger as he lit a cigarette and pulled on it, letting the smoke curl up around him.

"Hardly. What are you doing here?"

"My job. Which is to keep an eye on you—" Halloran's eyes—not glowing as they had been last night—looked over Caliban in boredom. "Who's this?"

"Ny, when did you get a boyfriend?" Nymeria almost gagged at Caliban's remark.

"By the Nymph, no! I have better taste than that." Halloran seemed unbothered by Nymeria's comment. "Caliban, this is Halloran Draig. He's going to be..." Nymeria hesitated and Halloran raised a brow. "Working with us. Halloran, this is Caliban Ortega. My partner—working partner." Neither man made a move to shake hands.

"You're a demon."

"Good observation, human."

"Ny, why are you working with demons?" Caliban's tone grew more concerned as Halloran chuckled.

"You haven't told your partner. You don't seem to trust him."

Nymeria snarled. "That's enough from you, get in the car." Halloran didn't move and Nymeria narrowed her eyes.

"A new murder has occurred and we must be quick if we wish to be there before the police corrupt the scene."

Halloran got up and went to the passenger side. He paused as his hands touched the handle. "Why is there a child in the back?"

"I'll explain that as well!" Nymeria snapped going into the driver's seat. Caliban sneered at Halloran as he made his way into the back next to Gen.

6

The Red Light District

The silence in the car was thick enough to cut with a knife. Nymeria had explained everything to both men and while Halloran seemed content to remain above everything, she could feel the quiet anger roll off Caliban. Caliban had turned when she spoke about the deal. Like most of the humans in Ghenna, he didn't like half-demons. Gen had curled up tighter into her blanket, pulling it up over her head. Occasionally, Nymeria would reach behind her so Gen could hold her hand for reassurance, something she used to do with her nephews when they were little. But every time she would do so, Halloran would look and she couldn't tell what the look in his eye was: Amusement? Mockery? Some weird sense of superiority? A dark cloud of arrogance hung around him and he was impossible to read. She hated it.

"So." Nymeria broke the silence. "Harlo—"

"You call me Halloran, that's my name," he snapped and Nymeria had to suppress an irritated sigh.

"Alright then, Halloran, how did you find out about this

before the cops? Who is your informant?"

Halloran looked over at her. It felt like he was trying to peer into her soul. "Imani."

How well-connected was she?

"She can't be everywhere at once," Nymeria countered.

"She has people that can be," Halloran said smugly.

"So she's the brains of your operation?"

"Precisely, good to know you're not only a pretty face."

Nymeria bristled. Asshole.

"Arwen is the face, Imani is the intelligence and I'm the fear."

"The full quote is the muscle," Caliban interrupted, and Halloran's brows furrowed as Caliban spoke.

"True, but that would imply Imani or Arwan cannot fight. They're both more than capable." Halloran straightened up, a small smirk on his face. "My presence and prowess in battle have lent me a reputation to be feared. People are scared of me, as they all should be." Nymeria and Caliban shared a look. Halloran was going to be an absolute joy to work with.

"The child wants you." Halloran's voice broke the silence, Gen was reaching out for Nymeria's hand and Nymeria put her hand behind the car seat. Halloran stared down at the child and Gen shrunk into the blanket even more. He turned to face the road ahead. She squeezed Gen's hand tighter, just a fraction. She may not be fond of the child, but she knew what it was like to be a scared little girl wanting for someone to hold her hand. She wasn't mean enough to deny an eight-year-old that.

Halloran had given them directions to the centre of the city but as they drove, the cathedral casting them in shadow, Nymeria knew the area more and more: the red light district.

"You sure there's a crime here and you're not wanting a quick fu—" Caliban glanced down at Gen. "Bit of fun?"

Halloran snorted. "If I wanted to seek my own pleasures, I wouldn't need to pay for it." Nymeria turned the corner, seeing a bunch of men and women standing outside a block of flats. Halloran hadn't been lying.

Nymeria and Caliban were often called out here; murders weren't uncommon for those living in the red light district and poorer areas but they were mainly called for muggings and violence against sex workers. "Alright, enough bickering. Your lead was right, Halloran."

"I know."

Nymeria had to bite back a retort as she exited the car. "Stay here, okay? I'll check on you in an hour," she said to Gen and she nodded. Nymeria slammed the door behind herself, shivering at the crisp air.

"You should have taken your jacket off the girl," Halloran commented. Nymeria didn't bother to reply.

The crowd let out a sigh of relief and Nymeria's lips twitched into a smile. She recognised many of the faces, that was how often she got called for help, and there was one woman who ran this small tight knit community. "Nymeria, darling. We must stop meeting under such horrible circumstances."

"It's good to see you too, Evelyn." Evelyn, a much taller red-haired middle-aged woman pulled her into a hug which Nymeria reluctantly accepted. She was already dressed to the nines, a full face of makeup and a silken robe tight across her body, the strap of a lace corset peaking out from underneath.

When Nymeria first arrived in Ghenna, with no money to her name, it was Evelyn who picked her off the street and gave her a roof over her head.

"Darling you look a mess!"

"Oh wow, thanks," Nymeria said flatly and Caliban chuckled behind her.

"No, not like that. When was the last time you slept or ate?" Nymeria felt a flush of embarrassment, she truly did look awful, she could see the knots in her hair.

"I've been busy the past few weeks." A half-lie. She had spent most of the past week in one bar or another when she hadn't been working. It was usually Caliban who picked her up from those bars when she was too drunk to drive or walk.

"You know I always have a plate ready for you and Ortega." Evelyn smiled at Ortega but her eyes lit up seeing Halloran. "And you have a new pretty man with you," she purred, and Halloran grimaced.

A few gasps erupted from the small crowd and, looking closer, she noticed many new faces. A lot of them were half-demon and it was these people reacting to Halloran. But the gasps and murmurs were more out of fear than respect. 'The Iridescent Dragon,' she heard frequently as well as 'The Prince of the Hells.' The rumours were true. She felt a sharp prickle of uncertainty down her back; he was staring at her, almost daring her to do or say something. So she turned to meet his gaze and stared him down. He didn't react, yet she could have sworn the corner of his lip twitched upward.

"We have a job to do here. We're dawdling." Halloran pushed

past Nymeria and she stumbled back. What was he doing? "Where is the dead?"

His bluntness took Nymeria and Evelyn off-guard. "I—" Evelyn stammered.

"Well?" he said impatiently. Nymeria pushed in front of Halloran and she felt his gaze bore into the back of her skull.

"He's new, ignore him. Lead the way, Evelyn."

"Of course. Make way my babies, this is the law we help, not the one we hinder," she instructed and the crowd parted.

Caliban, Halloran and Nymeria followed after Evelyn and into a large apartment complex. Some of the apartments were clearly just for living whilst others had many loud and pleasurable moans and sighs coming from them. Those doors were marked with the depiction of The Nymph, the god of love and pleasure. On some, it depicted their male form and the others their female form. But all depictions were naked and surrounded by pink roses. The group began to ascend the large spiral staircase.

"We think it occurred sometime early this morning," Evelyn started. "The neighbour of the victim, the poor man, heard a commotion he said."

She paused. "So there's a witness?" Nymeria had to suppress a smile. This was massive, finally a strong lead. "Do you know where this neighbour is?" she asked a little too eagerly.

"Two. We took the neighbour down to one of our doctors due to the shock of it all. I'm told he would be happy to talk to you in a day." A day. That could work. Nymeria would have wanted him straight away, but this was an annoyance she could deal with.

"We found him at nine this morning. His first client of the day came by—knocked three times and let himself in when no one answered." Evelyn's voice hiccuped slightly.

Nymeria frowned. She hated this part of the job; the comforting. She was barely able to understand her own emotions let alone another person. Nymeria looked to Caliban and he strode past her to walk alongside Evelyn and put an arm around her shoulder.

Halloran fell into step beside her. "Are you determined to make this as difficult as possible?" Halloran hissed.

Nymeria blinked. "Excuse me?"

Halloran glared down at her. "Do not act stupid, tempestuous woman. I took control of the situation whilst you were dawdling."

Nymeria shook her head and scoffed. "I was getting information. It's all good seeing the body but unless we get background details, it won't help the case." Halloran could be as pretty as he wanted but his personality instantly made him unattractive.

"We're here for a job, not for chatter. That was what you were doing," he remarked in that ever-belittling tone and then stomped ahead. Nymeria felt anger boil in her gut and she climbed the stairs two at a time, stopping in front of him. Her gaze was hard and angry.

"And I don't appreciate you interrupting me and trying to take over. I'm in charge here. You may have been Prince of Hell once, but here you're Prince of nothing, you arrogant man!" she snapped.

Halloran's gaze hardened and his lip curled into a snarl, the most emotion she had seen on his face since she'd met him. "Tempestuous woman," he snarled and pushed past her, his hand on her shoulder shoving her to the side. Her back hit the bannister with a thud. Bastard.

Nymeria stalked after him, catching up with Caliban and Evelyn at the top of the staircase. They approached an open door at the end of the corridor, the last apartment in the complex.

"Where is the other witness? The one who awoke the neighbour?" Caliban asked.

"He fled." Evelyn scowled. "Caused a scene, screaming and crying on the way down which is how the rest of the complex found out what happened. He was some finance guy that visits often, keeping things hush hush from his wife, no doubt."

Nymeria almost laughed. That sounded about right. Evelyn swallowed thickly. "I can't bear to look at it again. I'll be out in the hall, just in case the police show up."

Caliban nodded. "Thanks, Evelyn, you're a gem as always."

Evelyn blew a kiss at Caliban.

Nymeria smirked and Caliban frowned. "Getting friendly, are we?" she teased.

"Not now, I'm still mad at you," he sneered. It would pass. They would be friendly again in a few hours.

"No judgement from me," Nymeria muttered, slowly crossing the threshold into the room. And just like that the atmosphere switched.

Any light-heartedness and joviality was snatched up by an air of heaviness and the stink of death. Caliban gagged but Halloran didn't react and neither did she. Nymeria was used to the smell of death, she had smelt worse on a battlefield where hundreds of dead had lay before her. Unlike those times, this apartment could be littered with traps. A tripwire could be placed easily or a pressure pad under a creaky floorboard. Halloran walked in front. "I am checking for danger," he said pointedly.

"I wasn't going to say anything," she replied curtly. Halloran methodically went from room to room and Nymeria waited, Caliban by her side, gun in hand.

"Clear. The body is above the bed."

Good, one less issue to deal with. Nymeria rounded the corner, this was not the sight she expected. She had seen many brutal killings but this was almost artistic in the most macabre sense of the word. The body was sunk face first into the wall, the back exposed to the room. The spine was removed and the ribcage was brought back outward like a blossoming flower. This time, however, the hole was now filled with various organs. The same rune was drawn into the wall.

Caliban gagged as he rounded the corner. "How the hells did someone manage that?" she muttered.

"It's quite impressive," Halloran agreed.

"There's something seriously wrong with both of you," Caliban said between coughs. He wasn't entirely wrong there.

"These runes, are they familiar to you?" Nymeria turned to Halloran.

"Now you want my inference?"

"Just answer the question."

"Yes, they are. They look like summoning runes."

Summoning runes?

"Any ideas on what?" Nymeria asked, watching as Halloran approached. He flexed his hand, closing it into a fist and then opening it.

"Hard to tell, the ritual was incomplete."

Nymeria frowned and walked up to him. The runes looked the same but something was off. "There were three bodies last time," she mused.

"At the other ritual site?"

"Yes."

Halloran rumbled deep in his chest. "So it's an incomplete ritual. Perhaps your killer was scared off when the dead one's morning visitor knocked." Nymeria found herself nodding, much to her chagrin.

"Seems likely," she mused. "Either the killer will move on or come back and add to this little collection."

"That is...most likely," Halloran grumbled.

Nymeria almost felt like gloating.

"No," Caliban interrupted, standing up as he had been peering under the bed. "Not right." His face was pale.

Nymeria frowned and got on her hands and knees, peering under the bed. Staring back at her were two faces, half-sunken into the floorboards, vacant eyes staring back at her.

Nymeria jumped and pushed herself upright. "Shepherd guide them." She swallowed thickly and heard Halloran snicker. "They're dead. They won't save you now."

Nymeria turned on her heel. "Will you—"

But she paused, frowning as she heard a commotion from outside the apartment. All heads snapped towards the noise. Nymeria took the lead. She left the apartment and leaned over the railing, her knotted hair almost obscuring her vision from the officers at the very bottom of the stairs, arguing with some of the local residents. She couldn't quite make out what was being said but that didn't matter. They started ascending the stairs.

Nymeria pushed herself back from the bannister. No point in going down, that was a one way ticket to getting arrested. "What's the plan?" Caliban asked quickly.

"You get out of here. I'll take the crime scene photos," she ordered.

"And leave you to get arrested? No way—"

"I've got it, Ortega. I gotta make sure Halloran doesn't try to kill them!"

"He doesn't listen to us, just leave him!" Ortega urged.

"Hello? Who's there?" one of the officers called up.

"If he gets arrested, I'm gonna have half of this city's half-demons or worse on my ass. Go!" Caliban grunted, not looking happy but tore open the door to the neighbours, shouting quickly ensuing.

She rushed back into the crime scene, turning the camera on quickly. "What's going on?" Halloran demanded. Nymeria snapped as many photos as she could. She reached the bathroom and paused, hearing the creak at the top of the stairs.

"Shit, we're out of time," she whispered. "We need to

hide!"

"Hide?"

"Officers are nearly here." Nymeria looked around frantically, no time to go out the window. They would be caught before leaving the apartment. Her eyes landed on a small wardrobe nestled into the wall. Fuck it, she had hidden in worse places.

Her eyes widened as Halloran took a few steps towards the door. "You may choose to run instead of fight but I shall not—"

Nymeria grabbed his bicep and pulled him back. "We cannot kill the police!" she snapped and shoved him into the closet.

"What in the Hells are you doing?!" he hissed as Nymeria slid in next to him, slamming the wardrobe door shut. The cramped space was only slightly illuminated by the light filtering through the slats.

She shifted against Halloran and he hissed. "When did the infamous general and hunter become a coward—" Nymeria's hand slapped over his mouth and his eyes narrowed, glowing slightly.

"Shut up!" she hissed quietly, shifting again so their chests weren't touching as much. Despite his lithe build, she could feel the hard muscle underneath his shirt. Halloran's hand wrapped around her wrist, the one covering his mouth and she felt his grip tighten. If the officers hadn't swung the door to the apartment open, she was sure he would have snapped her wrist.

Both of them froze as they heard the steady footfalls of

the officers entering the room. Nymeria should have been listening in to what the officers were saying but Halloran's gaze and presence was overpowering; she could feel the daggers in her skin and she glared back. She heard a deep rumble and her eyes narrowed, looking outside the slats of the wardrobe door but the officers had only just arrived in the bedroom. It was coming from Halloran. It was a clear warning: *get your hands off me.*

It was a challenge and one Nymeria couldn't resist. Her nails of the hand over his mouth dug into his cheek, lightly pricking the skin. She smirked imagining the crescent-shaped marks it would leave on his face; *make me,* was her wordless reply. She could have sworn his eyes darkened or rather lightened as the glow in them intensified. Nymeria flinched as his hand suddenly reached out, preparing herself for a strike, a punch but she didn't expect his hand to brush under her nose, slightly spreading the damp blood over her upper lip. The nausea hit her all at once and her hand shot out to grip his arm to steady herself, her head swimming, vision blurring, and her scars overwhelming hot. This damn curse, it wouldn't let her have even a little fun.

She let go of his face, his hands grabbing her shoulders. She hadn't realised she was swaying until her head knocked against the back wall of the wardrobe. She froze. Halloran froze too and so did the officers. "Anyone in there?" one called and she heard the familiar click of pistols being pulled out of holsters and loaded.

"You are far more trouble than you're worth," Halloran growled.

"Come out with your hands u—" The officer was cut off by Halloran slamming the wardrobe doors open, sending one of the officers sprawling on the floor. The other was so startled he didn't have time to react as Halloran grabbed the gun out of his hand, twirled it around effortlessly and pistol whipped him across the temple. At least he was efficient.

Nymeria stumbled out after him, smacking the gun out of his hand. "We need to go!"

"Why would we when we can—"

"I wasn't suggesting! Do you want the whole of the GPD on us?! On Arwen's tail because you're too impulsive?" That silenced him and his lip curled into that snarl as he grabbed her arm and pulled her towards the window, sliding it up and half pushing her out and onto the fire escape outside.

Nymeria staggered out, her vision swimming in and out of focus. She heard a set of heavy footsteps follow after her and Halloran's hand roughly grabbed her, practically dragging her up to the roof of the building. "Move!" he demanded. Her feet stumbled along, her vision swimming and her nose bleeding more. "What is wrong with you, woman?! You didn't think to mention anything like this before we got into trouble." He begrudgingly had a point.

"Keep moving," she hissed as they dropped to the roof of the next building, Nymeria falling to her knees but still, Halloran kept moving, her knees scraping against the tiles. She hissed, feeling blood dampen her jeans.

"I should be telling you that!" Halloran snapped.

As they approached the edge of this new building, she could vaguely make out the shape of her car parked below them. "What the hells is going on?" She vaguely heard Caliban shout up to them. But unlike the previous roof, there was no fire escape this time. They were trapped.

"We're stuck!" Nymeria winced.

"No, we're not." She felt Halloran's hands under her armpits and he lifted her off the ground. "What the hells—"

"You can land on your feet, right angel?" he hissed.

She screeched but her words were lost in the wind as she felt herself plummet towards the ground. As soon as her back hit the windshield of her car, she blacked out. For the last few seconds before she lost consciousness, she could hear a whining scream from within the car and then strong arms picked her up.

7

The All-Seeing Private Eye

The first thing Nymeria felt as she woke up wasn't the throbbing in her head. It was the comforting warmth that surrounded her, like a hug, and if this was what death was like she would have embraced it a long time ago before the curse. But much to her annoyance, her eyes did flutter open. Nymeria instantly recognised the interior of her office, the headquarters for the All Seeing Private Eye. She groaned as she sat up, recognising her desk. The old red leather sofa was digging into her back uncomfortably. As she righted herself, the world spun wildly and she pressed her palms against her eyes.

Her private office was a medium-sized room with wooden floors and brick walls, a few filing cabinets and a computer at her desk. Apart from that it was fairly unassuming and empty. Behind her metal grey desk was a large circular window that overlooked the city, the cathedral looming ominously in the distance despite the deep golden sunlight filtering in. It had to be mid-afternoon. Nymeria rolled her shoulders and felt something slip off her; it was the brown blanket.

The doorknob to the office jiggled a few times before swinging inward. Nymeria could only make out the messy tumble of black hair before Gen crashed head first into her chest, little arms wrapping around her tightly. Nymeria wheezed, her hand awkwardly patting Gen's back. "You alright?" she asked and Gen pulled back a little and nodded eagerly. "Where is Caliban and Halloran? Did they get away?" Gen nodded. "You weren't scared around them?" Gen shook her head, her face falling. That was going to be something they needed to work on. Nymeria was surrounded by men most of the time, she couldn't have Gen hiding under her legs anytime one approached. It would get in the way of the investigation.

Nymeria frowned. Something about Gen's hair seemed off. She raked her fingers through the now uneven strands, messily chopped at varying lengths. "Did someone cut your hair?"

Gen shook her head and pointed at herself, grinning widely.

"You can't be doing that! You could slice a finger off."

Gen cocked her head and shrugged.

"You should have waited for me. I would have taken you to a hairdresser." Nymeria flinched at the scolding tone in her voice. She sounded so much like Mel telling off Cyrus and Alvaro.

Gen pointed at herself and then made a finger-cutting motion. She had done this before, maybe many times. Did no one ever look after her? It made her heart clench in a way she didn't like.

Nymeria breathed in deeply, dismissing the feeling for now.

"What have you been doing then? Whilst I was unconscious?" Gen left the office and Nymeria could hear some clear arguing, definitely male voices. Caliban and Halloran could wait, the sound of their voices was already giving her a headache. Gen returned a few moments later, this time with a small whiteboard and a marker; she must have been exploring her offices, those small whiteboards were in the storage unit, behind a locked door. She had to have used her magic. Gen wrote on the whiteboard then turned it around to face Nymeria; *Been hiding under the table or here, I only left to go pee :(.* Nymeria couldn't help the small smile that crept onto her face. "Thanks... for keeping an eye out." Gen grinned and Nymeria ruffled her hair. That child's smile was infectious.

She slowly stood up, swaying slightly and a small hand gripped two of her fingers. "I'm up, I'm okay," Nymeria reassured her as she pushed open her office door.

"Caliban, you're gonna say something you'll regret!" Arwen warned, his eyes narrowed at Caliban who was pacing in the makeshift bullpen, the only objects in the space being Caliban's desk, a coffee station and a giant whiteboard and corkboard they used for case details.

"Something I'll regret? You should be the one pissing yourselves. Your kind—"

"Careful," Halloran snarled, both half-demons straightening up, bodies tense.

"No no, Harlo let him finish. Let him dig his own grave." Arwen's voice dropped, becoming a snarl as well.

"How about we all calm the fuck down?" Nymeria hissed,

walking into the bullpen. All eyes turned to her.

"I told you she would pull through. She wasn't concussed." Imani's voice from behind her made her jump slightly. "Sorry." Imani smirked from her seat at Caliban's desk.

"Are you okay Ny?" Caliban asked, his fists clenched and he didn't move an inch.

"Perfectly fine. What the hells is going on here?" she grumbled, fixing Halloran with an icy stare.

Halloran looked impassively back before his cold eyes darted to Caliban. "You need a tighter leash on your dog."

"Dog?!" Caliban marched over to him as Halloran pushed himself off the wall but both Arwen and Nymeria stood between them.

Nymeria grabbed Caliban's shoulder, her back against Arwen's back. "Leave it Caliban! He isn't worth the energy."

Imani scoffed, remaining seated at Caliban's desk. "Trust the princeling to cause trouble."

"Not helpful Imani," Arwen said, annoyed. "Besides, we're supposed to be working together. Even more fighting won't help."

Caliban stepped back and Nymeria let go of his arms. She felt Arwen relax behind her.

"Fine. But I didn't throw the first punch," Halloran sneered, going back to leaning against the wall.

Nymeria hadn't even noticed the bruises that scattered Caliban's face and the black eye. Once he backed away, she looked over to Halloran who had a bruised cheek, it was clear who had won the fight.

"I can fight my own battles"—she shot Halloran a harsh look— "which will be dealt with later. But I came to an agreement and struck a deal with Arwen here, so we all need to calm down," Nymeria commanded and Caliban's eyes widened.

"You made a deal with a demon? Are you nuts?!"

"We need this deal. Otherwise, you can find yourself another job," Nymeria snapped. All eyes were on Caliban. A muscle in his jaw ticked and his knuckles whitened again.

"We're going to talk."

"Fine, but it will be later."

Imani coughed. "Can we finally move on to what we all came here for? The information on the murders."

Nymeria cleared her throat and gestured to the cork board. Pinned to it was a map of the city and on top of the map was a picture of the docks murder and a few other locations highlighted in red sharpie. "As you know, there have been five triple this month alone. All at different parts of the city." Nymeria pointed to each location. "We only managed to get to the docks crime scene. Myself and Ortega got to the others too late or were kicked off before getting evidence."

"So you barely have anything?" Imani spoke up, her tone more curious than accusatory.

Nymeria bit the inside of her cheek. "We know where the other murders took place." She gestured again to the other crime scenes, all spread at random points across the city. "We don't have any details on them, but we do know that the police seem adamant to pin the murders on the half-demon population. They may be right—"

"They're not," Arwen objected.

"We can't rule it out," Nymeria said sternly, half turning toward Arwen, his face a cold scowl. "Truthfully, no one knows who this killer is; it could be human, it could be half-demon, something could have crawled up from Hell. We don't know," she argued. Arwen crossed his arms and slumped back in the chair he had pulled up, wincing and rubbing his arms.

"Just because you have your bias doesn't mean—"

"Oh, I'm the biased one? Funny coming from an angel." Arwen smirked and Nymeria felt her stomach drop as Caliban's eyes shot to her.

"Nymeria, what does he mean?" Caliban's voice was quivering with barely concealed anger.

"Not now. Later," she urged, her temper on the verge of snapping.

"Hello, General." Arwen smirked and Nymeria shot him a look.

"Anyways, despite what happened at the brothel"—Nymeria sighed, biting the inside of her cheek again—"Halloran was helpful."

"He was?" Caliban almost laughed and Arwen gave Halloran an approving nod, to which Halloran didn't reciprocate.

"You went to a brothel?" Arwen's eyes widened and he elbowed Halloran's side. "Look at you being adventurous and having fun, my little brother, who would have thought?"

Halloran rolled his eyes and shuffled away from Arwen.

"He could vaguely read the runes at the murder site." Nymeria gestured to Halloran and he straightened up.

"They're summoning runes. Summoning what is unclear, but whoever is doing this wants to bring something from the

Hells. What that is, is anyone's guess."

"But it's demonic summoning runes?" Caliban urged and Nymeria bit her tongue as the tension built again. She didn't expect this much backlash from this collaboration. She had always known Caliban was wary of half-demons but she didn't know his hatred ran so deep that it would interfere with the case.

"It seems that way but it could also be a human doing the summoning. A human could have made a deal with a demon who then gave them magic just as easily as if a half-demon was doing all of this."

"What about an angel?" Arwan suggested and Nymeria shook her head.

"No, an angel wouldn't do something like this. Angels are sworn to protect humans from things like this."

"And kill anyone who doesn't fit their self-righteous image," Halloran snarled. "Your kind are glorified murderers."

"Halloran!" Arwen warned and Imani stood up.

"I was not a murderer!" She scoffed, yet she felt that deeply uncomfortable sinking in her gut again. "I was upholding the Faith and keeping people safe from harm."

Halloran snorted. "Are you sure? The nightmare of all demons is what we used to call you. The monster hiding under our beds"

"Did I ever appear in your nightmares?" she challenged, looking Halloran dead in the eyes. He remained silent.

"I'm confused." Caliban rubbed his brows. "How does a human have magic? It's been outlawed since the Destroyer attempted to take over Elysium."

"They make a deal. With a demon usually. Magic is passed through blood," Arwen explained. "Blood is the most powerful thing in this whole wide world. It can make and shape everything we see. The Creator made the other gods, shedding some of his blood and moulding them into being." Arwen looked at Nymeria to take over. After all, the intricacies of angel society weren't common knowledge to humans and most demons.

"Angels are the children of the gods. Why they wanted us, I don't know. They never stuck around and it's not like it's done out of love with another god or human. We're forged."

"Forged?"

"Yes, the Smith, god of Forgery, makes us with our parent god's blood and whatever our parents want to throw in there to give us power." Nymeria hated how her throat tightened. "I was forged from a dying star. My sister used to say I was plucked straight out of the darkest night during the brightest full moon of the year. The first sun angel in three millennia."

"And now you're a fallen angel," Imani whispered. Nymeria hadn't realised she had wrapped her arms around herself and forced them down by her sides.

"Yes."

"What did you do?" Imani's tone wasn't spiteful, not like the burning look she could feel Caliban give her from her side.

"It doesn't matter. It won't change a thing."

"But it did stop you from having any power," Halloran spoke up. "Most of the fallen angels get sent to the Hells. They get eaten up pretty quickly but they still have some amount of magic, even if it's weak. You don't have anything, do you?" His face still held that coldness but there was something akin to interest sparking in his eyes.

"I was cursed before I fell. A new curse," Nymeria said, her throat so tight she could barely make a sound. There were only two known curses in existence, both were created when humans were bestowed magic by the Destroyer; the curse of vampirism and the curse of lycanthropy.

"By my sister, the darling high priestess"—Nymeria's voice dripped with venom—"created one just for me. Curse of pacifism, she called it. It stripped all the magic from my blood and placed a sickness within me. I cannot do any harm to others and none shall come to me and if I try, well, I bleed for it or worse pass out entirely." Nymeria's voice was raw and she couldn't look at anyone. Instead, she fiddled with the cuff of her shirt. The room was silent.

"The high priestess of Elysium can make curses?" Arwen said slowly.

"That and more. Melantha has always been more skilled in the arcane and with her words than a sword."

"A curse-maker is a bad thing?" Caliban asked slowly. His naivety was endearing.

"Even amongst the angels, certain magics are forbidden. The first are curses, due to their association with demons. The second is magic of the body; mind controlling and blood magic. The third is the magic of reality; anything to do with time and the bending of reality or space. Which brings me to the most important thing I've found during these investigations." Nymeria pointed at Gen, who shrunk behind the door. "Her."

"Your daughter?" Imani raised a brow.

"Not my child. I found her in a shipping container at this fifth murder site." Nymeria pointed at the map. She was grateful that the attention was off her. "Whoever is doing these murders had her brought in especially."

A dark silence fell over the room. "Do you think they did anything to her?" Arwen asked, his voice gruff and he looked pained. At least they could all agree that Gen deserved better than what had already happened to her.

"I don't know. She can't talk, but that's not the most interesting thing about her." Nymeria leaned forward a bit to get a better look at Gen. "Come on." Gen shrunk behind the door until only one eye peaked around the corner.

"We aren't gonna hurt you," Arwen said and stood up, wincing as he crouched down. "I may not have the prettiest face but I'm not too bad a man. Promise," he said, grinning at her.

Gen met Nymeria's eye and she crouched down with a sigh. "You can stay right by me. I won't let anything bad happen, I promise."

Gen rushed to Nymeria and wrapped her arms around her middle. This was not what she had in mind. Awkwardly, Nymeria lifted Gen up and placed her on Caliban's desk next to Imani. As soon as Nymeria shifted away, Gen grabbed her hand and with a sigh Nymeria stayed by the little girl's side.

Nymeria tugged at her hand. "Go on. Show them." Gen looked up at her, confused as if saying '*You told me not to show anyone.*' "Yes I know I said that, but you can show them." Gen pouted and then rubbed her hands together, her tongue sticking out as she concentrated, looking at the corkboard. A small crack soon appeared in the space in front of the corkboard and split open just as one appeared in front of Gen. With a grin, she reached through—her hand appeared through the other portal by the cork board and she plucked the picture off it before pulling her hand back, both portals sealing behind her.

The room fell silent.

"But she's human," Halloran said slowly, tilting his head as he stared Gen down. Gen hissed as she cut her hand on the paper.

"May I?" Imani held out her hand to Gen.

"Go on," Nymeria said quietly and Gen gave Imani her hand. Imani leaned down, her tongue wiped over the cut. Gen squealed and pulled her hand back, wiping the saliva on the table.

"Definitely human," Imani confirmed.

"Could have said what you were gonna do first," Nymeria snarled and Imani simply shrugged.

"I won't apologise for efficiency. It may be an unusual method of detecting what someone is but blood never lies." Nymeria had to agree she did have a point.

Gen shrunk into herself, shifting so Nymeria was in front of her. Nymeria cleared her throat. "Yes, a human that can perform forbidden magic but can't read—"

"—And tomes are given to those who make pacts with demons. It's the only way for humans to gain magic and there's not a chance that this girl can read one of them or provide the blood sacrifice needed to strike that deal. This girl is something new entirely," Halloran interrupted. "You're a fascinating little human."

Gen's lips twitched into a smile. But Nymeria wasn't smiling.

"But more importantly, she's the first human in history to be born with magic. It's safe to assume that whoever our killer is wanted her for her magic. She's the key to everything going on. As long as she's with us we have the upper hand."

8

Confrontation

"So what, you're gonna use her as a hostage? As bait?" Imani scowled.

Nymeria didn't answer straight away, chewing on the inside of her cheek. She was going to use Gen to solve this case and afterwards, they would all go their separate ways. But as she looked down into Gen's wide eyes staring up at her, she felt a twinge of something in her heart. An old feeling, one she didn't want to recognise.

She turned her head away. "We keep her safe. She can draw out the killer. All the other victims have been adults, she was the only child. I imagine our killer will be very desperate to get her back. Desperate people make the worst mistakes and that's when we strike."

"That's a sound strategy. But what do we do?" Arwen asked.

"We lay low for a few days. Might be good to start by trying to track down whoever found the last person. Some finance man that frequents the red light," Nymeria said and Imani stood up.

"I can get some suspects but it may take a day or two."

"That's fine." Nymeria nodded and Arwen stood up as well.

"I can help out. See if any half-demons in the red light district know anything. They'll be more willing to talk to me anyway."

"Take care. Try not to be the next victim," Nymeria dryly joked.

Arwen paused, cocking his head. "You can make jokes? That's something you can do?!"

Nymeria gave him a blank look. "Get out."

Arwen held up his hands and left. Imani followed behind him, chuckling.

A simmering anger hung in the air as the door clicked shut behind. Before Nymeria could even turn around to confront Caliban, his hand had already tightly grasped her arm and pulled her into her office. His grip felt like a burning wound and she wanted him off but she was frozen.

Shutting the door behind him, she sighed as she heard the lock click into place, this was going to get messy. Nymeria let out a small breath of relief when he let her go and instinctively crossed her arms over her chest, leaning her hip against the desk.

Caliban ran both his hands up and down his face, messing up his hair. "How long have we known each other, Mercury?"

She was in trouble if the surname was being used. "Two years."

"Two years," he repeated. "I always thought it was weird you never mentioned anything about home or family, no matter how many times I asked. Despite the fact that I told you every little bit about myself; my divorce, my childhood, everything! And it turns out I don't know you at all!"

Nymeria remained quiet, letting Caliban pace, letting him yell and scream at her.

"I told you I hated the Faith." Nymeria felt a hot flash of anger. It didn't make sense; he was allowed to not like the Faith, but it somehow felt that he was saying he hated her as well.

"But all this time you've been a part of it!"

Nymeria barely held in her flinch as his hand smacked against the door in frustration. Nymeria caught the movement of Halloran lifting his head from where he stood in the bullpen. "Arwen said you were a general, is that true?"

"You've already made up your mind about me. Why bother asking?"

Caliban looked appalled as he stopped pacing and finally faced her, standing mere inches away. His breath fanned her face in angry puffs. "Because we've been friends for two years. Worked together, been shot at together, solved cases together. Does all that time mean nothing to you?" Nymeria hated how her throat bobbed, she closed her eyes, desperately trying to stop her mind from going to that dark room with the chains.

"I could ask you the same thing. We spent all that time together and you're throwing a tantrum because I kept my secrets to myself. Which I'm entitled to do, I don't owe you that." It was growing harder for her to keep her voice neutral.

"I'm not angry you have secrets. I'm angry that you don't trust me! I'm angry that I'm a good friend to you and you treat me like shit!" he seethed, some saliva splattering on Nymeria's cheek.

"I didn't tell you because I knew you would react aggressively, I knew it would cause more problems than it's worth." Her eyes narrowed. "Now I know I was right to be cautious."

"Of course I'm aggressive, I don't know you at all! I could excuse how everyone looks down at me when they learn I'm working underneath you. But you treat me like shit as well! Is it a thing that angels, or sun angels—whatever you are—treat humans like shit?!"

Nymeria knew there was no point trying to explain, it would just wind him up more. But once every few millennia, a strange phenomenon would happen; when the Smith made an angel—perhaps it was an extra drop of blood or an object too powerful was included in the mixture. Whatever it was, it would birth a Sun angel, capable of great power and great destruction, a herald of the Faith, the chosen protector of Elysium and the closest thing to a god amongst angels. That was what Nymeria had been.

"They said you were a general. A warlord! How many people have you killed? Tens?"

"Hundreds," Nymeria replied curtly, her gaze stern whilst he took a few steps back.

"Hundreds. You killed for the Faith but you won't give me, someone who matters, any sense of respect. You won't help keep me and my people safe and instead work with the enemy?"

Hundreds. The word bounced around her head, it was monstrous when he said it like that. But she'd never thought of it that way, not when a sword was first thrust in her hand at fourteen, not when she went on her first mission for the Elysium council at sixteen. It was what was expected of her, her duty to live up to, her whole reason for existing, surely there was nothing wrong with that?

"No, I don't feel bad." She couldn't tell if she was lying or telling the truth. "I never told you who I was," she started, clearing her throat, "because I didn't want you to know me."

Caliban laughed, the sound cruel and angry. "I don't know who you are!" he mocked. "Ha, actually I know!"

"Careful," she warned.

"How many nights have you called me, so drunk you can't even speak let alone drive your ass back home. I was the one who got you and stayed with you. Whilst you were sobbing about god knows what, throwing up and then drinking more! You're a shell of a person and an alcoholic. You know what, Zai is right. Maybe I should be the one running this business because you're an emotional mess of a woman—"

Nymeria slapped him, his head jerking so quickly she heard the muscle pop in his neck.

"Get out," she said quietly.

"Do you want me to pack my desk as well?"

"Do what you want. I don't care."

Nymeria turned to face the large window overlooking the city. She heard the door open and slam shut, Caliban's footsteps fading into nothingness.

She let out a shaky breath. One less person to worry about. Who was he to tell her that? She just liked to drink when she was stressed. Admittedly, that was all the time but she wasn't an alcoholic and she wasn't a mass murderer...

That uncomfortable feeling in her gut stirred again and she dismissed it. No. No, she wasn't any of those things.

The door opened.

"Not now, Halloran."

"The child was concerned."

Nymeria had partly turned around when she felt arms gently tug on her sleeve. *'You ok?'* Gen had written and Nymeria nodded.

"Clearly not," Halloran said and Nymeria scowled.

"Your eyes are very expressive. Your face is calm but your eyes tell the truth." Halloran sounded far too smug.

"Why are you still here anyway? Surely you have to get back home?"

Halloran sighed. "That's why I'm still here. My brother is altering the agreement slightly. Since you have no magic and can't protect yourself, he worries the killer may strike you directly. He wants me to guard you twenty-four hours a day."

"So you'll be living with me?"

"Unfortunately."

9

Not a Family

Nymeria's fingers flexed against the steering wheel. The tension was so thick that a knife would struggle to cut it. Her eyes were solely focused on the traffic in front but she could feel Gen's eyes flicker between herself and Halloran. Halloran was leaning back in the passenger seat, arms crossed and looking out the window. They were all sulking, even Nymeria could admit that.

Before they set off, Nymeria had a rather intense conversation with Arwen over the phone. She had almost screamed at him. She had spent enough of her life being undermined by plans made behind her back, and she didn't intend to relive that. Arwen had yelled back that it was just a precaution, not trying to control her but instead safeguard an asset. If she died, this whole investigation went in the gutter. He had a point. But she didn't like the idea of someone leering over her. Especially being anywhere near her when she was asleep. Halloran was an asshole, sure, but she didn't think he was capable of anything as malicious as that. But then again, she had been proven wrong once before.

"I...apologise."

Nymeria frowned, there was no way she had heard that correctly. "I'm sorry?"

"I..." Halloran looked pained as if putting aside his pride hurt him physically. "Apologise. For throwing you off that roof."

She'd heard him right.

"But I wouldn't have thrown you off that roof if you had been forthcoming about your situation." There it was. A more rational part of her would have apologised as well, a more strategic approach to keep the peace with her newfound allies. But that also meant vulnerability; by opening up and showing the ugliness inside her, allies quickly became friends and Nymeria didn't want friends.

"I'm repeating myself a lot today," She grumbled. "I don't owe you, or anyone, my whole life story." Nymeria felt her teeth grind together.

"I don't wish to hear it. There's only so much arrogance and superiority in the name of the Faith I can stomach." Halloran grunted and Nymeria rolled her eyes, focusing back on the road. "But myself and Arwen were under the impression that you had magic. You could do something that angels were born with: heal faster, at least cast some magic, even fight! But you're weak, powerless, no better than a human. Which puts you in a lot more danger than we anticipated."

Nymeria's teeth grind together. "You know what—"

"Stop that!" Halloran said, sounding surprised.

She heard a slap of a hand against fabric. Nymeria looked behind her, Gen hit Halloran's arm again, a scowl on her face. "Enough!" he barked, his hand grabbing Gen's when she went for another strike. Nymeria's hand shot out, grabbing his wrist.

"Let her go," she warned. Halloran's eyes met her, a heated anger simmering between them. She was prepared to pull this car over if need be. Halloran's other hand shot out and Nymeria braced for a strike but she felt the car harshly turn inward as a car honked at them as it drove past.

"Eyes on the road, otherwise I'll be driving," Halloran said sternly, letting go of the steering wheel and Gen's hand with a huff. The girl sunk into the backseat, pulling the blanket up around herself.

"And there goes any confidence she had. Thanks," Nymeria sneered.

"Not my fault your child is undisciplined. Can she not fight, like you?" Halloran's sneer and arrogant smirk were not lost on her but she did keep her eyes on the road.

"She's eight!"

"Your point?" Halloran sounded genuinely confused. "I was wielding a sword efficiently by the time I was nine."

"Where did you grow up, on a battlefield?"

"No. The Hells, so a close second."

Nymeria didn't reply to that. She couldn't even imagine what growing up in the different circles of the Hells would have been like at such a young age.

"Fair enough."

"No scathing retort? It was your kind that forced my mother back to the Hells. Arwen and I were barely walking at the time.

I thought angels loved to laugh at those in the Hells from atop your golden towers."

Nymeria felt her vision turn red.

"Don't speak to me of Elysium!" she shouted. The red vanished as she heard a squeak from behind her. Gen pulled the blankets tighter around herself. Nymeria sighed, letting her head hit the headrest with a thump.

Silence filled the car. Nymeria exhaled as she turned the corner and parked outside her apartment building. Nymeria fished around in her pocket and pulled out her keys, tossing them back to Gen. "Let yourself in. You remember the way?" Gen didn't respond. She hastily left the car and ran into the building. Halloran looked over at Nymeria expectantly.

"Can we agree to not shout at her or argue around her?" she asked, looking Halloran in the eyes.

"Why is she so scared? She has a determination like you do, why does she hold herself back?"

"I don't think she knows it."

This was maybe the most civil conversation they had so far. "But I found her in a storage container. Clearly, she had been trafficked, I don't think I have to explain to you why people would traffic little girls aside for her powers."

Halloran's face hardened and his Adam's apple bobbed. "I see." Nymeria swallowed hard as well, her fingers tapping the steering wheel.

"She's been through a lot. She deserves a moment of peace here, in my home. She's been through enough conflict being orphaned and—" Nymeria felt bile rise in her throat. "Creator forbids, whatever else."

Halloran was quiet for a moment. "Fine. I can agree to those terms. But that does not make us friends."

"Isn't the saying keep your friends close and your enemies closer?" she half-joked and she heard something she hadn't expected: Halloran chuckled. It was a hoarse sound, as if he didn't do it much or at all but it had an almost enchanting lilt to it. "Oh and one more thing."

Halloran's face fell and he scowled again.

"If you're gonna smoke, do it on the fire escape. I don't need my apartment stinking of brimstone and smoke."

"Fine."

Wordlessly, the two left the car and made their way into Nymeria's apartment complex. The building was not luxurious or even close to being clean, the wooden floor had many scuffs and the wallpaper was chipped and peeling. The walls were thin enough that the traffic outside could be clearly heard and a heavy scent of mildew hung over the building like cobwebs in an abandoned house. Halloran didn't hide his disdain, sneering at everything. The floorboards groaned in protest as they ascended the stairs.

"You couldn't afford somewhere nicer?"

Nymeria huffed a laugh. "Banishment from Elysium doesn't come with a severance package."

"You didn't use some extra tactics to stabilise yourself financially?" As they crested the first set of stairs, she paused and gave him an incredulous look.

"When you came up from the Hells did you threaten people to give you money?" Nymeria asked and Halloran raised an eyebrow.

"My brother's organisation encroaches on a lot of different territories."

"Gang is what the police refer to it as."

"Same thing," he dismissed and then continued, "It is easy to intimidate humans and weaker half-demons will give us whatever we want as long as we protect them." Nymeria could feel something boil in her blood. She could feel it call out to her *'Slay the monster, you're a heretic for even tolerating standing next to him'*. She pushed it down but it still simmered angrily.

But every time she blinked she would be back to being a fourteen-year-old girl, being taught the Codex back to front by members of Melantha's clergy who had a binary view on the Codex, and they would tell her what the actual meaning of the words on the pages meant. Nothing was up for interpretation. For a brief moment, she wondered if Melantha kept her Codex or their family one, or was it burnt along with the rest of her belongings when she was imprisoned? A small part of her hoped it wasn't, a greater part hoped it was.

It took two more sets of stairs to reach the top floor and her apartment. Nymeria opened the first door and stepped inside. She needed to clean up. "This is—"

"Don't—"

"—A mess," Halloran sneered. "I didn't think angels lacked basic hygiene."

Nymeria rolled her eyes. "Well you're living here now so you can help," she dismissed, walking farther into her apartment. A pattering of footsteps and then the spare bedroom door opening and closing. She sighed. She would have to build Gen's confidence back again. Nymeria turned back to Halloran who was looking at the beer and wine bottles that were overflowing her bin. She felt heat flush her cheeks in embarrassment. "I like to have a drink."

"Yes, I can see that," he said, his voice barely concealing the judgment in his tone. Halloran sighed, begrudgingly rummaged through the kitchen drawers and pulled out a bin bag. At least he wasn't entirely uncooperative.

"And this"—Nymeria patted the sofa—"is going to be your new bed."

Halloran turned to face her and instantly scowled. "That's a poor joke."

"I don't have another bed. Are you gonna deprive Gen of hers?" Nymeria challenged, a small smirk blooming on her face as she saw Halloran's lips curl into a snarl.

"Why can't I have your bed?"

"Absolutely not!" She scoffed. "I only give up my bed for friends and as you stated earlier in the car, we aren't."

Halloran sighed in defeat, and for Nymeria, it felt like she had finally one-upped him.

"I suppose you'll deprive me of your washing facilities too? If you have any," Halloran retorted and her smirk fell.

"My shower works fine, but I'm going to use it now. Make yourself comfortable," she said, turning on her heel. She grabbed a hoodie and leggings from her sparse wardrobe and headed back to the bathroom. It was just next to her bedroom and like the rest of her apartment, it was messy. Even the wooden flooring had dust bunnies and the white tiles had a layer of grot on them. Nymeria cleaned up a little bit, making sure any scissors and razors were out of the way of Gen-sized hands.

Nymeria looked at herself in the mirror: she needed a shower and a haircut; her skin felt sweaty and gross. Usually, she would have left washing until she needed to or Caliban said something. She had a child and a man living with her now, she begrudgingly had to make some effort with herself. With shaky hands, she took the gloves off then unbuttoned her shirt and shucked off her jeans. She tried to ignore them at first, instead focusing on her dull brown eyes which once glowed golden,, fueled by the magic of the sun.

She'd been the sun a lifetime ago. Now, she was a mutilated autonomous corpse of a woman. The chain scars criss-crossed her entire body, across her legs and thighs, her stomach and back, her breasts and along her arms. Nasty blots marred the scars every few inches where the chains had been embedded into her skin. Just staring at them, she could feel the agony twisting along her bones, stripping flesh from muscle and holding her up like a prize pig at the butcher house. Nymeria spat in the sink. Melantha deserved nothing but spit and pig shit.

She spent much longer in the shower than she meant to. Washing body, hair and scars until her skin was raw and her hair untangled and clean. Truthfully, she did feel better for it. Nymeria changed and left the bathroom, a cloud of steam following behind her. Halloran was not on the sofa nor in the kitchen and neither was Gen. The kitchen was also much cleaner than how it had been when she first stepped into the shower.

"You can't live under the bed."

Nymeria frowned. Halloran was in Gen's room? She quietly approached the cracked door and lightly pushed it open, not making a sound. Peaking through the crack, Nymeria could make out Halloran standing at the foot of Gen's bed, looking down at the floorboards. "If you were trying to surprise attack me, hiding under a bed is a fool's strategy. It's most likely where an adversary would check first."

She realised he wasn't looking at the floorboards but rather at someone underneath the bed, someone she couldn't see. "You cannot stay under there, Genevieve," Halloran scolded and a small hand reached out and swatted his boot.

"Alright, Gen it is. But that wasn't very polite." Nymeria could hear the squeak of the marker on the whiteboard and Nymeria had to bite back a laugh when she saw what Gen had written *'You are not very polit. You are mean to Ny and I dont kno your name'*.

Halloran sighed deeply, "What has my life become," he whispered as he sank to one knee then another and lay flat on the floor.

"My name is Halloran Draig. I'm going to be staying here with you and your...guardian." For a few moments, all was quiet until Halloran sighed and Nymeria could already imagine the scowl on his face as he pushed his pride aside for the second time that day. "I apologise for scaring you. It wasn't my intention. Your guardian is a jarring, stupid and tempestuous woman."

"Jarring, stupid and tempestuous? That's almost a compliment." Halloran shot upright so fast the usually composed man almost stumbled over his feet. His mouth pulled into a thin line.

"I didn't see anything." Nymeria held up her hands and turned on her heel. "Gen, you want takeout?" She heard a pounding of footsteps as Gen almost crashed into her legs, a big grin on her face. "Alright, you choose," Nymeria said fondly but Gen was looking at her with big round eyes and scribbled on her pad. '*Pretty.*'

"Go on and order food," she dismissed despite the small fuzzy feeling in her heart.

"Yes, you'll need your strength." Both Nymeria and Gen cocked their heads. "Your training begins tomorrow," Halloran said, leaving no room for argument. "I'm going to teach you to fight."

II

The Best Of Devils And The Worst Of Men

10

Rooftop Sessions

In her mind, Nymeria could visualise the corkboard and all they had learnt so far. Five crime scenes, the same runes and three bodies at each. But one big question hung over this whole investigation—why? The killer wanted to summon something, sure. But what would that achieve? Were they trying to prove a point? The demon attacks were putting a strain on the city as is. Summoning something may just break it beyond repair. There were far too many unknowns, and she didn't like it. The biggest being why Gen was involved. A million theories ran through Nymeria's head and each made her stomach churn. She needed more information and she could only get it when they found out who the man who had found the red light district victims was. Halloran, striding over to Gen, snapped Nymeria out of her thoughts.

"Hold the sword tighter and keep your wrists up. Otherwise they may break if your attacker is stronger than you."

Halloran took a few steps away from Gen, scooping up a training staff; Gen looked down and placed her hands farther apart. He twirled the staff in one hand and got into a fight stance.

"I shall go very easy on you, but remember that your enemies will not." Gen shuffled her feet apart as she got ready, inhaling deeply before running forward with a small yelp, swinging at Halloran's hip in a wide arc. Halloran lightly side-stepped, parrying the light blow.

Gen slowed and pouted, looking down at the staff.

"Why did you stop?" Halloran scolded, taking a few fast swings at her. "You never give up and never stop attacking until your opponent is defeated."

Gen backed up, barely parrying the first two strikes, and the third knocked her onto her back.

"Otherwise, you end up dead."

Gen frowned and stood back up, her hair falling in front of her face. Nymeria stood up from her spot on the rooftop's rimmed ledge, stretching her muscles. She walked over to her, taking a spare hair tie out of her jean pocket and crouching down behind Gen, grabbing a fistful of her black hair and tying it back into a small ponytail.

"It also helps if your hair is out of your face. You can focus on looking like a pretty warrior princess once you can fight effectively," Nymeria reprimanded lightly, her hands adjusting Gen's grip on the staff and then pushing her shoulders upright. "Having good posture also helps. Footwork is the first step for good combat; keep your feet apart like this at all times. It means you're less likely to fall, and light feet mean you can move faster and expose weak points."

Nymeria stood up and took a few steps back. Gen turned to look back at her.

"Go on. Remember, light feet and if all else fails and you're without a weapon, bite, kick and scratch the hands and eyes."

Gen nodded and turned to face Halloran. Just then, Nymeria's phone rang. She plucked it out of her pocket, not even checking the caller ID. "Hello, Nymeria Mercury speaking."

"You're always so formal picking up the phone."

Nymeria groaned. "You better have good news for me, Arwen."

"Is my presence not good news? Just popping over to make sure you and Harlo haven't killed each other already. Let us in already, it's cold out here," he said, his voice barely hiding his annoyance. She could faintly hear his fist banging against her apartment door.

"On my way," she said, hanging up on him. Nymeria approached the building ledge and swung her legs over, landing on the rickety and rusting fire escape that attached itself to the side of the building. She quickly stepped down one set of stairs and then another, almost tripping over her feet.

Sliding through the lounge window, she heard another series of knocks on her front door.

"Yes, yes, alright!" she called, unlocking the front door and wrenching it open. Not only was Arwen there, his usual charismatic smile on his scarred face, but also Imani, who looked more tired than usual.

"I've been a crow for way too long." She stretched out her back, hands on her hips. Nymeria opened the door wider, and the two strolled in.

"This is nowhere near as bad as Halloran described. He made it sound like a pig sty."

Nymeria ran her tongue along her teeth. "Oh, did he now?"

"Don't let him rattle you," Arwen said warmly, elbowing her. "I was half expecting to find him brooding in a corner. Where is he?"

"Training Gen."

Both of them looked stunned, like they had just seen pigs fly.

"I have to see this," Arwen said, a smile already falling over his face.

"Go out the open window and up the fire escape." She could barely make out Arwen's broad form; he moved much quicker than she would assume for someone of his physique.

Nymeria chuckled and went to follow, but Imani's hand caught her wrist. "Can I have a word?"

Nymeria looked to the window; she didn't want to leave Gen alone for long. She knew how she reacted with men and didn't want to push her luck by leaving her with one nice and another not-so-nice man who shoved Nymeria off a roof.

"What about?"

"Halloran." Imani's eyes were pleading, like she had something crucial to say. But if it was so important, why weren't the boys involved? Nymeria's eyes furrowed, but she closed the window. Imani let go of Nymeria's wrist.

"Thank you," she started. "I realise you may think of me untrustworthy—"

"Because of your curse? You haven't tried to drink my blood without asking, you're one of the most polite vampires I've met."

Imani laughed; the sound was a dark and alluring melody. "I'm only polite to friends, you're lucky to be one."

Nymeria raised a brow. "Friends? I believe we've had two conversations."

Imani shrugged. "Fair point. My curse has led my life to be a solitary one." Her voice became quiet. "I used to be the person to host block parties, birthdays, any kind of celebration and have friends over every weekend." Her tone turned bitter. "Now I'm reduced to nighttime skulking and shadows."

Nymeria went quiet, feeling a painful surge of memories of her childhood on Elysium. How she would tail Melantha around, sneak into the training arenas to catch a glimpse of the warriors sparring and when she was much older, attend the lavish banquets and feasts held by the Council.

"I know what that's like," she muttered, pacing anxiously.

"I can imagine." Imani's eye was watching her. "And because of that, because of our similarities in our struggles with the...changes done to us."

Nymeria paused and turned to fully face Imani, her hands on her hips.

"I feel a need to warn you about Halloran."

"Halloran?"

"He's not to be trusted."

Nymeria laughed, shaking her head. "Obviously."

"Good, I thought you would have enough sense as to not trust him already. But he shouldn't be anywhere near Gen, not with how important she is to this whole case."

That caught Nymeria's attention; she had history with

Halloran. Hatred? Or disdain for what he was?

"You don't trust him because he's a demon? Well, half of one?"

Imani shook her head. "No! I've met plenty of good half-demons thanks to Arwen."

Nymeria's first reaction was to scoff—there weren't any good half demons—but that feeling in her gut resurfaced, and she pushed that down. Why, now of all times, was she second guessing herself?

"It's thanks to Arwen that I'm alive now."

That broke Nymeria out of her thoughts. "Arwen is your curse maker?"

Imani sighed, her hand touching her eyepatch. "No, no, he saved me from my curse maker."

Nymeria frowned but remained quiet. She had learnt by now that when interviewing witnesses or suspects, it was better to let them talk first and then pick out discrepancies.

"Halloran brings death everywhere he goes and doesn't care who gets hurt or how many lives he ruins along the way." Imani's voice was like a hot blade, spitting with hate.

"He killed you?" Nymeria pieced it together.

"I used to live in Sodom," Imani hissed.

The calamity of Sodom. Nymeria didn't know all the details; it happened during her imprisonment. Sodom had been known as the Guardian city, not too far from one of the ward sights. It was a tourist hotspot despite the immediate danger. What she did know about the calamity was that for a few hours, the wards protecting Sodom had fallen, and from it rose an army of demons which slaughtered the city led at the time by a Prince of Hell, Halloran, who supposedly burst through the centre of Sodom itself.

"I was a tech support agent. I was just about to start my shift when it happened. I literally just walked out of the door, sipped my latte and then it happened." Imani's voice was distant.

"Sodom fell into the Hells?"

"Straight into the third circle. I woke up with glass in my eye and my body broken." Imani breathed in deeply and wiped a bloody tear from her eye. "Blood is the most powerful thing in this world, but it's also the most corrupting."

Nymeria swallowed thickly, her face had fallen more and more as Imani talked.

"Arwen has always been more human than demon. I saved myself from my curse maker but it was Arwen who saved me from blood-lusted insanity. But Halloran...Halloran who caused all of this in the first place? He hasn't done a thing," Imani spat. "If it means it will give him strength, power, or anything to leverage himself, he'll take it. He hasn't touched you because you don't have anything, but Gen does." Imani took a deep breath and Nymeria went to the kitchen, picked up a tissue box and passed it over to her.

"Thank you, my mascara is too expensive to waste on tears." Both women chuckled lightly, but the heavy sadness and anger were not leaving. "The point of me telling this isn't for pity. It's a warning. Halloran is the worst of men and the best of demons. Be careful, before he ruins another life."

Silence hung in the air. Nymeria knew Halloran had been a cruel man—a cruel demon. But to destroy a whole city was unheard of for a single demon to do, let alone a half-demon. Part of her blood boiled; she should strike him down and avenge those who had been killed in Sodom's destruction. But was she so different?

Of course she was. Nymeria had killed those who wanted to harm the council, harm the innocents of Elysium and the continent, she had done everything for a higher purpose. She wasn't like him at all, even if it was hundreds, she had a reason. But a small part of her spoke clearly—she was made a fallen angel because of a perfectly constructed lie. Could Melantha lie about her life's purpose as well?

"Well, I can't protect Gen by myself. So, on one hand, I do need him. But on the other hand, with him so close, I can keep an eye on him. Stop him from any more secret destruction he may have planned."

"Keep your friends close but enemies closer? Very strategic, General."

Nymeria chuckled bitterly and shook her head. She turned her back to Imani and opened the window. "I'm no general anymore, I'm just a fallen."

"I think you're a woman doing her best. We're both women trying their best, isn't that enough?" Imani's words stilled Nymeria, and her throat felt heavy.

She sniffed. "You coming outside?"

"I can't. It's daylight. And I used a lot of my magic trying to get here in the first place. I'm far too tired." Imani sighed.

Nymeria frowned and walked to her bedroom, rummaging

through a few drawers. "Would a very big umbrella help?"

Imani's eye widened and she smiled. "That may just work." Nymeria also wanted to talk to Imani, and there was no better time than this.

Nymeria knew her next words may backfire in her face. "Halloran said you're the informant for the gang, right?"

Imani paused, her hand a few inches away from the umbrella. "Yes, why?"

"I have something I would like you to look at. Something that I don't want Halloran or Arwen knowing about."

"I work for Arwen, not you," she said defensively and Nymeria pulled the umbrella back.

"I know—but I don't want either of them handling it because you know about curses more intimately than they do."

Imani quirked her brow. Nymeria had put her money on the fact that intrigue would pull her into doing this favour.

"My curse resides in the scars I have on my body." Nymeria's voice was quiet, shame heavy in her words. "Not in the blood, like you. As well as limiting my ability to do anything, the curse also protects me."

"Protects you? From what?" Imani interrupted, her mouth formed in a small 'o' of curiosity, her fangs poking out slightly.

"A few nights ago, before the dock murder. I went to a church—"

"You can do that?" Imani interrupted, and Nymeria couldn't deny it was a question she had been asking herself.

"Apparently...I was attacked by a demon, and the scars incinerated it."

Imani's eyebrows rose. "Incinerated? Are they charged with magic?"

"Pretty much." Nymeria shrugged.

"You want to see if it can be removed? Nymeria, no one has found a cure for curses. Ever."

Nymeria sighed. "I know. But with how different my curse is, maybe there's a chance. A chance to figure out how to reverse it. It's not to do with the case but I wanted to ask you because—

"I'm not a demon," Imani interrupted.

Nymeria swallowed thickly, feeling a hot rush of embarrassment across her body. "I get it. I was a woman of the Faith as well, my family was devoted to the Scribe and our family Codex had seven generations on its pages." Imani swallowed thickly. "It was destroyed when Sodom fell."

Imani cleared her throat again. "My point is, some demons like Halloran are bad, awful, but not all of them. It took a while for me to realise that, but Arwen helped. Maybe he can help you."

Something in Nymeria's blood screamed in outrage at the suggestion. She didn't have a life like Imani's—it took her a while to get used to humans, but demons? She couldn't see that happening.

"Why the church?" Imani asked, snapping Nymeria from her thoughts. "After your fall, I would have thought you would hate the Faith?"

"I...don't know," Nymeria admitted, her voice quiet, vulnerable like a scared child. "My entire life was the Faith.

Every waking moment—except the few I stole for myself—was dedicated to upholding the Faith." A lump formed in her throat. "Never mind, let's join the others."

Nymeria made her way to the window and stepped outside, opening up the giant beach umbrella. Imani climbed out after her, shoulders relaxing after a few moments. "It's nice, you know? Working alongside another woman. I end up surrounded by way too many men when working cases." Nymeria's voice was soft and quiet, losing its usual harshness.

Imani laughed. "I can imagine. I feel it as well. I love Arwen, but spending too much time with him does give me a headache." They both laughed as they joined the other three on the rooftop.

"—That will be enough for now. We shall continue later." Halloran's voice was cold.

Gen slumped onto the floor, back against the ceiling.

"You got yourself a little fighter in the making," Arwen said proudly. "Especially with such a good teacher."

Arwen clapped a hand on Halloran's shoulder, and his lip twitched up into a smile.

"She struggles with timing and with the weight. She may be able to just about defend herself against a drunken child," Halloran said coldly, and Nymeria thought for a moment.

"How about we try a bow instead?" she suggested. After all, that had been the first weapon she had trained with. "It's long range and not as precarious as a sword, but teaches more discipline than a gun."

Halloran sneered a little. "I suppose..."

Arwen shook him lightly. "Oh, come on! It's a great idea!

Tell you what kiddo, I'll buy you that bow. Consider it a present from your Uncle Arwen." Gen sat up, a massive smile on her face.

Nymeria smiled and shook her head, feeling another rumble from her pocket. How many people were gonna ring her today? Nymeria unlocked her phone, it was a text from Caliban: *I'm sorry for what I said. It was nasty, but I've made up for it. I found that witness from the red light murder.*

11

The Interrogation of Michael Sutton

The drive to the All Seeing Private Eye had been a quiet one. Nymeria had stopped along the way at a children's clothing store, picking up an array of clothes from shirts and trousers to dresses and skirts; all to Gen's liking. The girl had been grinning from ear-to-ear the entire time. Especially when Nymeria bought her a large, long-limbed white and black lamb plushie with beady black eyes and patchwork hooves. Surprisingly, when Nymeria had gone to pay for it all, Halloran had pushed her to the side, his card was already out of his wallet. Whilst the others seemed to be somewhat content with his answer, Nymeria was sceptical. It was almost like he felt responsible for her, that he knew something about Gen that she didn't.

All the excitement from getting new clothes and toys had tuckered Gen out, which was the exact point of doing it in the first place. Nymeria locked the door behind her, peering in on Gen one last time as she lay wrapped in her blanket in the backseat, the lamb clutched close to her chest as she slept.

Good, Nymeria didn't want Gen to see what she had to do. She needed information from that witness, and she was more than happy to have Halloran break bones to get it. Arwen and Halloran waited for Nymeria at the front door to the office building.

"He's already up there?" Halloran asked, back to his usual cold and distant attitude.

"Caliban has had him up there for about ten minutes. Imani went up to help soothe him, apparently he's quite jumpy," she muttered and Arwen chuckled.

"I would be too if a PI dragged me to a remote location in a shady part of the city." What Nymeria and Caliban usually did was interview witnesses at their current location so that they were to cause less panic, but Caliban hadn't done that this time. Instead, he pulled the man out of work and into the office. She assumed he didn't want him running off.

"I meant to ask," Halloran started as they entered the building and made their way into the elevator that took them to the top floor. There was no sound outside it, the rest of the building had been empty for a long time. Nymeria groaned, bracing for a scathing comment. Her finger went to press the button to the top floor. "Why do you keep the lights on at night?"

She paused. "How do you—"

"I can see the light appear under the door at night. Or have you forgotten you let me sleep on the couch like a dog?"

"The lady likes her privacy. I can't blame her, I wouldn't share a bed with you either." Arwen's comment did make a smile curl up her lip. His charm was rubbing off on her, it was annoyingly infectious. "I knew you could smile." Arwen chuckled.

"That still doesn't answer my question," Halloran interrupted as the elevator doors opened with a small ding.

"If you answer why you keep on referring to yourself and others as dogs then I'll tell you." Nymeria stepped out of the elevator and turned to face them both. They looked very uncomfortable as if she had said something sacrilegious. Nymeria raised a brow and Halloran pushed past her and towards the office. Arwen followed after him, stopping next to Nymeria.

"Best not to bring that one up again," he whispered.

"Why not? He can make remarks all he wants, but I can't?" Arwen's hand tightened on her shoulder.

"No, I'm not saying that. What I'm saying is that he has a lot to deal with but he's trying his best. Just be patient with him, please?"

"Like what?"

"Not my place to say." Arwen sighed. "If he wants to tell you, he will, but it's not my place. We all fuck up and his fuck ups are bigger than most."

Nymeria frowned but followed him into the office.

The two walked into the bullpen. Looking up, she could see the witness—a typical clean cut looking finance guy who probably spent his weekends perfecting his business cards—sat on the sofa in her office. Standing in front of him was Caliban who turned once the door behind Nymeria shut. He left Imani in Nymeria's office and came out, looking like a kicked puppy.

"Hey..."

"Hi."

Out of the corner of her eye, Nymeria could just make out Arwen and Halloran looking at each other awkwardly, pulling a face.

"Listen, I'm really sorry— "

'Save it." The damage had already been done. "Let's just focus on the case."

"Next time we go to that shitty dive bar you like, drinks are on me," he bartered.

Nymeria's lips twinged upward into a smile. "Even if I run your card dry?"

Caliban chuckled and shook his head. "I wouldn't expect anything less."

Arwen cleared his throat, and Nymeria straightened up. "Anyway, who's our guy?"

"Michael Sutton, thirty-four, financial advisor for some tech company in the business district in central Ghenna. Found him based on descriptions of him and his car from the other red light residents and Evelyn. Not many people have a McLaren in this city, and even fewer with a personalised number plate."

Nymeria whistled lowly. "Wish I had that kind of money."

"Don't we all," Caliban muttered, looking pointedly at Halloran and Arwen. Neither of the brothers responded.

"I'll start us off," Nymeria instructed, her eyes darkening, and she let her jaw set firmly. "If I need help, I'll ask, but don't talk over me and"—Nymeria looked between all three men pointedly—"no fighting."—She punctuated each word with a point of her finger. "Any of you start any sort of squabble, you're all going out." Nymeria pointed at the window in her private office.

"But you can't—" Arwen started, and Nymeria shot him a look.

"Out the window. You can save your childish squabbling for afterwards," she said sternly, turning to open her private office door as Halloran chuckled. The sound brought a smile to her lips but she quickly forced her mouth into a line as she pushed it open.

Imani turned to face her and the three men.

"Ah, good, the cavalry is here." Imani smirked and took a few steps back, leaning her hip against Nymeria's desk. Halloran and Arwen stood near the door and Caliban leaned next to the large window, the rings on his finger glinting in the sunlight. Nymeria grabbed her desk chair and dragged it in front of Michael, straddling the back and resting her folded arms upon the top.

"Michael Sutton, yes?"

"That's right, sweetheart."

She felt her skin prickle, not because of the demeaning name but because for a brief moment he looked repulsed to call her that.

"Nymeria will be fine." Her voice was sharp and curt. "Do you have any idea why you were brought into *my* offices today?" Nymeria suppressed a smirk as his lips twitched downward and he shifted uncomfortably.

"Not really. Your co-worker said you wanted a chat. I had assumed it would be a solo one." His eyes flickered behind her.

"Usually, but times change. Speaking of time"—she leaned to her desk and pulled towards her a notepad and pen—"tell me what your day was like on February 8th?"

"February 8th? It was a normal working day. Woke up at six thirty, had breakfast, went to work until five pm, went to the gym, and then back home."

Nymeria made some brief notes of his schedule. Now was time to make him confirm his story before poking holes in it.

"You didn't go out for lunch or dinner?" Her golden-brown eyes met his and he looked down, caught in his lie like a mouse in a trap.

"I left the office for lunch. But I went to the big cafe on the corner of Parkrow Street."

Nymeria made a note of that too.

"Interesting," she mumbled again, tapping her pen against the pad. "So, between leaving your home and going to work, you made no other stops along the way?"

"That's right." To the untrained ear he would sound certain but the slight high-pitched lilt at the end of his words made Nymeria's suspicions grow.

"So you didn't stop at the red light district?"

His pupils widened ever so slightly.

"What? No! I—" He laughed nervously. "I would never. I'm a respectable man, I would never mingle with people so—"

"I don't want to hear whatever is about to come out of your mouth," Nymeria interrupted. "Just answer my questions."

"No! I didn't," he said firmly, his eyes darting around and quickly looking away when they landed behind her. "You have no proof!"

"Huh. Funny that. We have multiple witness statements

describing your car and yourself entering one of the sex worker blocks."

"Just witness statements? You're gonna prosecute me based on that?!" Michael laughed. "Please, sweetheart, you're gonna have to do better than that." His eyes flickered once again behind Nymeria, and she ran her tongue along her teeth in annoyance. He wasn't going to respect her, fine. She wasn't above pulling out the big guns.

Nymeria looked behind, and both Halloran and Arwen seemed very amused, cruel smiles on their lips. As much as her blood screamed at her to wipe it off their faces, for the sake of the interrogation and perhaps her twisted amusement, she could indulge them. Just this once. Arwen's eyes locked with Nymeria and he quirked a brow. She nodded and Arwen stepped forward. Halloran slowly walked next to the couch, sitting on the arm. Michael shifted away from him nervously, just as Arwen sat next to him.

"Mind if I have a seat?"

"Uh—"

"Thanks." Arwen smirked and Halloran's lip curled into a smile. Nymeria turned her head to look at a frowning Caliban but he made no objection. He simply paced past the large window, the ring on his finger glinting in the afternoon sunlight.

"Now Michael—I can call you Mike right?" Arwen's usually charismatic tone had changed somewhat, a smooth dark edge now underlying it. Nymeria had heard that tone before when she struck the deal with him.

"Sure?"

"Excellent. Now, Mike, that's a nice suit you have there." Arwen's hand came around his shoulders and gripped Mike tightly. "You work somewhere really nice, right?"

"Financial district—"

"Xander?" Halloran reached down and pulled at the man's lanyard, an ID badge hanging from it with his picture, name and job description written in plain black text. "Fancy company," he sneered and Nymeria could practically taste Michael's sweat in the air. Xander was a very profitable tech giant, her phone was made by them and she was pretty sure most computers used in Ghenna too.

"Working for Xander tech as a financial advisor?" Arwen whistled. "That must pay very well."

"It—um, it does," Michael stammered out, and Nymeria looked down, biting back a smile. Arwen was a natural at this. How often did he do interrogations to do this so naturally?

"I bet it does." Arwan chuckled, slapping Michael's shoulder. "It pays so well because I'm pretty good friends with your boss," he said, his laugh ending abruptly. "Very good friends."

"Such good friends, in fact"—Arwen's hand squeezed Michael's shoulder tightly—"that I get his latest tech before it hits the shelves. I gotta have the latest toys to run my own business. Don't I, Imani?"

"Yes you do. It would be in your best interest to answer the investigators questions." Her tone was clipped and Nymeria smirked at her when she saw Imani yawn, purposefully flashing her fangs at Michael. His Adam's apple bobbed.

"But—"

Arwen let go of Michael's shoulder. "I'm not a violent man, nor a bully. I like to run my business on my own moral principle: Things can often be talked through first, not everything needs to be settled violently."

Michael relaxed, his shoulders slumping.

"Sometimes force is necessary, but it will never be by my hand." Arwan inclined his head towards Halloran. "I'm not for violence, but my brother is."

Michael looked up at Halloran, who had his arms crossed over his chest, the button-up shirt he was wearing pulled taut over his arms and chest. "So you tell me, Michael Sutton, do I need to use violence?"

"No, no you don't." Michael's voice quivered and Arwen smirked, his eyes twinkling mischievously as he stood up and walked over to the door, peering out the office.

"Then answer the investigator's questions," Halloran said firmly, unmoving from his position. For once, Nymeria was thankful for his presence.

"What were you doing at the apartments that early in the morning?" Nymeria questioned again.

"Don't humiliate me—"

"Nothing to be embarrassed of if you like men—"

"I don't!"

Nymeria sighed. Hateful idiots would still point the finger, saying they, along with the demons, were the cause of the gods leaving or dying. She had passed many a street preacher prattling on about how 'a lack of faith that was found in bodies of the unworthy'. Those street preachers were all idiots. The gods they worshipped often didn't conform to human expectation of gender or sex. Nymeria was tempted to curse them out when she passed them by. "I really don't care if you like men or not. I like men and women, so you're not going to receive judgment from me," Nymeria reassured, and Michael calmed down. "I want to know why you were there."

"You know why!"

"I need to hear you say it."

"Fine. I had an...appointment with one of the men there."

"You were there for a hookup first thing in the morning?" Halloran confirmed, and Michael frowned.

"I find I can focus on work better afterwards."

"And you found the body?"

Michael froze, wringing his wrists. "Yes...Oh Shepherd guide him, poor Paul...We only had a casual thing, but he was so nice. He often invited me on nights out. He knew how anxious I was, going to bars by myself. I don't have a lot of friends."

"What did you find?" Nymeria interrupted, her pen danced over the pad as she made notes.

"I heard it—the cracking, the sawing."

Her pen paused. "You saw the killer in the act?" Everyone straightened up, and Nymeria could feel all eyes, including her own, boring into Michael.

"I didn't stick around to figure out who it was—"

"What did he or she look like?" Nymeria pressed.

"Tall, average build? Whoever it was, they were wearing all black and had their face covered," Michael rambled, tears welling in his eyes. "They had a saw and—" His hand covered his mouth. "They had this book in hand?"

"A book?" Nymeria pressed. "What kind?"

"Leather bound from what I could tell and old looking with runes—" Michael didn't get to finish his sentence. There was a high-pitched whistling sound, and then the loud shattering of the window. The bullet struck Michael in the temple, and Nymeria felt warm, wet blood splash over her face.

12

A Lead

Nymeria lurched backwards, her back hitting the floor hard and a sharp pain radiating up her already bruised spine.

"Take cover!" Caliban yelled, pulling out his pistol from his waistband, pressing against the wall. Another sharp whistle sounded, as did a grunt of pain from above her. She opened her eyes enough to see Halloran looming over her and felt his hand grab her arm and drag her out of the office, Arwen scrambling after them, his head bowed.

"What the fuck was that?" he yelled as soon as they got to the bullpen, Halloran slumping down into Caliban's desk chair.

"There goes our only lead."

A ball of shadow enveloped the office like a blot of ink on crisp white paper. But Nymeria was not concerned about that at the moment. She bolted out of the offices and down the stairs. She was not going to wait for an elevator now, not when Gen could be in danger. Nymeria couldn't explain the feeling that motivated her. That drove her to take the stairs two at a time and burst through the front door, rush to the car, rip the door open and scoop a frightened Gen in her arms, holding her tight to her chest. Her fingers dug into the girl's clothes and she rushed back inside. Gen whined and pulled at her shirt desperately. "It's okay, it's okay." Nymeria repeated the words like a mantra as she went back up the stairs and into the bullpen.

"The hell did you go—" Arwen barked as she opened the door, but went quiet seeing Gen in Nymeria's arms.

His features softened ever so slightly, but an uncharacteristic grimace still graced his face. Nymeria sat on the floor of the bullpen, her back against the wall as Gen nestled in her lap, shaking. Nymeria looked back up to her office, the ball of shadow still surrounding it, enveloping the room in an impenetrable darkness. The bang of her office door nearly made her jump, and from the darkness emerged Imani, pulling Caliban out with one hand. A stream of shadows danced through the air like silk in a breeze from her other hand.

"Our shooter fired twice more into the shadows. They're trying to get you," Imani said pointedly, her eyes locking onto Nymeria.

"How the hell did the killer find us?" Halloran barked.

"Your agency is small, the first place they should be looking is the damn police station," Arwen snapped, pacing.

"They've been following him," Nymeria said, running through every logical possibility of what led up to the events that took place a few moments ago. Keeping her arms securely around Gen. "The killer knew his face. He could have been stalking him for all we knew." A heavy silence filled the room as a new question came into play.

"How did they know Michael was coming here?" Imani voiced the question on everyone's mind. All eyes landed on Nymeria, and she moved Gen off her lap but let the girl keep an iron grip on her hand, Gen's small fingers wrapping around one of her much larger ones. "If they were stalking Michael, they must have seen Caliban talk to him," Imani rationalised.

"How did they know Caliban was a PI or anyone important?" Arwen blurted.

Caliban and Nymeria's eyes locked.

"Unless they've been watching the crime scenes? They must have seen us at the docks." Caliban's words made Nymeria's blood run cold. How long had the killer been following them? Did they know where she lived? Was Gen now in danger? Her fingers closed around Gen's hand as she felt the girl shake.

"Then the killer could know where Gen is," she said quietly and Gen gasped.

Halloran shook his head. "They haven't been by the apartment. I haven't sensed any other presence aside from the three of us."

Nymeria sighed in relief. "Then that means they don't know the exact apartment. But it doesn't mean they don't know the building."

"Fuck, they could have seen you training Gen," Arwen said and Nymeria could feel her teeth grind.

"Arwen, do you have men to spare?"

"To keep tabs on the apartment building? I'm already on

it." Arwen had his phone pressed to his ear, and he stepped out of the bullpen and into the halls.

"You think the killer would have moved on by now?" Imani asked and Nymeria nodded.

The shadows slithered to Imani's hands and buried under her skin, her veins in her arms darkening until the sunlight filtered through. Everyone held their breath, waiting for another shot, for someone else to fall down dead, but all they were met with was the whistling wind from the now shattered window in Nymeria's private office. Nymeria stood up. This was going to be a mess to fix and an even bigger mess to explain to the GPD why there was a dead body in her offices. She paced in the space between the desks, running her hand across her temple.

"What do we do?" Caliban asked, his voice urgent and hoarse. "Nymeria, what do we *do?!*"

"Let her think!" Halloran snapped, groaning as he adjusted his posture in Caliban's chair.

"Okay." She tapped her fingers against her forehead. "Okay. Caliban, Halloran you two take the body and get rid of it."

"Any preference?" Halloran asked, already standing up. She was surprised he took orders so readily.

"I don't care. We cannot have the GPD asking questions around here. Cordero is begging for a reason to arrest me."

Caliban looked like he wanted to protest. His Adam's apple bobbed, and his mouth drew into a fine line.

"Anyone saw where the shots were coming from?" Nymeria asked, and Imani turned to face her, rubbing her wrist.

"One of the neighbouring blocks, second floor from the

top."

"How?"

"Vampires have good eyesight."

"Alright, you're with me. We're gonna see if he's still there or left anything behind," Nymeria ordered and Imani nodded.

"Yes, Ma'am."

"Take this." Caliban walked over to Nymeria and handed her his pistol. "I don't know how this... affliction of yours works..." he trailed off and Nymeria already knew what he meant.

"It's a curse, you can call it what it is. But thanks for the gun. Better to be safe than sorry. If the shooter is still there, at least I can use it as a warning." Nymeria tucked the gun into her waistband.

"Gen, stay here. Don't move unless one of us comes to get you." Gen nodded, hesitating for a moment before lurching forward and wrapping her arms around Nymeria's waist. Gen never had to speak to be able to convey what she meant: *'stay safe'*. Nymeria's hand hesitated above Gen's head but slowly came down to pet her head. "I'll be back before you know it." When she pulled her hand back, she noticed it was shaking and that her skin felt uncomfortably clammy as the familiar prickle of discomfort from being touched resurfaced. But what outweighed that feeling even more was a strange sensation that bloomed warm in her chest: it was something she hadn't felt in a very long time and the longing she had for it scared her. "I have to go now," Nymeria said, her voice harsher than she would have liked.

"Everyone, you have your jobs. We have to act fast, no more

dawdling."

* * *

"I didn't think Vampires had magic?" Nymeria asked between huffs as they crested the fifth set of stairs, neither had stopped sprinting since they entered the abandoned apartment block.

"I didn't think so either," Imani huffed. "But turns out if you consume demon blood, you absorb part of them."

"So, Arwen has shadow magic?"

"Who knows? I've never seen him use it."

"He didn't seem like the type. Usually, what type of magic someone has is based on two things: Bloodlines and what they truly think of themselves deep down. What angels are taught is that magic is a reflection of how we truly see ourselves." Nymeria panted as they crested the last set of stairs. Each angel's magic was usually connected with their god-parent's associated planet; children of the Crone, goddess of marriage and childbirth whose planet was the moon, had an affinity with water and ice-based powers. Whereas children of the Muse; god of medicine and the arts whose planet was Pluto often had mending. The actual specifics of what an angel's magic manifested as were determined by the individual's soul; how they truly saw themselves and what they were like

Nymeria thought about that a lot since she fell. Her magic had been a burning light; proud and deadly and full of hope. Just how she had felt in Elysium; happy, so certain she had been doing the right thing. But what would her magic be now? A slowly dying ember, she was sure. Spiteful, alone and fading.

She pulled the gun out of the waistband and double-checked that it was loaded as the two women waited just by the archway that used to hold a series of apartments, now gutted for reconstruction. "Keep your head on a swivel," Nymeria whispered, and Imani nodded.

"You know I'll sense someone before you do, right?"

"I was trying to be nice," Nymeria said tersely as she rounded the corner, pistol out and finger hovering over the trigger, waiting for any sort of movement.

The two walked slowly through the now large open space. Construction equipment lay scattered around, plastic sheets hung from the ceiling, and the smell of dust and cement was heavy in the air. Their footsteps ricocheted off the walls like bullets, and Nymeria had to resist the urge to whirl around at every sound. But despite what she was now, she was a seasoned warrior, and despite the spark of flight she felt, she knew better than anyone to stay still and push onward.

"Can you sense anyone?" Nymeria asked in a hushed voice, keeping her gun pointed in front of her, using the barrel to push past a plastic sheet that was hung up, covered in dust and grey paint. Imani walked a few feet away from her, heading in the same direction. Nymeria didn't have to say anything. Small shadows shot out from Imani's fingertips scouring every little dark crevice and hidden corner of the floor. Nymeria waited with bated breath for a few moments.

"All clear. Our killer is long gone."

Nymeria groaned and straightened up, tucking the gun back into her waistband. Another failure. She should have gone straight here as soon as Michael was shot, she should have been faster, quicker—

"Ny?"

Imani's concerned voice broke Nymeria out of her spiral. "Nothing. Just should have been quicker."

"No one is at fault for not catching them. We were all rattled." Imani shrugged, the shadows crawling back into her fingertips.

"If I'd been quicker, we could have wrapped up this case," Nymeria grumbled, swatting away more plastic sheets as she walked forward, moving closer to the windows to try and see how far away her office window was. If she could triangulate where the shooter had shot them from, then perhaps she could find some clues.

Nymeria looked out each window until her leg hit something, a briefcase lying on the floor next to the last one which was open. Nymeria frowned. That was odd. Why was a briefcase in the middle of a construction site? Her eyes glanced out the window, elevated and upwind of her office, with a clear view of her sofa. Michael's body was now gone, but the floor and walls were still bloody. Her attention returned to the briefcase. She pulled her gloves tighter across her hands; she didn't need her fingerprints on a piece of potential evidence. Slowly, her fingers snapped open the clasps with a click that echoed around the room. She heard Imani's footsteps jog up to her. "What did you find?"

Nymeria's eyes widened, and she felt her breath catch in her throat as she saw what was inside. A perfectly dismantled sniper rifle. Even the silencer was neatly packed inside. It wasn't quite catching the killer but it was a damn good lead. With careful hands she took the main body of the rifle out of the case and looked it over. But when she flipped it over, her stomach dropped. "What is it?"

Nymeria flipped the body of the gun to face Imani. Printed into the side of the gun was the GPD logo.

13

Bathroom Secrets

Nymeria was not letting that briefcase out of her sight. After showing Imani what was inside, the two women rushed back to the All Seeing Private Eye, showing their findings to the rest of the group. Arwen had offered to take it, as had Caliban, but Nymeria was insistent on keeping it close to her. This was the only concrete piece of evidence this investigation had; it had to be protected at all costs. A compromise was reached with Halloran being the one to guard the suitcase. If anything happened to her, at least their evidence wouldn't be compromised. But since the talk had ended and Halloran had now taken custody of the suitcase—which was now sitting in the footwell of the passenger side of Nymeria's car—Halloran had been uncharacteristically quiet. No smart remarks, no scathing comments on her failure to capture the killer when they had been so close. Just silence.

Halloran grunted and shifted; that was the one noise he had been making.

"You got something stuck in your throat?" She didn't turn

to look at him, but she could feel him glare at her.

"I am fine. Drive faster." Nymeria looked behind her to where Gen contentedly sat with her lamb plushie. She shrugged and looked at Nymeria, confused, and Nymeria shrugged back, both as lost as the other to Halloran's strange behaviour.

"Of course, your highness," Nymeria started, a sarcastic smirk on her face. "Would you like tea when we get back as well?"

Halloran sneered, and she looked over to take pleasure in it, but she had to do a double take. A dark stain was blooming across his shoulder and upper chest. "You got shot?!"

"It appears so."

"And you didn't think to stop and get aid?"

"Don't be dramatic."

"So demons are immune to infections, are they? And blood loss?"

"I thought you would be more joyful to see me bleed out," he groaned, now cradling his injured shoulder. She opened her mouth and then quickly closed it. She should be relishing just a little bit that he was hurt, but she wasn't.

"Well, if I let you bleed to death, or get an infection, I'd face Arwen's wrath."

That caused Halloran to chuckle. "Maybe my death will finally get him to break that bothersome oath of his."

Nymeria parked her car outside her apartment building and the three of them quickly made their way up the stairs, rushing past confused and disgruntled neighbours. Nymeria tossed her keys to Gen, and she opened the apartment door for them.

"Gen, you make yourself comfortable," Nymeria said as she pushed Halloran towards the bathroom, her hands on his back. He reluctantly stumbled forward.

"What are you—"

"You're not getting blood on my sofa."

Nymeria heard soft footfalls behind her. "Gen, it's gonna get bloody in there," she warned again, her voice cold, but that warm feeling bloomed across her chest as she saw Gen shoving her plushie into Halloran's hands, from the corner of her eye. Gen quickly wrote on the whiteboard '*Squeeze Lambo if pain hurt. I shall keep guard*'. Nymeria had to suppress a laugh as her face scrunched up with a determined look, as if guarding the bathroom was a life or death situation.

"Very well, little warrior." Nymeria chuckled. "Keep us safe."

Nymeria gently closed the door behind her. She heard a shuffling and then a small thump. Gen, taking her guarding duty seriously, brought a small smile to her face. From behind her, she heard Halloran clear his throat. "Why have you closed us in here exactly?"

Nymeria put her hands on her hips and turned to face him, his scowl boring into her and his eyes cold. "Well, I'm not having you bleed out on my sofa," she repeated and pointed at the bathtub. "Get in."

Halloran looked behind him, and his scowl deepened further. "You can't be serious."

"Very serious. Get in and get that shirt off."

Nymeria bent down, reaching for the cupboard under the sink and pulling out a first aid kit.

"If you wanted to get me naked, being less tempestuous

would be a good start." Now it was Nymeria's turn to scowl, and she turned to face him.

"My tempestuousness is part of my charm..." She trailed off as she watched Halloran unbutton his shirt and pull it off with a grunt, his arms flexing in the process, his lip curling up into a snarl. Of course, the rest of him would be as pretty as his face: his bare chest, abs and arms looked as if they were cut from the most beautiful marble. But as Nymeria's eyes flitted over his shirtless chest, her eyes landed on a scar; a massive, long scar that started above his heart and struck downward and diagonally, ending at his hip. But it didn't detract from how ethereal he looked; if anything, it made him look angelic.

A little dark voice spoke up from deep inside her, *'He is exposed before you, a pretty fool he is. Now is the perfect time to strike.'*

"Do you hear it?"

Nymeria was broken from her darkest thoughts and teachings. "Pardon?"

"The call in your blood. That tells you to harm me, just as mine calls to harm you." Halloran fixed her with a steely look.

Nymeria's brows rose. "You hear it too?"

"It often tells me to rip you to pieces and drink your blood, and sometimes I'm tempted to indulge it." Halloran's lip curled into a slight smirk, and Nymeria couldn't help but chuckle.

"Likewise."

"At least we can agree to not act on it; mutually assured destruction," Halloran proposed and Nymeria nodded.

"Fine. Mutually assured destruction it is."

Halloran moved back and sat in the bathtub, his legs hanging off the edge. "I'm not taking my trousers off."

"Thank the gods for that." Nymeria placed the first aid kit on the edge of the bathtub, standing between his legs. She slowly took her gloves off and rolled up her sleeves. "Can't believe you lugged a whole body around with a bullet in your shoulder."

"I am quite resilient," he said sharply.

"I didn't say you weren't!" Nymeria snapped as she opened the first aid kit with a sharp snap. "And perhaps I would get along with you better if you didn't have a permanent stick up your ass and act like everyone is beneath you!"

"I do not—"

"Yes, you do!"

A tense and heavy silence fell over both of them, and after a few moments, Nymeria plucked a cleaning wipe from the kit and grasped Halloran's injured shoulder. He flinched and remained tense as she wiped the area around the bullet wound. He hissed through his teeth. "Thought you would be used to getting patched up," she said quietly.

"Not in the Hells, my father would insist that I handle any injuries myself. If I died from them, then I was not worthy as his successor."

Nymeria frowned, and she felt something twinge within her as the call of her blood to harm him died down. "Sounds like the Destroyer is as ruthless as they say."

"It was a good lesson in resilience. I needed it when I was fifteen, I was weak."

"Perhaps, but I don't think a father should enforce a lesson like that on a child at such an age." Halloran remained quiet, but his eyes narrowed in thought.

Nymeria finished wiping the wound and tossed the wipe into the bin. She tilted him back and inspected it. "It doesn't look too bad, might just be a deep graze. I might still check if the bullet is lodged—"

"What was your father like?"

Nymeria paused. Her father? He hissed and she let go of his arm, not realising her fingers had been digging into his flesh, small indents left in their wake. "My father...I couldn't tell you. The Swordsworn just dumped me at the Mercury Estate, my sister was the one who raised me. Can't imagine it was easy for a child to raise another child," she said quickly.

"Hm, disappointing," he muttered, and Nymeria grabbed a needle and thread. "I was curious as to whether your father taught you to hate demons as much as my father taught me to hate your kind."

Nymeria missed the hole.

"Perhaps this hate is genetic," Nymeria mused, trying again to thread the needle. "Perhaps their hate has passed onto us. It was my father who defeated yours and cast him down to the Hells." The bitterness in her voice surprised even her.

"Surely it's not that simple," he argued, and maybe it wasn't that simple, but Nymeria didn't have an answer for him, so she remained silent.

Finally managing to thread the needle, she leaned in close. "Keep still," she warned and began to stitch him up. "What about your mother?" Nymeria asked softly. "Did she feel the same way?" She noticed a flash of something in Halloran's eyes; it was so fast, and she was so concentrated on stitching him up that she almost missed it. But it was an unmistakable look of grief.

"She was afraid, but never hateful. She couldn't hate anyone except me." His voice was cold but quiet, not holding its usual arrogance. "My mother was fiercer than most of the Destroyer's concubines, but more loving than any of them were to their own children. She wanted to give us a better life. Your kind threw her back to the Hells."

Nymeria felt a sense of guilt she couldn't place.

"I'm sorry."

"For what?"

"That she died."

Halloran's eyes narrowed. "No one is to blame for her death but me."

Nymeria's eyes widened, and she was tempted to push it, but the flicker of movement of his fists clenching around Lambo caught her attention, and she dropped it. This was a brief moment of peace they had, but he was exposed before her and she couldn't hold back the temptation to get a little revenge.

She continued the stitching, pushing the needle into his skin a little harder than she needed to, and smiled as he grunted.

"I thought we were having a moment of civility," Halloran said, his eyes boring into her.

"We are. Consider this"—she dug the needle in deeper until blood so dark it almost looked black, pooled from the wound—"reparations for throwing me off that roof."

He rolled his eyes, but the corner of them crinkled as his lip curled upward into the briefest of smiles. "Tempestuous woman."

"Arrogant man." She chuckled, and she could have sworn she saw his eyes soften. But just as quickly as they did, he snatched her wrist, the needle cutting into his skin as she did the last stitch.

"What are those?"

In her haste to patch him up and not get blood on her clothes, she had completely forgotten that the scars would be visible. An uncomfortable prickle crawled up her spine like a spider, and she felt entirely exposed without having to take her clothes off. "It's nothing—"

"It looks like something. Did you—"

"They're not self-inflicted!" she urged, pulling her wrist back, but he just pulled her in closer, Nymeria stumbled forward and braced her free hand near his head, their face a few inches apart, noses brushing.

"Then who?" His eyes flickered into a glow.

She twisted her wrist, his grip loosened and she pulled her hand free. "It was a long time ago. It doesn't matter now."

"Considering you always keep your whole body covered up, it seems like it does matter—"

"Shut up!" she shouted, pushing away from him and stalking to the other side of the bathroom.

When she turned to face him again, she was expecting anger on his face. Instead, he looked confused and almost uncomfortable, as if her outburst had not been the reaction he had expected.

Halloran cleared his throat and stood up, rolling his shoulders and inspecting the stitches. "Not bad. Perhaps you should become a tailor," he joked lightly, and the previous tension dissipated. Perhaps she shouldn't have yelled; it was an honest question, but it felt so visceral and hit a raw part of her, an open wound that had been bleeding since her imprisonment in Elysium. A wound that never stopped hurting, no matter how much time passed.

Nymeria couldn't look him in the eye, so she turned her back to him and opened the door. Gen stumbled backwards but caught herself on the door frame. "All sorted." She smiled down at her faintly and that uncomfortable warmth blooming in her chest returned as Nymeria saw Gen's gap-toothed smile.

Gen scribbled something down. *'Can we watch a film?'* Her first instinct was to say no, that they had work to do. They couldn't be caught slacking off, not when so much was at stake. Words that had been drilled into her as a soldier of Elysium and even more so when she was general. Even when she had been off-duty, she always had to maintain appearances, become the epitome of a woman of faith, just like her sister was. But she was always bad at it, and now she had none of that pressure and those expectations on her shoulders. But she also realised Gen had probably never done this either, and who was she to deny the child some sense of normalcy?

"O-okay." It felt strange that her voice came out in a stammered whisper.

Gen scrambled to her bedroom and Nymeria walked into the living room. She couldn't remember the last time she did something that was just to relax—besides drinking. She heard heavy footsteps from behind her, and feeling Halloran's breath on the back of her neck made the hairs on her nape and arms stand on edge. But he made no move to speak and neither did she.

Silence filled the room until Gen returned, giggling happily as she dragged her blanket onto the sofa. Nymeria moved to sit at the opposite end of the sofa from Gen, picking up the TV remote.

"What do you want to watch?" Gen giggled and reached for the remote, and she passed it over. Halloran hovered behind the sofa, that aura of coldness and stoicism now returned, their brief moment of understanding pushed away as he maintained a distance from her and Gen. Gen looked behind her and patted the sofa spot between her and Nymeria but Halloran shook his head.

"No, I will make some food." His face maintained its cold harshness. "If we continue to eat takeaway like we have for the past four days we'll grow sluggish, and if we are sluggish, then it will be all the more easier for enemies to surprise us." Nymeria's stomach churned when she saw Gen pout, her face scrunched in annoyance as she turned to face the TV.

Nymeria's brows knitted together. "You can cook?"

"Of course I can. I was a beggar before I was a prince, my mother made it a top priority that myself and Arwen could take care of ourselves if anything happened to her when we were children." He walked into the kitchen and started rummaging through the cupboards. Since he started staying here, Nymeria had made a quick shopping trip, and for the first time, there was fresh food in her cupboards and her fridge was fully stocked. Nymeria turned to the TV and saw Gen had picked out a cartoon. Not her first choice, but she wasn't going to ruin Gen's fun.

"You wanna watch it?"

Gen nodded.

"Alright then." She leaned back against the cushions as Gen pressed play.

She was surprised how entertaining the film actually was, and the characters quickly grew on her as the film progressed, but she couldn't fully focus on it. Through the film, Gen had been awkwardly inching closer to her, shuffling herself along the sofa. A small smile curled up Nymeria's lips as she lifted her arm, and with a happy squeal, Gen snuggled into her side, hugging her close. For once, she would allow a modicum of that warm feeling that bloomed in her chest, above her heart, to sweep over her. It was pleasant, and as she looked down at Gen, who was intently watching the film, she felt something akin to protective nurture sweep over her, and she realised she would walk through the Hells if it meant keeping her safe. But she also felt bad. Bad that she hadn't taken the opportunity to ask Gen about herself. She knew nothing about this child.

"Can I ask you something?"

Gen nodded and reached over to grab her whiteboard and marker with a yawn. "Where are you from? Do you remember before..." Nymeria wasn't good at the delicacy of these situations. "Before...you came here?" she said slowly.

Gen shifted closer to her, her leg bouncing in place. Nymeria's thumb rubbed small circles into her shoulder. Gen's hands shook as she scribbled something down and turned the whiteboard back to her: *'Don't no. Not big like this citee, smaler'*

Nymeria was painfully reminded that she definitely had to get Gen into education and read up on sign language.

Gen quickly added another sentence, *'I used to liv in an orfanage'.*

Nymeria assumed as much; those in the care system were far more susceptible to trafficking than children from stable homes.

"Anything else you can tell me? Anything that might help us capture our killer, any information, no matter how small, can help me and Halloran keep you safe." Nymeria hadn't intended to ask about the case, but she couldn't help it.

Gen was quiet for a moment, worrying her lip between her teeth until the skin split. *'Befor portal happend and they kept me away from other kids, I wuld sneek around office' of the one's in charge'*

Nymeria grinned, knowing Gen was always so playful made her happy, but her face fell when more words appeared on the board.

'Me and alot of kids were from a place called Sodom'.

"You're from Sodom?!"

A sharp crack of splintering glass sounded from the kitchen, and Nymeria whirled around. Halloran swore under his breath but she couldn't make out what he said, the shattered glass of one of her cups decorated the kitchen tiles.

"The hells was that?"

"Nothing," Halloran snapped and stormed past them and into the bathroom.

"Do you—" Nymeria started to ask.

"No."

Any semblance of common ground they had had now crumbled away. Nymeria frowned. He was acting like a wild animal—skittish and unsure. She supposed she was one as well—angry and defensive. But it was clear that both of them were deadly and both destined to never get along.

A tightness formed in Nymeria's throat. Gen was from Sodom. She might have been there when Halloran destroyed her city. Had he killed her parents? Eaten them in front of her eyes? Nymeria frowned. She doubted that, otherwise Gen would not be as comfortable around him. Was he responsible for the way she was now? What else could he be hiding from her? Did he know more about this case then he was letting on? But as soon as that last thought entered her mind, she dismissed it. Halloran had made it clear he hated this deal, hated her. He wouldn't benefit from impeding the investigation. But it did prove that Imani's hypothesis was right; Halloran would only do what benefitted him.

Gen tugged on Nymeria's arm, and she saw Gen had written a new question. *'What was yur home lik?'*

Nymeria didn't like how her heart hurt. She hadn't realised how dry her mouth had gotten until she licked her lips. "My home..." She focused on the sound of Halloran moving around in the bathroom, the sound was a pleasant distraction from resurfacing memories of an always dark dungeon and rattling chains, of unwanted touches and grabs and—

Gen elbowed her, and Nymeria hadn't realised she had been holding her breath. "My home was not a nice place. I was taught to fight, younger than you are now. I was raised to be the best of angels and—"

Destroy and kill anyone who defied the Faith by words or by existing as a product of the Destroyer.

"—Uphold the Faith."

Gen frowned and scribbled down another sentence. *'So you didn't get to do things you lik?'*

She hadn't really thought about it like that. She had been raised to maintain an image of a lady of the Faith, the most powerful angel. But was that all she had been taught to like or did she actually enjoy any of it? Had she enjoyed anything of her own volition without being prompted or feeling obligated to do it? She felt a sharp prickle in her gut, and she had a sudden craving for the bottle of wine in the fridge. Nymeria got up, untangling Gen from her and quickly walked to the kitchen, bumping her shoulder against Halloran in her haste to get to the fridge and grab the bottle. She frantically poured herself a large glass. She could feel Halloran's judgmental eyes on her, and she didn't care; she just needed to push those memories down as far as they would go.

As soon as the wine slid down her throat, Nymeria felt the tension in her shoulder ease. Gen's chin was resting on the back of the sofa as she watched Nymeria, and she sighed.

"It wasn't all bad," Nymeria said, but she found herself trying to convince herself more than anything. "The Elysium council would host these grand banquets; roast pork drizzled in honey, wine from the children of the Nymph, greens covered in butter." She could almost taste the food on her tongue. "Lots of dancing too. It was the only time I was expected to dress regally and not in heavy armour and leather."

"I would have thought the fearsome general would only like bloodshed and heavy armour," Halloran grumbled, and Nymeria shot him a look, but she didn't have the energy for a quick-witted retort.

"I was a general who liked the heavy armour and fighting, true. But I'm also a woman who likes pretty silk dresses and dancing," she said softly.

Nymeria took another long sip of wine as she saw Gen happily squiggle something on the whiteboard *'Do you stil hav them? Can I see?'*

Nymeria's face fell and she looked down at the wine, swilling it around the glass. "No, all of my belongings would have been burnt when I was cast out." There was a bitterness in her voice as she took another long sip.

14

Of Demons And Clergymen

Nymeria rubbed her eyes for the umpteenth time that hour, her vision blurring and her eyes watering as she replayed the same video on how to ask 'How are you?' and 'I am well.' in sign language. The investigation had been out on pause since the chaos at the offices and to fill an otherwise boring void, she had bought textbooks on learning sign language and basic spelling and grammar, going all the way from pre-school to an eight-year-old level.

Nymeria straightened up, rolled her shoulders, wincing as her muscles popped and ached. "Hello! And welcome to Signs with Sid, today we'll be learning—" A flicker of movement caught her attention and a pencil flew across the table and clattered onto the ground.

"Gen! What have I said!" Nymeria snapped and the girl jumped. Nymeria looked at the piece of paper in front of Gen, a basic grammar and spelling test she printed off the internet, now marked with numerous frustrated squiggles. Nymeria sighed and ran a hand down her face. This wouldn't be the last time this would happen, she was sure of that. Nymeria had memorised the entire Codex by the age of seven. If she could do that, then Gen could learn how to communicate. She could make out a few correct spellings of 'besides' and even a correct compound sentence. It was progress, slow, but still progress.

"Give it here and get ready for bed." Her voice was hoarse and tired.

Gen pushed her chair out and walked around the kitchen table, fiddling with her fingers as she approached.

'*Are you mad?*' Gen slowly signed.

"No, I'm not mad. Just tired." Nymeria sighed, leaning over to pick up the pencil and toss it onto the table.

'*Anything—*'

"No, I'm just tired!" Nymeria snapped again and Gen took a few steps back. For whatever reason, Nymeria felt her heart sink.

"You're not in trouble and you haven't done anything. I'm just frustrated because of the case."

Gen nodded before awkwardly shuffling away. Nymeria picked up the sheet of paper that Gen had scribbled on. Reading the girl's handwriting was half the battle. She couldn't wait until the others next visited, at least then she could have a break.

Caliban, Imani, and Arwen had been around frequently during the week and keeping his promise, Arwen had gifted Gen a bow. A small one and basic training model, but she had squealed so loudly when Arwen handed it to her that Nymeria's ears had rung for the rest of the day. Building a makeshift target on the top of the apartments had been surprisingly easy, cobbling together some old furniture, and Caliban had managed to grab an old target sheet used in GPD training ranges from a former police friend of his. So far, no arrow had completely missed. Nymeria felt proud that her assumption Gen would be a natural archer was true.

Hearing the front door unlock, swing open, and the familiar smell of cigarette smoke invading the apartment made Nymeria tense. Halloran was back. He had been distant since their argument and had all but estranged himself from Gen.

This was the daily routine; he would wake up before Nymeria or Gen, silently keep watch over the both of them from some distant corner and then step outside the building to speak to one of the many guards now surrounding the apartment complex, or spend a few hours smoking. Then, he would sulk for a few more hours in the night before going to bed.

When their eyes met as he crossed the threshold, they both paused for a moment, before he continued to the sofa. Nymeria tilted her head down and started ticking and crossing the spelling sheet.

She had only started on the second question, where Gen had used the wrong kind of 'there', and she felt her vision blur and her body tilt forward, sleep creeping over her mind. She pinched the skin of her hand until she felt a jolt of energy wash over her. But as she ticked the next question, her pencil arched drawing lines across the question box below. She felt the pencil fall out of her fingers as she slumped forward.

Nymeria had expected to wake up on the kitchen table with

horrible back pain and paper sticking to her face. But instead, she was in her bed, the sheets pulled up to her shoulders. How did she end up here? She stumbled out of bed and over to the kitchen table, the chair she had been sitting in was tucked in and the papers now neatly stacked. Nymeria frowned as she looked down. It was marked with comments in handwriting which wasn't her own and was far too neat to be Gen's.

Her mouth opened, Halloran's name on the tip of her tongue, but her phone, left on the kitchen table from the night before, started to ring loudly. She snatched the phone and pressed accept.

"Hello?"

"Hello Miss Mercury, this is Lucy, Mr Alighieri's secretary. He is requesting a meeting this morning. He wants an update."

* * *

Nymeria had texted Arwen and Imani if either of them could accompany her instead, but much to her dismay, both had said they had meetings to attend to. The tension in the car was coming to a slow boil, but Nymeria made no move to speak; Halloran had been the one to overstep, if anything, he should apologise to her. But the silence was grating on her nerves.

"Are you going to stop having a tantrum?"

He snorted and sneered at her, "I am the one having a tantrum?"

Nymeria's gloved hands flexed against the steering wheel. "Yes. You haven't said two words to me this past week, yet you take me to bed when I fall asleep at the kitchen table."

Halloran stiffened.

"It really wasn't difficult to figure out it was you."

Halloran kept his eyes facing forward, as did Nymeria, but she could see the faintest of pink dust on his ears from the corner of her eye.

"If you hate me so much—"

"I do not hate you! If I did, I would have said; I find you brash and hotheaded, jarring and persistent on being my adversary at every turn," Halloran spat, and Nymeria felt exposed once again in a way that made her skin crawl. "I don't know what I find more jarring: your attitude or your persistence on keeping everyone at arm's length."

"That's not true!"

"Yes, it is, and it's only a matter of time before you do it to Gen, and that's not fair to her." Halloran's voice had risen to a thunderous anger, his eyes glowing. "Your emotions control you when it should be the other way around. I don't agree with Caliban on anything except this, you do push anyone away who tries to get close to you—"

Nymeria opened her mouth, but Halloran held his hand up.

"You don't want to get along with me, fine. This gods-damned deal will be over soon. But you are not going to do that to Gen because that girl looks at you like you are the sun itself, which you are. I'm not entitled to know what those scars are about, what happened to make you fall, but that does not mean you get to be angry with everyone around!"

Nymeria closed her mouth and parked the car off the side of the road. Looking in Halloran's eyes, she could have sworn he wanted to add a few more words onto that sentence.

"What about you?" Nymeria pressed. She knew she shouldn't say the next sentence but it was bubbling on her tongue.

"What about me?" Halloran warned his voice low.

"You act cold and callous to everyone, you accuse me of pushing people away, and yet you do the same! Not even the child that wants to give you a chance, the child that has a magic she shouldn't have because of your actions! Don't even get me started on what you did to Imani, you destroyed her life!"

His nostrils flared, and Halloran got out of the car.

"You need to take responsibility! For Imani and Gen!" she yelled as he slammed the car door.

Nymeria gritted her teeth together and closed her eyes, inhaling and exhaling deeply. Calm, calm, calm, she chanted internally. She couldn't scowl and be in a mood when meeting the mayor, not when she had a big favour to ask him and had to be on her best behaviour. Nymeria planned to ask if she and Caliban could raid the GPD headquarters for evidence. After sitting on the case for a week, all roads led to the police. Whether they were providing weapons to the killer or the killer was a member of the GPD itself, unless Nymeria got concrete evidence proving they were directly involved, the case would grow cold and fall through. Nymeria tightened the straps on her gloves and exited her car. Halloran stood a few paces away, smoking his second cigarette of the day.

"Stub that out before we get past the gates." She walked past him and she could feel his gaze burn into her back.

Walking to the gate, pressing the intercom and going through the gates had all been an awkward affair. The anger still bubbled between the both of them as Nymeria approached the front door, not bothering to check if Halloran was following after her. But it opened before she was even within ten feet of the door.

"Miss Mercury!" Zai's smile was still as beaming as the last time she saw him but now it jarred on her already grated nerves.

"Mr Alighieri," Nymeria said curtly, and then cleared her throat, forcing a bright smile "Glad we could meet again. Mr Ortega couldn't attend this morning as he's busy."

What Caliban was actually doing was making sure they had all the warrants and gear necessary to raid the GPD. "So I have my...'friend.'" Nymeria gestured and stepped to the side, turning to Halloran who had his brow raised in a silent 'friend? That's what you're going with?'

"Draig."

"Alighieri."

The silence was thick enough to cut with a knife as the two men stared each other down, Nymeria awkwardly caught in the middle. Perhaps, she should have done this alone. Bringing one of the city's most notorious gangsters may not have been a smart idea, but Nymeria wasn't going for smart at this moment. Instead, she was going for intimidation, and what was more intimidating then the former Prince of the Hells?

"You have a strange choice in companions, my dear," Zai said, and Nymeria felt her eyes widen.

"Perhaps, but we live in dangerous times, and I need all the protection I can get." She almost vomited in her mouth admitting that. Zai's eyes narrowed as he looked between her and Halloran, and Nymeria hoped she could still salvage a working relationship with him.

"Very well. I can understand your concern," Zai said in a steely tone that was unlike the ever-smiley and beaming mayor. Nymeria didn't miss how his eyes landed on Halloran.

"But I can easily recommend more suitable bodyguards for you." Zai turned on his heel and re-entered his home, and Nymeria followed behind him. She could feel Halloran breathing down her neck with how close he was.

"That won't be necessary. But I appreciate your generosity," Nymeria said quickly and the mayor looked at her from over his shoulder and smiled.

"He's very good at his job and charges a decent rate." Nymeria shrugged, hoping her nonchalance would make her lie more convincingly.

"I see." Zai led them to a small lounge room off the main foyer, ornate white wooden doors already swung open and pinned back. There was a small glass coffee table, with carrot cake and a steaming pot of coffee in the centre. The table was surrounded by cream coloured chairs and a sofa, extravagant oil paintings on the walls. "I've had back to back meetings for the past few days, and you caught me in the middle of cleaning. Allow me to tidy things up, but in the meantime, help yourself to some coffee and cake." Before Nymeria could even reply, Zai was quickly walking down the hall and away from them.

Nymeria made her way to the sofa and sat down, leaning against the arm and tucking her legs in close. She reached over and grabbed a slice of cake. She couldn't remember the last time she had cake.

"I'm not resuscitating you if it's poisoned," Halloran chimed, and Nymeria looked up. He was leaning up by the wall closest to the open doors.

"Why would he poison it?"

"Men like Zai are cowards; poison and deception are not above them."

Nymeria rolled her eyes. "You're hardly a shining paragon on morality," she sassed back as she chewed the cake and swallowed. She grimaced, it wasn't even good.

"Excuse me?" A small and timid voice spoke. "You're the investigator, right?"

Her eyes flitted to the door. A girl no older than sixteen stood there, dressed in a long-sleeved red top and ankle-length skirt, her leather shoes shone in the light. Nymeria's eyes zoned in on the emblem on the shirt, in pale blue stitching was a crystalline stork, the symbol of the Muse, goddess of the Arts and Medicine. Beneath the crystal stork was the phrase, 'Ghenna all girls school'. Nymeria realised this was Eleanor. The girl she had briefly seen the last time she came here.

"Yeah, that's me. I'm just waiting for your father—"

"Can I have a quick word?" she blurted out.

Nymeria straightened her back as she noticed the girl pick at her fingers. She was clearly worried about something, and anyone who could give insight was someone who could provide a new lead.

"Yeah, of course." Elanor moved so quickly over to Nymeria it was almost like she was in a rush. She lowered herself to sit next to her.

"Speak quickly then," Halloran said coldly and Elanor instantly sprung upright. Nymeria glared at Halloran, his cold stare was fixed on the girl as if daring her to make one wrong move.

"You—You're a—" she stammered, and Nymeria looked up at her. Eleanor's eyes were wide and all the colour drained from her as if she'd seen a ghost. Or better yet, a creature so horrible, so vile that it had her frozen with fear. But she was just looking at Halloran.

"I'm a what?" Halloran's voice had a bite to it that even she hadn't heard.

"A demon." Eleanor's bottom lip wobbled, and Nymeria knew if she didn't intervene, Eleanor would run straight out of the room.

"That I am," Halloran confirmed, and Eleanor inhaled.

"Ignore him." Nymeria gently grabbed her elbow. The tension left her shoulders. "Right now, he's harmless." Nymeria stared down Halloran. "Aren't you?"

Halloran's eyes briefly met hers, and he relaxed. "Fine," he snapped, and Nymeria could feel Eleanor's body tremble under the grip she had on her elbow. The girl sat down, still picking her nails.

"See? He looks scary, but he's more of a guard dog." Eleanor laughed at that, and Nymeria almost laughed at Halloran's briefly annoyed expression.

"You said you wanted a word?" Nymeria needed to have control of the conversation. She didn't know how long it would be before Zai returned and she had a feeling Eleanor would close up. Why else would she ask to speak to Nymeria privately?

"My father has been acting strangely," Eleanor said quietly. "I'm sure it's just stress because of my mother's disappearance. But ever since she's been gone, he's been spending more and more time alone or speaking—well, more like yelling—to Chief Cordero."

That caught Nymeria's attention. "Zai and the chief haven't been getting along?"

Eleanor nodded. "I've heard him more than once screaming down the phone, and I've heard the Chiefs' name but not much less. I'm sure the Chief is doing something wrong with my mother's disappearance and the other murders. If he was doing everything right, surely the killer would be caught by now," Eleanor ranted, and Nymeria couldn't help but agree.

"And your father? No abnormal behaviour?"

Eleanor vehemently shook her head. "No! He's always busy running the city, and especially since the murders started, he has taken solace in the gods more so than ever! Even the Swordsworn."

Nymeria felt something click in her brain. The Codex proudly displayed in the foyer was one of the Creator. "But your family Codex is of the Creator?"

"Yes, but surely you too would pray to the Swordsworn for protection in times like these. I'm sure it's for my own well-being, me and my dad only have each other," Eleanor urged, but the franticness in her voice made Nymeria curious if she was trying to convince Nymeria or herself.

"Perhaps your father is losing his mind," Halloran said so bluntly that even Nymeria cringed.

"My father is not losing his mind, horrid Hells creature!" she snapped, but her voice quaked with fear. Halloran took a step forward, and Eleanor reached under her shirt and pulled out a set of prayer beads, white and gold beads on a rope cord and on the end was a seven-eyed owl.

Eleanor held the beads out in front of her. "Back! Stay back."

Nymeria was speechless and Halloran chuckled bitterly, a burning look in his eyes like he wanted to strike her down.

"You think those little beads will do anything? Many of your kind have held those to me. It never stopped me from striking them down and tearing the flesh from their bones," Halloran leered, and Eleanor's hands shook.

"Can we all—"

"Ellie?" A voice sounded from the door and Nymeria felt the colour drain from her face as Eleanor rushed to her father. "Is everything alright?"

"Why is one of those things here! They don't look like how the Codex describes. Why does it look human?" she ranted, and Nymeria was so stunned she didn't know how to react or what to say. Halloran may be an asshole but he was trying to help this case, he wasn't the enemy here. But Nymeria studied Eleanor's face as Zai held her close and consoled her. Did the Codex instill this much fear and distrust for those who looked different? Who acted differently? Truthfully, she couldn't remember; it had been five years since she last read a Codex. But surely, it didn't instill this much fear; she had only killed those who were threats to the Faith, according to the Council.

But it was Melantha and the council that betrayed her, and it was the same Council that educated her growing up. Did she use to be just as hateful, if not more so? And why, after everything, was she still trying to defend the Faith that had ruined her life? It was the same old wound, she realised. One that was raw and bleeding, and no matter how much she hated it, hated Melantha, it was still there, a mark on her, on her mind.

Nymeria suddenly craved at least two bottles of wine. "Ellie, go upstairs, will you? I'll have a quick word with the investigator." Zai's tone left no room for argument.

Nymeria got up and followed Zai, as did Halloran. Eleanor sprinted up the staircase, briefly looking back at Nymeria, as if she had more to say, but she made no move to pull her aside. Nymeria lost sight of her as she walked down the corridor.

"The half-devil can wait out here," Zai said dismissively as he swung the doors to his office open and gestured for Nymeria to enter.

"Halloran."

"Sorry?"

"His name is Halloran," Nymeria said sharply, and Zai's eyes narrowed. Halloran took a step closer to her from behind, his chest almost brushing her back.

"Doesn't matter what its name is, I'm not having a criminal in my office where I keep all important documents relating to the city."

Nymeria might have taken his words at face value earlier, but after Eleanor's display, it was making the gears in her head turn. If Eleanor, a former nun in training, was so frightened from seeing a half-demon just standing, what was Zai, the former archbishop of Ghenna, teaching her?

"If it makes you feel better, he can stay by the door. But like I said, he's here for my protection. Nothing nefarious." Nymeria tilted her head up and looked up at him. "Right?"

She could see his eyes flicker down to her and she felt a shiver run through her as their eyes locked for the first time.

"Of course." Halloran cleared his throat and looked back at Zai. "Nothing nefarious."

Zai frowned but relented as he stood aside, letting them both enter his office.

Nymeria sat down and recounted everything that had happened: the brothel murder, the witness, the assassination and most importantly, the rifle. Throughout her explanation, Zai seemed contemplative as he watched her speak, elbows on his desk and his finger steepled as he stared her down as if trying to strip her soul bare and find the truth underneath. "I see. The police force has been more of a hindrance than a help?"

Nymeria nodded. "Exactly."

Zai suddenly stood up and ran a hand down his face and into his hair, mussing his perfectly styled comb over.

"I didn't want to think that the police would be involved, but they must be. I gave Cordero strict orders to work with you, so you can both work on this case. But with him directly going against orders and his less than satisfactory progress on the murders and my wife's disappearance..." Zai suddenly looked a lot older and tired, as if the weight of the world was on his shoulders.

"You think Cordero is the killer?" Nymeria confirmed, and Zai froze for a moment.

"I hope not. I hope the killer is just some half-demon, that no upstanding citizen of Ghenna would be capable of such a thing, but the facts are piling up." He seethed, Zai's gaze flickering past her, and Nymeria didn't need to turn around to know who he was looking at.

"I did want to ask you something," Nymeria interrupted. Now was her chance, and since he was starting to see some sense, this was her *best* chance. "With all this evidence piling up, I think it would be best if a small team—just myself and Caliban Ortega—conducted a raid on the GPD to see if they have any missing rifles to start, and then go through their files see if they have anything suspicious that can be linked to the murders. "

Zai nodded. "If you get a warrant, and raid during the day, you risk them hiding or destroying anything. But if you were to do a more covert operation during the night...If anything were to happen, I can turn a blind eye. I'm also going to be hosting a charity gala over the weekend to raise money for those affected by the murders. I know Cordero will be there; it would be the perfect time to take him out," Zai urged, leaning on his desk, hands splayed in front of him. They had a plan, and in just a few days, once they got even more evidence and had Cordero in a corner, they would finally have their answers.

15

The Break-in

"Are you seriously considering stealing files the police might have on you?" Caliban snapped, slamming his hands on the kitchen table, sending a few diagrams of the police HQ layout floating onto the floor.

"Why not? It would be the perfect opportunity," Imani said smoothly, examining her nails whilst Caliban looked at her as if she'd grown two heads.

"We're doing this to solve murders, not for you to do clean up."

"And why can't we do both?"

Nymeria rolled her neck and rubbed her eyes, sticking her fork in her take out box and eating the last of chicken noodles. This argument between the two had been going on in circles for the past hour.

"It would be opportunistic," Halloran grumbled and Caliban shot him an equally dirty look. "Of course you would agree.

"I don't see what the problem is." Arwen shrugged, his voice muffled as he chewed his food. "We do what we want if we have a few extra minutes. But only if it doesn't jeopardise the main objective."

"The problem is that it can put us in even more legal trouble. This break-in is risky enough without any side quests!"

Nymeria sighed and stood up, grabbing one of the manilla folders and walking around the table.

They all went quiet. Over the two days they'd been planning this break-in, these fights had been happening all hours of the day and Caliban was almost always the instigator.

"If you have all finished squabbling like children, can we please focus on the planning?" Nymeria's patience was waning fast.

"But—" Caliban started to speak but the manilla folder cracked over the back of his head. Nymeria wobbled on her feet and she felt a strong hand gently grab her forearm to stabilise her.

"No buts—" Nymeria shot a hard look to the others. Arwen removed his grip and raised his hands in surrender. Halloran looked away and Imani shrugged. "I know better than to mess with the boss."

Nymeria caught a sliver of movement from the couch, the eyes and top half of Gen's head was peaking over. Gen wanting to be involved had been another problem. No one wanted to leave Gen by herself, so Nymeria often sat her on the sofa with a worksheet. Sometimes Imani, Halloran, and Arwen would help her learn her sign language, and they were trying to learn as well. With a little guidance from Gen, all could have a basic conversation with her. The only one who would not do this was Caliban.

"Are we being too loud? Sorry," Arwen said softly and Gen shook her head.

"Can we go to the cornerstore?" she signed.

If Nymeria had to overhear anymore arguing, she was going to kick all of them out of her apartment.

"Sure. Get your shoes on," she spoke and signed back.

"What are we going to do about their ridiculous plan?" Caliban asked harshly.

"Do what you like. If it doesn't affect the main objective, do whatever."

Nymeria walked over to the table, taking her jacket off the back of the chair and pulled it on. Caliban made a noise of protest but was cut off by Arwen.

"I knew you would see sense." Arwen stood up and put his hands on Halloran's shoulders. "I bet our warrior here has been restless."

Halloran shook his head but Nymeria could make out a faint smirk on his lips. "Some progression in this case is long overdue."

Arwen rolled his eyes. "Come on, you can admit you're itching for a fight." Arwen stepped to the side and lightly punched Halloran's side. "But maybe you've grown sloppy."

Halloran stood up to throw some soft jabs of his own and Arwen retaliated. It was like watching two wolf pups play fight with each other.

However, it all stopped when Arwen's hand ended up around Halloran's throat and both brothers froze, a chilly breeze flowing through the kitchen from the nearby open window. Nymeria frowned. They both looked as if they were frozen in time. She couldn't even tell they were breathing until whatever spell had fallen over the brothers seemed to vanish and Arwen hastily pulled his hands away, stuffing them in his pockets.

"I didn't mean to—" Nymeria had never heard Arwen sound so panicked.

Halloran's throat bobbed. "I know."

"I'm sorry."

"You don't need to be."

Nymeria frowned. What was that all about? She couldn't dwell on it as Gen's hurried feet rounded the corner and eagerly bounced by the front door. Wordlessly, Nymeria opened it and let it shut behind the two. The two crossed the corridor and down the stairs, Gen squealing on the last step and Nymeria just managed to see her tip forward. Her hand shot out, catching Gen's wrist. "Careful!"

Gen stumbled to her feet. "Need to get the landlord to look at that." Nymeria scrutinised the offending crooked staircase. She squeezed Gen's hand and walked outside and down the street in Ghenna's warm evening spring air. Only when the bell of the cornerstone chimed and warm light washed over them, had she realised she was still holding Gen's hand. Gen was looking around but she lacked the usual excitement she had when the two went on a corner store run. Nymeria looked down at their hands, how much bigger her hand was to Gen's, how much more scarred and battle-worn it was. Nymeria gave her hand another squeeze and walked further into the corner store.

"Anything in particular you want?"

Gen shook her head.

"Why did you want to come then?"

Gen wiggled her hand out of Nymeria's. *"I didn't like the fighting. Why do you all hate each other?"*

"I don't hate them," Nymeria admitted, walking past the aisles holding baking goods and condiments until she stood outside the aisle lined with snacks.

"But you all argue."

"We do," Nymeria admitted.

"So you hate each other."

Nymeria shook her head. "Not necessarily, people argue all the time. Doesn't mean you hate them. I disagree with Caliban a lot but I like him. Imani and Arwen too." Nymeria reached for a packet of wine gums.

Gen face scrunched into a frown. *"That's confusing. Being an adult sounds confusing."*

Nymeria chuckled. "It is, Luckily you got me to help you when you grow up." Nymeria cringed. Why would she say that? It came so naturally and it didn't feel like a lie. But their time together was limited.

"What about Halloran?" Nymeria's hand paused.

"He's rude and arrogant."

"But he keeps us safe! Surely that makes him the nicest."

"We have a complicated history."

A brief silence fell over them. Gen must have realised she wasn't getting any more answers. Nymeria reached for a packet of chocolate covered marshmallows and tossed them down to Gen. She knew by now they were her favourite.

Nymeria walked down towards the cashier, pausing at the alcohol section, eyeing the fridges containing bottles of various sizes and colours. But in the mirror's reflection she could see the worried face of Gen, ringing her hands together. That face was able to compel Nymeria to move on and go straight to the counter, the first she had ever done that.

Gen tossed her marshmallows onto the counter as did Nymeria with her wine gums. *"Does that mean you and Halloran can never get along?"*

Nymeria frowned and she answered truthfully. "I don't know."

* * *

The sun had set long ago and Nymeria had forgone her usually stylish attire for an all black ensemble and a ski mask. She knew the GPD would have guards and cameras, and whilst Imani had said she had some of the gangs' tech experts on standby to disable the camera, Nymeria wanted to be extra careful that their identities weren't leaked. The plan with Zai would be all the more difficult if they got caught.

"You have everything?" Nymeria asked for the seventh time, and Caliban looked at her like he was going to slap her. "Fair enough," she said quietly. Nymeria turned around at the sound of soft footsteps from behind. Gen was dressed in all black with her own ski mask.

"Gen... We've talked about this," Nymeria said dismissively. "You aren't coming."

"*Yes, I am,*" Gen signed with one hand, tucking her makeshift ski mask under her elbow. Nymeria crouched and slowly signed back while speaking.

"No you aren't. You're a child—"

Gen shook her head. "*All I do is sit here whilst you, Halloran, Arwen and Imani do all the working,*" Gen signed rapidly, a scowl on her face and angry tears brimming her brown eyes. "*What good is all this magic I have if I never use it? I can help, why won't you let me,*" she signed, an angry shout leaving her lips.

Nymeria clasped her hands together, trying to stem her temper. She was stressed enough as it was with planning, she didn't have the time nor energy to be angry with Gen. "You're the most important thing—" She paused, *to me* she wanted to say, and it was on the tip of her tongue. "To this case. You're wanted by the killer, for whatever reason. I cannot allow anything to happen to you."

"*But—*" Gen started to sign, and Nymeria pressed a finger to her lips.

"No, this conversation is over. You're a child, you never should have been exposed to anything like this!"

"*But you were,*" Gen signed. "*You were doing all of this and more at my age!*" Gen smacked Nymeria's arm, and Nymeria grabbed her wrist.

"You don't want to be like me," Nymeria warned and the way Gen's eyes widened in hurt made her heart cease. Nymeria wanted to console her and apologise, she didn't want to be harsh. But she knew how Gen would turn out if Nymeria abused her powers. She would end up like her when she was younger: Egotistical and deluded. Gen was a good child, a brilliant one. She didn't need to be anything like her.

"You're staying here and you're not going to leave this flat." Nymeria stood up, picking up a duffel bag as she and Caliban left the flat, locking Gen in behind her.

Nymeria looked up to the ceiling and sent a quick prayer to the Crone to keep that unruly child well behaved.

"Damn, didn't think I would see you be a mama bear," Caliban teased as they walked down the stairs, and now it was Nymeria's turn to look at him like she wanted to smack him.

Caliban held up his hands. "Sorry, mama bear. Don't rip my organs out."

Nymeria rolled her eyes and slapped his shoulder. Caliban chuckled.

"Besides, afterwards, we can have a nice drink."

It reminded Nymeria that she needed to ask him about why he was so insistent on drinking with her. Had the revelation that she was an angel had shaken him that much? Was he going through something? She didn't have time to ask, now they had to focus on this break-in.

The two made it down the stairs, out of the building and to her car. Halloran was sitting on the hood, smoking, and Nymeria let a small half smile creep up her face whilst Caliban cleared his throat.

"I thought we agreed it would just be two of us."

"We did. But it's my job to keep Nymeria safe." Was that the first time he said her name instead of woman or her? She liked how he said her name, like it was a rare silk or a precious jewel.

"I'm capable of doing that—" Caliban started, but Halloran quickly cut him off.

"Are you? Last time I checked, you're a human who can be

outshot by an eight-year-old girl. I, at the very least, have magic."

Caliban scowled and looked like he wanted to burn a hole through Halloran's face.

"He does have a point," Nymeria agreed, and Halloran's eyes widened, as if he had been expecting her to fight him on this.

"Fine. But we're only getting information pertaining to the case, no evidence on the gang's crimes," Caliban said sternly and went to the backseat of the car, dropping the duffel bag at Halloran's feet.

"What crimes?" Halloran chimed. "We're just good, honest businessmen."

Nymeria let out a small huff of a laugh, going to the boot, but Halloran took the duffel bag out of her hands. She raised a brow, but he simply shrugged. Nymeria made her way to the driver's side, and just as she opened the door, she could have sworn she heard a crackling sound.

"Doors locked and boots closed?" she asked, closing the driver's side door. Halloran tossed the duffel bag into the boot, not looking inside it before joining her in the passenger seat. Nymeria started the car, a shaky exhale leaving her. This was perhaps the riskiest thing she had done in her two years on the continent, and it sent her blood pumping in an old way that made her smile.

* * *

The drive was short, and they parked a few streets away from the GPD HQ. The three took all of their belongings up to the roof of the neighbouring building, and Nymeria looked out over the edge to see the GPD HQ. All lights were off except the faint glow of a flashlight shining through the skylight over the bullpen. Brian Parker, the GPD guard, was on duty tonight just as Imani had said. Footsteps came up behind her and an earpiece was thrust in front of her.

"Showtime," Caliban said, and Nymeria lifted part of her ski mask to clip the earpiece over her ear and tap it twice. A horrible ringing sounded at first and then cut to a crackling voice.

"This is Draig customer service, how may I help?" Nymeria couldn't help but laugh at Arwen.

"Customer service huh? You send Halloran to do all the heavy lifting," she chimed, pulling the ski mask back down and making sure it was comfortable against the earpiece.

"Well, that's his job," Arwen deflected. "Also, as beautiful as my face is, even with a ski mask, the scar is pretty visible. If anything went wrong, I'd get caught and identified in no time, and then my whole business would go under. Which isn't fun for anyone."

Nymeria sighed; he did have a very good point.

"Halloran checking in."

"Caliban checking in."

"Imani here," she said over the comms. "Are we ready to move out?"

Nymeria looked back over her shoulder at Halloran and Caliban, and their eyes were wide, looking at her.

"Why are you—" A flicker of movement next to her caught

her eye, and Nymeria closed her eyes. No. No, this wasn't happening. She slowly turned around. She wasn't going to see Gen when she opened her eyes. She looked down and opened her eyes to see a very smug Gen, smirking up at her.

The gods were truly dead if even the Crone couldn't control this unruly child.

"Why are you—" She started to shout and then cleared her throat. Her anger flared like hot lava, bubbling under her skin. "Why are you here after I—"

Gen was still smiling and despite how angry Nymeria was that she went against her words about her safety, Nymeria was also incredibly impressed.

"How?"

"I portaled," Gen signed. *"I just want to help! I didn't mean to make you upset!"*

Nymeria slowly turned her head to Halloran, whose eyes widened in surprise.

"She's getting much better at sneaking and going undetected. Good job."

Nymeria could hear the smirk in his voice.

"No! Not a good job!" Nymeria scolded. "I gave you an order!"

Gen flinched, *"Well I'm here now. Make use of me, I want to help,"* she signed, her hands shaking.

Nymeria stood back up and paced across the roof, she couldn't deny the strategic value of Gen's magic. But her heart didn't want to turn her into a weapon like she had been. But she could be of use, just this once. Would a single moment of indulging her truly be that bad?

Nymeria put her hands on her hips.

"You stay here—" Gen's hand started to move.

"—But! It would be very helpful if you could portal us from here to there." Nymeria pointed to the skylight and the bullpen within. "Just long enough so we can get in and as soon as we're all inside, give us twenty minutes exactly then reopen them. If none of us come through during that time, you stay here and Imani and Arwen will come get you. Do you understand?" Nymeria's voice strained with concern.

Gen nodded, a naive eagerness in her eyes that Nymeria was all too familiar with.

"Alright," Nymeria said into the earpiece. "We're moving out."

"Yes, ma'am," Imani said on the other end. "Camera's going out in three...two...one. You're in the clear."

"Wonderful. Gen."

Gen nodded and held her hands out in front of her. A few seconds passed as a small crack in the air above the roof grew larger and larger before splitting open, showing the bullpen.

"Remember, twenty minutes." Nymeria frowned when she saw the over eager grin on Gen's face and her bouncing on the balls of her feet. She shook her head, closed her eyes and jumped into the portal.

As Nymeria entered the portal, she felt a strange sense of lightness overcome her whole body. As she opened her eyes, Nymeria felt a sense of awe wash over her she hadn't felt in years. She could see shades of silvers and purples that she couldn't name even though it was one the tip of her tongue. Objects floated around she had never seen before, which undulated and stretched unnaturally. It was a beautifully odd place. But just as soon as she saw all these things, they vanished as she stepped into the bullpen. As Caliban and Halloran bumped into her back, she heard the crack of the portal as it disappeared behind her. At least Gen could follow that order.

Nymeria turned to face the two men and nodded. They all knew the plan. "Everyone is through," Nymeria muttered into the earpiece.

"Heard you, good luck," came Arwen's voice, all humour gone from his voice as he focused.

Each person had a job and Caliban was to head to the armoury and check their loaning system. He nodded at Nymeria before walking into the dark corridor. Nymeria's job—now Halloran's as well—was to raid Cordero's office. Any sensitive information was bound to be held there, similar to how Nymeria kept hers in her office before the murder of Michael.

Nymeria walked on the balls of her feet to Cordero's office door. She could practically hear her covert mission teacher, a badgery old man who was a descendant of a child of the Shepard yelling in her ear, '*Feet light and magic ready, child. For you may be getting hunted whilst you are doing the hunting.*' Every time she was spotted, he would cut an inch of her hair off—a universal punishment in all of her training. She didn't make many mistakes.

Nymeria's hand wrapped around the door knob and shook it. The door rattled but didn't open. Of course it was locked, and they didn't have the time to pick locks; that guard could be around the corner.

"Halloran, break it." White crackling magic surrounded Halloran's fists.

"Quietly," she added.

"I'm not an amateur," he chastised. His fingers twitched and a spark of lighting surged forward, hitting the doorknob. It clattered uselessly to the floor. For a few seconds the air hung still and they both waited for the blare of an alarm, or the sound of heavy footsteps from the guard, but nothing came.

They both stepped into the office, and Nymeria immediately went to the desk, opening drawers and pulling everything out and onto the desk. Halloran moved behind her, his hip against hers as he used the same method he did to open the door on the filing cabinet. She pulled out papers, notebooks and pencils, and riffled through all of them, trying to find anything. She came across notes on the other officers in the bullpen: how Officer Lim was exceptional for a recruit, how Sergeant Sharp was struggling in her new role and more. But none of that was what she was looking for.

"Anything?" Imani spoke over the comms.

"Not yet," Halloran replied, cursing under his breath.

"Caliban?" Arwen asked.

"Negative, still looking," he replied and Nymeria felt her heart hammer against her chest. They needed something, *anything*.

The tense silence was broken by loud whistling and heavy

footfalls of leather boots. Nymeria froze for a split second before ducking under the desk and grabbing Halloran's wrist, pulling him down as well.

"Why are you always pulling me into cramped spaces?" Halloran whispered, and Nymeria scowled.

She pushed herself as far back as she could, until she was half curled in on herself and Halloran, who must have heard the footsteps as well, crowded over her, his hand at either side of her head, their chests touching. She could feel his breath on her neck, goosebumps raising over her skin and she shivered. Nymeria closed her eyes. She needed to focus, but it was so dark in the office and she hated feeling a presence looming over her. But she also wasn't there, as her mind pulled her into darker memories that she wished to forget.

"Please not now..." she quietly begged, squeezing her eyes shut. She could hear the rattling of chains, the way hands would squeeze her bare body and the hot breath of someone she used to know behind her ear and—

"Easy." Halloran's voice was like soothing balm over a burn, and she slowly opened an eye. His eyes glowed slightly in the dark, and they held the softest look she had ever seen.

"Easy..." he said again, and his hand brushed her cheek, as if an electric shock had passed through them. She flinched away. "What is—"

"I'm fine," she whispered as a stream of light coasted over them, highlighting Halloran's face in a way that made his cheekbones more pronounced and his jawline sharper; even through the ski mask, he was truly the most divine thing she had ever seen. He was so close she could see his pupils blow out.

"What?" she whispered.

"You're...Nothing." Halloran cleared his throat and even in the darkness she could see how his cheeks and ears were red.

"I'm nothing?"

"That's not—Never mind."

The sound of footsteps slowly retreated, and Nymeria felt his hand pull away from the back of her head. When had he even moved his hand to cradle her head? As soon as silence fell over them, Nymeria heard a small struggle, grunts of effort, a shout, then a thump.

Silence returned.

"Caliban?" Nymeria whispered into the earpiece.

"Don't worry, that was me. The guard won't be an issue for about... half an hour."

Nymeria sighed in relief, at least that gave them a bit more free reign.

"You can move," Nymeria said quietly, and Halloran cleared his throat.

"Right."

He stood up and straightened his shirt. She rolled her eyes and started to get up when his hand came into view, palm up. She looked up at him and took his hand.

A moment passed as he helped her to her feet, and then another. She cleared her throat and pulled her hand back.

"Find anything?"

"Not yet. Just old files pertaining to other cases. You?"

"Nothing." Nymeria returned to the main desk drawer and pulled it roughly

"There has to be something—" She could have sworn

she saw a flicker of movement from the back of the drawer. Nymeria pulled again, and she saw it. Excitedly she grabbed each side of the drawer, and pulled it out, setting it on the floor. Halloran crouched next to her.

"Is that—"

"It's a false bottom."

She pulled it out, a thin piece of wood coloured exactly like the desk. She placed it next to the drawer on the floor and inside the false bottom was several documents. Nymeria pulled them out and quickly thumbed through them.

'Mariam - 16 - used at park site' and attached was a picture of a young human woman.

'Charlie - 21 - used at brothel site.' Another picture of a human boy.

'Clarice - 26, Armen - 19, Sven - 15 - used at pier site.'

These were showing the names and ages of all the victims for the murders. But something struck her as odd—the wording—'used', as if Cordero had done it himself. But even more disturbing and gruesome were the photos. Each document had several photos of the crime scenes and the victims in their final moments, blurred images of eyes wide in terror. Bloody faces and even bloody hands trying to push away at their attacker. Mouths pulled back in what was most certainly a scream or at least trying to. In the other images some were freshly dead, blood still bright red but eyes vacant of life. Trophy pictures.

"Nymeria, I'm about to be your favourite person!" Caliban's voice crackled over the earpiece. "That rifle we have? Last checked out by—"

"Chief Morgan Cordero? Yeah, I practically have a confession here," Nymeria said. She felt giddy with excitement. She got him. She got the killer red-handed. This had to be more than enough to show Zai. She heard the familiar crack of Gen's portal in the bullpen.

"Time's up!" she said over the earpiece. The two of them ran out of the office, the portal crackling brightly in front of them. Caliban rushed past both of them, and Nymeria wasn't far behind.

In the blink of an eye, she was back on the roof, Halloran behind her, and she heard the crackle of the portal shutting behind her.

Caliban ripped off his ski mask, and Nymeria followed suit; both grinned at each other. "We did it!" Caliban beamed. "We did it, we got the fucker!" he cheered and he rushed forward scopping her up into a hug, spinning them both.

Nymeria squealed, feeling a jolt of uneasiness. She did flinch but she didn't push him away. As Caliban spun her around, she caught glimpses of Gen celebrating as well, jumping up and down before hugging Halloran's leg—unable to quite reach his waist. Instead of pushing her away, he ruffled her hair.

But Nymeria wasn't celebrating. Truthfully, she saw nothing to celebrate. The man who was in charge of protecting this city was its biggest threat. At least, that's what all the evidence pointed to. But one question was already plaguing her mind; *why?* Morgan Cordero was a hero amongst the police force. He was a stickler for following the law to a T, at least, that's what she knew of him. Had that been a lie? Something about this didn't sit right with her, but it was all she had to go off.

Morgan Cordero had a lot to answer for.

16

The Vampire's Den

After breaking into the GPD, Nymeria had been hoping for a good rest the following morning. She hoped to rise well after the sun, and maybe go to a nearby bakery and pick up some fresh pastries. Something sweet, almost domestic and entirely foreign to her. She trusted Halloran enough to make breakfast for Gen; his cooking was, begrudgingly, delicious. But no, her dream of a soft muffin would not come to be as Nymeria was awoken to the sound of her phone buzzing angrily on her bedside table. Her hand smacked the table a few times before her fingers curled around the device, and she answered.

"Hello?"

"I thought you would be up already, investigator. With you having a child and all," Imani teased over the phone, and Nymeria smiled.

"Please say you have good news for me if you're calling me at"—Nymeria checked the time on her phone—"six in the morning."

"I do. I managed to pull some strings and with a lot of

persuasion, I may have something."

Nymeria sat up. "Oh yeah?"

"I would prefer to talk in person. Prying eyes and ears are around every corner."

"Alright then. Send me the address."

Nymeria's phone vibrated as a text was sent.

"I'll be over in an hour. This will have to be quick, I've arranged with Caliban to be at Zai's home by 10 am."

"Don't worry, this shouldn't take too long. Talk to you in a moment."

Imani hung up, and Nymeria got up fast, washing and dressing, ignoring Halloran's confused grumble of bewilderment.

"I'm seeing Imani," was her rushed reply.

* * *

Nymeria was confused. She looked between the warehouse she was parked outside of, and then at her phone. She wasn't sure what she expected a Draig 'production house' to look like, but a run-down, falling apart building near the docks was not it. She got out of her car, double-checking that she locked it behind her. She casually walked up to it, which looked very abandoned on the outside, like the rest of the warehouses by the docks: the walls were covered in ivy, mould and graffiti. Nymeria rattled the side door and it didn't budge. "I swear to the gods Imani..." she grumbled, ringing Imani again but receiving no response. The 'no signal' bar in the top right corner of her phone felt like a taunt.

She tried the door again, her fingers wrapping around the

handle, and she pulled, but this time her eyes narrowed and her brow furrowed. As her fingers wrapped around the handle, Nymeria noticed a shimmer, and she felt a strange tugging feeling, almost sticky like she was putting her hand through molasses. Nymeria twisted it, and her wrist looked like it was covered by a fine, clear sheet: distorted and unclear. Nymeria stepped back. "What the hells?"

"There you are!" Imani smiled mischievously, clearly pleased with whatever trick she was planning or rather had someone else pull. Nymeria frowned. Imani looked like she had walked straight out the wall.

"How—"

"Illusionary magic," Imani relented. "The docks are one of the only parts of the city which is a mobile dead zone, making it the perfect place to set up shop for any under the radar business." She smirked. "Ayako, lift the veil for a moment," Imani called to someone over her shoulder. The door pulled away from Nymeria and into the wall, as if it was sunken into the molasses like magic before disappearing entirely. Nymeria blinked in surprise. She hadn't even sensed any magic in the area.

"Not bad," she mused, walking up to Imani, who opened the real door for her. Nymeria walked through, and Imani followed behind her.

"Demons are as natural with magic as angels are." Imani chuckled. The inside of the warehouse seemed to be much bigger and cleaner than the outside. There were multiple half demons—some looking more human—the only telling features of their heritage being unnaturally coloured eyes or strangely textured skin like scales, prongs of slime. Whilst others could have passed for full demons with their long horns or fins, black sclera, sharp teeth and the odd prong or bump visible through clothing. Despite the wild differences, all of them were talking with each other, sharing coffee and making jokes like they were at a regular office job. But for the slightest moment, the room went still when she entered. Nymeria didn't miss the beat of silence that passed as all eyes were briefly on her. They were just as weary of her as she was of them. Only five years ago, she would have decimated this room of life simply for the fact they were breathing, and even now she felt the need boiling in her blood to do just that.

"Well?" Imani barked and Nymeria could have sworn a few of them jumped as everyone went back to work.

"They aren't used to visitors," Imani apologised, gesturing for Nymeria to follow behind her. Wordlessly, the two passed through the cubicles of half-demons, up a set of rickety iron stairs and into a refurbished office. Imani had a new money aesthetic taste in decor that Nymeria could appreciate. Black walls and carpet, with a modern glass desk at the far end and a small window overlooking the warehouse below.

Nymeria walked over to the desk, pulling out one of the black chairs and sitting down. "I'm afraid I couldn't be of much help." Imani folded her hands in front of her. "I looked through our database back to front, I went to the local library and went through all the archives I could find to see if there was anything about curses. I checked new and old, I fell asleep reading history textbooks, and I couldn't find a single thing."

Nymeria slumped back in her chair. "So you woke me up at

6am for nothing?"

"Not quite."

As if on cue, a knock sounded at the office door.

"Come in."

A half-demon walked in, one of the ones that looked more demon than human. Webbed fingers, fins on his cheek and neck and a grey-purple colouration to his skin, which made his short black hair look even darker. He looked like he could have been related to that Gluttony demon that attacked her in the church all those weeks ago.

"Imani." He smiled, but when his black and yellow eyes landed on Nymeria, his face fell, and he looked like he wanted the ground to swallow him whole. "Mercury."

"Oliver, Nymeria. Nymeria, Oliver," Imani said briskly, and Nymeria inclined her head.

"Oliver here is our artefact expert. Any weird things we brought from the Hells he examines to see if we can make use of any of it."

"Most of it is junk." He chuckled nervously.

"I thought he could have a look at your scars."

Nymeria half-turned to face Imani. "Are you serious?"

Imani blinked. "Yes? Just a brief physical, see if it's anything he has seen before."

Nymeria scowled and shifted in her seat, becoming hyper aware of the individual threads in her shirt and the scratch of her trousers against her thighs.

"It will only take a few minutes," Oliver spoke up, his voice was warm and Nymeria hated that. The pity. She wanted to slap it out of him.

She could bear it for just a few minutes. "Fine."

Nymeria stood up and took off her coat. Oliver moved closer, pulling rubber gloves out of his pocket and onto his hands. Imani walked towards the door, pulling it open.

"Stay!" Nymeria's voice came out as an urgent plea. Imani paused for a moment and then closed the door.

"...Okay?"

"Whenever you're ready." Oliver's voice was quiet.

Nymeria inhaled sharply and slowly popped each button, cursing as her trembling fingers got stuck on the last one. Slowly, she pulled the shirt off her shoulders, and a very quick and quiet gasp passed between Oliver and Imani. Nymeria had to bite her cheek to stop herself from the shout that bubbled in her throat.

She could feel the judging looks, the unspoken questions on their tongues and she hated it. She felt exposed like they were examining her soul and it made her cringe. Her fists curled at her sides, knuckles turning white.

Tentatively, Oliver pressed a hand to her shoulder, easing her forward. "I just want to take a look at your back."

Just like that, with a motion so simple, Nymeria was back in that dark cell surrounded by clinking and burning chains, cruel laughs and hands pushing and pulling her into whatever position they wanted.

Nymeria hadn't realised she had struck Oliver until he called out in surprise. Spots danced in her eyes, and her head swam. A shattering sound reverberated around the room.

"No!"

Oliver groaned, leaning on the desk, the fractured photo frame by his feet. Nymeria pulled her shirt back on. "Get out!"

she seethed, and Oliver looked between Imani and Nymeria. Nymeria's lips pulled back into a snarl like a frightened dog, her hands gripping the diary planner on the desk and she launched it at him. Oliver shielded his head, the planner landing against his outspread palms. He quickly rushed out.

"What the hells was that?!" Imani snapped, her voice quivering as her hands dove between glass shards and picked out the photo within. Straightening out with the urgency like it was a living, breathing thing.

"Why are you getting worked up over a photo?" Nymeria deflected. Her fingers trembled again as she buttoned up her shirt. "Fuck sakes."

Nymeria looked at the glass desk, her eyes pulled to the photo. It was Imani and a handsome black man holding each other. Imani's hand facing the camera, showing off a glittering diamond ring.

"Didn't know you were married." Nymeria hadn't seen Imani wear the ring. She knew the topic would be sensitive, but right now she didn't care; she just wanted Imani not to ask her about the whys of what happened.

Imani stiffened. "I wasn't. But I was engaged. Then Sodom happened."

"Do you ask all your friends to strip around strangers? If so, I can see why he left." She snapped.

Imani stopped moving, and the room suddenly felt darker.

"Tell me, do you know what it's like?" Imani stood up. "To wake up with glass in your eye and your body broken, only able to turn your head to see the love of your life being feasted on by demons?" she spat. "I wasn't alone when Sodom fell. Omar came after me, as I forgot my keys."

Nymeria didn't answer.

"I was the perfect target for that demon. Euphoria, it called itself. It wanted to indulge in curses, become a curse master, it said. The curse process of dying and being reborn as an unholy creature is an excruciating one. It wanted to play god. Sometimes it would leave me without blood for weeks at a time, just to see what would happen. Other times, it would force so much down me, it's like I was high and I would be like that for days. Only until it got bored and cast me to the Ring of Wrath, which is where Arwen found me."

Imani stood up, throwing the picture down.

"Is that what you wanted to hear? Is that good enough for you? Because you only that to get a reaction from me, which is really fucking cruel."

Nymeria should have kept her mouth shut, but she had wanted to hurt someone else in the moment, and now she felt ashamed that she had lashed out at all.

"Yes, it is," Nymeria replied. She had started this and she would own it. This was what happened every time; someone would poke a little too deep and she would lash out.

"Get out," Imani said sternly. "Don't request any more favours again because next time I'll deny it and tell Arwen straight away. That can be your shitstorm to deal with."

Nymeria didn't say anything else; she got up and walked out.

Rushing down the stairs two at a time, almost tripping over her own feet, Nymeria slammed the door to the warehouse open and breathed out deeply, staggering forward until her hands latched onto the rails that separated land from sea.

Her heartbeat was in her ears, her vision blurred as she pushed those visions down. No, not visions, memories. Memories of those horrid three years. Three years where the almighty Swordsworn could have turned the city of Elysium to rubble and freed one of his daughters. Roughly ten per cent of the population of Elysium were actual children of gods, the rest were angels who had children with other angels. The Swordsworn's inaction had only shown her just how replaceable she was. Her father, with all the power in the world, chose not to save her. At least that was what she had thought until she escaped and arrived on Earth. Only then had she learnt that the gods had been dead and Elysium had vanished from the skies.

Nymeria gagged and vomited over the rail, her bile being swept away by the lapping waves. Nymeria crouched down, her hand still gripping the railing, and she pressed her forehead against the rusting metal. She needed a drink. She needed to forget. Her chest was so tight she couldn't breathe, choked gasps leaving her mouth. It felt like something rotten was inside of her, and she truly considered ripping her insides out just to make this horrible feeling stop. She stayed like that for what felt like hours, until the memories faded and she could breathe again. On shaky legs, she stood once more, wiping the mixture of tars and snot on the back of her hand. She could deal with the mess later. Now she needed a drink.

Nymeria staggered around the corner and was surprised to

see a crowd. "What's going on?" she half-slurred as she approached.

"Cops," one half-demon said to her. "A friend of yours?"

Nymeria ignored the jab and pushed past the crowd.

"—I won't ask you again. What are you doing here?" the cop snapped, a half-demon with red eyes had his hands up and out in front of him.

"I'll tell you again, I'm just on the way to the fish market."

"And you're taking the scenic route then, huh?" the cop said accusingly.

"I'm literally just walking. Do you stop everyone walking down the street?"

Nymeria's eyes narrowed; it was the same demon who was the bouncer inside Greed, the one who had checked her over before she met Halloran and Arwen for the first time.

"Hey, what's going on?" Nymeria called, stepping closer to the half-demon than the cop.

"Mercury? What are you doing down here?"

Nymeria glanced down at the name tag on the officer's uniform—Lim—the exceptional new recruit according to Cordero's files. "Hey, Lim."

He was being friendly to her. He must be new.

"Just checking out the area." Nymeria wrapped an arm over the half-demons shoulders. "Hey man, how's it going?"

The half-demon frowned, almost pulling away.

"A friend of yours?" Lim's shoulder relaxed, and the half-demon leaned into her hold.

"Yeah, she's my partner?"

"Yeah, newest recruit for the All-seeing Private Eye," Nymeria lied. "Just have him patrolling the area."

"Yeah, that's right," the half-demon said. "We cool man?"

Lim took a few steps back. "Yeah, we're cool. Sorry for the trouble. You tell your rookie to walk in more well-lit areas. Never know what kind of trouble he may find himself in," Lim warned. He walked back to his cruiser.

"Pussy," the half demon snapped.

"What was that Hells-spawn?" Lim snapped back, stalking over with his hands on the gun at his waist. Nymeria stood between the two men.

"Easy! No need for a fist fight over insults. How old are you both, five?!" she yelled. Neither man was looking at her, instead having a stare off like bulls about to rip each other to shreds. The animosity made her feel better.

"You need more gun discipline if your hands are going to your waist at an insult," Nymeria snapped at Officer Lim. He flinched as if she struck him.

She then turned to the half-demon. "You need to cool it. Can't have my investigators going off and starting fights during investigations," she said calmly, cocking her brow upward *'play along'* she tried to communicate.

He fixed her with a steely look and exhaled sharply. "Yeah, you're right boss. Sorry."

Officer Lim walked backwards towards his cruiser, not taking his eye off either of them until he got into it, fixing the half-demon with a steely look before speaking into his radio and driving off.

The half-demon quickly pushed himself away from Nymeria. "Thanks," he said curtly.

"Don't mention it."

He fixed Nymeria with a judgmental glare. "Why did you help me out?"

"You were a person in trouble, being unjustly pestered by the police."

The half-demon chuckled. "You make it sound like it's a rare occurrence. That's the third time this week. The last cop who pulled me over told me it was because I looked suspicious walking down the street. I was just shopping!" He kicked the wall and sighed heavily, his shoulders shaking.

"Alfie?" a soft voice said.

Nymeria looked over her shoulder. A very pregnant half-demon woman appeared through the disguised door, pushing past Nymeria and heading straight to Alfie. She was a short woman with dark hair, a beanie over her head, which Nymeria noticed was barely hiding two bumps on the tops of her head—poorly concealed horns.

"Are you alright? The cops aren't giving you a hard time, right?" the woman fussed.

"Ayako, hun, I'm fine. Just a misunderstanding." Alfie put his hand on Ayako's stomach. "You shouldn't even be here. Arwen has given you time off for a reason."

"I know, but I hate being at home by myself."

Nymeria cleared her throat. She really should not be here for this conversation.

"I should go. Take care." She started to walk past them, but Ayako put her hand on Nymeria's shoulder.

"Thank you for helping my boyfriend. He's so reckless and never knows when to keep his mouth shut." Ayako shot Alfie an accusatory glare.

Nymeria couldn't help but laugh.

"No worries, just doing my job."

"It's a good job. You're helping my kind, actually doing what you should be."

"Which is?"

"Looking out for people. Trying to maintain law and order. We half-demons, we all know what you are doing. You're becoming something of a local legend despite the fact you're... " Nymeria knew what she was going to say. "Anyways, thank you. For doing the right thing. Keeping all of us safe. I can't imagine how difficult being the last of your kind is."

Nymeria felt weird, she hadn't been thanked like this before. It felt wrong. She was doing good now, but if this was a few years ago, she would have killed this very nice woman on the spot without a second thought. All the half demons she had met seemed so normal... not at all like the wrathful, faithless, mad creatures she had been brought up to believe they were or the ones she had killed. They had lives and ambitions just like she had. It made her wonder... She shut that thought down quickly, her throat dry and a lump forming in it. She needed a drink.

Her phone rang loudly, breaking the silence and her thoughts. "I've gotta go, but take care." Nymeria nodded at both of them and quickly walked away, almost sprinting to her car and getting in. Answering her phone with shaking hands, "Hello?"

"Hey, it's me." Caliban's voice was sharp over the phone. "Where are you? I'm already at the mayor's gates."

"Oh shit! Sorry, didn't realise things ran over."

"You hung over?"

"No, I was sorting out something with Imani."

"What kind of something?"

"A personal something." Nymeria turned her key in the ignition of her car.

"Why are you so eager to get me drinking more anyway? You've mentioned it twice now."

"I can't look forward to having a drink with a friend?"

"Considering you usually don't like it when I drink, it's just a weird change of heart."

Nymeria's car rumbled to life.

"I'm just trying to get things back to how they used to be between us," Caliban said, his voice melancholic. "I don't mean anything else by it."

"Alright. I'll see you in ten minutes. Alright, see you soon."

"Bye."

17

A Trap Of Extravagance

Later that morning, when Nymeria finally arrived at Zai's estate, and wobbled up to the door (she may have indulged in a bottle of vodka she kept hidden in her car) she was quite surprised that Caliban didn't start shouting at her like he had done at the offices a few weeks back. He gave her a resigned look, pressed the intercom and they were shortly let inside. Eleanor was still eating breakfast when they almost threw all the evidence they had gathered in front of Zai and after looking over it for only a few seconds, he came to the same conclusion as they did: Morgan Cordero was the killer.

Arwen had been exceptionally pleased that the killer was not a half-demon. Although, according to his sources, tensions were still high between half-demons and humans, Arwen was confident that they would come to an end as soon as Cordero was caught.

Nymeria had asked if Cordero would still be coming to the gala; surely he would have been scared off by now. But apparently not, as Zai had eased her worries. Thanks to Imani cutting the camera's, the knocked-out guard, and no signs of forced entry, the security guard had gotten the blame for trying to steal police documents and was currently in jail with a pending court date. Nymeria felt quite bad, but the bail was so high that she couldn't afford to pay it. Maybe once Arwen paid her she could get this guy out—a small apology.

Three nights after the break-in, it was time for the gala. Considering she was expecting things to get hairy and a potential chase, she opted for one of her nicer suits. She didn't wear dresses anymore; they often showed off her scars, and that led to questions she didn't feel comfortable answering. The deep crimson suit and its matching trousers complemented her hair nicely, which was tied back into a ponytail for once; a black polo neck covered up all the scars and matched her black leather dress shoes. She pulled a few strands of her hair down to frame her face, looking at herself in the dresser mirror.

"You look...good."

Nymeria jumped and turned around to see Halloran leaning against the door frame of her bedroom.

White dress shirt underneath a grey waistcoat and matching trousers. It suited him very nicely, and it hugged him so well he must have had it tailored.

"You look"—handsome—"good." She didn't even try to hide how her eyes looked over him.

"I thought you said you liked pretty dresses," Halloran said, and Nymeria blinked in surprise.

"Pardon?"

"Last week, when you and Gen had that movie night. You said you like pretty dresses. I thought a gala would be the most opportune moment to dress up." He didn't sound judgmental for once; instead he seemed curious.

"People see the scars if I wear a dress."

"It's more than just your arms?"

"They're all over my body." She looked down, fiddling with the gold rings adorning her fingers.

"Why hide them?"

"Don't be an asshole—" she started to scold but he held up his hands.

"I'm being serious. Why hide them? They're a testament to your strength. Endurance. Of what you have overcome. Isn't that something to be proud of?"

She had never thought about them like that. "Not everyone will think that way," she corrected, and Halloran frowned.

"Then those who don't think that way are fools."

Nymeria cleared her throat. "Then why don't you show off yours?"

Halloran chuckled. It was annoying how much she enjoyed the sound. "My attendance is already going to cause a stir; going shirtless would get me quickly escorted out." He raised a brow. "You want to see me shirtless again? In front of strangers? I didn't think you were so crass."

"I was just trying to prove a point—you know what? Never mind!"

Halloran's phone buzzed, and he fished it out of his pocket. His thumb swiped across the screen. "Right on time for once, Arwen is here."

"I didn't know he was picking you up."

"Picking us up," Halloran corrected. "You're an associate of the Draig business now, I can't have you showing up in that old monstrosity you call a car. It would make us look bad."

Nymeria tilted her head to look him in the eye, but his head was turned away, fixing a burning hole into her wall. She was starting to think he didn't care about his reputation. No, that seemed a bit too straightforward, and Halloran was anything but.

"Whatever you say," she said nonchalantly, a small smirk on her lips.

Nymeria walked into the lounge, and Gen gasped when she saw her. Nymeria did a small spin.

"How do I look?" Nymeria signed.

"Beautiful," Gen signed back.

Nymeria strode over and scooped her into a hug. "You gonna behave and stay here this time?"

Nymeria felt Gen nod against her shoulder.

"You promise?" she asked again, and Gen pulled away, holding out her pinky finger. It was such a sweet gesture, and she hooked her pinky around Gen's.

"Good."

"We really have to go," Halloran called by the door. "Stay safe, Gen."

The two wordlessly left the apartment and walked down the stairs, and when Halloran opened the complex door, a limo waited outside. Nymeria's eyes nearly bulged out of her head. "Over the top, much?"

"I voted for a Jaguar, the limo is..." One of the back windows rolled down, and Arwen's russet-haired head poked out.

"Come on, love birds. We have a party to attend." Nymeria rolled her eyes, and the limo door popped open. Nymeria clambered inside.

"Evening." If Imani hadn't said anything, Nymeria wouldn't have noticed she was there, despite how stunning she looked. Imani looked like a vision of grace. Her usual eyepatch was replaced with a brown glass eye, a shimmering gold dress hugged her body, a slit revealing her legs.

"Evening," Nymeria replied curtly.

An uncomfortable tension descended over the occupants of the limo.

Caliban cleared his throat, dressed in a casual black tux. "Not bad."

"Not bad yourself." Nymeria's lip twitched into a smile.

Halloran knocked on the driver's window and the limo started to move.

Imani crossed her arms over her chest and looked out to the dark streets. Nymeria became fixated with the cufflinks on her suit: silver swords.

"Anyway," Arwen spoke up, easing the tension, "I'm due a compliment." He pouted. He was sitting opposite her, dressed in a burgundy suit not too different from her own, but also not too different from what he usually wore.

"Not dressing up?" Nymeria raised a brow.

"You can't top perfection." He gestured down his body, but his lip quirked downward when he took in what she was wearing.

"Not dressing up either?"

"Nah, I don't look good in dresses," Nymeria deflected. "Besides, I have a feeling Cordero isn't going to go quietly. Better to be prepared."

Arwen chuckled. "Ever practical." Nymeria didn't miss how Arwen's gaze lingered on Halloran, who shot his brother an unamused look. Arwen waggled his eyebrows in reply, and Halloran scoffed.

She had no idea what secret message was passing between them.

"We need clear communication from here on out," Caliban chastised. "No more...whatever that was."

Imani started to hand out earpieces.

Nymeria chuckled and shook her head. She felt a small pang of sadness in her chest. After tonight, the deal she made with Arwen would be resolved, and she wouldn't have to see any of them except Caliban again. But that made her realise something else, what was she going to do with Gen?

* * *

Nymeria used to love big events like this. She used to be the centre of attention—dancing with multiple men and women and then taking one or two to her bed at the end of the night. Recalling those memories didn't feel real, and she was almost convinced they were just elaborate dreams she had conjured during her imprisonment to keep herself sane. Now, she hated being the centre of attention—all these people were naive to what was going on, the real reason for this gala, or simply didn't care.

The Alighieri Museum had been transformed into a formal event. Whilst all the exhibitions were still up, fairy lights had been strung up between podiums and railings and the main centre floor had a small string orchestra next to the mammoth skeleton. The classical music brought an air of sophistication to the room that made Nymeria's heart ache for simpler times, but the pop up bar next to the extinct fish exhibit soothed that ache quickly.

The team had split off to their separate corners of the museum. Imani was up on the top floor, sticking to the shadows and conducting surveillance overlooking the main floor. Caliban was by the live small orchestra, keeping an eye from a distance while nursing a drink in his hand. Arwen had opted to keep an eye on things from the bar, conveniently enough, but also use the time to get as many free drinks as possible. Nymeria was on the main floor, waiting for Cordero to show his face, and Halloran was supposed to be with her but had disappeared almost as soon as they had entered. Zai had let her know that Cordero seemed to be running late but was going to show, he was certain.

Nymeria finished off her third champagne flute of the evening; the aftertaste was horrible. Elysium wine was lightyears better but that didn't stop her returning to the bar and sliding next to Arwen. He elbowed her lightly. She looked down at where he was leaning his elbows on the bar, his eyes focused on the back mirror; Nymeria was pleasantly surprised he was doing his job and not just getting drunk on the mayor's salary.

"Relax, he'll show up," he whispered.

"And if he doesn't?"

"We break into his house and threaten his wife and kids." Arwen shrugged like it was the most logical solution. "Imani already has his address."

"You have a backup plan and didn't tell me?" Nymeria narrowed her eyes at him.

He quietly thanked the bartender who passed Arwen his drink with a frown. "My own precaution. I trust your judgment and your plan but a reserve is always necessary."

Nymeria was slightly stunned; she expected such words from Halloran not Arwen. They truly were brothers after all.

"Sorry to interrupt." Both of them turned to see Zai standing behind. With how impeccable Zai dressed daily, his baby blue suit didn't make him look any more or less good-looking. "I was wondering if I could steal away the hopeful hero of the hour, just for a few small words."

"Of course." Arwen's voice sounded similar to how he had talked to Michael.

Zai offered his arm, and she took it.

"What do you want to speak about? If it's about Cordero..."

"No. Nothing about that." Zai led her to the centre of the room and began to sway with her. Nymeria cringed.

"We really shouldn't, I should be focused on waiting for—"

"Why not?" he interrupted, his tone leaving no room for argument. "My dear, I also want to discuss your plans for after this." He spun her lightly.

"Ny, what's going on?" Caliban asked over the earpiece.

"After this business is wrapped up, you'll be looking for work again, no?" Zai's tone was so silky smooth Nymeria could feel goosebumps awaken on her skin.

Nymeria opened her mouth to speak, but as the music crescendoed, he dipped her. A gasp of surprise left her mouth instead of her explanation.

"Things aren't going to get better between the humans and half-demons; it's going to get worse. But I can keep you out of harm's way. Work for me." The thinly veiled demand made Nymeria think he already thought she was going to agree without questions. A few weeks ago, Nymeria may have seriously considered his offer. It would set the All Seeing Private Eye in a position of esteem for being associated with the mayor, not to mention the diplomatic immunity within the city. But with how Zai had spoken to Halloran last time they met, she had an inkling she wouldn't be actually helping people.

"I will—" She stopped talking as Zai's face leaned closer to her neck, and he slowly brought her upright.

"You would look a lot prettier in a dress," he whispered, his breath brushing her neck. "Greens and blues would suit you. By my side, you could do whatever you wanted—what is that?" He pulled the top of her polo neck down slightly, and she pushed away from him, taking a few steps back.

"Nothing." He must have seen the scars.

"These are quite unusual. How did you get them?" His tone had turned a lot colder. Before she could answer, a firm hand wrapped around her waist and Nymeria found herself pulled behind a lithe yet muscular body.

"Does there seem to be a problem?" Halloran's voice didn't hide the sheer loathing this time, spitting out his hatred like a viper.

"Halloran Draig," Zai addressed indifferently. She couldn't see Halloran's face, but it must have been something fierce, as Zai's eyes widened and he took a step back. Halloran's hand pulled Nymeria into his side, his thumb caressing the material above her waist.

"Is there a problem?" he repeated.

"No." Zai cleared his throat and smoothed back his hair, quickly taking a few steps back. "Do consider my offer. Carefully." Zai disappeared into the crowd.

"Thanks," Nymeria said, breathless. She hadn't realised she'd been holding her breath.

"What offer was he talking about?" Halloran snapped, his eyes narrowed, full of a distrust she hadn't seen in a while.

"A potential job after this case."

"Hm. I see."

"I was considering my options," she deflected.

"What is there to consider? Accepting his offer would give your agency the standing and funding you'd need."

Halloran's logic made sense, but she felt conflicted. Perhaps because it would mean she would most likely be sent to take down the gang. She didn't want to do that. Even though they extorted, kidnapped, and maybe even murdered people to gain power in the city's underbelly, and they were clearly not good people, she wouldn't betray them. Over the weeks, in that short amount of time, they had become her people.

"I'm not in the habit of betraying those who help me out," she whispered and Halloran's brows rose.

"I see."

"Look lively, Cordero is here," Imani said over the comms, and

Halloran removed his hand from her waist. They both looked behind themselves and saw him enter, flocked by some of his officers—twelve at first count and all dressed up. Instead of going to the main floor like they thought he would, he immediately turned to the right, heading towards the stairs.

"Imani, be ready, he's heading to you," Nymeria said through the earpiece. "Caliban—"

"Already heading up on the other set of stairs, Arwen is with me."

Halloran and Nymeria followed a few feet behind. Cordero and his officers crested over the top of the stairs, Arwen and Caliban already standing in the middle of the path. When he turned around, Nymeria glared back at Cordero's confused eyes. A few officers drew guns and Halloran's fists were encased in white crackling lightning.

"Are you sure you want to do it like this? I'm not above killing you," Nymeria offered, one hand up but the other hovered to the concealed gun in her waistband. A buzzing in her head warned her of the curse, coiled and ready to strike.

"I'm not going to be taken in," Cordero said firmly, but his voice trembled slightly. "Just let me speak to Zai."

"No," she cut off. She spotted a flickering of movement from the shadows and saw a glint of a red eye.

"All you had to do was not get involved!" Cordero shouted, pulling out his own handgun and aiming straight for Nymeria. Her eyes widened, hands wrapping around her pistol, and she could feel a slight simmering pain within her. "All I needed was the girl, and everything would have been fine. You just needed to stay out of the way!"

Nymeria heard the shot fire and felt a searing pain across the back of her hand. The museum erupted in screams.

18

My Justice Is Quicker

Everything happened so fast. She felt the burning in her hand as the bullet sliced down her knuckles, down to her wrist. She felt Halloran's hand grab the back of her jacket and pull her behind him. She just managed to see Imani descend from the shadows, her arms wrapping around one of Cordero's officers, white fangs protruding an inch out of her lips, mere centimetres away from his exposed neck.

Then time seemed to catch up.

The screams were the first thing she heard, and she could hear a manic stampede from the main floor as everyone rushed and panicked, desperate for an escape. Nymeria gripped the gun tighter, the burning in her blood starting to boil as the curse took effect. Breathing deeply through her nose and grinding her teeth, she forced the feeling down as much as she could. It was bubbling and churning like a hot-spitting fire that threatened to drag her into the depths.

The second thing she could hear was the gunshots. Three sounded, one behind Cordero's group and two from it. But the first clear thing she saw was Imani's arms pulling an Officer into the shadows, hearing a scream and then a spray of blood from the darkness. The blood cast a beautiful arc in the air among the dispersed crowd, and she could finally focus. Halloran grunted as an officer punched him, and he swung his fist back, lightning tailing after his arms, striking him in the ribs, followed by the cracking. Caliban had taken cover behind a display case holding an ancient clay vase, and fired at another officer, who was taking shelter behind a display case holding a wooden mask. He fired back and she heard a loud "Fuck!" from Caliban as glass cascaded down over him.

Nymeria took a few steps forward, scanning the chaos for Cordero. A flicker of movement caught her eyes. Everything seemed to blur. It didn't matter—nothing did but Cordero. Cordero who was already at the far end of the hallway and turning around the corner. She took only a few steps forward, loading a clip into the gun when she felt cold metal press against her temple.

"Freeze!"

But she had a job to do. This may be the only opportunity she would get to catch him and she would rather condemn her own damn soul than let Cordero slip through her fingers. In the blink of an eye, she spun the pistol in her hand and twisted her body, striking the handle against the Officer—Sergeant Sharp, his badge said—and he dropped to the floor, blood pooling from his temple. Nymeria groaned in pain, her vision going white for a second, and she stumbled back, holding onto the railing. She had to focus, had to fight.

Despite his delirium, Sergeant Sharp raised the gun at her—and the way he looked at her, like she was a beast, something to be feared—it sent a jolt of familiarity through her; it made her feel powerful, and that feeling was a terrible addiction. One she used to chase when hunting the damned and relishing the fear in their eyes as they drew their final breaths, breaths they didn't deserve because those who denied the Faith were not worthy of her light, that was what she had believed so wholeheartedly. She was staring down at a heretic—a human one. She had never considered humans to be heretics before.

She heard a snap of fingers just as Sharp pulled the trigger followed by the click of the barrel. Then another click.

"Damn." Arwen chuckled. "Seems you're out of luck."

Sergeant Sharp's head jerked back as a bullet landed in his temple and his body followed suit. Nymeria looked over to the display case, and Caliban reloaded his pistol.

"Always looking out for you." Caliban smirked at her.

Arwen turned to Nymeria and placed a hand on her shoulder. She felt a light tingling run over her as the familiar thrum of magic stirred her soul.

"Don't let him run! I want that bastard strung up!" Arwen patted her shoulder and squeezed. "Don't die, Harlo will kill me."

Nymeria didn't nod or reply, she took off down the corridor.

"Nymeria!" Halloran shouted behind her, but she didn't stop moving forward. She couldn't afford to let Morgan leave her sight for much longer.

"She's fine!" She heard Imani snap, followed by the sound of slicing flesh.

Just before she turned the corner, the room visibly darkened and she caught a brief sight of a massive ball of shadows surrounding the group of remaining officers. Both Draig brothers' eyes glowed white against the darkness. They were demons who had grown up in the Hells, darkness was more familiar to them than light was to her. The ball of shadows fully formed around the group and Nymeria could no longer see anything, but she could hear the shouts and sounds of carnage—wild shots and precise punches and fangs ripping flesh.

Nymeria rounded the corner and heard the rattling of a door before she saw Cordero pulling at one. Their eyes met.

"Morgan!" she shouted, lips snarling and her eyes focusing on him, ignoring as a bullet whizzed straight past her, clipping her ear. She lifted the gun and fired, her vision going black again and her body slack. She just managed to put her arm out to catch her fall against a wall. She knew if she pushed herself too far she would pass out completely.

"Come on General," she hissed to herself, her vision still blurry as she pushed herself off the wall. She could make out the shape of the gun in her hand and the shape of Cordero running farther into the museum. "You've done this before, a hundred times over. What's once more? One more slaughter won't save your soul, redemption is too far away for you," she seethed despite not knowing what she was saying. She staggered after him.

Nymeria's strides grew more confident and quick. This was familiar, and she knew exactly how to move now. As she turned another corner, she saw a shadow duck behind a door and quickly slam it shut. She ran forward, pushing the stand that read 'Exhibition in progress—come back soon!' to the side and yanked the door open. Thin plastic sheets draped over marble statues, packages wrapped in bubble wrap and tape saying 'Delicate—handle with care!' and the thick scent of fresh paint and oak hung in the air. At the far end of the room, by large floor-to-ceiling windows, a stone lion statue was under construction. But not a single sound could be heard. Quietly, she grabbed a spare ream of bubble wrap, tore it, wrapped the material around the ornate handles and tied it. If Cordero wanted to leave this room, he would have to make a lot of noise to get out.

Slowly, Nymeria slunk further into the room, sticking to the outer walls, her eyes darting into every shadow, looking at every reflection and at every flutter of the plastic sheets. She moved on the balls of her feet to be as quiet as possible, her footsteps barely making any sound against the hard oak floor. The silence was more deafening than the very faint sounds of carnage. She made one full rotation around the room and then moved inward. Now patrolling around the first line of displays, but there were so many cabinets, statues and displays, each casting a shadow Morgan could be hiding in. Her finger was taut against the trigger, not shaking, not flexing, perfectly still and disciplined.

She heard the scampering and fast footfalls of someone running, and she lifted the gun. Nymeria could hear a ringing in her ears as her vision spotted, *'you are weak now, to not be able to lift a weapon is a disgrace.'* And she couldn't help but agree with the burning shame and anger that flared in her blood and soul. Five years ago, she would have kicked in the door, ripped the statues and paintings down, thrust her twin blades in every shadow and bathed the room in a light so bright it would have melted Cordero's skin straight off the bone.

She heard the skimming of something against the ground nearby and turned to look but didn't shoot blindly. This was cat and mouse, and he was trying to lure her out. Rounding the corner, she saw a penny, heads up on the ground.

"You think I'm stupid?" she called out. She was more offended that he thought she would die so easily, be so easy to deceive. The rage burned brighter within her.

"You can stop this. Let me go. I didn't want to get this deeply involved!" Cordero's voice ricocheted off the walls, impossible to identify where the noise was coming from.

"A demon promised you power? You want to worsen the division between humans and half-demons? We know it's you—we know your first victim was probably Lucille Aligihieri. The one thing I cannot fathom is why? Why do all of this? Why go after Gen?" she called out, hearing her own voice echo around.

"This isn't about me! Things aren't going to stop with me. But if you let me leave, I can still save my family, please!"

Nymeria shook her head; on too many occasions had she heard the same words from people just before she took their lives. He had a family, sure, maybe he wanted to spare them from the imminent fallout, but he still had to face justice.

"What about the families of those who were killed? Their

families are ruined forever because of you! And you think you deserve to go back to yours? Neither of us is leaving this room until one of us is dead!" she spat.

Cordero roared in anger, and the display case behind her shattered as a gunshot blasted through the air. Her hand flew behind her to shield the back of her neck. She saw a flicker of movement as Cordero ran from behind a statue, and she fired three shots wildly, chipping statues. A marble arm was knocked loose, shattering against the wooden floor.

"Come on, Cordero, you've killed fifteen people! Is your aim that bad, or are you not used to your victims being able to fight? Is that why you targeted the weakest, the most vulnerable, like Gen?" she roared, following the direction he had run in, taking cover behind a large marble statue of a man and woman in a naked embrace.

"If you left that girl alone, just let me take her in! None of this would be happening! You just had to steal the one person that was crucial to all of this, the one person they needed, to execute this plan!" Cordero's voice sounded much closer and she crouched down, moving around the statue. Cordero's back was facing her as he was crouched in front of the statue.

"She was crucial to this plan, and now, because you have her hidden, more people had to die, and suffer! I didn't want to get someone her age involved, but her magic was crucial to the plan, and those slimy bastards at her orphanage would do anything for some under-the-table cash—"

He was still unaware of her presence.

"I didn't know what those men would do to her."

Nymeria froze, and she felt anger course through her like she had never felt before. Red hot, setting her blood boiling and prickling under her skin, making her shout and scream and curse. This anger was cold, like a frozen dagger to the heart. It made her seethe silently. All she wanted to do was rip that dagger out and drive it into Cordero's skull.

"Or the other people in those shipping containers. I was just doing what they told me to keep my family safe. But more had to die because you had that child hidden somewhere! That Sutton boy would still be alive if not for you!"

Nymeria rose to her full height, behind him and pressed the gun between his shoulder blades. She felt Cordero tense beneath her, but she didn't feel any sort of satisfaction with holding his life in her hands.

"You knew...When I asked you at the station if you knew anything about her, why Genevieve was so scared, you lied," she seethed, her voice shaking in anger, her finger slowly pulling the trigger back inch by inch. "I'm not going to bring you in," she promised.

"I thought you lived by justice?"

"I do. My justice is quicker."

Cordero twisted his body around, his elbow knocking the gun to the side just as Nymeria pulled the trigger, the bullet shattering the wooden flooring below. The curse seared through her like a brand against her skin, and it was far too much.

She could feel her back hit the floor as she passed out. She felt pressure against her neck, but she found she didn't want to fight. The darkness was so gentle, it was the most at peace she had felt in two years, and she just wanted to slip further and further into its embrace. Perhaps sleeping forever wouldn't be so bad.

"Wake up!" a male voice said from the darkness, and she slowly felt her mind and consciousness return to her. Everything was dark. She couldn't see but she could feel someone in the darkness with her.

"Finally," the voice spoke, and it almost seemed familiar, like she should know who it belonged to, but didn't at the same time.

"Is this how you fight? To show your belly like a dying pig to an opponent unworthy, a man of all things, not one of light or darkness!" The voice was enraged, and Nymeria couldn't understand why she felt so embarrassed by it. She felt hot hands on each side of her face. "Get up, my child. Fight! Fight!" The hands dug into her face, she could feel the nails—no, claws—break the skin as it pulled her through the blackness faster and faster, as if she was being catapulted through her own mind.

Her eyes snapped open. Cordero loomed above her, shielding his eyes with his arm and moaning in pain, his skin red and peeling off his face. Even Nymeria winced at the searing heat from the orb of fire, as it combusted in on itself. Nymeria looked down at herself; her scars remained dim, like they hadn't activated. What was going on? Nymeria bolted herself upright, her vision swimming as she clutched her head.

"I cannot stay, for my prison pulls me back. I shall give you this one pass, this one protection. Never disgrace yourself like that again, General," the voice spoke, growing quieter before being snuffed out like a flame.

Nymeria rose to her feet quickly, almost falling over. She swayed as she stood up and then backed up. She couldn't brute force this. She had been given a chance to do it over, she needed a new strategy. So she went back to the corners of the room, keeping to the shadows.

She had to act and think fast; whatever the voice had done wouldn't last forever. Desperately, she looked around, trying to find something, anything she could use. She winced. The light from the setting sun blinded her as she looked at it through the large glass windows that lined the back wall of the exhibition. Including, the lion statue. Nymeria had a plan. It was a stupid plan, one that could go wrong quite easily, but it was better than hiding, and she wasn't letting Cordero get away again.

"Mercury!" Cordero roared, and Nymeria wasted no time climbing up the scaffolding as quietly as possible, feeling the iron bars creak under her weight and dust crawl under her suit. Her jacket ripped as she jumped to reach the lion's head. She needed to get to the top, because that was where a small makeshift crane holding several planks was now resting. Nymeria fumbled with the cable. She couldn't see a generator to start up the crane, not that she had a key for it anyway.

"Fuck it," she whispered as she slowly moved the small platform holding the planks off the lions head. They swung in the air, the planks knocking together, and the cable went taut. Cordero's footsteps got closer.

"You won't keep me from my family!" he shouted, his voice

cracking and Nymeria almost replied 'likewise.'

The footsteps got closer, and Nymeria shifted so she was lying atop the lion's head, trying to make her body as flat as possible. The head of the marble lion obscured most of her vision, but she could faintly make out the shape of a body walking below her. He needed to get closer.

"Where are you?!"

Just a bit closer.

"You've left me no choice. I didn't want to do this to you."

Just a few more inches.

Cordero stood directly in front of the window.

"I'm sorry it had to come to this."

This was going to be the stupidest thing she had ever done. Nymeria leapt off the lion's head and grabbed the platform. The momentum pushed the platform faster and faster, and before Cordero could spin around to defend himself from the commotion, her feet planted into his chest, and she kicked him back. Her vision spotted for a few seconds, and she let go. The platform and Cordero crashed into the window. The glass sprayed everywhere, and a shard cut her cheek. The sudden wind blew her hair back, her jacket fluttering open around her. Cordero yelled, his knuckles bone-white as he held onto the side of the window, one leg on the frame, the other flailing wildly behind him.

Her vision was still slightly spotty as she rushed forward, grabbing Cordero by the shirt and pulling him up slightly.

"Who is they?" she demanded.

Cordero looked wide-eyed between her and the four-story fall behind him. “They have eyes on me, on Zai, on this whole city. You let me fall, they’ll know, and they’ll come for you!”

“Who?!” she screamed in his face.

“You already know who,” Cordero warned. He swallowed thickly, and Nymeria could make out tears in his eyes. He was afraid, she realised. Afraid of death.

“Liar.” Nymeria pushed Cordero back and let go of his shirt. Cordero screamed. There was a slam and then nothing. She didn’t look away as his body splattered against the concrete.

“Ny?”

Nymeria turned around; Caliban, Imani, Arwen and Halloran were standing behind her. “Did he—”

“He’s dead.” Her voice was hoarse, and a collective tension eased from the group.

“Holy shit, we did it!” Caliban chuckled, putting his hands on his knees, his chuckle growing into a roaring laugh.

Arwen sighed in relief, sinking to the floor. “I would thank the gods, but they’re dead...See—” Arwen patted Halloran’s knee. “Told you she would be fine.”

Halloran said nothing.

“This is wonderful news!”

Nymeria almost jumped as she heard Zai’s voice and flinched as his arm wrapped around her shoulders.

“I knew you could do it. My faith never wavered for a second.” He beamed, the warmth not quite reaching his eyes.

Zai walked her away from the window, Caliban on her other

side. "We've made it, Ny! We're gonna be legends from this!"

She looked over her shoulder, Imani, Arwen and Halloran left behind.

"Go," Halloran said. He didn't sound angry nor cold but something else entirely. "Enjoy the adoration." He forced the words out, almost spitting and she could see his Adams apple bob. But as their eyes met, he looked away.

Nymeria was still picturing that look in his eyes. As she stepped out of the museum main entrance and into a swarm of flashing camera lights and reporters shoving microphones in her face and asking questions, she realized what that look was; it was regret and bitterness.

19

The Draig Estate

Nymeria had been answering questions for what felt like hours. "Yes, Cordero was the killer, we're certain. No we don't know his motives at this time but we're sure he acted alone. I'll not be accepting any more jobs for a few more days, myself and my partner Ha—Ortega, need to rest after such an intensive investigation. But we'll be back open soon."

Caliban had invited her out for a drink but all she wanted to do was sleep for a year. She almost fell to her knees and slept on the floor when she swung the apartment door open. The only thing that kept her upright, was the feeling of arms around her waist.

"Hey." She sighed. "It's done. I got him. Cordero can't hurt you." Nymeria dropped to her knees, hearing the small sobs wrack Gen's body.

"Shh," she shooed, her hands cupping Gen's face. "This is a happy moment, okay? You're safe."

Gen shook her head. *"But what happens now?"* she signed. *"I don't want to leave. Where is Halloran?"* Nymeria didn't reply.

What could she say? She didn't know what would happen either, or what she should do with Gen. She wasn't her child and with the case resolved, she had no reason to stay with her.

Nymeria wrapped her arms around Gen and pulled her in close, hugging her tight as Gen cried. Nymeria didn't want to let her go.

"I don't—" Nymeria's voice came out hoarse, and she cleared her throat. "I don't think Halloran is coming back. How about we watch a movie tonight?"

Despite the film being an upbeat one, there was a melancholy to the apartment. Gen would constantly look over her shoulder to the door throughout the night, but he never came. By the time midnight arrived, Gen was fast asleep and Nymeria picked her up, cradling her against her chest. Nymeria stroked her hair, untangling the knots as she walked to Gen's bedroom, opened the door, crossed the room to her bed, and placed her under the covers. She tucked Lambo in beside her, and her thumb brushed Gen's cheek.

"You must have cursed me," she whispered. "You must have, because ever since you crashed into my life, I've known nothing but rose-coloured happiness. I didn't want this to happen, because I knew doing what was right by you would be the hardest thing. The right thing is to send you away, but I don't know if I can do that." Her voice cracked. She smoothed her hair back and left Gen's room.

Nymeria didn't know what time she fell asleep but she awoke early in the morning by her door creaking open and a small shape scampering in. She sat up slightly, aided by the lights she always kept on. Gen climbed on her bed and lay down behind her. Nymeria slumped against her pillows and just as sleep took over, she felt Gen draw letters into her arm: *'Don't leave me, Mama.'*

Nymeria reached behind her and smoothed Gen's hair, her thumb brushing the top of her head until they both fell asleep.

* * *

The slam of the front door awoke Nymeria with a jump. She felt slightly delirious, an unusual airiness surrounded her like a weight had been lifted off. She heard footsteps walking around the living room. Nymeria sat up as the bedroom door swung open. Halloran stood under the frame and leaned against it like he had done the night before. He looked tired, like he hadn't slept well at all. "Do you have a habit of bursting into women's bedrooms?"

Halloran smirked. "Not usually."

Nymeria's annoyance at him for not showing up last night and upsetting Gen in turn outweighed how attractive he looked when he smiled.

"Don't make it a habit."

Gen sat up, rubbing her eyes. She squealed seeing Halloran, tripping over herself as she clambered out of bed and ran up to him, hugging his waist.

Nymeria laughed at the sight. When she had seen him show affection to Gen after the GPD break-in he seemed so relaxed, but now he was as stiff as a board, as if he had never touched another being in his entire life. He looked like the epitome of a man unused to physical affection. "Yes, I...missed you too." His voice fell to a whisper as he patted Gen's head. The sight stirred something in Nymeria, that warm, blooming feeling she felt when Gen did something sweet.

Halloran slowly detangled Gen from him.

"I've just come by to collect the majority of my belongings."

Oh.

Nymeria swallowed a lump in her throat. "Right, of course. The deal has been concluded." Her voice was quiet. No wonder Nymeria felt so light and airy; she had fulfilled the pact with Arwen.

"Yes." Halloran's voice was tense, uneasy, like he wanted to say more. "The deal is done. You won't have to see any more of me, and we go back to our normal lives." Halloran's eyes flickered to hers, those stormy eyes trying to pierce through her very soul. "Doesn't that make you happy? We'll finally be rid of each other."

Funnily enough, despite how long she had waited for this moment, being rid of him wouldn't make her happy.

"I'll miss your cooking. It was your one tolerable trait," she said softly. His lips quirked up into a half smile, which was all too familiar by now.

"Perhaps I'll miss that smart mouth of yours, tempestuous woman."

Nymeria couldn't help but laugh, and when she looked back at Halloran, his ears were slightly pink. "But we needn't say goodbye just yet, though."

"What do you mean?"

"Arwen is hosting a dinner tonight at our home. A celebration for completing the investigation. You are, of course, invited and so is Gen. But if you have plans with Zai—"

"I don't," she interrupted. "I don't have plans with Zai or Caliban or anyone else."

Halloran's eyes widened slightly and then softened. "Good. I'll let Arwen know. All you need to bring is yourselves and something to eat or drink."

Nymeria frowned. "So Arwen is hosting but isn't cooking?"

"Arwen not cooking is a blessing." He shrugged. "I've taken up the role instead."

"Well, I would be a fool to turn down good cooking. Gen?"

She nodded eagerly and pushed past Halloran and into the apartment. She could hear cupboards being opened.

"I'll leave you to it then." Halloran turned his back to her and walked away. A few seconds later she heard the front door close.

Nymeria got dressed and washed for the day, and when she entered her living room, she frowned. Halloran had left his duffel bag behind.

* * *

Nymeria and Gen spent the day deciding what they would bring to Arwen's dinner. Nymeria's first suggestion had been to buy something pre-made from the local corner store but

Gen had pouted and signed that: *"They should make an effort."*

So they compromised. Nymeria bought some top-shelf whiskey as well as ingredients to make chocolate cupcakes. Gen tried her best, she really did, but by the time she was done making them, Nymeria's kitchen looked like a crime scene.

During the drive to the Draig estate, Nymeria had to swat Gen's hand multiple times from eating the cupcakes, once catching her licking the icing.

"That one is yours now." She chuckled, swiping the icing across her finger and smearing it across Gen's cheek, an uproar of giggles coming from Gen.

"Turn left." The automated voice of her phone's map app broke the laughter. Nymeria followed the instructions, down a bumpy track. The directions Arwen had texted her had taken them thirty minutes out of the city. The forest was so quiet it was unnerving, just like the black iron gates she drove up to. Through the headlights she could faintly make out a large estate house that almost blended into the twilight.

"I'm gonna kill Arwen if he sent us to a haunted house," she murmured.

As if on cue, the black iron gates slowly swung open, and Nymeria drove through. The tyres crunched on the gravel as she parked up near the black oak door. The Estate was made of dark wood and stone, imposing from the outside. Nymeria had to wonder if the place had been bought by Halloran with how much of a brooding aura it exuded. The two got out of the car and walked up to the door. Both shared a look and then stared at the angry-looking silver dragon head knocker on the door. Nymeria's hands tightened on the bag containing the whiskey as she reached forward, grabbed the knocker and let it drop.

Barely a second passed before the door opened to Arwen's smiling face.

"The lady of the hour!" He beamed and what she hadn't expected was for his tree trunk-like arms to wrap around her and bring her into a hug.

"I didn't think you would"—she wheezed as he lifted her off the ground—"still be in your emo phase, living in a vampire's castle." Arwen laughed heartily, and the smell of alcohol on his breath hit her like a train. He roughly set her down on her feet and stepped back, gesturing for them to come in.

Whilst the outside was dark and imposing, inside the Draig estate was much warmer. Cosy dimmed lights, dark oak flooring and green walls and plush carpeting gave the house a more homely feel.

"Come to the kitchen." Arwen led them down the corridor, a right turn and into a modern looking kitchen, twice the size of the one in her apartment. A large dining table, big enough to seat twelve next to floor to ceiling windows that overlooked the forest surrounding the house. A massive kitchen island divided the dining area from the kitchen.

Imani was pulling back the foil on several containers of food, and Nymeria's stomach rumbled at the smell. "Before you take another step—" Imani sounded so serious that Nymeria froze, Gen bumping into her leg. "What did you bring for dinner?"

Nymeria's hands wrapped under Gen's arms and lifted her

up, Gen thrust the container of eight chocolate cupcakes towards Imani.

"Will you deny this little face food? Cast her out into the night?" Nymeria teased and Imani's lip twitched upward before falling, she took the container out of Gen's hands.

"This is acceptable, you may join."

"It would be unlike you to turn down strays, Sayyid."

Nymeria set Gen down, scurrying to the island, climbing on one of the stools and setting the container of cupcakes on top. Nymeria turned around to face Halloran, in a red button-up and black slacks, he looked as he always did: arrogantly regal but there was an air about him that he didn't hold before, she didn't know what to call it but she could see it in the way his eyes softened as they landed on her.

"I don't turn away people who need help, Draig. Perhaps you can take a page of empathy from your brother's book," Imani hissed.

Halloran's eyes hardened and narrowed when they focused on Imani. The two stared each other down—Imani's burning hate was frozen by Halloran's cold indifference.

Arwen laughed nervously, stepping next to Nymeria, blocking Halloran and Imani's view of each other.

"Come on now, this is going to be a nice evening. Let's not ruin it with petty squabbling."

For once, Nymeria remained quiet.

"Fine," Imani said, pulling the foil off the remaining containers with much more force than needed. The tension eased slightly. The brothers went to talk and Gen was signing. But Nymeria could only focus on Imani. She had to set things right.

Nymeria grabbed Imani's arm as she pulled away. "Can I have a word outside?"

Imani frowned but nodded. Nymeria placed the carrier bag down on the ground and wordlessly, the two women left the kitchen and walked back outside. Nymeria closed the door so hard behind her the knock jiggled.

"Please don't ruin my night." Imani sighed.

Nymeria shook her head. "No, no, it's nothing to do with that...Actually it's everything to do with that."

Imani crossed her arms over her chest. "Then what?"

"I want to apologise." Nymeria hated how stunned Imani looked.

"You want to apologise?" she repeated back.

"Yes, for what I said at the warehouse. It wasn't nice at all and..." Nymeria paused, taking a deep breath in and pushing that rising feeling of shame aside. "I don't like people looking at me, touching me, anything like that. I know you were trying to help, but it became way too much and I just exploded, and turned into the worst person." Nymeria paused her ramble.

"Now it just sounds like I'm trying to make excuses for my behaviour."

"It does," Imani said critically, her eye narrowing.

Nymeria sighed. "I'm bad at this. My point is, you're right. Us women should stick together. The world sucks and people want to hurt us at every turn. The least we can do is have each other's backs and not hurt either of us like the world wants to and I'm sorry."

Imani paused for a second, but to Nymeria, it felt like a lifetime.

"Okay. I'll forgive you." Imani's tone was quiet. "But no more nasty comments again. Especially about him."

Nymeria nodded. "It was uncalled for. I'm truly sorry."

"You need to find a way to deal with that; your anger, the way you lash out. One day you'll do it to the wrong person and really break some bonds. Bonds you won't be able to recover."

Nymeria felt as if she'd been scolded, the embarrassment crept up the back of her neck in a hot blush. "I'll work on it."

A brief silence fell over them until Nymeria chuckled.

"You know you really sound like a therapist sometimes." Nymeria felt her heart flutter as Imani smiled, shaking her head. A pretty chuckle left her lips.

"Yeah, well, I've been seeing someone. A therapist, someone," Imani quickly added.

Nymeria raised a brow. "I didn't know human therapists would treat a vampire?"

Imani shook her head. "No, the gang has their own in-house therapists and doctors. We have a demon woman working with us—Ayako. She's really good with illusion magic, and she puts charms on those wanting education so their appearance looks human for a few hours before they need a top up."

Imani took a step closer. "But a few of us in the gang do have our own..." Imani pursed her lips as if she was struggling to find the right words. "Therapy group? We basically meet on Thursday afternoons and talk about our issues. It's nice to vent."

Nymeria smiled painfully. It sounded nice. Maybe it would be nice to talk to someone. But talking meant exposing those soft and squishy parts of herself that could be damaged even more than they already were. Nymeria's apprehension must have shown on her face. Imani reached out for her hand and Nymeria let her take it. Imani placed her other hand atop their conjoined ones. "No one will say anything."

"I wasn't worried about that."

"No. Of course not." Imani scoffed. "But if that was something you were worried about..." Imani squeezed Nymeria's hand; Nymeria hadn't realised her thumb was rubbing over the back of Imani's hand. She had almost forgotten how nice it was to hold someone's hand.

"I would give anyone who gave you grief a stern talking to...maybe even a little bite."

Both women laughed.

"I can't promise anything, but I'll think about it." And for once, Nymeria meant it.

Imani smiled and then shivered. "Let's get back inside, it's getting cold, even for me." Nymeria smiled and followed Imani through the door.

The two entered the kitchen, and Arwen smiled at them both. "You two were out for a while."

"Girl talk," Imani deflected. "Not something you would know about."

Gen rushed up to Nymeria, tugging her hand and quickly signed, "*Their present! Don't forget!*"

"That reminds me." Nymeria picked up a glass whiskey container from the spare bag she brought. "This is a little thank you gift for the resources and funds, and helping me solve this case." Arwen grinned and took it out of her hands, looking it over.

"Very nice." His lips quirked up into a smirk. "You got Halloran's favourite brand?"

Nymeria felt heat prickle up her neck. "I didn't know—it was the first one I saw." She shrugged.

Halloran pushed himself off the door frame and took the bottle from Arwen's hands. "This is very nice. Thank you."

"Damn you got a thank you. That's the nicest thing I think I've heard him—"

Arwen doubled over as Halloran punched him in the gut.

20

The Cold Burns

The dinner was lovely. Imani had brought all the vegetables so Halloran was in the kitchen cooking steaks. Gen had pulled a stool from the island and sat next to him. The sight had stirred that familiar warmth in her, especially when Halloran would clumsily sign with one hand whilst flipping the steaks with the other, Gen adjusting his fingers or hand when he got a word wrong.

Once the wine started being poured—by Arwen since he was banned from cooking—any previous tensions left.

"So angels don't have physical wings?" Imani asked, and Nymeria laughed, her cheeks red, but whether it was from either the wine or laughter, she couldn't tell.

"No! Of course we don't. Can you imagine how wide doors would have to be?" Nymeria shook her head, shoving the last of Imani's grilled greens into her mouth.

"They're more like manifestations, we can make them physical to give us flight. They bleed, and you can feel it when feathers are ripped out, but they can be unsummoned with a snap of the fingers," she explained.

Halloran's eyes widened. "So you can't rip an angel's wings out?"

Nymeria shook her head. "Technically no, if you try to saw them off, they'll disappear once removed but the pain will still be felt." Nymeria looked at Gen next to her who looked a little queasy at the conversation.

"But each angel's wings are different—the colouration and pattern on the wings often look like birds found on the continent. Urban legend says that those with wings like a raptor will become the most deadly of angels, whilst those with prey bird wings will be weaker."

"What were yours like?" Gen signed and Nymeria paused. It was almost hard to remember what they looked like but she could remember the feel of them.

"They were white with black-brown markings from the middle to the tips on the underside, completely black-brown on top," Nymeria spoke slowly.

"Like an osprey?" Imani spoke up, and Nymeria snapped her fingers at her.

"Exactly, like an osprey."

Arwen stood up with a grimace on his face and he walked around the table. Placing his hand on Nymeria's shoulder, he said, "Can I have a word? It will be quick, I promise."

Nymeria wiped her mouth with the back of her hand.

"Don't worry we'll be back soon. Just business talk," Arwen reassured and she followed.

Arwen led her out the kitchen, down the hall, up a flight of stairs and to the third door on the right. Nymeria followed after him and into a large spacious office. It wasn't too dissimilar to the office she saw at Greed but somehow, this one felt more lived in and homely. Perhaps it was the paintings on the walls, or the broken clock on the desk, its hands twitching back and forth.

"Thanks. I just wanted to have a chat." Arwen went behind the desk, pulled one of the draws and took out a small tube. He rolled up the sleeves of his shirts. Her eyes widened, the burns weren't just on his hands but also his arms, and she realised they must cover most of his body. He pushed the cream over the burns and began rubbing it in, letting out a sigh of relief.

"I'm sure you know the itch," Arwen said, focusing on rubbing the cream into his skin, "that comes when scars get irritated."

Nymeria frowned "How do you—"

Arwen raised a brow. "I trust you a lot. I invited you into my home after all. But I needed to make sure you weren't keeping secrets."

Nymeria looked away, running her tongue over her teeth.

"I'm annoyed, but I would have done the same thing," she admitted begrudgingly.

Just how much had Halloran told? Had he mentioned their moment when she patched him up? Or the GPD break-in? Had any of those moments been real, or was it a ploy to get more information out of her? She understood the why, but she condemned the methods.

"Good, at least we can come to an understanding on that. I'll admit, I was worried about your reaction. But hopefully, now we can come to another agreement."

Nymeria leaned towards him.

"I would like you to work with us again. Permanently." Arwen's tone had switched to business.

Nymeria scoffed. "Are you asking me or telling me?"

"Asking." His voice was sharp and quick, like he didn't want her to misinterpret his words. "I'm asking you because I trust you. I respect you and I would very much like to see more of you. So would Harlo."

"Right," she said sarcastically. "And Halloran is an angel."

"I know my brother well. I don't see him tolerate anyone's attitude the way he does yours. He doesn't look at other people the way he looks at you, and he doesn't let them get close," Arwen insisted and she shook her head.

"Back to the topic. Why?"

"Well, the first reason is that you're a useful asset by yourself. Caliban drags you down."

Nymeria didn't answer but she did scowl at him.

Arwen sighed. "And also because we're all better people when together. I've noticed it, Imani has too, and I see the change in you as well. You look happier, less tired. We have a good team—maybe more than that here, and I'd like to keep it that way." Arwen looked so hopeful.

Nymeria swallowed a lump in her throat.

"I don't know. Zai made me an offer." Nymeria hated the way Arwen looked at her—he knew. His eyes held that resignation of hearing something you didn't want to hear but knew was coming anyway.

"Halloran mentioned, but I hoped it was his distrust talking."

"I haven't made a decision."

"Why?"

She paused. "I don't know. You bringing the gang into my life made everything complicated." She struck her foot out and lightly kicked his shin, her vision blurring for a second. "Damn you!"

Arwen sighed, his relaxed attitude replaced by something far more serious.

"Things are gonna get worse in Ghenna, if not across the continent for half-demons. Did you even know they found some half-demons stripped, hanging from the ceiling in the subway?" Arwen growled, pulling the sleeves of his shirt down harshly, the material ripping. Nymeria felt her stomach churn. A crime like that wasn't random mugging gone wrong. That was calculated and hateful to a degree that Nymeria was ashamed she was familiar with. "One of them was one of my men, Alfie. A bouncer at Greed."

Nymeria felt her stomach drop to her feet. Alfie, the half-demon she had protected from a police officer just days ago. Alfie, who had a very pregnant girlfriend. Now he would never get to meet his unborn child, never get to be a father, a loving partner. She had to find Ayako, somehow, help her out if she could.

"I didn't." Her voice was caught in her throat.

"I suppose you wouldn't," Arwen said coldly.

"Any motive?"

Arwen barked a cold laugh. "You're kidding, right? He was killed because he had funny coloured eyes and never knew when to be quiet. Doesn't help that beaming bastard Zai is encouraging this behaviour by calling us Hells-spawn," he ranted and then paused, smoothing a few strands of red hair back. "The police just chopped them down and found a ditch to put their bodies in."

Her blood turned cold. "I'm sorry—"

Arwen shook his head. "I have a fight coming in the next few months, if not a war. I just hope you pick the side your heart is on."

A tense silence fell over them. Zai had said the same thing; things were truly going to get worse.

"Your scars. How did you get them?" she asked after a while, pulling her knees up to her chest. As if her words took the air from his lungs, he slumped into the chair.

"Feels like a lifetime ago. I can barely remember a time without them. I didn't know you could get freeze burns until I spent two years in the seventh ring."

Nymeria frowned. "How did you get there?"

He wrung his wrists. "That's a long story," he dismissed and she knew what he was doing.

"I have time."

Arwen smiled, a soft, genuine smile.

"Our mother was called Niamh Draig and she was determined to give us a human life. She told us she lived in the countryside before she got sent to the Hells the first time. We lived up here for only a year or two before the angels found us and forced us back down. Do you know what it's like being constantly on the run? Being raised to either kill or be killed, not because our mother wanted us to be deadly, but only because it was the only way to survive down there. I didn't want any part of it. I wanted desperately to cling onto the goodness of humanity that mother spoke about. About her dream home, a large estate in the middle of a forest."

Arwen wiped his eyes.

"Perhaps it was my refusal to fight that made Halloran hate me when we were kids. He picked up the load for our mother and me. We definitely would have died without him."

Nymeria didn't say a word, she put her hand on the desk and turned her palm upward. Arwen clasped her hand. Nymeria realised they had similar scars—just in different shapes.

"Our father found us soon enough. We lasted a while. I tried to see my mother as often as I could, but she was sent away with the rest of the Destroyers concubines. I never saw what he did to them but I could hear it, we all knew what was going on."

Arwen fiddled with the cuff on his shirt.

"Do you know that, every fifteen years, dear ol' dad holds a tournament? A battle to the death, of all his children. The strongest is the winner, and the winner crowned his heir. They become the second most powerful devil in the Hells. It's what all of us should want, but I didn't. I'm not a good devil. When I was thrust into the arena, Harlo left my side almost immediately, and I'll admit, I cried. I was scared."

He squeezed Nymeria's hand and brought his knees up to his chest.

"When your magic is altering probability, that makes all the difference in a fight to the death, but even luck runs out eventually. It was the only time I had to break that promise to my mother, and what did violence get me? Halloran winning the tournament and sending me and mum straight to the seventh ring—" Arwen's voice cracked.

"Betrayal and Treachery. Lake Iscar." She had heard of the frozen wasteland with a singular frozen lake, where nothing could truly survive without consuming whatever living things were left.

"I tried to keep us safe but I was too weak after Halloran banished us. I was barely conscious when I heard the demons breaking my mother's bones and eating her."

Nymeria felt sick to her stomach.

"How are you still talking to him? Are you not angry?" she asked, outraged for him.

Arwen chuckled. "Oh no, I did try to kill him. When he eventually got cast down to the seventh ring, two years later. I didn't know I could turn into a dragon until that day—that was how much I hated him. A black iridescent dragon and a red dragon tearing each other apart above Lake Iscar. 'The battle was felt across the Hells,' the other half-demons have told me. Only when he willingly surrendered, when I had him pinned under the water, did I realise he regretted everything. Halloran never backs down from a fight, but in that moment, he didn't struggle and didn't fight. He grabbed my wrist, wrapped it around his neck and let me drown him. He would have let me kill him if it meant showing how sorry he was." Arwen sighed.

"It took a long time for us to get to where we are now, a journey across every ring. But the hardest thing you can do sometimes is forgive them."

Nymeria sighed. "Some things you can forgive people for. But some things are too unforgivable."

Arwen nodded and squeezed her hand back. "You know, I work out a lot—"

"I can tell."

Arwen shook his head.

"My point is, it helps me feel good about myself. I'm not as pretty as I used to be." He chuckled dryly. "But working out helps me take out any of that anger I have. Maybe you can join me on my next session?"

Nymeria smiled. "I would like that."

Arwen smiled back and squeezed her hand once more before standing.

"Come on, if I keep you away for too long, Harlo will become jealous."

Nymeria rolled her eyes.

The walk back down the corridors and stairs was a quiet one and Nymeria couldn't help but replay Arwen's words in her head. Half-demons were just like her. Cast out, abandoned. They had so much more in common than she had ever considered, and the thought didn't disgust her.

As soon as Nymeria entered the dining room after Arwen, she knew something was up immediately. If Gen's grinning face and eager bouncing in her chair were not enough of a dead giveaway, then Imani's failure to hide a smirk was.

"Why do you all look like that?"

"Like what?" Imani said, leaning forward, her arms on the dining table.

"Like you're hiding something." Nymeria crossed her arms over her chest and smirked.

"Perhaps we are." Halloran smirked, his arms crossed over

his chest as he leaned back in his chair, one leg over the other knee.

"You see"—Arwen walked behind the back of the door and picked up a hangar, a dress bag dangling from it—"a little birdie told me that you lost all of your possessions when you fell. Including all of your fancy dresses."

Nymeria's heart slammed into her throat, her hands falling to her sides.

"Can I—" Her voice wavered, and her eyes stung as Arwen handed her the hanger. Nymeria didn't realise her hands were trembling until the zipper caught on the fabric of the bag as she pulled it down. But once it was fully pulled down, she hesitated. A part of her thought it was some cruel trick, but that was definitely a glimmer of silver silk she could see. Slowly, she pulled the dress off the hanger and away from the bag. The dress was soft silver—almost blue. Just by looking at it at eye level, she could tell it would be a perfect fit.

"How? When?"

"Gen told us your favourite colours," Imani interrupted. "I guessed your measurements, Arwen paid."

"But," Arwen added, "it was Harlo's idea."

Nymeria looked down at Halloran who was taking a very long sip of his wine.

"This was your idea?"

"I mentioned it in passing," he dismissed.

Nymeria was speechless; she just stared at the dress, rubbing her fingers over the material. "Thank you, truly."

Halloran grunted, his ears crimson.

By the time Nymeria was driving back to her flat, she had to pull over several times to wipe her eyes. Gen didn't understand why she was crying. Nymeria didn't expect her to understand it, not fully. It was silly to be crying over a dress of all things, it was just a piece of fabric. But it looked so much like the dresses she used to wear, nowhere near as grand or expensive, and certainly not tailor-made. But it was like she'd been given a piece of her old self: a happier self.

Nymeria parked the car outside the flat, and Nymeria tossed Gen her keys.

"I'll be up in a moment, I just need a minute."

Gen wordlessly scrambled out of the car. Once Gen was out of sight, Nymeria reached for the dress, patiently sat in the passenger seat and took it out of the dress bag, holding it up to her, smoothing the material down as if she was wearing it. A smile pulled at her lips. This was the first time in a very long time that she felt beautiful.

Nymeria got out of the car, putting the dress back into the dress bag. Her nostalgia was sharply broken by the sound of a smash. It sounded like something fragile like a glass or a lamp. Nymeria looked up towards her apartment building. all the lights in the windows were off, except her own. Perhaps Gen switched them on when she entered their home? Nymeria frowned, picked up her dress and walked into the complex.

Nymeria was lucky that her neighbours weren't a noisy bunch, but this was a new kind of silence. It was almost sinister, waiting and predatory, like a hunter aiming down a gun at an unsuspecting deer. She felt like a deer. Her footsteps sounded like gunshots in the quiet hallway, and she fished in her back pocket for her phone. She held the phone behind her as she entered her home, but the two individuals she saw sitting on her sofa, one holding Gen still by her shoulder, made her drop the phone.

"Hello Aunty."

21

Sins Of The Mother

Cordero had been right. He said they would come for her. She thought she'd been the last one, spared by whatever fate had consumed the angels since she'd been imprisoned, but apparently not. Two angels, in all their armoured horror, were in her apartment. One stood up, brown hawk wings behind him, in a flash of red magic. The other's hand tightened on Gen's shoulder and she whimpered in pain.

Nymeria was frozen.

"Forgive the discourtesy of playing in the shadows." The angel who stood rolled his shoulders back, gold and silver armour freckled with gold and black blood. Angels were supposed to strike fear into the hearts of demons and wary caution to humans. Their armour reflected that. Large and heavy plated, hiding any inch of skin or hair. The plates were designed to look more like scales than metal. But the most chilling part was the helmets. They had been her own design; expressional, eyeless masks of gold. The wearer could see out of them but no one could see inward, the voice of the wearer distorted enough that they didn't sound human nor demon but something far more terrible and otherworldly. "My intent was to face thee head-on. But alas, thee were not here at the hour of our arrival. We had been waiting some time, loathsome kin."

Nymeria frowned. She recognised that voice. It was much deeper now. Back then he had been a boy, both of them had—boys who had been enlisted into the army upon her sister's insistence.

"Alvaro." Her eyes narrowed, and she turned to the angel still sitting on the sofa. "Cyrus."

"Aye," Cyrus confirmed. "Tis indeed us, disgusting traitor." Nymeria's teeth ground together and for once, that flare of her blood didn't call for her to harm; it wept. How could you betray them? Your faith—Nymeria closed her eyes and exhaled, silencing it. She never betrayed the Faith.

"Whatever lies my sister told you—"

"—Our mother does not lie, she is impossible of sin. The High Priestess knows all." Nymeria reached into her back pocket. Cyrus laughed and stood, pulling Gen close to him, which nearly sent her flying. Angels were so much stronger than humans, a simple punch from Cyrus could shatter Gen's chest.

"Thou'st want to engage in blades?" Cyrus laughed, the sound making the hairs on her arm stand up. "Then thou are mine to vanquish," Alvaro spat hastily, looking over his shoulder to Cyrus. Gen made a squeal and tried to run. Cyrus' gauntleted hand grabbed her by the back of the neck, lifting her off the ground.

Nymeria rushed forward, Alvaro's arm wrapping around her middle and tossing her back effortlessly as if she weighed as little as a cat. Nymeria cried out as her back collided with the wall. She could feel the small crater left behind her, her vision spotting and swimming. Her hands trembled as she reached into her pocket, precariously unlocking her phone, scrolling to a random contact and pressing call. She cried out as a gauntlet grabbed her hair, pulling the roots. Her phone clattered behind her as she was dragged forward and tossed over the sofa, tumbling over and onto the coffee table. Wood cut into her skin as it splintered beneath her. Gen's screaming and Cyrus' words were drowned out by the ringing in her ears and the blood pooling underneath her. Alvaro leered over her. Everything snapped back into focus when Cyrus picked up Gen, tucking her under his arm.

"Don't touch her!" Nymeria screamed, grabbing the disjointed leg of a coffee table, ripping it off and swinging it at Cyrus. He laughed and took a step back, opening the window. In a burst of green magic, fluffy dappled wings like a long-eared owl appeared behind him. Hearing Alvaro's footsteps behind her, she swung around, aiming for his face. Alvaro caught the table leg in his hand, his fist closing and snapping it in half.

"Worry not!" Cyrus goaded.

Nymeria felt Alvaro's fist connect with her face and her mouth filled with blood.

"I would ne'er keep a mother and child apart. Thou shall both cometh to the homeland." Cyrus jumped out of the window and spread his wings wide.

"Yet first, apostate, thou shall become reacquainted with

thy kin," Alvaro leered, whispering in her ear. "How long they hath missed thy flesh and taste."

Her eyes widened and she froze, a blood-curdling dread settling into her stomach, Alvaro wrenched his fist back and punched her once, twice and by the third time, she was unconscious.

* * *

The shaking of the ground woke Nymeria first. Her vision swam so violently that when she tried to open her eyes, she closed them again, rolling her head forward. She moved to stand, kicking her legs out only to accidentally sway herself lightly, her toes skimming the ground. She forced her eyes open in a panic, it was dark. The rumbling sounded again and she felt dust and debris from the ceiling falling into her hair and mouth. Nymeria strained her ears and she made out the very distant sound of a train horn. She had heard rumours of the abandoned train tunnels underneath the Ghenna subway but didn't know they were real.

"Thou art awake." Cyrus chuckled. Now that her eyes adjusted to the darkness, she could make out other shapes—six others excluding Alvaro and Cyrus.

"Whilst we await orders—" Cyrus took the helmet off. He had his father's black almost blue hair that cascaded down his shoulders, a few natural streaks of blonde running through. His poorly maintained facial hair looked like it would itch. But what made Nymeria's blood run cold was that he had golden eyes like his mother and warm-toned glowing skin. Nymeria felt it boil within her as she looked into those eyes; it was not hatred or rage, those words didn't do what she felt justice. It was all-consuming, threatening to blister her skin and spew from her mouth like an undying flame. It was wrath, pure unadulterated, untempered wrath.

"—haply the wilful apostate wanten to confess her sins?" he leered, his face inches away from hers.

Cyrus raised his brows, expecting an answer. Nymeria mumbled something and he scowled, grabbing a fistful of her hair and yanking her head back. Nymeria hissed. "Address thou betters with grace. But such a grievous imposition is commonplace from a devil's whore!" he hissed, spit hitting Nymeria's face.

"How do you know so much?" Nymeria hissed, looking past Cyrus. Gen was tied to an old oil drum, chains around her middle and unconscious, her chest rising and falling slowly. Alvaro was leaning against it, his hand resting upon a long sword strapped to his waist.

"It is not our duty to kill her, brother," Alvaro chimed. Cyrus rolled his eyes and turned, facing away from Nymeria.

"I am aknown." He whined like a bored child—in a sense, they both were. The last time Nymeria saw them, they had both been fourteen. They couldn't even be twenty yet. "But mother didn't say mirth was banished from our presence."

"If thou kill her—" Alvaro warned.

"I shan't!" Cyrus promised, and Nymeria shook the chains above her. They were wrapped tightly to a rusted pole above her.

"Thou having to kill her to restore our lineage is all thou speak of!" Cyrus groaned. "Thou want a hobby."

"And thou needest take the words of the High Priestess and

the general seriously." Alvaro pushed himself off the barrel, taking his helmet off. Alvaro looked almost identical to Cyrus, but his hair was buzzed short and he had an ugly scar across his lips that ran down his neck.

"Mother and father shall not forswear us harming the apostate." Their father was the general? Ulysses, her former right hand when she had been general, was the one to replace her? It was so obvious that was what Melantha would do. How had she not thought of it before? The dry and mad laugh crawled up her throat, spilling uncontrollably from her lips. All eyes were on her. One helmeted angel took a few tentative steps forward. Alvaro held out his hand and he approached.

"Amused, whore? Forsooth, are thou truly so corrupt that us discussing how I shall regain our family glory once I slaughter thou amuses you so?" Nymeria laughed again, the sound ending in raucous coughing.

"Stupid boy, there is no glory in slaughter," she spat. "Our family name—" Nymeria's head snapped to the side with the force of the punch.

"Speak thy name Mercury again and I will have your lying tongue!" Alvaro roared.

She turned her head back to face him and laughed. She couldn't quite see, her hair hung in front of her eyes, but she could hear the unsheathing of weapons.

"Our name," she seethed, spit bubbling with each word, "is a foul name. Mercury is the name of bastards and traitors. A name of self-righteous heresy." The wrath was overflowing, puppeteering her mouth, she couldn't stop herself, not that she wanted to.

"All of you."—she lifted her head— "all are willing traitors. I did kill Nasir Pluto, but not because of power and not because I was going mad. I was following orders, much like you all are now! Orders that hold no loyalty to the council once they have no use for you! I've seen the hypocrisy and hate of the Faith and I'm so glad I have no part of it!" she screamed. She could see the angels spread out around her, circling her with raised weapons. It was now she noticed contraptions on her nephew's waists—small containers like old gas lanterns with a fire burning inside. Roiling in on itself—not the ball of flame that had appeared above her when Cordero tried to kill her—this was a bright, hopeful fire. A fire that Nymeria knew all too well. How was her magic, the power of the sun, trapped into a lantern?

"You!" she growled, sounding more like a snarling beast than a woman. "All of you with your self-righteous hypocrisy!"

She vaguely saw Gen stir awake from the corner of her eye.

"The sky will fall upon you all one day and the Sun shall sear your flesh and destroy your golden towers and I will laugh as your hubris crushes you!" she screamed.

"She has gone mad," she heard one of them mutter.

Nymeria snapped her head towards the speaker. "If madness is truth, then I am indeed mad!" She rattled the chains above her head. "And here is another madness! Any one of you, even your cowardly simpering bastard of a father, could become general of Elysium and not a single one of you would ever be as feared or great as I was in my decade as general!"

The speaker from before stalked forward. "Apostate I will

have your head!"

He swung his sword down, splitting part of her shirt open but Nymeria swung forward, bucking her hips upward, dodging the second strike. She brought her left knee up, hitting the pommel of the sword and forcing it upward before kicking out at the blade with her right foot. The blade sank into his jaw and part of his neck. His eyes bulged and watered and he let out a shocked and joked cry, as if he couldn't quite believe what had just happened. The sight made Nymeria chuckle before her head hung forward, immediately pulled into the familiar deep blackness of the curse's punishment. This time, she didn't have the mysterious helper from before. She did it herself, and that filled her with a macabre sense of pride. Much quicker than before, her consciousness returned. Her vision focused on the angel lying dead before her, a pool of blood around his head and neck, his fingers twitching slightly. She felt a warmth wash over her, like that of a warm hug.

A smirk curled its way onto her lips. She hadn't felt this wave of pride in a very long time and she let it wash over her like a tidal wave. "Well? Which one of you brave and loyal devotees of Melantha is next." she jeered, but none of them moved. "Come now, you've all had a turn with me before during my repentance. So come on—" Her voice rose to a shriek, scratching raw. She heard a sob and Gen was bawling, wriggling against the restraints. She didn't want her seeing this but if they took their anger out on her, maybe that would give Gen enough time to escape and find Imani or Arwen. Nymeria didn't want Halloran or Gen to see whatever they would do with her. The circle around her closed in, weapons shaking.

"Who the fuck is next!" she screamed. They all hesitated.

Gen managed to wriggle one rope up and over her head. She opened her mouth to scream again but it was silenced by a boom of thunder, the noise so loud it rattled her chest. Nymeria looked up to the stone ceiling but no dust cascaded over her head. The angel's weapons, which had been pointing at her, turned to behind her. Nymeria looked over her shoulder as best she could, only to find a large, dark tunnel. It was impossible to see into but she could hear a shout and then another boom, this time much closer. She could pick up a rasping growl at the end. The sound wasn't thunder, it was a roar.

"When did the other six leave us?" Cyrus said quietly to Alvaro.

"Half an hour ago," he growled. All weapons now pointed to the tunnel as the angels moved past her and formed a small semi-circle around the tunnel entrance.

Heavy steps, then a snarl echoed around the room. Whatever it was, it sounded very large and very angry.

"What is that?" Alvaro whispered, his voice shaking.

Two angels charged forward and that was when Nymeria saw it. A small white light appeared far above their heads. It grew brighter and brighter, the light illuminated a black scaled snout and eventually, the scaled head of a dragon with four horns—two which curled back down its neck.

It was common knowledge, amongst angels at least, that powerful demons could transform into horrible creatures—Basiliks, Griffons, Giant wolves and Lions. But the most powerful of all demons could transform into Dragons. The white flames billowed downward as its mouth opened into a cruel and wicked smile. Two of the six angels were caught in the flames, shrieking as metal fused with their skin and cooked them alive. The smell of burnt flesh almost made her gag.

"Stand strong!" She heard Alvaro bark, but she was no longer looking at the scene behind her. A few angels flew around the cave but Nymeria was wriggling, trying to get her wrists free, inching the chains off the rusted pipes inch by inch.

"Gen, get out of here!" she yelled as another hissing breath of fire licked under her feet, spreading outward to the oil drum, the flames burning the ropes surrounding Gen. Gen wiggled against her restraints, her shaking hands trying to pull the burning rope off her.

The heavy thud of draconic footsteps shook the ground beneath her before coming to a stop behind her. She could feel hot breath tickle the back of her neck, a deep melodic rumble from the dragon's throat. She froze, waiting. Waiting for the fire to burn her or sharp black teeth to pierce her flesh or crush her entirely. Instead, the giant snout went above her, and one massive fang the size of her forearm snagged the chain holding her. With the slightest flex of the dragon's jaw, the chain broke. Nymeria cried out as she fell onto the cold floor, her muscles screaming in pain. She rose slowly to her knees, but the dragon's snout ducked down under her chest and quickly lifted her to her feet.

Nymeria looked up at the dragon as it pulled its head away,

snapping its jaws at the angels that flew around its head. They flew above and under the dragon, swiping their spears in its direction, trying to get close enough to get a single hit in. The beast walked forward until she was underneath its belly, the ground shaking so violently with each footstep that she nearly fell over. But now she could see a strange peculiarity with the dragon's scales; they were black but they had a sheen to them. A blue, red, green and purple shimmer, the colours undulating across the dragon's whole body. An iridescent dragon. Now that Nymeria thought about it, it made sense. Demons absorbed power by consuming other lesser demons and powerful ones often had visible changes to them. She was almost embarrassed she hadn't put the connection together before as she gazed at the iridescent scales. Scales which were a colourful symbol of power—a symbol of hundreds of bodies consumed. So much power that it could turn a half-demon's hair a mismatch of white and black and his eyes a silver-white.

A white light flitted between the scales of the dragon neck and a jet of white fire bellowed from its mouth in a wide arc, angels shouting in panic and narrowly managing to dodge the flames. Halloran's draconic eyes glanced her way briefly. She would recognise those silver-white eyes anywhere. His jaws clamped around one of the angels and he wasted no time shucking the carcass down his throat before snapping at the others now flying around him, breathing another billow of flames across the sky.

But a shriek of fear snapped her out of the chaos playing around her. Nymeria rushed forward,, avoiding the odd sword swing and stomping of scaled feet. She slid next to Gen, pulling the now barely held together ropes off her body. The flames almost touched the oil drum.

Nymeria grabbed Gen and pulled her away, only getting about a foot away before a deafening blast sounded where Gen had been. Both of them shrieked, the heat licking at their backs and the force of the explosion sending them to the ground.

"Are you okay?" she asked breathlessly, her hands clearing Gen's face of any dirt, the girl only nodding eagerly. Gen's hands smoothed across Nymeria's wrists. Nymeria stood up, pulling Gen with her. But she was forced to let go as a body slammed into her, grabbed her arms and lifted her into the sky. Nymeria lashed out, kicking at Cyrus, who dropped her and then caught her again by the leg.

"Stupid whore!" he spat, and Nymeria punched at him, Cyrus chuckling as her punch wildly missed. He flew higher and higher, dangling her above Halloran's maw, a torrent of flame building in his mouth but when his eyes landed on her, the flames died in his throat and a front claw swiped at Cyrus, chipping his pristine armour. The angel let go of her leg.

"Foul creature!"

Nymeria's eyes widened as she plummeted towards the ground, Halloran darted forward, a claw reaching for her but then recoiled and roared in pain. Nymeria could just see a cruel smile on Alvaro's face as his sword pierced into his scaled neck.

But Nymeria didn't hit the ground, she heard a cracking, a feeling of weightlessness and then she found herself stumbling backwards, her feet on the ground. Nymeria opened her eyes and she just saw the portal close. She looked down and saw Gen throw her hands out. Nymeria looked between the girl and the angels, noting a rather bewildered Cyrus looking around for Nymeria.

"Gen," Nymeria panted. "You said you wanted to be useful right?"

Gen nodded.

"No better training than on the field," she muttered. Nymeria couldn't protect her from this, so she may as well use it to their advantage.

Two angels flew above Halloran, diving downward aiming for his eyes.

"Those two!" Nymeria instructed and Gen made two portals. The angels flew through them and ended up skewering each other on their spears, a look of horror and confusion on their faces. A thunderous boom of white magic blew the rest of the angels back and Nymeria stood in front of Gen as the shock wave hit them, sending her staggering forward. A body slammed into the ground nearby and Nymeria moved Gen behind her as Cyrus stood up, his eyes nearly bulging out of his head as a snarl graced his lips. "Thou dare to disgrace myself? My brother? You! A devil's whore!"

He stood up, picking up his spear. "I'll kill your bastard and then you," he screamed. Gen screamed as well and flung her arms out, a portal forming and Gen crying out as she willed it forward. The portal encapsulated Cyrus and forced him to now be where Halloran had been. The dragon, now a demon once more, traded blows with Alvaro. The harsh sound of a blade slicing the air, and fists beating on metal made

Nymeria's stomach drop. Halloran caught a sideways slash of the blade with his hand and sent a lightning infused punch into Alavaro's breastplate, the sound causing a thunderous boom.

Cyrus turned around, snarling, and roared, rushing back through the portal, thrusting his spear forward. The tip of it pierced Nymeria's belly and she cried out, wincing. But before the spear could go any deeper, the portal closed. Nymeria grunted, the spear a sharp cold pain in her belly, but her heart dropped as she fully opened her eyes. A pair of arms, both from the elbow down, were still tightly grasping the handle of the spear. Cyrus wailed from the far end of the chamber, curling in on himself as a fountain of golden blood poured from the stubs that had been his forearms.

"Cyrus!" Alvaro shouted, turning his back on Halloran for a second, and that was all Halloran needed. Two more thunderous punches ricocheted around the tunnel and Alvaro crashed into the wall next to Cyrus, leaving a dent in the brick. Nymeria staggered forward, her hand on her stomach as golden blood seeped between her fingers. With her free hand, she pulled the spear out of her stomach with a cry, letting it clatter to the ground. Halloran wiped his fists clean of angel blood on a corpse and took two steps towards her nephews.

"Halloran!" she called out, hunched over, Gen's hands on her side helping keep her upright. Nymeria looked down at her wound for only a second and when she looked back up, Halloran was in front of her, his hands gripping her shoulders.

"Are you okay? Are you hurt?"

Nymeria looked down at her wound.

"Never mind, a foolish question," he said quickly, pulling Nymeria's arm over his shoulders, he grunted and slammed his free hand over his neck. Nymeria could just make out black blood seeping between his fingers in light rivulets.

Just as he did that, Nymeria heard a thump next to her. Gen was face down on the floor.

"Gen!" Nymeria lurched forward and rolled Gen onto her back. The girl's eyes were closed, blood trickling from her nose.

A blinding golden light cast over them all, and a golden portal opened up.

"Foul, disgusting loathsome beasts!" Alvaro screamed as a sobbing Cyrus staggered through the portal. The fire in the gas lantern burned brighter.

"But fret not. I shall cleanse thee of thy sins and flesh for neither of thou are worthy of mother's goodness." He unlatched the lantern and the fire flowed from the lantern into his gauntlet which shimmered with bright magic.

"Do you recognise thine heat? Thine sun? After mother rescued your abused magic, she moulded a phylactery and gifted it to us, her sons, her most devoted."

The fire built bigger and bigger as Alvaro moulded it with his gauntlets. All the light in the room being sucked into the ball of fire, all air being sucked towards it. Nymeria knew what he was going to do, she had used the same move many times to wipe out areas of demons.

Nymeria grabbed Gen. "No!" she screamed, lifting her into her arms and sprinting away.

Halloran sprinted past them both towards the tunnel, making it into the entrance before she could. The light was so blinding Nymeria had to close her eyes, but her blood turned to ice as her foot snagged on a corpse. She fell down, her head jerked upwards and her eyes locked with Halloran. By the way his face fell, they both came to the same realisation at the same time. They both knew she wouldn't make it in time.

"Burn!" Alvaro shouted, dropping the orb and stepping into the portal, the gold portal swirling around itself and dissipating into sparks of gold magic.

"Hold on tightly!" Nymeria yelled as the orb pulsed three times. Nymeria curled her body over Gen, trying to keep every scrap of her as shielded as possible. Nymeria closed her eyes tightly, feeling a body wrap itself over hers as they were bathed in a blinding light.

III

False Prophets

22

Desecration Of An Angel

Nymeria was surprised when she awoke. She was convinced that would be it. That her own magic would kill her, burn her to a crisp. Yet, as her consciousness returned to her, she found she was very much intact. Not a single burn on her body from what she could feel. The only injury was a dull throbbing from her stomach. But she wasn't in her bedroom. The room she was in was fairly barren, with wooden floors and ceiling but familiar deep green wallpaper. She sat up. Her muscles ached as if she hadn't moved for hours and the hair that fell in front of her face was matted. How long had she been unconscious?

The soft duvet shifted and pulled around her as she swung her legs over the side of the bed. It felt as if someone was caressing her waist and thighs, she cried out and pulled the duvet away. She could have sworn she heard a chuckle of an angel saying *'You can give us a little more.'*

But no one was there, just an auditory hallucination or an old memory half realised. Only now did she realise she was wearing a shirt which was a few sizes too large. The door swung open with a crack against the wall, Halloran's fists already ablaze with thunderous magic.

"Nymeria?" he breathed out, his features relaxing. "No one else is here," Halloran said firmly, leaning slightly so he was back in her line of sight. Nymeria nodded but her eyes were looking everywhere but him or Gen.

Her breath was catching in her throat, her skin felt too hot and clammy and her stomach churned. She vaguely made out Halloran calling her name, but she couldn't hear anything except how her own heart hammered against her chest. They had found her. The angels weren't dead, they had just been hiding. They knew where she was, and had tried to drag her back. By the gods' mercy, she didn't know what they would do to her but she could not relive the repentance through flesh. She hoped they would just take her head because they would come again. Now that they had seen her, they would never stop—

"Nymeria!"

She finally looked up at Halloran. Her eyes burned and she relaxed them, not realising how wide they had been.

"Yes?" Nymeria's voice came out a whisper.

"Are you alright?" His voice was the gentlest and quietest she had ever heard.

"Yes," she lied. He didn't look convinced for a moment.

Gen barrelled into the room, her eyes lighting up when they landed on Nymeria. She squealed, a noise Nymeria would have enjoyed but now it just made her head throb. When

Gen wrapped her arms around her waist, squeezing Nymeria tightly, it just made Nymeria shiver in disgust.

"Gen, not now," Nymeria said sternly, grasping the child's shoulder and pushing her away. But Gen made a sound of indignation, holding Nymeria tighter, her shoulders shaking.

"Gen I said enough!" Nymeria shouted, and pushed again, harder than before, so hard that Gen fell back onto the floor, a surprised gasp leaving the girl's lips.

Everything and everyone fell silent for a moment. Gen's chest was heaving, tears streaking down her cheeks. Nymeria was frozen. She hadn't meant to push her that hard. Nymeria's lips moved a fraction and she took half a step forward, but Gen had already scurried to her feet, rushing past Halloran. When Nymeria and Halloran's eyes met she saw an emotion in them she hadn't seen before: confusion.

Shortly afterwards, Imani and Arwen came in, consoling her about her kidnapping. Arwen mentioned something about her moving into the Draig Estate much to Gen's delight. But Nymeria wasn't paying attention. Truthfully, her mind was a whole world away, replaying those memories; foul memories of her repentance. It would never leave her mind, not that it left it before. Before yesterday, those events would replay on the back of her eyelids or when she was surrounded by darkness. Now they wouldn't leave her even when wide awake. She would stare at empty spaces as the memories played, not noticing she had been stuck in the same rigid position for a few full minutes until someone shook her out of the trance.

As she finished her second bottle of wine of the day, she knew what she had to do. It was well into the night by now, everyone had either gone home or retired to their beds. It was a beautiful full moon outside. Maybe if yesterday hadn't happened, she would have taken Gen out to see it. But she wasn't going to do that. She hadn't spoken to Gen all day, nearly driving the girl to tears. It would hurt now, but Gen would deal with it. Besides, if Gen was angry with her it would make Nymeria leaving all the easier. Arwen and Imani had brought over her limited belongings and she hadn't unpacked them from the duffel bags they arrived in. She zipped up the duffel bags after having changed into a pair of joggers and a hoodie. She quietly opened the door and closed it behind her, walking on the balls of her feet to be as quiet as possible.

She passed Arwen's and Halloran's doors with ease but the last door, the one at the top of the stairs, she paused at. She hadn't realised her hand was reaching for the doorknob until she felt the cold metal underneath her fingers. She pulled her hand away. If she spoke to any of them, she would never leave.

Nymeria made her way down the stairs and out of the door. She had ordered a taxi to arrive at the nearest bus stop. The only downside was that she would have to walk through the woods. At least that's what her phone told her. It was cold. Cold enough that she wished she had another layer on. She continued onward through the forest, but she grew increasingly more annoyed as each little leaf and twig snagged on her clothing as if trying to stop her, trying to pull her back towards her family. She shouted in annoyance after a while, swatting at everything and snapping a few branches as she stumbled into a clearing.

"Fuck off," she shouted. "Everyone just fuck off!"

Despite the fact she was standing still, she heard two footsteps behind her as someone stumbled into the clearing.

"Where do you think you're going?" Halloran's voice was hoarse and strained. Nymeria clenched her fists at her side. If she faced him she would never go.

"I'm going to ask you once more." His voice was a growl, a threat. "Where are you going?"

The duffel bag that had been on her shoulder slid down her arm, hooking into her elbow.

"No." He sounded hurt. She thought he wasn't capable of that. "No, you're not going."

"I have to." She turned to face him, the duffel bag dropping onto the mossy ground. "I have to go!"

"You don't get to leave!" he yelled, walking up to her until there was no space between them. His finger jabbed into her chest. "You don't get to leave Gen behind. You don't get to abandon her after all your preaching about taking responsibility!"

Her heart stung but she turned on her heel, picking the duffel bag up but Halloran snatched it out of her hand and tossed it to the side.

"Why are you here?!" she yelled. "You're no longer obligated to follow me. Our contract is done!" she spat, moving away from him but he grabbed her arms and pulled her back, his fingers digging into her arms.

"And I don't know why I do!" he spat back. "But I'm glad I did follow you because you clearly need sense spoken into you!"

Nymeria struggled against his hold, her hands scratching her own wrists, hitting his arms and slapping his chest, he only caught her hand after she slapped him across the face. "STOP IT!" he roared and she felt herself shrink.

His jaw set stiff and swallowed heavy, his hands that were tightly squeezing her wrists moved upward, his thumbs opening up her palms.

"You haven't shown cowardice at any other stage of this whole investigation. Why now, as soon as you see your own people?" Nymeria looked down and shook her head.

"I'm sorry, but I can't let you hide from this."

"No—"

"This has been the one thing hanging over you since I've known you. Did your scars happen because of them? Are they the reason you don't sleep in the dark?"

"No. No, stop it," she begged pathetically, trying to pull away but his hands kept her close, his thumbs rubbing circles into her palms.

"No." His voice was firm and steadfast. "I need to know because If I'm going to follow you I need to know the kind of woman I'm following. I also—" His voice cracked. "I need to know why you would abandon your child."

Her throat constricted and she looked up at the sky. "It's ugly, what I did and what happened to me."

"I don't care, tell me anyway." She met his eyes and she realised he hadn't once looked away from her face.

"Okay." He finally let go of her wrists.

Nymeria took a few steps back, looked to the sky once more

and breathed in deeply.

"I was general of Elysium, as you know. I was an arrogant and stubborn thing. I was treated like an idol because I could hold the Sun in my palm and because of that I thought I was above every rule." For the first time in a long time, she allowed herself to remember the full sequence of events.

Nymeria soared through the clouds, osprey-like wings stretched wide, half a dozen armour-clad angels behind her and Ulysses to her right.

"Cheer and be merry! You get to see thy wives and children!" she called back. A series of cheers sounded from her men who soared through the clouds behind her, weaving and diving happily. Nymeria grinned behind her helmet and rolled through the sky over to Ulysses.

"My friend, I can feel your frown from here!" she leered, nudging his raven-black wings with her brown and white ones.

"You get to see your wife and sons soon!"

Nymeria could feel Ulysses eye roll. "For that I am filled with joy. But I suppose your good mood has an ulterior motive."

"Yes," she said mirthfully. "I shall also enjoy silk sheets and a full belly."

"No companions in thy bed?" Ulysses joked, nudging her with his wing. "That's unlike you."

"Well now that you've tempted me."

Ulysses groaned. "It was merely in jest."

"Am I not allowed an indulgence?" she challenged.

"A woman of your status—"

"Should not what? Enjoy the comfort of another?"

"You know what I mean," he warned. The platoon banked downward, the floating island of Elysium coming into view.

Almost home.

"Our last campaign was a long one. I would rather not have it spent with Council gossip and your sister's complaints."

"Then simply don't listen. The council are a bunch of pompous cunts. I'm half convinced most of them have never read the Codex." She felt Ulysses tense next to her.

"I'll pretend to not hear that."

They soon landed in the inner walls of Elysium where the grand palace stood, the Creators Requiem. Wings disappearing behind them as they peeled their heavy armour off, Nymeria sighed as the weight was released and she could feel the leathers underneath. Her long braid of maroon hair swung downwards, the end hitting her lower back.

"I was such a stupid girl." Nymeria paced around the clearing.

Halloran watched her carefully, like she was a caged animal. "To think I was above the rules, above expectations and the Faith itself. But—" Her voice cracked, on the edge of a sob. "I would never have expected any betrayal from Melantha."

"When is our Father returning?" Nymeria heard a whining voice say from inside the teaching room. The Mercury Estate was a grand one; carved from Obsidian despite the gold and white interior. Nymeria didn't understand why Melantha had her children homeschooled, but never questioned it. Her sister always knew what was best, and always made the correct decision. She was the one who communicated directly with the gods. The most powerful member of the council besides her. The other councilmen were dogs compared to the two of them.

"Nevermind Father, what about Aunty Ny?" Nymeria smiled, she loved her nephews but Cyrus was her favourite. A little loud-

mouthed and rebellious, much like herself. She was surprised the boys did not use formal speech with their Governess. Speaking colloquially was only accepted amongst close family.

Nymeria flung the door open. "Why don't you ask her yourself?"

Cyrus beamed and rushed up to her, he nearly barrelled her over. Nymeria grinned and wrapped her arms around him. "Oh I've missed you both." She held out her arm as Alvaro ran to hug her as well, she pressed her forehead against each of theirs, a sign of affection to loved ones and family among angels. Cyrus and Alvaro were sweet boys, and she missed training them.

"Where's Father?" Alvaro asked, resting his chin on her shoulder.

"Tending to a few tasks I left him. He will be back soon. Now, where is your mother?"

Nymeria ignored the governess' protests as the twins eagerly dragged her through the halls.

Melantha was in her usual spot, the sunroom, her eyes closed as the sun shone over her. Her golden hair sprawled out like a halo over her, her features more softer and angelic than usual. Melantha had always been the most beautiful woman Nymeria had ever seen.

"Boys I'm napping," she grumbled. The two teenagers giggled and left, shutting the door behind her. Nymeria approached quietly and Melantha threw her arm over her eyes. "Boys!" she said sternly.

"I'm sorry Ma'am," Nymeria joked. "Perhaps I should come back later." Melantha rose and turned to face her, golden eyes that matched Nymeria's opening, a tired grin crossing her face.

"Your campaign was successful?" Nymeria frowned, why

wasn't she greeting her with a hug or a forehead touch as usual?

"Indeed. Be happy, me and your husband are back safe!" she gushed, taking the steps forward and pressing her forehead against Mel's. Mel smiled and pressed her forehead back.

"Forgive me, darling sister. My days have been long and the council is unforgiving. The gods are truly testing me." Melantha sighed and sat down, Nymeria sat opposite. Melantha ran a hand down her face and reached next to her, a stack of letters on the table that Nymeria had not noticed before.

"Aren't the boys too young for proposals?"

"They are. These are all for you and a bigger stack the week last."

An uneasy tension filled the room.

"You need to marry."

"So my future husband can take my title of general whilst they pump me full of babies. I think not," she dismissed, standing up and walking to the pot of jasmine tea Melantha always had prepared when she was in the sunroom. Nymeria poured one for herself. Melantha shook her head and stood up.

"You are not above tradition, Nymeria. Above law."

Nymeria frowned, her face scrunching. "I never said I was."

"We have a duty, as women of faith. We have bodies for nurturing—"

Nymeria tuned out her rambling. For as much as she loved her sister, she did spout sanctimonious bullshit at times.

"Never doubt my loyalty and devotion to the Faith." Nymeria turned on her heel, her hand cupping Melantha's face. She leaned into the touch. "I am as devoted as any. But my path is serving through the slaying of our enemies, a path of blood and glory.

Yours is bringing life into this world and my nephews are gifts." Her voice was earnest. "But your path is not mine."

"But you still go see your women and men tonight?" Melantha said, her voice cold like ice. Nymeria pulled her hand back.

"Ah, so that's what this is really about."

"Your Proclivity—"

"Proclivity?" Nymeria snapped back. "Is that what you're really calling it? You make it sound like a sickness."

"It's not becoming of a woman of our prestige."

Nymeria shook her head and quickly left, closing the door behind her.

"You had a few lovers?" Halloran inquired and Nymeria stopped her pacing, she hadn't realised the ache in her legs so she sat down, the damp moss seeping into her leggings and making her shiver. Halloran came over and sat next to her, bending one knee and resting his arms atop it.

"A few, men and women, but there was one who was special: Cerys. A daughter of the Nymph, freckled skin, sapphire eyes and pink-silver hair. She was so beautiful and we saw each other more than any other. She refused to be mine. I never understood why until I got to the Continent." Nymeria smiled sadly. "She was far too good for me. I often had to sneak out of the estate to go see her and she would always have a window open for me to climb through."

Halloran smiled. "She sounds like trouble."

Nymeria laughed. "She was! We were as bad as each other and the council hated it." Her smile slowly faded. "She should have stayed far away from me."

Usually, grand banquets were held for celebrations: Births of direct godly descendants, marriages, or in this case a successful campaign against heretics. The great hall of the Creators Requiem was lined with three benches pushed to the far walls of the room. Each bench was lined with the most exquisite food and drink imaginable whilst a live orchestra played and guests danced in the middle, angels of the highest standing in Elysium. Despite it all, Nymeria was bored out of her mind. It was all polite conversation, tight-lipped and never revealing too much. The only interesting parts would be gossip but none of her friends who indulged in such had arrived yet—or they weren't invited.

"Lady Mercury. Thou do not wear a veil this evening?"

Nymeria had to suppress an eye roll. The Patriarch of the House of Uranus—Benjamin—was an older gentleman who was as pious as he was nosy.

"Do not concern yourself." Nymeria pulled her braided hair over her shoulder. Her silver sheer veil, pinned to her head with a golden jewelled headband was weaved into her braid.

"See? I still wear'th one." Benjamin narrowed a wrinkled amber eye.

"My lady you haven't forgotten the protocol—"

"I haven't." She sighed, taking a long sip of honey wine. "I still wear'th a veil as you can see. But this fabric is fine and expensive. I would hate to dirty it whilst eating and drinking and they make conversation much harder, wouldn't thou agree?" Benjamin opened his mouth and closed it, the great ornate doors opened once more and a single woman walked through.

Benjamin scowled. "Odd, Lady Cerys was not to attend this evening."

Nymeria frowned. "She was not invited?" Cerys loved these events.

"It was one of her many brothers' turn to attend this evening."

Nymeria could just see Cerys smirk in the parting of the red veil attached to a rose-gold circlet. Her dress was a deep crimson adorned with emeralds. The skirt was long with a leg slit and the top was two red strips of the same material that covered her chest. As always, Cerys was a vision. But instead of coming over, she danced in the centre with the others, their eyes meeting now and again. An old familiar dance, this was for Nymeria.

"You shall have to excuse me, Lord Uranus, I am being beckoned."

She didn't give him a second glance but she could feel his eyes watch her and others. Her silver silk gown glimmered like sea waves as she rounded the bench and approached the floor. Twirling and weaving between dancers, much like she was on the battlefield. Both dance and warfare were an art. Her focus was locked on a single target and with a spin, her hand wrapped around a freckled waist.

"Lady Venus," she greeted.

"Lady Mercury," Cerys' smooth and seductive voice replied and Nymeria couldn't help but smile.

"I trust you have not missed my presence too much." Nymeria's voice dropped to a whisper as they danced, twirling and swaying to the music.

Cerys' hands stroked up Nymeria's arm, her nails scratching lightly which made Nymeria bite her cheek. "I did not come here for you," Cerys whispered.

"Did thou not?" Nymeria teased.

"No, I did not." Cerys sounded annoyed but her smile told Nymeria otherwise. Cerys did like to play games.

"My darling, you are an awful liar." Nymeria grinned.

Cerys spun on her heel, but Nymeria pulled her back gently and dipped her low, Cerys giggled wildly, her hand caressing Nymeria's face.

"Ny!" she whispered.

"What? Let it cause a scandal. What will they do? Scold their general?" Nymeria chuckled and Cerys laughed as well. "Brave you are and loyal. Perhaps I need to be reminded of your other talents?"

Nymeria felt her cheeks heat up.

"Now who is causing a scandal?"

Nymeria straightened up, bringing Cerys with her. Cerys interlocked their hands and started pulling Nymeria out of the grand hall.

"You only just arrived, you do not wish to feast?"

Cerys shook her head. "I only snuck in so I could feast upon someone more delicious." Cerys squeezed Nymeria's hand as they left, raucous gossip behind them.

Once they left the grand hall, the two walked down the halls and out the giant front doors. They both looked around, making sure no one was around. Nymeria then scooped Cerys into her arms, her hands interlocking below Cerys' ass. "I missed you terribly," Nymeria admitted between warm and longing kisses.

"As did I." Cerys giggled between kisses. "Even though I shall be the one in trouble. I cannot help but be drawn to you my love, like a moth to a flame."

"That following morning, I received a summons to the council. I arose quickly, armour on and when I reached the Council chambers in the Creators Requiem, it was just Melantha. She said that her suspicions of a heretic amongst the Council had been founded." Nymeria sighed, running a hand down her face. She noticed Halloran's eyes hardened not with anger but with worry. As if he had already pieced together the series of events

"I found it odd that Nasir Pluto was the heretic. He was a charitable man, one of the few who had a relationship with his godly parent and acted as mediator during Council meetings. He was also a dear friend. He never told of my escapades with Cerys. But why would I have ever thought that Melantha was trying to deceive me? That she would cause me harm? She was Melantha, kindly and virtuous." She spat the last words like venom. "She could do no wrong."

Elysium was the entirety of the heavens according to humans and demons, but this was not true. Elysium was merely the capital, the rest of the heavens consisted of floating islands, far higher in the sky, closer to the stars than the continent. Nymeria flew by herself, her wings cutting through a waterfall, the spray was a comfort against her skin as she flew up and landed in the garden of one of the many houses of Pluto. The Muse, the Nymph and the Crone had the most children and most of them liked to live close to Elysium, if not in the capital itself. But Nasir didn't—which meant he did not have many guards or servants, roles taken up by younger and less powerful members of his house. Nymeria dissipated her wings, her twin blades drawn as she stalked through the unkempt garden.

Nymeria frowned. Nasir was usually well-kept. Had the corruption of heresy turned his mind into mush? Would he even be sentient or raddled with demonic maddening rambles? She had

been hoping for more of a fight, a challenge. Killing a madman felt like butchering a lamb—no glory would be had. Nymeria's fist smashed through the glass door of the conservatory, grabbed the door handle and pulled it open. The conservatory was empty, a thin layer of dust over everything and she frowned. Was he even still here?

Nymeria stalked through each room of the house, overturning furniture, ripping cupboards and wardrobe doors off their hinges.

"Where are you, heretic? Face my blade!" she screamed, sparks jumping from her hand as her blades glowed in a simmering anger. As she ascended the stairs, she heard a scampering of feet. Too loud to be a mouse but not quiet enough to be a demon. The two blades snapped together, transmogrifying in a flash of light into a glimmering bow. She pulled the molten drawstring back and an arrow of dazzling sunlight formed. She saw a figure and released the arrow, missing the target but the whole dark hallway exploded in bright light.

She heard a cry as the figure was blinded but Nymeria stalked onwards. That had to be Nasir. "Nasir, the shame of Pluto!" she called as she ripped the door he had been hiding behind off its hinges. Nasir was dressed in the purples of his house, groaning as one hand covered his eyes and the other in front of him feebly feeling around. Nymeria grabbed him by the collar, hauling him off his feet with a single pull off his shirt.

"Nymeria please!" he begged, his hands clenching against the golden chest plate. "My dear friend!" His knuckles whitened against the chest plate and Nymeria felt her eyes start to water at the corners.

"No! You are not a dear friend, we are not friends. I do not

befriend traitors," she spat, lifting the hand now holding a blade and pressing the tip against his neck. "Why?" Her voice was raw with barely restrained anger. "Why would you betray everything we hold dear? Why would you choose this?"

"I have to do this!" he pleaded, his own eyes watering. "Please my friend, lower your weapon and let me explain. Let me show you my findings." His shaky hand, skin much darker than her own, closed around her wrist. "Please, my friend."

Nymeria backed away, body still tense and ready to strike. Nasir smiled, his eyes shimmering with hope and she hated it. Hated that he looked at her like he had a way to escape. She was the hunter of the damned, anyone considered damned by the council would meet a quick end by her hand. Nasir turned his back to her, his hands rummaging over the scattered files and pages on his desk. "For a few months now, I've been hearing whispers of a plot, a conspiracy. I thought nothing of it at first, just high society gossip. But then I felt an itch. An itch to dig further, deeper." Nymeria looked down at the blade, letting the familiar warmth of her sun magic flow through her and into it, the blade starting to dimly glow as if held over a blazing fire.

"But I found that it wasn't just a conspiracy. I found more and more evidence of the High Priestess taking ancient and forbidden tomes from the Scribe collection in the capital and whispers of her private prayers in the chapel. The Lady Melantha is up to something—"

"That's enough," she barked, and Nasir started to turn towards her.

"Don't. Face your maddening works, words of heresy. I cannot let you live, the High Priestess demands your blood. But for the

sake of our friendship, the cut will be clean. You will not feel a thing."

"Nymeria, listen! Something is—"

She swung the sword and his head tumbled off his neck in a single strike, the wound cauterising instantly.

"Nasir tried to warn you," Halloran said and Nymeria stood up, circling him like an anxious caged animal.

"I know that now. I can see that now. I'm shocked at myself. I was so blind so..."

"Indoctrinated?"

Nymeria stopped. The word felt like a punch to her gut. Indoctrinated. During these past weeks, it was the one question about her past and the Faith that had been bouncing in her head. Had she ever really enjoyed following the practice or had she simply been told to love it? As a girl, had she ever really enjoyed her duties? Did she feel good about the hundreds of bodies of angels and demons that paved the road behind her? Had she wanted to kill them or had she simply done as she was told to do? Like a good soldier, a good butcher. A sudden realisation hit her so hard that she nearly fell to the ground. Had she ever had a thought during her upbringing in Elysium that was her own? Or was it all Melantha's whisperings that Nymeria had proudly declared?

"Sit down before you fall over," Halloran said and reached her, but she batted his hand away.

"No, I need to stand and pace for this next bit."

"Why?"

"Because if I'm still—" Her voice broke and Nymeria inhaled deeply, wrapping her arms around herself. "I'll feel them. I always feel them in the dark."

Halloran frowned and straightened up, resting his hands in his lap. "What do you mean?"

"The following morning"—Nymeria ignored his question—"I was arrested in the family estate on the council orders. My trial was midday the same day, on charges of high treason. High treason is only called for crimes against the council or the gods. The most common reason for the charge is—"

"Murder of a council member?" Halloran murmured. His eyes widened. "Melantha didn't—"

"She did."

"You don't have to push and pull," Nymeria snapped at the guards flanking her. She was surrounded and she could barely see past them.

"Quiet, Traitor," one behind her spat. One of her soldiers, she had overseen his training when he was first introduced into the army. "You will get your justice soon enough."

"How dare you! I am the Swordsworn's justice made flesh and you shall receive due punishment once this mistake is cleared."

Nymeria was very familiar with the judgement chamber in the Swordsworns temple, it was where all trials were held. Seven marble podiums, one for each council member were positioned in front of a marble statue of the Swordsworn, at least twelve metres high, and where he should be holding a sword, he instead held the scales of justice. The guards surrounding her split to the far corners of the room, their hands on the hilt of their weapons. Nymeria shivered. She had been pulled from her bed without being given a chance to dress, still in her nightgown from the night before and her hair unbraided and unbrushed. She certainly looked a state, her hair would most certainly be matted after this and it would be a pain to fix.

"General Nymeria Mercury," Benjamin Uranus spoke, his hands braced on either side of his podium. "You are being charged with high treason for the murder of Nasir Pluto, how do you plead?"

Nymeria blinked. She was confused. Why were they charging her for something she did on their orders? "Not guilty, of course."

"And why of course?"

"Because it was the council who gave me the order." Nymeria swivelled to face Melantha. Nymeria felt a cold pang of fear shoot down her spine. The look of disdain and shame Melantha was giving her, she had never seen anything like it. "Melantha, tell them." She laughed nervously but the only reply she got was hateful silence. "Melantha?"

"I have no recollection of this."

"Mel?! Tell them."

"But if I may, councillor. I fear my sweet sister is suffering from a disease that has plagued our kind for generations. One that is caused when we think we can become the gods themselves—madness."

"Is that so?"

Nymeria's eyes widened, if she was found guilty she would be imprisoned, and tortured for believing she could become a god. But she had never thought that. She knew that to be true.

"If I may your graces."

Nymeria felt her stomach drop as Ulysses stepped up to her podium.

"I am aware I am only taking this position to fill in for the accused but I may have some evidence that may support my wife's claim."

Mel nodded and Benjamin gestured for him to continue.

"The accused spoke to me in confidence when we returned from our latest crusade from the Hells. I believe her exact words were 'The council are a bunch of pompous cunts.' and 'I'm half convinced most of them have never read the Codex.' "

Nymeria knew she stood no chance so she simply fell silent. She had ruined the council's ego, the greatest sin to them. She prayed to her father, begged him, and pleaded that he would save her.

"Nymeria Mercury, you will be stripped of your rank and title—" The Council member for the House of Saturn spoke.

"Father please—" she whispered, her hands clasped together, as much as the cuffs would allow.

"Your possessions will be given to your sister."

"If you can hear me. If you are there, if you have ever been there," she quietly begged.

"I sentence you to imprisonment in the Creators Requiem until further notice. Any potential co-conspirators will be sharply questioned."

"I need you now. More so than ever. Father please!" She sobbed.

All she was met with was silence. The marble statue looked down at her impassively as she was dragged away, kicking and screaming as she was sentenced to imprisonment in the dungeons until further notice.

"Looking back..." Nymeria rubbed her wrists. It was like she could feel the manacles even now. "Despite the title, the rank, the prestige and the big lavish estate..." She licked her lips. She needed a drink. "I was just a stupid girl. A stupid, pompous, arrogant girl who had been told since birth she would be a pillar of the Faith." She crouched down, her hands digging at the dirt, pulling at flowers and roots and ivy. "A guiding light to any believer, and it's ridiculous that I thought that. Because who am I?! Just a woman at the end of the day," she yelled, her hands plucking and raking at the ivy and dirt, marring the entire outer ring.

Halloran was quiet as he stood. "You were sent to the prisons? Is that the dark room you hate?"

Nymeria froze, looking down at the dirt on her hands and it felt, as it always did, that it was all over her body. She wiped her hands on her leggings, but it was still there under her fingernails. "Before my imprisonment, I had never seen Melantha use magic. She has Blood magic."

"How do you know?" Halloran's lips trembled like the words came out before his brain could shut him up.

"That's how she stripped the magic from my blood. It was so strange, seeing all of your blood in front of you—stripped of its magic, a molten lava—and then shoved back inside of you."

She screamed, metal chains digging in further to gaping holes in her arms, legs, ribs and chest. She felt herself pass out for the second time in five minutes, the chains wrapping around her bones so painfully that caused her brain to shut off. When she came too, her nightgown was sticking to her sweating skin despite the cell being so dark and so cold. She could only make out Melantha by the red misty magic flowing from her hands—separating golden blood from molten magic—her magic being stored into a lantern on Melantha's hip.

She blacked out again.

When Nymeria woke up, she was forced awake by Melantha's hands caressing her head, her thumbs stroking her cheeks. "Why did you do this? Why did you make me do this?" Her voice was soft but cold.

"I- I Didn't," Nymeria whimpered, crying out as she moved just an inch and the chains scraped against her bones, the sensation so foreign. The accelerated healing of an angel hadn't left her and she could already feel the entry points for the chains scabbing over. How long had she been unconscious? An hour? Two? Maybe a few days?

"You know I didn't—I would never," she blubbered.

"I know."

It was so dark that Nymeria couldn't make out Melantha's face but could see her golden eyes, narrowed with hate. Looking at Nymeria like she was not her sister but instead a rat, vermin. No, she was less than that.

"You were a good soldier. The best my forces have produced." Melantha's hands dug tighter into her head and Nymeria gasped in pain. "But you spit on our family name. The family name I have spilt too much blood for to be brought down by your folly and promiscuity. Not now when plans I have spent decades building are so close to fruition."

"What? But I followed every order. Did everything you—"

Melantha hand shot down and gripped Nymeria's jaw.

"When will you realise this is not about devotion to the fucking gods!" Melantha screamed.

Nymeria trembled. The last time Melantha yelled at Nymeria like that was when she had smashed a plate when she was seven years old.

"I have sacrificed too much for you to stop me. So many councilmen have wanted me to reign you in for so long and I only

abstained because you posed no threat. But with your blatant disregard for the responsibility you have as a child of the War god, everything you do reflects onto me and I cannot have it ruined by your brazenness, your arrogance and worst of all, your whoring."

Nymeria shook her head. "It wasn't any of that. It was love—"

Melantha slapped her, the sting hurt worse than the chains.

"So many men's egos I have had to satiate because of your rank and title and the shame you bring our family. I should never have made you general. That was my last mistake."

She hadn't earned it? All those hours spent training as a child, the punishments, the beatings to make her better. None of that mattered because she had been given the title based on her blood not her skill.

"But there is a way you can atone. That they may forgive you."

Nymeria could only whimper, her eyes could faintly make out a flicker of movement and she saw four men. Not that she could make out who they were but she did notice how undressed they seemed. Their hands on their belts.

"It seems fitting that your repentance is in the same manner as your sins. Sins of the flesh shall be redeemed with repentance of the flesh."

Nymeria shook her head, once and then repeatedly. Melantha gestured for the men to enter her cell and they did. Nymeria's head was pulled back and arms pulled her further into the darkness.

"You shall only be redeemed when I say so." Melantha left.

Nymeria grabbed a branch on the outer edge of the clear.

"Sometimes it would be one at a time. Other times it would be multiple at a time. Sometimes I would pass out and one would still be there, still going. "

She slammed the branch into the tree until it splintered

at the tip. "But you know the worst bit?" she screamed, slamming the branch again, a larger chunk splintering off.

"That at first, I was eager! I wanted to repent for whatever sins I had committed, despite the fact I didn't know what I did wrong." Nymeria's voice shook. "I still don't know what I did wrong." She wiped her eyes.

"I recognised all the voices after a while. Some of them were guards around the estate or the Requiem, others were soldiers I had trained myself when they were recruits. Others were fucking council members!" She slammed the branch again and again until it was nothing but splinters. "BASTARDS!"

"What about Cerys?" Halloran hadn't spoken a word, yet his voice was hoarse.

Nymeria stopped, her fists digging into her palms until she could feel gold blood drip down them. "A day or two must have passed I think. Ulysses brought me her head. 'A head every week of those who believed your poisonous words and were corrupted by your flesh.'" Her voice broke and she nearly sobbed. "I started to look forward to the heads, one a week. It was the only way I could tell that time had passed. I grew angry that they stopped after the eighth one."

Nymeria sobbed. "Gods, she didn't deserve that." She turned away from him, smoothing her hand over her stomach. "Her death was in vain because I gave up all too quickly. I gave up after the heads stopped coming and I grew angry at that because I could no longer track time. When I finally escaped, I wished more than anything that the fall from the heavens would kill me. I wanted the humiliation to end. I wanted them to stop using my body to reclaim their egos."

Nymeria hadn't realised she had been shouting until her throat was sore. "Because that's all it was. They just wanted to humiliate me. Put me in the place they thought I should be in." Nymeria's hands smoothed her stomach again. "I had only ever done as I was told. Killed, tortured and maimed hundreds. Destroyed families and decimated bloodlines just to become the 'general of whores'. That's what they called me."

Her lip quivered and she curled her fingers over her stomach, digging through the material of the hoodie. Nymeria didn't look at him but she heard him stand up.

"How did you escape?" His voice was still so soft, so gentle.

"After a year, I think I formed a plan. Every day, I would move an inch, until a chain link popped out of my flesh. Sometimes when I would have visitors they would..." She felt bile rush up her throat and she swallowed it back down. "Use the chains to move me around, more links would rip through my flesh. Eventually, I stopped getting visitors and I was simply forgotten about, the key was hung just a hand grasp away from my cell. So when all the links were ripped out, I reached forward and grabbed it. I wanted to die, so badly. I prayed the fall from the Bethesda Chamber would kill me."

"The Bethesda Chamber?" Halloran asked.

"It's a massive chamber of grey marble with a hole in the floor. Once fully opened, and if you go through, you're trapped in an arcane tunnel. The waves of pure arcana push you down out of Elysium and into the Hells when set to the correct location. But I didn't wait for it to open fully. As soon as I saw the clouds and sky again I jumped."

He nodded, looking down at the ground.

Nymeria's throat tightened, her skin clammy and her fingers dug harder into her stomach. For the past two years, she had been living in a state of shock, in limbo. Not living, not dead, just surviving, pushing down any reminder of what she had been through with a drink. But speaking aloud what had happened made it real. In that moment, the shock that had lasted for two years gave way: only grief and anger were rising through her at a rate that threatened to consume her.

"And out of everything that happened—" She let out a choked sound close to a laugh, she could feel her eyes wide, tears leaking down them. "Do you know what I realised? All of my achievements, my reputation, the sanctity of the Faith and the purity of the name of Mercury are all a lie. I've done more harm to people by being my sister's tool, the council's tool, to further their own self-interest. I'm probably the biggest cause for all of the hatred and separation in this world—I killed anyone who thought differently than what my sister wanted, killed half-demons and demons just because they looked different, because everything I was taught is that you were all evil. I was never allowed a single individual thought or feeling and when I did indulge myself I was tortured for it for three years," she wailed.

She dug her hands under the hoodie, tearing at the skin of her stomach.

"Nymeria stop that!" Halloran hissed.

"No." Her nails dug in deeper and deeper, leaving golden lines and then small droplets of blood.

Arms shot around and she felt a body against her back and

pale hands grab her wrists pulling them flat against her chest like she was praying. "Stop it." She tried to fight against his grip but she was tired. She was so, so tired.

She felt his breath against her ear, "You were indoctrinated your whole life and every bit of your autonomy was taken away from you. You can be angry, you can cry, scream, rip up the ground and turn this whole forest upside down. But what you cannot do is hurt yourself." His voice sounded pained, hurt even angry.

"Let me go! If I can dig inside myself I may find a part of myself that belongs to me! Something untouched by them!" she screamed, the tears flowed down her face and once they started they wouldn't stop.

Nymeria wasn't sure how long she screamed, how long she wailed, when she had stopped crying or even when she started. She hadn't realised her legs had given out until she was gasping for air, her throat sore and chest aching, her heart hurt and she wiggled one hand out of Halloran's iron grip and placed it over her own. The air had grown colder; how long had she been crying and screaming? An hour or two by her guess. After some time, Halloran let go of her other wrist and wrapped his arm around her stomach, his face pressed into her hair. In truth, she hadn't noticed he was there until now.

"You're still here?"

"Yes."

"Why?"

Halloran paused. "I don't know," he finally said after a few moments. "My mother used to hold my brother like this when he would have panic attacks as a child. I thought it would help."

A silence fell over them, not quite uncomfortable but not comfortable either.

"I can't let what they did to me happen to Gen." Nymeria sniffed, wiping her eyes. "I won't allow her to be a target."

"And you think running will stop that?" Halloran interrupted and she knew he was right. Gen wasn't even of her blood but just the knowledge that Gen meant something to Nymeria, meant that Melantha would continue to order her demise.

"You don't need to run," Halloran spoke again and Nymeria looked up at him. His hair was messier than usual, framing both of them in a shallow dark curtain. "You don't need to run," he repeated. "You have Imani and Arwen, they'll take care of Gen. And I..." Nymeria felt her heart clench. "I'll look after you."

"I don't need looking after," Nymeria whispered; She could see just how sharp his eyes were, like a roiling storm about to release its first crack of lightning.

"Yes, you do," he whispered sternly. "You taught me that even the best of warriors need a shoulder to lean on."

"When did I say that?"

"You didn't say anything. It's something I've noticed. Your eyes are—"

"Expressive?" she interrupted. He let out a huff of laughter, the warm breath making her shiver slightly.

Halloran leaned away and Nymeria missed his warmth. His arm started to move away from her stomach but she grabbed his bicep. She felt Halloran flinch beneath her touch.

"Stay. Just a while longer," Nymeria pleaded. There was a beat of silence that felt like it could have stretched on for hours.

"Alright. Just for one night."

"Just one night and then we can go back to hating each other."

Nymeria looked up at the night sky, the full moon bright and beautiful.

"Melantha said I was born on a night just like this one. During the brightest full moon of the year."

Halloran laughed and she turned slightly to face him. "What?"

"Nothing. Just that I was born during the eclipse." Nymeria laughed lightly as well. They were true opposites.

23

A Family

The walk back to the Draig estate was a quiet one. Neither of them spoke a word, but a word didn't need to be shared. Even now, something was different between the two, a shift in dynamic that hadn't been there before. A shift that Nymeria didn't want to give voice to because if she spoke of it, much like before, it would make it real. Judging by the rigidity in Halloran's shoulders as he opened the front door, looking back at her over his shoulder but quickly looking away when their eyes met, he was just as much a coward as she was.

Wordlessly, she stepped inside behind him and as soon as she had taken her shoes off, Arwen was already coming down the stairs. His hair was loose, going to his pectorals which she could now see as he was dressed only in a pair of grey sweatpants. He hadn't been exaggerating when Arwen had told her the burns covered most of his body. The only place they didn't seem to touch was the sliver of skin around his waist and then downward below his sweatpants.

"Why don't you have a shirt on?" Halloran criticized and

Arwen shrugged.

"I was asleep, as most people tend to be at three in the morning. I can wear what I like." Arwen's white eyes flitted between the two of them, a smirk gracing his face as he crossed his arms over his chest.

"What were you two doing up and about at three in the morning?" he asked, as if he already knew the answer. Nymeria's cheeks reddened, her mouth opened but Halloran beat her to it.

"Don't be juvenile. We went for a walk."

Nymeria was pleasantly surprised he didn't expose her real intentions straight away. She mouthed a 'thank you' and he nodded ever so slightly.

"Huh." Arwen ran his tongue over his teeth. "I've personally never been for a walk at three in the morning. Especially not one's where my clothes get dirty with mud and I look quite as dishevelled as you do."

Nymeria frowned and then looked down at herself, mud covering her knees. She could feel the dampness soak through the fabric.

"I'm going to bed." Nymeria's eyes met Arwen's as she passed him, a shit-eating grin on his face as he wiggled his eyebrows at her.

She shook her head and ascended the stairs.

She heard Halloran grumble behind her. "We were not—"

"I'm just surprised you're freaky like that is all. In the woods, really?" Arwen teased. There was the brief sound of flesh hitting flesh and a wheeze from Arwen.

Nymeria crested the top of the stairs, passing the first door but then she paused. She could have sworn she heard something. There it was again, a high pitched sound, stuttering. Nymeria felt her heart sink down to her stomach. It was crying. Nymeria's hand paused on the door knob, she took a deep breath in, a short exhale and then opened the door.

Nymeria stood in the doorway for a few seconds, letting her eyes adjust to the darkness. Gen was bundled in a bed much too big for her, the duvet wrapped around her so that she could only see the top half of her face. Her eyes were red and wet with tears. Nymeria took a few steps into the room.

"Gen I—"

Gen buried her head under the pillow, pulling the duvet tighter around herself.

Nymeria sighed. She didn't know how to approach this or what to do. She wasn't equipped to be a mother. She wasn't like Melantha who had taken to motherhood like a duck to water.

Slowly, Nymeria rounded the bed and crouched down, staring at Gen, silently praying she would look at her. But she stubbornly refused, pulling the pillow even tighter over her head. Nymeria sighed again, running a hand over her face. She looked down the bed and on the other side, Lambo stared back at her, with its judgemental beady eyes. She suddenly had an idea. Nymeria reached over, grabbed Lambo and placed the plushie back down on the bed. Gripping its back she shuffled the plushie closer to Gen, the bed bouncing slightly. Gen peeked out from under the pillow, her eyes curious but cautious.

"I don't know what I'm doing," Nymeria admitted, moving the plushie as it was talking. "When it comes to taking care of you or myself. I don't know how to keep you safe, and the closer you get to me the more danger you'll be in. But you're impossibly close to me. I care for you as if you were my own." Nymeria hesitated. "Can I tell you a secret?"

Gen nodded.

"It frightens me how much I care for you."

Gen pulled her head out from underneath the pillow, her hair sticking up in all directions.

"And sometimes—most of the time—when I get frightened, I lash out. It feels like everything reaches a boiling point and then—" Nymeria lifted Lambo's arms to its head. "Boom." She dropped Lambo's arms. "I shouldn't have pushed you earlier. I'm sorry."

Gen pushed Lambo aside and lurched forward, wrapping her arms around Nymeria's neck.

Nymeria returned the gesture, scooping her up, climbing into the bed and setting her in her lap. "You've wormed your way into my life. I would very much like for you to stay in it."

Gen leaned away and nodded.

"Alright then. You can stay with me."

Gen beamed and snuggled into Nymeria's chest. Nymeria smiled, burying her face into Gen's hair and kissing the top of her head. A flicker of light from outside caught Nymeria's eye and she lifted her head. Someone had been listening in. She heard the distant sound of footsteps and a door open and close. The door to the room she had been sleeping in when she awoke the previous day.

* * *

"Harlo!" The shout startled Nymeria awake, jerking upright. Her hair fell onto her face and she swiped away a few strands that caught on her chapped lips.

"Harlo! You around here?" Arwen's voice was unmistakable. Gen yawned against her chest and snuggled closer.

"Stay here," Nymeria whispered, shifting Gen off her lap and into the bed. Nymeria threw the covers off and wrenched the door open. Looking down the corridor she saw Arwen peering into the room she had been sleeping in.

"Everything okay?"

"I don't know, Harlo isn't around."

"He didn't go to bed this morning?"

Arwen shook his head. "I'm sure he did. He's an early riser, likes to get some reading in before we go to work. But he isn't around and even if he did go out, he would leave a note or a text."

Nymeria frowned. Had he left because of their talk last night? Had he regretted his words?

"What did you two do last night?" Arwen's voice dropped and Nymeria blinked in surprise.

"We talked."

"In the woods? Alone? At three in the morning and you both came back dishevelled?" Arwen's voice was dripping in disbelief. "If you two are fuck— " Arwen looked down and past Nymeria. She followed his gaze to find Gen standing behind her. That girl was getting very good at sneaking up on people. She felt a glimmer of pride flash through her.

"—Cuddling. I don't mind, I really don't."

Nymeria shook her head and dropped her voice to a whisper. "We talked last night. I told him some things about how I ended up here and also about"—Nymeria gestured over her heart—"feelings"

"So no argument or fight?"

Nymeria shook her head.

Arwen ran a hand through his hair. "My little brother is a fucking mystery even to me." He paced down the hallway, paused at the end, and turned around. "I have some paperwork to fill out today. I can keep an eye on Gen if you can get in your car and look for him." Arwen paused again. "If you want to look for him. I know you're still choosing your options and—"

"I'll find him," she said, quicker than she would like.

Nymeria wasted no time getting washed, changed, and hopping into her car. Nearly dropping her keys on the floor as she rang Imani.

"Hello? Girl, do you have any idea what time it is?" Imani croaked over the phone.

"Small, probably non-emergency." Nymeria heard shuffling on the other end.

"What is it?" Imani sounded much more alert.

"Halloran has gone missing. Hasn't left a note or anything. I was wondering if you could track his phone location. You do have his phone number right?" Nymeria turned the ignition and her car rumbled to life.

Imani scoffed on the other end of the phone and the sound of footsteps followed by the creak of a chair. "What kind of information broker would I be if I didn't have the numbers and IP addresses of everyone in the organisation and who we work with?"

Nymeria paused her hands hovering above the steering wheel. "Does that mean you have mine?"

Imani didn't answer.

"Here we go. Got him, looks like he's a bit out of town...Huh. That's odd."

"What is it?"

"He's in an abandoned church dedicated to the Swordsworn."

24

Atonement

Nymeria parked outside the old church. The one she had visited all those weeks ago. She had visited a shrine to her father in a moment of desperation, a moment of confusion and rage, just like the night before. The difference between those two nights was that, for the first time, yesterday she actually had someone answer her and she had finally found some semblance of solace: in a half-demon of all things.

She squeezed the steering wheel again. She didn't know where the conversation with Halloran was going to go or why he was at a church dedicated to his father's sworn enemy. But he had been there for her last night, it was only right she returned the favour. Nymeria got out of the car, chucking her jacket back inside onto the driver's seat. Over the past few days, it had grown much warmer. When this investigation first started, it had been the first few days of February. Now, it was almost May. Nymeria walked through the rickety old gate, the hinges squeaking in protest. Her feet crunched against the gravel and her hand paused against the iron knocker, hesitating just a moment before pushing the door open. The door screamed in protest, some of the wood cracking and splitting, covered in slashes from where the demon had attacked her. Only a few short months ago, she would have distrusted any half-demon immediately. Adversity brought the most unlikely of people together, turning would-be enemies into almost family. Nymeria's footsteps echoed like gunshots in the church.

Halloran was hardly trying to hide. She could see the back of his head, sat in the front pew, his hands in his lap, a curling wisp of smoke swirling around him.

"You aren't allowed to smoke in church, you know," Nymeria spoke up, slowly walking up until she stood next to him. Despite his chuckle, Halloran's eyes remained fixed ahead of him. He plucked the cigarette out of his mouth, tossed it to the floor and crushed it under his heel. He leaned back in the pew, legs spread.

"It's also not proper to man-spread in a church," she joked and Halloran sighed and leaned forward.

"Then how do you do it then?" His question took Nymeria by surprise.

"Pray?"

"Yes."

She felt a jolt of uncomfortable shock rock through her. "You want to pray?"

Halloran nodded, looking up at her.

"If you don't—"

"No, it's okay, I can show you." Her voice was quiet and she took a few steps towards the partially destroyed offering table. "Come."

Nymeria went around it gathering the dirty candles and straightening the wicks, placing two on the dirty surface. She looked around the debris for any prayer beads but none were found.

"We may have to improvise this. Usually, you hold some prayer beads."

Halloran said nothing but stood awkwardly.

"Lighter?"

Halloran approached, pulling a metal lighter out of his pocket and lighting the two candles. Nymeria knelt in front of the table, and Halloran followed suit. She placed her elbows on the table and clasped her hands together. Halloran copied her.

"So, what are we praying for?" Nymeria asked, her voice barely a whisper. It felt wrong to speak so loudly in such a quiet and sacred space. But like the demon had said before, this place was no longer sacred; it was just a hollow husk of a dead faith.

"Forgiveness." Halloran's voice was hoarse like he had to force the words out.

"Forgiveness? For what?"

The silence was deafening, stretching on for minutes. Nymeria turned away from Halloran, bowing her head. After what felt like an eternity, Halloran finally spoke:

"I've been told all my life I am the best of devils and the worst of men. Now I don't want to be either. I've been told this by my mother who was afraid of me, my father who exploited my gift for bloodshed and conquest. By every other half-demon alive who still sees me as the feared Prince of the

Hells, the Iridescent Dragon. The demon who razed a city and dragged it down to the Hells. A demon who installed fear into the masses. All those things made up who I am now and I was fine with that. That was my place, the consequences of my actions, in my quest for security and control. But now I don't want any of that, none of that is what I want to be known for."

"What's changed?" Nymeria asked and he turned to face her.

"You. You came into my life."

Nymeria felt her lips part, her tongue darting out to wet them as they had suddenly dried.

"All my life, I have known my place in this world. Beneath the gods, the angels, even humans. I've been told I am violent, dangerous, and the son of the Destroyer is all I'll ever be and I"—his voice grew to a yell—"was content with that." His shoulder shook with anger. Or was it confusion? Nymeria couldn't tell. But she remained silent. He listened to her, so she would listen to him.

"But you—you showed me that life can be more than what everyone says you should be. You've made things complicated. Now I am here, in the church of my father's sworn nemesis, praying for forgiveness for wanting something I don't deserve, not even in a thousand lifetimes. You have given me hope for something I cannot have."

Nymeria straightened her back. "Why not?"

Halloran scoffed and shook his head.

"I'm serious, why not?"

"After everything I've done? Do you think I can have a normal casual life? With a partner, a child? Have friends and family? Have people over for dinner on the weekend?" His voice was full of disbelief like she had just told him she saw a pig fly.

"I think if you really want those things you can have them. Not without conflict, not without strife and hardship. But you could have those things, if you're willing to fight for them," she said slowly. The fire light cast his face in an angelic light that made him look so much younger. For the first time, Nymeria actually saw him.

"I hate you for making me want what I cannot have," he seethed and Nymeria turned her head, instead focusing on the dancing flames of the candles. The flames twisting and writhing together like dancing lovers.

"Maybe I could have those things in a less cruel and miserable world. But that's not the world we live in."

Nymeria nodded. "We do live in a cruel and miserable world," she agreed. Transfixed by the flames, two flames on two candles. One a darker shade of silver than the other. One more chipped than the other and taller. Both unconnected. But yet, they burned and danced together.

"But perhaps this world—a new world—one without ever-present gods and sanctimonious angels, can be one where we finally get to have the things we dared not have before?" The words felt poisonous on her tongue and her blood simmered. It didn't roar like it had done in the past at the slightest hint of blasphemy. This time it was a gentle warmth; comforting. Simmering.

"Be careful," Halloran warned, his voice teasing. "That's blasphemous talk."

"Maybe. But what really is blasphemy in a godless world?" she challenged, the words flowed freely off her tongue like water.

"Fair point."

"But you're talking like you have already admitted defeat before you've even started to fight for what you want," she chastised and Halloran sneered. "How badly do you want something if you won't fight for it? Not even try, I thought you were a man of action," she chastised.

"I am," he growled.

"Then fight!"

"I don't know how!" he boomed, his voice echoing like thunder in the empty church. "This is a battle where I don't know the enemy, nor the strategy! It's infuriating." Halloran sighed. "But you know."

That caught Nymeria off guard "Do I?" She scoffed. "I'm hardly the most well-adjusted person."

"Perhaps not, but you're the most human person I know. The only one, in fact, who will tell me things matter of factly and will actually talk to me like I'm a man. Not the former Crown prince of the Hells."

She could begrudgingly admit he did have a point there.

"So how do I approach this battle?"

Nymeria blinked. "You're asking me for my opinion?" She never thought she would see the day, maybe Cordero had killed her and she was still in that weird Limbo state.

"Typically, when one asks another for their opinion it means they value it. So, how do I approach this...topic?"

"Perhaps you should apologise to those you've hurt first?" Nymeria suggested but instantly regretted the words once she had said them.

Halloran quickly cut her off. "Apologising to Imani would be akin to slapping her in the face. Asking her for forgiveness would be an insult in itself."

"What about Gen?"

Halloran was silent for a moment.

"Gen deserves to know how she got her magic," Nymeria said softly. "We both know the only way she got her magic is by drinking demon blood and she would have been in Sodom at the time of the calamity. It was more than likely your blood. She's a part of you whether you like it or not."

"I know," Halloran rumbled, his knuckles turning white as he held his hands tighter together. "I just don't know how to explain it to her."

"The beginning would be a good start."

Halloran smirked and chuckled. "Fuck you."

The two laughed for a small beat. Halloran swallowed thickly. "I never thought I would see her again. Gen, I mean."

Nymeria remained silent and when Halloran looked over she raised her brows: *continue*. "I had burst through the earth, brought Sodom to the Hells and I remember feeling so proud of myself, surveying the carnage, the blood, the suffering. I was so proud of what I had done because I knew it would make the Destroyer proud. I would get that desperate lick of affection that every boy wants from their father. Then I heard crying."

Halloran paused, his throat bobbing.

"Not the usual crying of those regretting their actions or lack thereof. It was innocent and truly frightened. I searched and searched, and moved some rubble with my claws and that's when I saw her. I had never seen a human baby before. I had always been told they were annoyingly loud and weak but no one mentioned just how innocent they were. How untouched by the world."

Halloran held out his hands like he was cradling an imaginary baby.

"This tiny creature had done no wrong whilst I had done so much. I brushed my snout against the baby and it giggled. 'Genevieve' was engraved on the blanket. This tiny creature deserved a chance at normal life above the Hells, a chance I never got. I scooped the child into my jaws and climbed back out of the hole that was Sodom. I flew a few miles away and placed her by a road, now long deserted. She was so pale that I bit my lip and trickled some of my own blood into her mouth. The colour returned to her and I left back to the Hells."

Halloran ran a hand through his hair.

"I think I knew right then I would eventually fail my father. But I didn't want to believe it. I think both of our destinies are to be disgraces to our fathers legacy."

Nymeria sighed. "We were born from a feud between our fathers which has lasted hundreds of years. And despite all that, here we are, having a conversation and praying in a church. We're both responsible for a little human girl, who needs both of us."

Halloran stood up, rolling his shoulders. "I hate that you fill me with hope."

Nymeria swallowed thickly, she opened her mouth, closed it and then opened it again. "Perhaps in this new world, we're allowed to hope for forbidden things. If you, me, Arwen and Imani can come together and form...this strange bond we all have. A bond that by the Codex shouldn't be possible. Then why can't we all hope for other things?" Nymeria felt as if she had ripped her chest open, exposing all her insides with those words. She held her breath as Halloran's gaze flitted over her.

Their eyes met but he had a distant, faraway look in his eyes. As if he wasn't entirely there. Nymeria stood up and his eyes flickered back into focus. "Apologies." Halloran's voice was quiet as he cleared his throat.

"None needed," she said a little too quickly.

A beat of silence. Then a question that had been on her mind for many nights since her conversation with Arwen bubbled up her throat and past her lips before she could stop it.

"Why did you betray Arwen?"

Halloran sighed deeply, running a hand through his hair and his frown deepened. "When did he tell you?"

"When he took me to his office after dinner."

Halloran sneered.

"Not to talk badly about you," Nymeria added. "I asked how he got his burns. He answered and it spiralled from there."

Halloran turned his back, pacing up and down the centre aisle, between the broken and dusty pews. He paused halfway, placing each hand on the corner and leaning on the pew benches which groaned in protest. "I hated him," Halloran said simply, looking down, his hair hanging over his face.

"I hated that he never fought. I was always the one defending myself, our mother and him from demons, even as a child. I hated that our mother loved him more because she was afraid of me. She always told me that I've always looked too much like our father. I hated that I had to hunt. To protect our family by myself. Do everything that he should be doing and he was beloved for it. Because Arwen couldn't do anything wrong, Arwen was just a sweet boy, Arwen looked just like our mother and was so much more human than I would ever be. He had all the love and I—" His voice had steadily risen to a bellow. "I had none of it. No love."

He stood up straight, his knuckles turning white as he gripped the pews. The wood beneath his fingers cracked. "Until my father found us. The day his guards found us and dragged us to the Harrowing Palace. I killed three of his guardsmen at the age of twelve. He was so impressed he gave me food. So much food I didn't know what to do with myself. I ate until I threw up." His hair framed wildly around him, making him look dishevelled. His eyes widened in anger, teeth gnashing together. "I should have known better; everything comes with a price with him. But I was an angry boy who had finally gotten riches beyond my wildest dreams, so when the tournament came around, I could take out my anger on the one who caused me the most pain. Arwen."

"I had a sword, Cahir, my most prized possession. Forged from obsidian made from the lightning of a superstorm and infused the souls of the worst of the dead. I sliced that sword through his stomach, a shallow wound. At the moment, I didn't know why I was so hesitant to kill him. So I tossed his injured body to servants and ordered them to send him to the seventh ring. Hoping whatever writhing devils lay there would finish him off. After that, my father had me crowned as Prince of the Hells. After the ceremony, my mother slapped me and kicked me until I ordered my guards to cast her down to the seventh ring as well."

Two loud cracks resounded around the empty church and Halloran staggered forward, cursing under his breath and chucking the splintered wood onto the ground. "You tell me, angel. Is a demon who tried to murder his brother, murdered his mother, dragged a whole city to the Hells and killed and consumed countless others—is that someone who can really be forgiven and start anew?"

Nymeria slowly approached. How was she supposed to answer that question? She was no saint herself, she had done just as much harm as he had done. Who was she to pass judgment on his sins? She stopped when she was chest to chest with him. She reached for his face and he pulled away, his scowl deepening. "What are you doing?"

"Fixing you up. You don't pull off the messy look."

Her hands reached into his hair, pushing the majority back as it had fallen forward and then moving individual strands to frame his face. Nymeria was focused on how the black and white strands curled around her fingers. She had never realised his hair had a slight waviness to it up close, making it look like undulating strikes of lightning.

Nymeria's hand moved a large chunk of his hair forward, her palm sliding across his scalp. She could have sworn, despite the movement being so quick, that he had leaned into her touch, his head tilting into her palm as if he was seeking warmth.

"There," she whispered, his hair now framing his face as it usually did, in its wolf-cut style. Her hands remained by his head and it felt natural for them to be there, caressing him.

"Thank you."

Nymeria's eyes widened slightly and she lowered her hands.

"If I stopped you from your wishes and desires, intentionally or not. Would you do to me what you did to Arwen?"

"No." His reply was instantaneous.

"Would you do it to Genevieve?"

"No."

"Then you can start anew. But you need to forgive yourself first," she said softly, walking past him and giving his bicep a soft squeeze of reassurance.

"Where are you going?"

"Back to my flat. You should text Arwen."

"I will." He sighed, the tiredness returning to his voice. "I just need a few more minutes."

Nymeria nodded and she looked up at the stained glass window of her father, which painted the two in a mosaic of blues, silvers and greens as the morning sun filtered through finally.

"Your father is always depicted with a helmet on," Halloran criticised.

"Indeed."

"Was he ugly?"

"Most likely."

Nymeria chuckled. She didn't know what her father looked like—he was always depicted as tall so maybe he was. She always imagined he would look like Melantha—long flowing golden hair and harsh golden eyes.

A loud crackling and sizzling caught her attention and before she could react a bolt of lightning shattered the stained glass window, sending glass shards flying outward. Nymeria's hand covered her head but after a moment, when she felt no cuts against her skin, she slowly lowered her arms. Her eyes looked over to Halloran, his hand smoking and his fingers slightly charred yet he looked unbothered as he shook his it out.

"My father would always say how much of a prick your father was. Now they seem as awful as each other."

Nymeria burst into raucous laughter. She had never felt a greater sense of satisfaction.

* * *

Nymeria slowly opened her apartment's front door, half expecting to see Cyrus and Alvaro waiting for her, weapons brandished. But nothing greeted her except silence and the sight of her shattered coffee table. She heard the crunch of something under her foot. Nymeria stepped off it and picked up the cream envelope, popping the seal. Nymeria unfurled the cream letter with gold trimmings with black cursive handwriting:

'Dear Miss Nymeria Mercury,

You are formally invited to dinner at the Zai family estate, along with a few influential members of the city, to celebrate the solving of the case and the beginning of a new age for Ghenna.

When: Tomorrow at 8 pm.

Attire: Formal.'

25

Following The Heart

Nymeria had sat in her car for the past five minutes, fiddling with the hem of her dress. Just as she thought it would, the silver silk clung to her like a second skin, highlighting the pronounced curves of her body but also the warmth of her skin. Truthfully, she didn't have anything else that was nice to wear and she didn't want to be caught wearing the same suit twice. Nymeria had turned her wardrobe upside down trying to find something to cover her body. The pair of tights she had tried on at first had holes in and ruined the leg slit, so she had scrapped that idea. But after pulling everything in her wardrobe out she found a pair of lace gloves. It wasn't quite what she wanted—her leg was still exposed and part of the dress was backless, but it was better than nothing. The black lace complimented her dress nicely anyway and covered her arms.

The steady rumble of a car coming to a stop next to her pulled her out of her thoughts. She couldn't hide in here forever. Her phone pinged and she opened up the notification from Imani.

'If you don't get out of that car I will drag you by your hair.'

Nymeria had found it odd that Zai had invited the Draig's and Imani as well but not Caliban. But after thinking it over, she could see why he would: trying to find peace before war broke out in the city and settle any differences was a strategic move. But it was not one she could have seen Zai pull, not with how he reacted last time a half-demon was in his house. But he was providing free drink and food and Caliban had offered to babysit. She would be stupid to pass up on such an opportunity.

Besides, she could use this opportunity to get Zai alone. Tell him her decision. She had picked a side.

Nymeria got out of the car, adjusting her maroon hair one last time; tied into an immaculate bun, two strands framing her face. She was a little wobbly on her feet as she walked to the grand door; she didn't wear heels often. Not as much as she would like to.

As she approached the door, a human man dressed in a standard black suit bowed his head at her and opened the door. "Miss Mercury, I trust your journey was uneventful."

She frowned. "How do you know me? Have we met?"

"You've been all over the news the past few days, forgive my intrusion."

She was still getting used to that. Still getting used to every human in the city wanting to speak with her about something or another. She didn't like it. She wished she had her anonymity, where no one knew or cared who she was.

Nymeria took a few steps forward. As soon as she felt the warmth of the room and the nauseating smell of high-quality perfume and champagne hit her face, the room fell silent. Just for a beat as all eyes were on her. There weren't many people attending, it was an intimate dinner. But the most influential people in the city were here. She recognised the head of Xander tech—Xander Laslow—the new chief of police, a man Nymeria didn't know, and an older man she did know; he was Zai's biggest financial backer in his last mayoral campaign.

The latter approached her, grinning warmly and revealing a row of yellowed teeth which complimented the few white strands on his hair that were slicked back. "Hello Ma'am, it's an honour to finally meet you."

"It's a pleasure. Mr?" Nymeria looked over his shoulder, trying to find Halloran, Imani or Arwen.

"Ian O'Hara," he said, his voice hoarse like he smoked a lot—or at least, much more than his body could handle. "What you've done for this city is truly remarkable. I hope we get to work together closely in the future." He grinned and Nymeria politely smiled back.

"Hopefully so. If the gods are kind."

She frowned, the words felt like acid on her tongue. Whilst the words coming from her lips were uncomfortable, at least now they weren't a painful reminder.

"There she is!" Zai's voice boomed. Ian stepped to the side as the mayor brushed past him and wrapped Nymeria into a hug. She froze, awkwardly patting his back a second later. She pulled away perhaps a bit too quickly, a flash of confusion in his eyes. "You look lovely," he purred. He took her hand and kissed her knuckles. The action sent such a strong sense of betrayal and disgust she snatched her hand back. Like she was doing something she really shouldn't. He frowned, his cheery disposition vanishing to something much darker, something she had seen in very few people. But it disappeared as soon as it arrived. Zai awkwardly chuckled, taking a step back.

"Everything alright?"

"Yes, can we talk somewhere? Privately?"

His eyes narrowed in confusion for a brief moment, before lighting up in excitement. "Right, yes of course. Please follow me."

Nymeria felt a strange apprehension wash over her. She needed to keep the mayor in her good graces. If she pissed him off, he would become a nuisance for any future investigations she would try and carry out, if not try and get her shut down entirely. She had seen his intention in that flicker of darkness that crossed his face when she pulled her hand back. He thought of her as a weak-willed woman who could be swayed by the promise of riches and luxury. A doting little pawn. He was a pathetic, scheming man. The second type of man she hated the most.

They walked into the office and Zai leaned against the desk, legs crossed at the ankle and arms across his chest, his shirt pulling taut.

"I've decided on your offer."

"You wanted to celebrate in private?" He chuckled, a smirk on his lips. "You're bold."

"No." Nymeria could feel the strands of her patience snapping. "I'm not accepting your offer."

Zai frowned, straightening up. "Excuse me?"

"I won't be working for you directly. I'll be operating as an independent business without any political ties."

He scoffed. "You don't know what you're denying."

Nymeria held her tongue. She wanted to call him out, tell him she had made a choice to work more closely with the Draig gang. To actually find a way to form peace between half-demons and humans. A younger her would have called him out, but she was not in a position of power; she needed to play things smart, not brash.

"The reason my business works is because I'm not aligned with any political side. I work for the people, like I always have done and will continue to do so," she urged.

"But can't you see how that holds you back?"

She frowned and he took a few steps forward, his hands caressed her bare shoulders.

"Doing what you think is good now may not be the best thing in the long run for your business." He leaned in close, his mouth above her ear and his breath fanning her neck. "Do you want to tarnish your business' name and your own by associating with criminals?"

"Do you want to continue the divisions in this city or actually make changes to make things better for all its citizens?" she challenged, her temper simmering into her words.

Zai leaned back, running a hand through his pristinely swept-back hair. "The Codex is clear on humans and half-demons not mixing."

Her patience snapped.

"Fuck the Codex. It's a dead book about gods who have been dead for over five years."

Zai looked as if she had shot him: eyes wide, mouth slightly parted and frozen.

"Times are changing. If you don't change with them, you'll be left behind to rot."

He sighed, a strange look of reluctance in his eyes. "Times will be changing. I'm sorry we couldn't come to a mutual understanding."

Nymeria turned her back and walked towards the door, opening it and pausing as she was halfway through. "Also it's a very bad look to be flirting with other women whilst your wife is still missing. Makes you look guilty as sin."

Nymeria walked out into the hallway, Zai following after her, grabbing her forearm.

"Listen here—"

"Excuse me." A dark arm linked with her own and Nymeria looked down to see Imani in a red dress with a strap top and two leg slits. "I believe my friend is needed somewhere else." Imani's voice was like silk but with a poisonous lacing like a dual-edged blade. "There isn't a problem here, is there?" Imani cocked her head, smiling, her fangs poking out.

"No. Not at all," Nymeria said, mirroring Imani's tone. "Isn't there?"

Zai let go of her arm. "No. There isn't. Our business is done here. I'll see you both at dinner." His tone was clipped and he bumped against Imani as he walked past her.

Once he was out of sight, Nymeria sighed. "Thanks."

"No problem. You look stunning."

"So do you."

Imani pouted. "I'm sad he didn't put up more of a fight. I'm parched."

Nymeria laughed and lightly slapped her arm. "Behave."

"Shouldn't I be telling you that?" Her voice dropped to a harsh whisper. "Arwen informed me of your forest excursion with Halloran.

Nymeria rolled her eyes. "It was not what Arwen thinks it was."

"Oh really? Care to share? Because to me it sounds like a hookup in the woods."

"We talked," Nymeria urged. "That's all. A heart-to-heart. We settled some matters."

Imani's eye squinted. "Hmm."

"I promise that's all it was."

"Your trust in him is misplaced." Imani's voice was sharp and suspicious. "You agreed with me on that."

"Yes, I did," Nymeria admitted. "But time changes, as do people. Not everyone stays awful forever."

The two walked in silence as they made their way back to the main foyer. Arwen, dressed in a red suit, was talking very animatedly to Xander Laslow's wife. His fingers tucking a strand of hair behind her ear, she covered her mouth as she giggled, a rosy tint to her cheeks.

But Nymeria was looking for one man and it didn't take long for her eyes to land on him, as if pulled by some unseen force. Halloran was by the grand fireplace, one hand in his silver suit pocket, the other holding a champagne flute. He looked up. Their eyes met for a moment and his lips parted slightly.

"It wasn't anything my ass," Imani sneered and Nymeria frowned.

"Imani—"

"You're an adult. Do what you like, but I'm warning you; he'll hurt you." Imani's heels clicked away.

Nymeria knew she should heed Imani's warning. She would be an idiot to not give it credence. But her feet led her towards Halloran regardless. Someone so evil would not look at her with parted lips and blown wide irises, like she was the most angelic thing he had ever seen.

"We look like we're matching," she said, taking the champagne flute out of his hand and sipping it, grimacing at the bubbly taste and artificial sweetness.

"We do. Not intentional," he grumbled, snatching the champagne flute back.

"You sure? Or do you only have one suit?" she teased. Halloran's lip curled upward. "I have quite a few. I'm not wasting the nicer ones on Alighieri."

"Fair enough."

Nymeria took the champagne flute back, her eyes locking with his as she took a long sip. Halloran's hand wrapped around her wrists, bringing the hand that Zai had kissed up close to his face as if he were scrutinising the lace material of her glove. "I saw you go off with him." His voice lowered to a whisper.

"Yes. I went to tell him my decision."

"Was talking all you did?"

"Would it matter if it wasn't?"

Nymeria smirked as a muscle in his jaw twitched.

"Don't play games with me."

His finger hooked underneath the material of the glove.

As entertaining as winding him up was, Nymeria didn't want

to ruin her evening by angering him too much or pushing too far. They had only just come to an understanding. A closeness they now shared because they had similar lived experiences that no one around them had been through.

"I'm only teasing." She chuckled, but his frown didn't ease. "We just talked. I told him my decision and then I left."

"And what is your decision?" His face was neutral but his eyes looked hopeful.

"I'll have to speak to Arwen but we should be working closely together again." Nymeria smiled and she saw Halloran's shoulders sag.

"A wise choice. You would have gotten bored working with Zai."

"Would I?" She chuckled.

"You would have missed my stimulating humour."

Nymeria's eyes widened. "Was that a joke?"

"I'm capable of such things." He chuckled along with her.

Halloran's eyes dropped down to the glove and Nymeria realised his finger was still tucked into the lace. He was waiting for permission.

"Fine."

Halloran wasted no time in stripping the gloves off her arms.

"You look much better without them." Halloran's voice was quiet. "More like yourself."

"Ladies and Gentlemen!" the butler's voice from earlier boomed across the room and the room fell silent. "Dinner will be served shortly. Will you all follow me into the dining room?" Eager chatter started up again as the other guests followed him in an organised fashion. Halloran and Nymeria walked at the end, a comfortable silence settling between them.

They were led past Zai's office and towards a set of double doors at the end of the hallway. Once close enough, Nymeria almost gasped. The room was immense, with a high ceiling with a mural of the heavens. Polished oak floor and a dining table large enough to host twenty people. But for tonight it would only hold eight. The table was covered in white cloth, cutlery, plates and origami napkins already out. It was an inviting scene.

"What do you mean I cannot sit down to eat? How will I get dinner tonight?" Nymeria heard Eleanor's confused protest just as Nymeria passed the threshold of the door, Nymeria looked behind her to see the butler blocking Eleanor's path.

"This is a special occasion, miss," the butler said, pulling the doors closed behind him as he stepped out of the room. "Not for you."

Nymeria and Eleanor looked into each other's eyes, and the moment they shared was brief. But Nymeria garnered a brief notion in Eleanor's wide, concerned, and confused stare. Something was not right.

26

A Charlatan's Dinner

Nymeria sat down next to Halloran and opposite Arwen and Imani. That look Eleanor had given her was replaying in her mind, over and over. Eleanor must have attended dinners and parties hosted by her father. It was expected of her, and surely Zai, who loved his daughter, would not let her go hungry even for a day. So why was she not allowed to eat this meal?

She felt a foot tap her leg and nearly jumped. Her gaze shifted to Arwen. "You good?" He mouthed to her. Imani and Halloran also looked over at her, concern in their eyes.

"Something isn't right," she whispered.

"What do you mean?" Halloran leaned closer to her.

"Eleanor isn't here?"

"Yes, and?" Imani whispered.

"If this was a normal, fancy dinner, surely his daughter would be here as a representative of his family. Judging by this whole house, he's hardly going to be content giving her a microwave meal or takeout whilst he has dinner."

Imani glanced to Arwen who met her concerned look.

"Why would Zai not want his daughter here, if not to keep her away from something?" Halloran finished her sentence.

"And we're going to witness what that something is," Imani added.

The doors opened again and the butler returned, carrying plates of food on his arm, setting each plate down in front of the guests. Nymeria stared down at the white meat, accompanied by some succulent looking vegetables all dripping in a rich sauce that looked almost purple. The other guests eagerly tucked in, chatting amongst themselves. Nymeria looked up at the table and met Zai's eyes. He was staring at her, leaning back in the chair, his food untouched as he drank a glass of wine.

"Don't touch the food," Halloran whispered.

"Wasn't going to," she replied, her eyes locked with Zai.

Zai straightened up and leaned forward.

"You're not allergic to anything are you?" His voice was loud and cast the room into silence. The other guests looked down the table, towards her: snobbish sneers and looks of disdain, whether it was because she had interrupted their meal or simply the company she was sitting next to.

"No, not at all," Nymeria said quickly, a tight smile pulling at her lips. Right now she was grateful that Melantha had been so strict with etiquette lessons when she was a child.

"It's usually rude to eat before the host, is it not?"

Zai stared her down, and then that charming smile graced his face. But, unlike before where it was just theatrics, this time it felt like a threat. A dark, sinister look in his eyes, different than last time.

Zai continued to smile as he brought the goblet to his lips. "True, but at least enjoy the wine."

Nymeria broke the gaze to look down at the glass cup of red liquid in front of her; the liquid felt like a taunt. "Drink. I insist."

Nymeria wrapped her fingers around the stem, the liquid stirring as she rested the glass against her lips. She cast a glance to Imani, her eye wide and body as stiff as Nymeria was. She looked over at Arwen who gave her an equally concerned look. Nymeria tipped her head back and let the wine slide down her throat. She could feel the tension in the room build to a stifling heat and she waited. Waited for a burning in her stomach and insides. She was sure she was about to find out. But as the seconds ticked by, nothing happened except the nice, warm feeling of wine in her system.

"Don't look so surprised." Zai laughed and the other guests joined in, even Arwen chuckled nervously. "The wine isn't poisoned."

The tension eased and Nymeria's shoulders relaxed, the other guests picked up their cutlery and began to eat once again.

"The food is, however." The room fell silent.

Nymeria blinked and stared down at Zai. The old man she had spoken to earlier coughed, shallow at first but then it grew into a raucous cacophony. The man put his hand over his heart, slouching over before collapsing. His face splattered with gravy, blood from his nose and mouth trickling off the plate and onto the white tablecloth.

Halloran tried to stand up, grunting with effort but he could not move an inch, his arms stuck to the arms of the chair. Nymeria looked down at him, a red glowing chain wrapping around his arms and she could see the same wrapping around hers, keeping her tied down to the chair. Her chest heaved, breathing quickening as she looked down, they weren't far off from being bloody. Covered in her blood like they had been in that dark cell.

"Nymeria, Ny!" Halloran barked sharply, Nymeria lifted her head looking in front of her. Imani shouted in frustration, a puff of shadow surrounding her, once and then again each time the chains around Imani's arms glowed.

Two more raucous coughs and then two thuds as Mr and Mrs Laslow slumped into their dinner. Zai had now stood up, a white and gold leather bound tome in his hand, the pages flicking by themself before stopping on a specific page. As Nymeria stared longer at the book, her blood turned to ice. The symbol on the book was one she was very familiar with: a silver sun with a shield and sword in front of it; The symbol of House Mercury.

Zai smirked at her, her shock and surprise must have been obvious. "I'm surprised you're so shocked. I've always been a pious man."

"Was it always you? The Murders?" Her voice trembled, not out of fear but with barely contained anger. It was building so fast inside, it was the type of anger she hadn't felt in five years. He played her for a fool, an idiot, and she had fallen for it. Every nicety he had shown her was to try and get her on his side. So he could claim an angel as his wife? An object? Or hand her back over to Melantha?

"Not always. You were right that Morgan Cordero was the murderer. I just needed someone to do the act itself. It would have been all too obvious if I was showing up late to meetings after a murder happened. He grew very pliant once I had his wife and child hostage. Well, he thought they were hostages. The things you can do with recorded footage to make it look live is truly incredible." Zai chuckled. He sounded so nonchalant, so casual, like he was discussing the latest sports results with friends.

Nymeria ground her teeth together.

"But now his family joined my wife under the docks. She was the first one to find out what I was doing. She threatened to take Eleanor. Stupid woman!"

"But I let you get the trail on Cordero after I had him shoot Michael Sutton. I told him to leave the gun behind. He was starting to regret his actions. Threatened to expose me. But you just had to side with the wrong people."

He sighed as if talking to a child who had made a mess of things. "I warned you throughout this investigation to side with the right people, the good people, and you refused at every turn. The Lady Melantha said you were defiant, a heretic. I didn't want to believe the Good Lady at first, even after bestowing me with this magic. I didn't want to believe that someone as ethereal as yourself, a lady of faith, could be disillusioned by deceivers, but sadly I was proven wrong. Even if you did side with me, I would have given you over to her. You need to go home, Nymeria." Nymeria's blood turned to ice and Halloran thrashed in his chair.

"And what is it that you want?" Halloran spat.

"The old world back. Change things to how they used to be. When everything was good and made sense and my city wasn't infected with subhumans," Zai spat, launching his wineglass at Arwen. Arwen grunted as the glass shattered against his head, black blood dripping from his temple.

"The Lady's instructions were clear, three sacrifices at seven sites across the city. That would be enough to prepare the city and then a magical conduit to bring the Hells up to Ghenna. But then you rescued Gen. You kept the most crucial piece of this from me. I didn't even know you had her until someone told me."

"Who?"

The doors opened once again and Caliban walked through, Gen screaming and struggling as he had her thrown over his shoulder. Her feet kicked his chest. "I have her sir, she is all yours."

Nymeria's stomach dropped to her feet. She couldn't even move, could barely breathe as she watched Caliban walk straight past her and put Gen down next to Zai. Gen immediately lunged away, reaching for Nymeria, but Zai pulled her back by her hair, reached behind him and pressed a pistol to her temple. Nymeria lurched from her seat, the chains rattling in protest, barely able to hold her back.

"I'm not the only one who yearns for things to go back to how they used to be," Zai said, pulling Gen in front of him. The book floated in the air, turning a few pages. Caliban bowed his head, looking down at his feet.

"You fool," Halloran seethed. Nymeria had never seen him so angry, his teeth ground together, lips pulled back in a snarl.

The chains rattled again and Nymeria could see a few links pulled taut, barely holding them together. "I should have killed you when I had the chance."

"And you didn't. That's on you," Caliban sneered.

"Enough. Prepare the bodies, then we can start the final phase," Zai ordered and like a dutiful soldier, Caliban drew out a knife and a hammer and walked to the old man. Stripping him off his clothes and then making the incisions. Nymeria watched in silence as Caliban pulled and tore at the skin, cracked the ribs and spine, pulled the organs and then remade his body into a macabre fountain. That wasn't the worst part of it; it was the fact his face and eyes remained stone-cold as he did it. Did he never care for humans, despite how much he claimed to or was he simply blanking this out? His body moving to its vile puppeteer's wishes. She didn't know which one was worse.

Gen whimpered and reached for her, for Imani, for Arwen and Halloran. Arwen groaned and tilted his head back and shook, a few pieces of glass falling from his hair.

"Damn, couldn't even give us good wine before you killed us," he groaned.

"I wouldn't waste my good reserve on foul-blooded men and night crawler filth," Zai spat, casting his attention to Imani.

Imani stared him down, a snarl on her lips.

"Why are you doing this?"

"Because the old world needs to come back. This ritual will bring the Hells to Ghenna for twenty four hours, and then Lady Melantha will banish them back. But to the average man, it will look like I'll be the one to do so. A mere man with the powers of the divine. Your kind will be sent back to where they belong and things can go back to how they should be."

"Bringing the Hells to Ghenna? You'll kill thousands!" Nymeria snapped, her voice warbling on the verge of anger, a familiar righteous feeling stirring deep in her gut that spat *heretic.*

"If a few hundred must die so a thousand more may live in a godly world of prosperity then so be it. It's a worthy sacrifice. One I'm sure they would understand."

Zai turned to Halloran.

"I really should thank you. The Good Lady Melantha said she was inspired by you dragging Sodom to the Hells. So I shall sincerely thank you only this one time."

Nymeria turned to face Halloran and his jaw was set tightly, his eyes a brewing storm of regret and anger. Nymeria tried to reach for his hand, but the chains stopped her index finger just short of wrapping around his.

"It's done!" Caliban said, wiping his brow and smearing blood across his forehead. His shirt was damp with blood and viscera, clinging to him like a sheer shawl. The intricate pattern on the table glowed bright red as Zai muttered words in a language Nymeria didn't know, casting his hand over the sigil. The ground shook for a moment before stilling and a red beam of light shot from the back of the dead, breaking through the ceiling and into the night sky. Nymeria looked outside as several more red beams shot into the air.

Caliban marched towards Nymeria and held the blade still coated in blood and guts of the now three victims against her neck. Nymeria held her breath, fearing if she breathed the blade would cut to the bone.

Arwen thrashed against the chair. "Don't! Not her, you can cut me, sear my flesh, whip me! I don't care. I'm the enemy! I'm the one you want!" he roared.

Nymeria kept her eyes open, flicking her gaze to stare up at Caliban. Caliban's eyes shifted away. "Look at me," she demanded. "Look at me!"

Caliban glanced down, his eyes darting around, trying to not meet her gaze. "If you're going to do it then do it. Make the cut clean at the very least. No need to make an even bigger mess than there already is."

"Stop it," he growled through gritted teeth.

"I'm not doing anything."

"Stop trying to make this harder."

"I'm not."

She could hear Imani and Halloran shout as well, but all she could focus on was the thundering of her pulse in her ears, her throat bobbing underneath the blade. Nymeria winced as Caliban pressed the blade tighter against her neck, gold blood trickling from the nick.

"Come on," Nymeria snapped. "You made your choice long ago. How long have you been a traitor? Since the Docks?"

Caliban pressed the blade tighter against her throat and Gen wailed.

"Since our argument. You always treated me like a tool and our argument proved that. But what should I have expected from an angel? You're just as much of a freak as they are. Lord Zai gave me purpose and made me feel that for once I was being heard, not just a placeholder. I can help shape a world where people like me are on top."

She wanted to yell at him that he was already at the top of the world. That men like him ran everything in Ghenna, controlled everything, and now they wanted even more? But two words tumbled from her mouth before she could stop herself. "You're pathetic."

The blade dug deeper into her skin, and Nymeria could feel more blood dripping down her neck.

"Caliban!" Zai barked. The blade pulled away from her neck.

"You've been loyal, Caliban. Like a dog. Unfortunately, Lady Melantha was clear in her instructions to tie up all loose ends."

Nymeria's eyes widened as she heard the rattling of chains and the familiar disgusting crunch of chains piercing through flesh, it was as if time stood still for a few moments.

"What? No! Zai, what are you doing?!" he screamed, his hands digging into Nymeria's shoulder, leaving bloody crescent marks on her skin. Her chair swung forward as Caliban was pulled away, her nose smashing against the table.

Nymeria pulled herself back upright and looked down at the table, quickly wishing she hadn't. Caliban's shirt had been ripped open and the chains kept him spread eagle, face down on the table. The knife floated above his back, poised, eager to draw on a new canvas. "Books hold so much power. The Codex shows us right from wrong and this book shows me magic that I didn't know existed. So much power, all at my fingertips." Zai's voice took on an airy quality as if he was high.

"Caliban Ortega, be my willing canvas. Witness the power of a prophet, with the gift of transformation." Nymeria could hear the creaking of chains next to her and the gentle opening of a door. Yet she couldn't take her eyes off the sight in front of her. The bright full moon shone down on Caliban's back through the red beams. "I gift onto you, Caliban Ortega: The Gift of Lycanthropy. The first creation of my new city."

27

Escape

Nymeria watched the knife plunge and carve Caliban's skin again and again. The slicing and peeling reminded her of pulling apart raw bacon from a packet before grilling it. Nymeria didn't know what language Zai was speaking in, one hand raised as golden magic swirled in the air like steam and poured into every slash and stab the hovering knife made.

She couldn't look away and by the lack of noise, the others couldn't either. It was a macabre play with an orchestra of Caliban's pleas and cries. But it was all over as quickly as the horrifying ritual had started. Caliban slumped against the table. Nymeria couldn't tell if he was breathing. Had the curse ritual worked or had he succumbed to his injuries?

"It's a glorious day," Zai said, pulling Gen along by her arm. She cried and tried reaching for Nymeria. "I'll make sure to have an obituary in the newspaper for you, Nymeria. 'Private Investigator mauled by Werewolf in a freak break-in.' And then, once that news grows old, everyone will forget about you. You'll have never existed. Just as Lady Melantha wants."

Zai walked to a door towards the back of the room and opened it, cold night air rushing in. "It's been a displeasure knowing any of you."

Gen cried once more before the door closed on both of them.

Silence filled the room but only for a moment. Caliban groaned, his back heaving and then it stilled. The chains dissipated into nothingness.

"Please be dead," Imani whispered. "Please, please be dead."

Caliban shot to his knees, screaming, bending backwards like he was possessed. Screaming incoherent madness, his fingers digging and scratching his skin like he was on fire. He was so loud that when delicate hands started pulling the chains away from Nymeria's arms and legs she jumped and thrashed.

"Please stop, it's me!" Eleanor's voice came as a shock to Nymeria.

"What are you doing here?"

"Helping!" Eleanor's fingers shook between the chain links and wet tears poured down her face. The clatter of something hitting the table gave both women pause, Eleanor looked up and screamed. Nymeria turned. Caliban's teeth and nails were scattered on the table, wails coming from his toothless maw as the bone of his jaw elongated and new fresh fangs pushed through his gums and claws where his nails had been.

As the last chain fell from Nymeria she bolted up, pushing past Eleanor as she reached Halloran, pulling the chains binding him down with quick precision and ease. Her fingers still remembered the quickest way to move chains along an arm.

"Are you okay?" Halloran said quickly.

"I'm okay, are you?"

"I should have killed him long ago."

"Not the time," Nymeria said quickly. They all had to get out before Caliban fully turned. Nymeria was fortunate enough to have never encountered a werewolf before, but she had been to the scenes of a werewolf attack. She had never seen blood coat a ceiling like fresh paint. Body parts were strewn around a three-mile radius of the crime scene and the culprit was found in the bedroom of the house, cradling the bloody dress of his infant daughter. Nymeria had heard a few months later that the suspect killed himself from grief. At least, Caliban didn't have anyone to lose now, he'd just lost himself. But a man without anything to lose was just as dangerous as one with something to lose.

More chains slammed to the ground as Arwen stood up and Eleanor quickly moved to Imani.

"Hurry up!" Imani snapped.

"I'm going—" Elanor was cut off by the sound of snapping bones and tearing muscles. Nymeria turned away, rushing to the door she had entered through and pushed it open. The double doors swung wide, and the butler from before stared at her with wide eyes.

"By the gods—"

Nymeria shoved the butler aside.

"Out of the way." She heard Arwen bark and the last set of chains snapped away. Nymeria turned around, Imani and Arwen rushing past her, followed by Halloran. Eleanor's back was to Nymeria and the teenager stared ahead as Caliban's muscles flexed and stretched, the skin cracking and peeling apart as a grey-furred haunched back ripped through the human skin.

"Fucking humans always freezing like a deer when something horrifying happens." Nymeria rushed forward grabbing Eleanor's arms.

"Instead of moving your ass!" she yelled. Eleanor's eyes widened. She gasped and ran with Nymeria. The two women pushed past the frozen butler. Nymeria ran with Eleanor towards the main foyer, the sobs from the teenager grating on her nerves.

"Why are you saving her? She could be in on this!" Imani shouted as Nymeria and Eleanor skidded to a halt with the others.

"Because she saved our asses!"

"You know anything about this?! About your father?" Halloran demanded, his voice angrier than Nymeria had ever heard it.

"I didn't, I swear!" Eleanor sobbed. Halloran's face hardened and he grabbed the back of Eleanor's head, fisting her braid. Nymeria could have sworn she heard a crack as Halloran's fingers dug into her neck.

"Don't lie to me!"

"I'm not, I swear! I tried to warn you last time! I thought Dad was just depressed! I didn't think—" Eleanor sobbed, her body shaking with each gasp of breath.

"Easy," Nymeria said sternly, facing Halloran, he looked at her from the corner of his eye. "We need her. Just because her father is a piece of shit, doesn't mean she is. Right?"

There was a beat of silence before Halloran hummed in agreement and let go of Eleanor's neck.

"You're coming with us," Nymeria snapped. "You're going to tell us everything you know about your father and this ritual."

Eleanor nodded, wiping her eyes. "I will. I prom—"

The sound that came from the dining room couldn't be described as a howl or a scream but a pained amalgamation of both. Like an animalistic scream of something dying and being born at the same time.

Nymeria heard a snarl, the pounding of paws against the oak flooring and the screams of the butler, quickly followed by the sound of glass shattering.

"Not a sound," Arwen whispered.

Eleanor clutched onto Nymeria's arm much like how Gen would. In the silence, Nymeria could faintly make out the snuffling and snarling of a werewolf outside. Imani pointed at the wall, slowly moving her arm in a semi-circle following the Werewolf as it moved around. Nymeria swore as she heard paws on the gravel of the driveway. They couldn't get to their cars. One escape route down.

"Eleanor," Nymeria whispered. "Where is the quickest escape route?"

Eleanor stammered over her words, she was barely holding back tears. "We have a back door to the garden. But we have to go back through the dining room." That would not be ideal. She didn't know how fast a werewolf could run but if it was already at the front of the house in a few minutes, Nymeria didn't doubt that as soon as it heard noise from the garden, it would run over to investigate.

"Any other ways to reach it?"

"Not unless we jump out of my bedroom window or the roof—"

"That's how we get out then."

"What?!" Eleanor squeaked.

"I've learned recently that humans can be quite durable if thrown from a roof." She cast a glare at Halloran.

The snarling and snuffling grew louder, and the door knob jiggled.

"Upstairs. Slowly," Arwen said quietly, backing towards the grand staircase. Nymeria followed, not taking her eyes off the door as the jiggling grew more intense.

"If he gets through the door," Imani whispered, "all of you get upstairs and get out. I can distract him."

"Fat chance," Arwen whisper-yelled. "I'm not leaving you behind."

"You won't be leaving me behind. I'll just keep the steroid-raging puppy entertained with a bird. Besides, you can't luck your way out becoming dog food." Imani shot back, fixing Arwen with an icy stare. "You saved me once, two and a half years ago. It's about time I repay the favour."

Arwen opened his mouth but no sound came out as the door slammed open. The werewolf walked through the door on all fours, a hulking beast of grey fur and black claws nicking the marble and tapping with each step of its paws, which were easily the size of Nymeria's head. The werewolf paused just for a second and looked up at the five of them. Nymeria held her breath. It still had familiar blue eyes but they were much angrier than she had ever seen them.

The Werewolf—Caliban—made that horrible roaring wail and rushed towards them, only to be enveloped by a cloud of shadow. Imani quickly shifted into a crow and flew around the shadow cloud, dive bombing in and out, shadows clinging to her feathers. Furry paws swiped at the bird as he snarled in frustration.

"Everyone move now!" Halloran ordered. Nymeria wasted no time, sprinting up the stairs two at a time, dragging Eleanor along, the girl tripping over her own feet.

"Where's your bedroom?" Nymeria yelled, not looking behind. Not even when she heard a squawk of pain and Arwen call Imani's name.

"Down here." Eleanor grabbed Nymeria's wrists this time and pulled her forward, Halloran hot on her heels.

"Imani—" Arwen called again and Nymeria could hear a pair of feet stop.

"Move. Imani has things under control!" Halloran barked, striding past her, pulling Arwen reluctantly along. Who was trying in vain to pull his hand free from his brother's iron grip.

"Just this door here!"

Nymeria's wrist twisted painfully as Eleanor sharply opened a door to her left. The four came to a screeching halt inside. For a teenage girl of one the wealthiest men in the city, Nymeria would have expected the room to be full of band posters and celebrities, makeup on her desk and maybe a few shirts and trousers scattered along the floor. But none of that was present—instead, the room was sparse with only bare necessities and too much religious iconography. A small altar to the Creator was at her bedside and the walls were decorated in sermons.

"So what now?" Eleanor's voice warbled. Halloran marched to the window, pulling the handle once then twice when it didn't budge.

He snarled under his breath, his eyes glowing as he put his fist straight through the glass, sending it tumbling downward to the garden below. "Everyone out, now."

Nymeria almost jumped, feeling a hand on her shoulder and a light airiness flowed through her, as if everything would be alright.

"A bit of extra luck. Just in case." Arwen flashed her a charming smile before heading to the window.

"Isn't the human phrase ladies first?" Halloran scowled as he passed his brother making his way to the door.

"And let the ladies hurt themselves when they land? No wonder you don't have a girlfriend," Arwen teased.

"A little more serious right now please," Nymeria snapped.

A roar made the four of them fall silent. Then came the sound of large paws quickly getting louder.

"Time to go!" Arwen propped himself on the ledge and leisurely tipped himself backwards. Nymeria turned the door's lock and took several steps away, the paws sounding like they were just outside the door.

Eleanor hesitantly made her way to the window, shifting so she was sat on the ledge. Nymeria could see her fingers tremble as she gripped the window frame. The door knob rattled and a growl of frustration sounded from the other side.

"Move it!" Nymeria barked and Eleanor whimpered.

"I'll catch you!" She could hear Arwen vaguely call. But still, Eleanor didn't move.

Halloran growled again. "Move!"

He shoved her out the window with one hand, Eleanor screaming as she fell. He leaned out the window, looking down at where she fell.

The door creaked as the werewolf slammed his body into it, and the wood splintered as he did so again. Nymeria rushed up behind Halloran, placing both hands on his back.

"Consider this payback," she whispered in his ear and she shoved him as hard as she could.

Halloran made a noise between a growl and yell as he fell forward. The door behind cracked, on the verge of breaking. Nymeria climbed onto the window ledge and looked back to see snarling teeth and angry blue eyes peering at her through a crack in the door.

Nymeria couldn't afford to waste another second, Caliban forced his body through the door, sending splinters scattering around the room. Nymeria jumped off the ledge.

28

Lycanthrope

Nymeria crouched and rolled forward as her feet hit the ground, the heels of her stilettos snapping and shards of glass raining down from above, cutting into her legs and arms. "Move!" she screamed at no one, running into the garden, kicking the stilettos off. A shame, they were cute.

The garden was large, full of beautiful flowers in a rainbow of colours. If circumstances weren't so dire, she would have loved to spend a day reading amongst the flowers. In the centre of the large garden were several construction vehicles; a digger, a few trucks and a small cement mixer all surrounding a huge hole that was easily twenty feet deep and was placed before a large statue of a seven-eyed owl.

Nymeria had a plan. She opened her mouth, Halloran's name bubbling on her lips but it soon turned into a cry of pain as she felt the familiar sting of sharpness piercing her flesh; it felt as if ten knives had pierced into her shoulder all at once. Caliban landed on her back, skidding her face across the dirt and grass. The two collided into a workbench and sent tools scattering across the ground, a few slipping into the pool. The jaws around her shoulder released for a moment and Nymeria rolled onto her back, holding her arm out in front of her just in time. She screamed as Caliban's jaws locked around her arm and he shook his head, her back cutting into the grass and dirt and the flesh of her arm being ripped to ribbons. Nymeria looked him dead in the eyes and they hardened as they met hers. This wasn't just werewolf bloodlust, he was taking out every bit of anger and resentment he had ever felt for her. Deep down in there, he had always wanted to lash out at her, this was just his perfect opportunity.

Nymeria's free hand reached around, her fingers gliding over the handle of a hammer, and struggling to wrap around it. She just needed to be a little closer. Their eyes met again and she paused, her teeth grinding together. What Caliban had done was unforgivable; he had betrayed her and handed her child off to a madman. He could rot in the Hells. Nymeria pulled her body to the side as far as she could, feeling the flesh of her arm shred. Caliban growled, lifting her off the ground with his jaws and slamming her back down with a force that knocked the air from her lungs. But he had done what she had wanted him to do. As if fate itself was on her side, the hammer jumped in the air with the force that Caliban slammed her down, moving it just close enough for her to grab.

Her fingers wrapped around the handle of the hammer and she felt her blood boil as she swung the hammer down onto Caliban's eye with all her might. Nymeria grinned as she heard the bone of Caliban's brow snap and break, his eyebrow splitting, bone jutting out of the fur. Caliban howled in pain, dropping Nymeria's arm and whining as he took a few steps away.

Nymeria scrambled, dragging herself by her good arm.

"Get him in the pool!" she yelled out. She couldn't see the others but she desperately hoped they could hear her. Otherwise, she was in trouble.

Her eyes widened as Caliban growled, stalking up to her. He lurched forward but a body landed on top of him and in the chaos of roaring and hissing, of fangs and claws, Nymeria could make out brown locs scratching and biting any part of Caliban's fur.

Nymeria staggered to her feet and from the corner of her eye, she saw a flash of russet and blonde hair. Nymeria's heartbeat was in her ears, blood thrumming in her veins.

"Get him closer!" someone yelled. She could do that. Caliban jumped in the air, a clawed paw catching the back of Imani's neck and throwing her away. Her body slammed into a hedge and flew through it. Nymeria froze when she heard a snap. She turned, and she could make out Imani's body on the other side of the bush, unmoving.

"Imani?"

Silence.

"Imani?!"

Nymeria heard the thundering of paws and hot breath on her neck, she turned back just to see pearly jaws framing her face and hot breath that smelt like death itself washing over her.

But Caliban paused mid jump, his jaws snapping close, his teeth brushing her skin. Nymeria looked down and saw two familiar arms wrapped around the werewolf's middle.

Goose bumps rose on her skin as she heard the deep draconic rumble she had heard in the subway tunnels.

"It seems you haven't learnt from our first fight. Fine. I'll teach you your place again." Caliban was pulled away and thrown back over Halloran's head.

Caliban lay sprawling and Halloran casually rolled up the sleeves of his shirt. The white of his eyes had turned black, his white irises glowing brightly. Caliban rolled back onto his paws and rose to his full height. He was easily twice the size of Halloran. He drew his head back and roared, spit flying from his maw.

"Even as a dog you're more bark than bite. Disappointing," he snarled. Halloran turned to face her, a silent conversation between them, '*Are you okay?*'

'*Fine.*'

He nodded and jerked his head towards the statue. Nymeria turned, Eleanor and Arwen were shuffling the statue closer and closer to the edge of the plinth it was on. Nymeria smirked, holding her injured arm. The cement mixer was just on the other side of the pool.

Caliban roared again and Nymeria ran as if all the demons of the Hells were chasing after her. Halloran roared back. Nymeria wanted to turn when she heard the sounds of crackling lightning and thunder, of Caliban's roars and Halloran's grunts of pain. She desperately wanted to look, make sure Halloran was alright, make sure the sounds of flesh being torn weren't his. But if she did look back, she wouldn't get to the cement mixer fast enough and perhaps the last time she would see Halloran would be with his throat ripped out.

That would not be her final memory of him. She intended to make many more with him. With Arwen and Imani and Gen. No one was dying on her watch, not again. Not like Cerys and not like Nasir.

Her hands wrapped around the handlebars of the cement mixer and she threw her whole body weight into the handles, the drum of the mixer spilling forward and dumping gallons of wet cement into the pool. Halloran roared and Nymeria looked over to him.

Halloran had Caliban's jaws wrenched open, and he pulled, the popping sound of bones dislocating and muscles being pulled far beyond what they were capable of. Caliban wriggled and swiped at Halloran, his claws catching on his shirt and ripping it asunder. Yet Halloran remained unflinching. Caliban growled, barely able to shut his jaws.

"Halloran!" Nymeria called and he looked up instantly.

His eyes glanced down to the pool and back up to her, he smirked. Halloran sharply brought his knee upward into Caliban's throat. The werewolf baulked and sputtered. Halloran drew back his fist, white lightning swarming around it as the wind began to circulate his body. Halloran uppercut Caliban, sending him into the air with a thunderous boom.

Caliban shot up a few feet. The draconic rumble from before

sounded and with a much smaller boom than when he shifted in the tunnels, two black iridescent draconic wings materialised from his back. Halloran shot into the air with the same wind, rising just above Caliban and slamming both of his feet into his skull with a loud crack. Caliban flew straight down into the pool landing in the cement with a wet slap, roaring and howling in outrage and churning up chunks of wet cement into the air. Nymeria peered over the edge and Caliban jumped up at her, a hair's breadth away from pulling himself up. But his wet paws slapped uselessly against the sheer stone sides of the pool wall and he fell back down with another wet slap.

Caliban flailed around uselessly, his movements growing more and more sluggish as the cement matted his fur and dried much quicker than Nymeria thought it would. The statue tipped forward, crashing into the pool and sending a spray of dust and cement up into the air. But as the dust fell, all was silent with only the steady hum of the red beams illuminating the night sky over Ghenna.

Nymeria waited only a moment, and when she didn't hear any other sounds from the pool she rushed to the bushes. "Imani?"

No reply.

She pushed her way through soil and thorns that nicked her skin and dirtied her now ruined dress. Amongst the broken plants, she could make out a spiral of locs. Imani's neck was turned at an unnatural angle, facing away from her, her body still. "Imani?" Nymeria's voice was barely above a whisper.

Imani's head jerked towards Nymeria, her neck snapping.

Nymeria jumped back, falling among the soil.

"Don't look so surprised," Imani rasped, sitting upright.

"I thought you would know only daylight and blessed artefacts can kill a vampire." Despite Imani's chastising tone, Nymeria had never been happier to hear it. She let out a huff of laughter, grabbed Imani's arm and pulled her in for a hug.

Imani hesitated for just a moment before wrapping her arms around Nymeria as well.

"You're such a bitch for scaring me like that," Nymeria joked, willing the burning tears in her eyes back.

"I'll try not to make a habit of it."

Jogging footsteps slowed to a stop behind them. "You girlies alright?" Arwen called and Nymeria pulled away from Imani. "All good."

"We're wasting time," Halloran chastised from afar and Nymeria watched him rip a part of his shirt off as he walked over. He grabbed Nymeria's arm and pulled her to her feet, the bite on her arm lightly bleeding, the healing factor already kicking in.

"Careful!" Nymeria hissed, her face softening as he wrapped the fabric tightly around the wound.

"It would be an inconvenience if you bled out."

They both knew she wouldn't, but she wouldn't deny the closeness. After all, it was the same reason why Halloran let her stitch up his bullet wound in her bathroom all those weeks ago.

"We're fine too by the way!" Arwen's voice was laced with annoyance as he pulled Imani to her feet.

Halloran grunted in dismissal. "Move. We've wasted too much time with the dog. Zai could be anywhere by now." His eyes were still dark and lightning was crackling and sparking between his fingers.

"I might know." Eleanor's timid voice sliced through the tension as she peered around the corner of the bush.

"Where?" Nymeria's voice was hoarse.

"Lately, in the evenings, he's been going to the old cathedral in the city centre. He was talking about renovating but now I think he may have been lying."

Nymeria nodded, marching past Eleanor and grabbing her forearm.

"What are you doing?!"

"You're coming along. Or would you rather wait for Caliban to wake up?" Nymeria snapped.

Eleanor's eyes widened and she shook her head.

"Come on, we're going now!" she ordered, marching onward as Halloran wordlessly fell into step beside her.

"What about your arm?" Arwen called.

"It'll heal."

She could barely feel the soreness any more, it was replaced by a desperation to get to Gen and anger towards Zai. She was going to kill him.

29

Last Stop Before The Hells

The car jostled again as Arwen pulled out of the Aligihieri Estate gates. Nymeria grunted as the laces of her boots slipped through her fingers, it was painful enough tying these laces with her bandaged arm still throbbing, golden blood leaking through the fine material that had been Halloran's shirt.

"Who taught you how to drive, a blind man?!" Nymeria snapped at Arwen.

"You wanna take the wheel, one arm?!" he snapped back, shooting her the most hostile look she had ever seen from him.

"Enough bickering. We need absolute focus," Halloran snapped at both of them, fixing Nymeria with a stare which was not as icy as the one shot at Arwen.

Nymeria looked away. He was right, they couldn't afford in-fighting, not at a time like this. Not when Gen's life was on the line.

"Halloran's right," Imani spoke, wedged between Nymeria and Eleanor. "We can't stop this if we're fighting each other. Last time we were, Caliban turned on us."

"You think it was even back then?" Arwen asked, his voice sounding more tired as he sped the car up. The darkened windows and buildings sped past them but that ominous red light cast a macabre glow over the city, as if a blood moon was shining down upon them.

"Dad was right," Eleanor whispered. Nymeria finished tying her boots. She was grateful she brought back up shoes with her now. Nymeria lifted her head and Eleanor's wide eyes were focused on her arm and the wet golden patches that had seeped through.

"You're an angel."

"I was. I'm a fallen one."

"Oh...But you have the blood of gods."

Nymeria paused and looked down at the golden splotches. Still bloody and still golden. Just like five years ago.

"Just because I have the blood of gods, doesn't mean I am one. I'm nothing close to celestial, nor do I want to be."

Eleanor's eyes narrowed. "If you don't want to be then why do you look so sad?"

Nymeria swallowed and straightened up, a heavy silence hung in the air.

"Because it hurts and it's allowed to hurt. I'm mourning the girl I used to be." Her voice warbled but she didn't hate it, because now it was a controlled release. Like the gradual lapping of waves rather than a burst dam.

The car suddenly rocked forward, Nymeria's forehead slamming against the back of the passenger seat.

"What the hell Arwen?" Imani snapped.

"The road is gone." His voice was quiet, as if stolen straight out of his lungs.

Nymeria pressed the window button down and stuck her head out. Where the road had been was now an empty hole, glowing red. Even some buildings were completely missing, replaced by holes, accompanied by some sort of noise she couldn't make out.

"What's the road ahead like?" Arwen called.

"Broken in parts, but be quiet for a moment," she replied, straining her ears and leaning further out the window. It was subtle but it sounded like the moaning and wailing of hundreds of people. Nymeria had heard that sound a few times when raiding the Hells—it was the sounds from the River of the Damned. Humans who died and unfortunately caught the Destroyer's attention but weren't attractive enough to be considered for the role of one of his concubines.

But the sound was getting louder and louder and Nymeria only realised how quickly it was creeping up on her until it was deafening. A crack sounded from behind and the car skidded backwards. Nymeria fell back between the open window and outside, the red glow behind her illuminating all she could see.

"Everyone out of the car now!" Nymeria screamed. With one hand on the roof and the other on the window, she slowly pushed herself through, inch by inch. The vehicle creaked underneath, almost in warning. It lurched back, as more ground fell away, almost at a ninety degrees now. Nymeria knew she had to act fast, it was now or never.

She pushed one arm through, her upper body then her lower, then one leg out. A loud crack and the wails grew to a deafening pitch as the slab of road she was on lurched again and the car fell back, her leg trapped in the window dragged along with it. Nymeria cried out as she was pulled along the road, just pulling her leg free as she felt the downward lurch. It fell into the red glow and was claimed by the Hells. Nymeria peered over the ledge, the wailing died down and the red glow was ever ominous, as if it was waiting to grab its next unfortunate victim.

"Are you alright?" Imani asked urgently, dragging Nymeria to her feet. Nymeria dusted herself off, looking up at Imani.

Imani's eye was wide with fright, sweat on her forehead and her hand clenched and unclenched around nothing.

"You good?" Nymeria's voice was quiet, as if they were both hiding from some unseen looming force.

"Yeah...Yeah. I'm fine." Imani sounded more like she was trying to convince herself than Nymeria.

"You can sit this one out," Nymeria promised, slowly taking Imani's thumb and forefinger and wrapping her hands around them. "I'm not asking you to come with me."

"I'm fine," Imani repeated, even less confident than before.

Nymeria didn't believe her but nodded anyway, squeezing her hand one more time. Women had to look after each other after all.

Nymeria walked forward. Halloran was pacing back and forth like a caged animal, Arwen peering at the red hole in front of them and Eleanor was sitting on the floor, trembling. "Everyone got all their limbs intact?" Nymeria called.

"All good," Arwen called back. "Are we moving?"

"We're moving," Nymeria confirmed.

Arwen took the lead, Imani next to him. Nymeria walked behind, Halloran falling into step beside her, walking so close their hands brushed every time they took a step forward. They all continued down the road, walking precariously around the large hole in the road, bits of tarmac being pushed into the hole under their feet with every step. The swirling red abyss was an alluring sight, it pulled at her from the corner of her eyes, urging her to stand still and gaze into its endless void.

But whenever she would feel that pull, a loud voice in her brain and in her heart would scream at her. Scream that there was someone right now that needed her, someone she had to save, someone she wasn't going to run away from. That was all it took for her to put one foot in front of the other and keep moving.

Nymeria stumbled forward as she passed the hole, a chunk of tarmac giving way under foot. A scream sounded behind her, and without looking, Nymeria thrust her hand back and wrapped her fist around the material of Eleanor's shirt, throwing her forward. Eleanor stumbled, her braid slapping against Nymeria's arm. The ground where Eleanor had stood slipped away into the red hole, a pop and burst sounding where a water pipe now spewed water downward.

"Thank you." Eleanor's voice warbled.

"You need to be more switched on. I may not be able to save you next time," Nymeria said, voice cold and disinterested. It was not a threat, but if Eleanor slowed them down any more then Nymeria might consider leaving her behind.

"What are you going to do to my dad?" Eleanor blurted out, her eyes widening as if she hadn't meant to say that.

Nymeria slowed her walk and dropped Eleanor's hand, letting it fall limp until Eleanor cradled her wrist.

"I'm going to kill him," Nymeria stated.

Eleanor's eyes widened and she reached out to grab Nymeria. She pulled her arm back swiftly. The group stopped walking and the tension in the air grew even heavier.

"You can't."

"I have to."

"Why?"

"Look at all this." Nymeria threw her hands up, gesturing to the crumbling city. "He would rather condemn every life here to literal Hells than accept that times are changing."

"He can change."

"People like that can't."

"What if he can—" Eleanor pleaded, her voice cracking as her eyes brimmed with tears.

"He can't," Nymeria spat, her teeth grinding together.

"Easy," Arwen said, his voice low. "We need to keep moving." Nymeria could see Arwen, Imani and Halloran continuing to walk down the road from the corner of her eye.

Nymeria closed her eyes, breathing in deeply and out through her nose.

"I know the kind of man your father is. He won't be able to accept peace. He sees anyone different from him—looks or otherwise—as a threat to his security. Many things are changing but the fact that this world is 'kill or be killed' is not one of them. The only real thing changing is who will end up on top at the end." Nymeria felt a pang of hurt in her chest as she looked down at Eleanor's wobbling lip.

"But he's still my dad." Her voice cracked, on the verge of

a sob. "He's all I have now. I swear he's not a bad man, he's just sick."

Nymeria's eyes softened. Once, she would have defended Melantha in such a way, many years ago when her life as she knew it was a lie but much simpler too. Such was the curse of blind love.

"I'm sorry your dad is a bad man. I know what that's like." Nymeria's voice was much softer.

Eleanor wiped her eyes with her sleeve.

"But he has taken my girl from me. He plans to kill her. I'll burn this city down before I let that happen," she vowed. "I'm going to kill him. But I won't make you watch. You can head back home or you can come and help. Many people are going to need it."

Nymeria turned her back on Eleanor and left; she only took a few steps forward before she heard the pattering of smaller feet quickly follow behind her. Nymeria smiled; Eleanor had a good head on her shoulders.

30

The Mad Bishop And The Fallen Angel

The state of Ghenna was becoming worse and worse the further the group traversed towards the cathedral. The usually depilated cathedral now had a bright eerie red glow surrounding the sacred ground around it that made it look like the gothic abode of a vampire lord rather than a symbol of the dead Faith.

The holes in the road became more frequent and grew in size. Buildings and cars were being swallowed whole, and humans and half-demons alike screamed and wailed loudly; most running in any direction away from the holes, only to fall through a newly formed crack. Some chose to hide on top of buildings or behind cars. Others simply knelt on the ground and prayed, as if dead gods would save them.

The group had taken to jumping between the holes and cracks and when they couldn't jump they would climb across using anything they could find; cars on the verge of tipping into the Hells, billboards to shimmy across, partially destroyed buildings to climb through. But each step brought them closer to the looming cathedral—closer to Gen. Nymeria hadn't known when she had taken the leader role but the closer they got, the more she rushed forward, sprinting and jumping between rooftops, billboards and chunks of land as if she was flying again.

"Nymeria wait!" Imani's voice was lost to the chaos as Nymeria kept moving forward. She could make out the cathedral doors by now, just a few more moments and she would be there. She would save Gen, scoop her up into her arms and hold her so tight that she couldn't wriggle away. A deafening boom sounded from the cathedral and Nymeria fell flat on her back, her ears rang and she could feel the magic of the shockwave rattle her chest.

But she withstood the ringing and pressure in her chest that threatened to keep her pinned. Nymeria gritted her teeth and pushed herself up, rising to one knee. A second shockwave boomed from the church. She tensed all her muscles and hissed as it rocked through and past her. But she held firm, staggering forward. The small tarmacked island she was now on rose higher into the air, buildings and chunks of land falling into the gaping red abyss. Other chunks of land, vehicles and buildings rushed past her; she couldn't count how many people screamed as they fell. She couldn't tell if the ground was sinking into the Hells or if her platform was being lifted higher and higher into the sky.

Nymeria ignored the blood dripping down her nose and pooling on her lips, ignored the rattling of her ribs as her breath wheezed from her lungs. She put one foot in front of the other and kept moving forward.

"Nymeria!" a faint voice called for her.

She looked around but couldn't see anyone.

"Nymeria!"

She peered over the edge of the rocky island and below, leisurely hanging off the side of a fallen apartment building was Halloran.

Nymeria opened her mouth "Wh—"

"The others are helping some people get to safety. Imani is out of action. She can't breathe."

"Go help them."

"No."

Nymeria's lip curled almost into a snarl. "I wasn't asking you."

"Neither was I," he yelled back. He had that look in his eyes again, the one she hadn't quite been able to place—maybe because she hadn't wanted to. But now, there was no denying what it was.

"You can't take him on alone!" He was right, she knew that.

"I don't intend on fighting him with fists," she called back.

"Let me come with you—"

"There are a lot of people out there who need help. Go back to Arwen, he's gonna need someone to do his heavy lifting." Nymeria started to turn away.

"I don't care about any fucking person in this city except you, Arwen and Gen! If you die—"

"I won't." She peered down at him. "I promise."

Halloran's jaws clenched and he ground his teeth together.

"You really are a self-righteous hero." There was no real

venom in his words and the corner of Nymeria's mouth curled up into a smile.

"Perhaps I am," she admitted. Halloran started to climb away, back the way he came. "Halloran?"

"Yes?"

"Don't die. This city would become so much more boring without you." He paused, his lip parting and Nymeria cleared her throat. "After all, where would I find someone who loathes me as much?"

"Loathing is that what we're calling it?"

"Yes."

He laughed wholeheartedly, his chest shaking. "Fine. I'll stay alive and you get our girl back."

Nymeria hadn't needed any motivation to keep going. But Halloran had fuelled her with determination. She didn't need to just save Gen, she had to live afterwards. Nymeria sprinted forward, jumping between small floating islands of debris, running across pipes and displaced buildings, swinging off of broken telephone poles and sparking electrical wires. It was with one final swing off a fire escape ladder, landing in a controlled roll, that she reached the cathedral.

The wailing was loud when she was traversing the ruined city but now it was at its crescendo. The sound threatened to make her eardrums bleed. She placed both hands on the ancient iron doors and pushed, the door swinging inwards. Nymeria had expected to see many things; most of them were of Gen gutted or already dead. Thankfully she wasn't.

The space immediately in front of her, stretching to each side of the cathedral and stopping just short of the altar, was a large swirling vortex of red and amber, lightning sparking inside it. That pull to just stare at it was stronger now than ever. Candelabras, pews, shattered stained glass and marble columns all floated aimlessly in the space between Nymeria and Zai.

Zai was hovering over the altar, his tome floating above Gen as he muttered words Nymeria couldn't make out. Gen lay on the altar, rope around her torso keeping her tied down despite the fact she wasn't moving. Her eyes barely fluttered open, her skin sickly pale and her chest spasming as purple magic, sparking and undulating as if it wanted to return to its owner, flowed into the gas lantern device she had seen Alvaro and Cyrus wear. Out of the device, Gen's magic flowed to the tome, the magic turning from purple to an obnoxious gold.

Zai gave an exasperated sigh. "You can never let things move as intended, can you?"

Nymeria's teeth ground together and she took a few steps forward until she was right on the edge of the vortex.

"The Good Lady warned me you would interfere, 'that the cur can never lie and be patient, she must act like the wind gives chase.' Another thing I doubted The Good Lady about and another doubt I shall receive due punishment for."

"Whatever my sister will do won't be anything in comparison to what awaits you when I get my hands on you!" Nymeria seethed, eyeing the surroundings. There had to be a way for her to reach the other side.

"I couldn't understand it at first. Why such an esteemed,

devout angel as yourself fell. But as I spoke to you more and more, I began to realise why; you're filthy. Full of the sins of the flesh, the sin of cavorting with the unholy. You're disgusting. A shame to your very kind and a tarnish on your father's name." Nymeria felt her blood heat up with such fury it frightened her. Her blood called to her again: '*This pretender dare make a mockery, a fool of you, slander and tarnish your name and person, you have fought so valiantly to uphold the true will of the Faith. Show him who you are, daughter of Mercury.*' It almost felt like someone else was speaking to her, an unseen ally and that warm feeling that she should know, blossomed over her.

"The only sinner I've met is you."

Zai snarled, his lip curling up like a feral beast.

"Tell me, former Bishop, have you ever read the Codex?"

"Of course."

"Front to back?"

"Absolutely." His snarl dropped, and his brows knitted together.

"So you would know then that at its core, the Codex held all the key principles of the Creator. To teach you humans lessons on how you should live, and how you should treat each other. Then you should know that at its core—it teaches acceptance."

Zai's eyes widened and she could have sworn she saw a bead of sweat drip down his forehead.

"Acceptance of differences, so on and so on. As a holy man, you know this." She paused for a moment, the passages of the Codex burning to the forefront of her brain as if she had read it yesterday. "'And these words I beseech you are of the utmost consequence. That there be nothing so hideous and loathsome to I as a false god or false prophet. That if discovered, thou faithful shall afflict judgment post-haste.'" Nymeria couldn't tell if she was slightly disgusted or impressed that she could remember it all by heart.

"That's"—Zai licked his lips, his chest rising and falling quickly—"that is not what that means."

"Yes, it is. I can criticise the Creator for many things but he never minces his words when it comes to who the followers of the Faith should be targeting. It's never been about half-demons. You just don't like people who don't look like you, and you preach that as gospel. He was right to give you instructions on how to conduct yourselves. You're all far to stupid."

Nymeria took a few steps back. "You know the due punishments for false prophets." Her grin fell and her eyes narrowed. She had to focus.

Zai let out a scream of rage, his fist clenching and the purple magic that had been flowing into the device paused and retreated into Gen, who stirred on the altar. Zai drew back his arm and cast it forward, a series of gold-red chains thrusting over the vortex. Nymeria ran forward, leaping off the edge and onto one of the floating marble columns, stumbling. Zai's eyes widened in surprise and he jerked his arm again. Nymeria didn't waste time looking behind her, jumping from the column to a pew, almost losing balance when she landed. The sound of the column being obliterated behind her nearly threw her off balance, as well as pieces of marble skimming past her. She gripped the back of it tightly, her nails chipping into the wood.

Nymeria pulled herself back, coiled like a tightly wound spring and then surged. Jumping between the pews, clambering up and over marble columns, the chains striking behind her with each jump. Nymeria jumped to another and lost her footing. She spun wildly in a circle, arms failing until her hand caught onto one of the floating candelabras. Using the momentum, she pivoted in a loose-footed spin and hurled it like a javelin at Zai, the pointed sticks colliding into his ribs. Zai screamed and was launched backwards, sprawling flat on the ground, two of the three sticks lodged into his stomach.

Nymeria jumped and landed on solid ground, falling to her hands and knees as the curse took hold and black spots dotted her vision. But she couldn't afford to stay down for long. Nymeria rose to her feet and staggered next to the altar, right by Gen's head.

"Gen!" Nymeria's voice came out a choked panicked shout as she rushed to Gen's side, leaning over the altar. Her hands cradled Gen's head in her hands, like the girl was made of fine china.

"Gen? Can you hear me?" Nymeria brushed strands of messily cut hair out of her face; her face was so pale it almost looked translucent.

Gen's eyes slowly fluttered open, eyes which were once brown now a bright purple. With each blink, they turned back to their original colour, yet flecks of that mysterious purple remained.

Gen's eyes opened fully. A brief flash of panic crossed her features and then recognition, a childish sweet smile gracing her lips.

Gen's gaze darted to the side. She wailed and Nymeria felt a sharp searing pain in her thigh. She sank to one knee, looking over her shoulder to see a knife sticking out of the back of her thigh, streams of golden blood pooling onto the floor. Zai loomed over her, a deranged snarl on his lips, his eyes wide and hair dishevelled falling onto his forehead.

"The Faith and its teachings will always be whatever I want them to be," he seethed, placing a hand over his stomach which oozed blood.

"People don't want to have their opinion, their own thoughts. They just want to be told what to do, like sheep and I"—Zai raised the knife and Nymeria rose to both feet, leaning on the altar—"am the Good Lady's ordained Shepherd of this land."

Zai brought the knife down and Nymeria's hand shot out, grabbing his wrist and using every bit of rapidly fading strength to keep the blade away from her throat, the tip of it grazing her cheek. Zai screamed in outrage, spit flying from his mouth. Nymeria screamed back, a sound of hatred that came from a dark place deep within her gut. Her free hand jabbed out, punching him in the stomach, her fingers digging into the open flesh where the candelabra had struck him. Zai screamed in pain and doubled over, his grip slightly faltering on the knife. But that was all she needed. Nymeria's hand wrapped around the handle of the blade and the curse immediately took effect. She swung forward, aiming for his eye, but she knew she missed when spots overtook her vision and she heard a shocked gargle from Zai. She wrenched her arm to the side, slicing through skin and muscle.

Zai wailed in pain and Nymeria felt his presence move away, she blinked back the spots in her vision. Zai was cradling his cheek, blood spurting past his fingers and his eyes full of tears as he drew his hand away. The side of his mouth was completely exposed, she could even see his wisdom teeth. Nymeria smirked. *There goes that obnoxious award-winning smile.*

Nymeria huffed a laugh, her ribs rattling with effort.

"Now you look as you really are, a charlatan." She chuckled.

Zai breathed heavily between his clenched teeth and ran at her, fist held high as chains surged towards her. Nymeria held her arm out.

The chains never touched her as Zai ran into the outstretched knife, the blade embedded firmly in his sternum. Zai looked down, coughing up blood which splatted across Nymeria's face. Nymeria let out a shaky breath and hobbled to the side, dragging Zai with her and then threw her weight to the side, Zai tumbling over the edge and into the vortex.

Nymeria peered over the edge, Zai's body plummeting down and down until he was nothing but a blip and then vanishing entirely. Nymeria breathed heavily, placing one hand against her bloody leg, blood oozing between her fingers. She half lay on the altar as she cut the ropes of Gen's body. She didn't get all of them off before Gen wriggled free and wrapped her arms around Nymeria's neck in a grip so tight it could strangle her. Nymeria patted her back and Gen released her, her brown eyes full of tears and the purple flecks still present.

"Are you alright?"

Gen nodded.

"It's alright," Nymeria wheezed. "I've got you."

A tremendous rumble shook the building and the vortex expanded further. Nymeria rounded the altar, taking a few steps back. Gen scrambled towards Nymeria as the altar tipped into the glowing red light and Gen screamed as she fell.

"No!"

Nymeria launched herself forward, grabbing Gen's hand and the other hanging onto the edge of the hole. The swirling vortex beneath them nipped at their heels inviting, them down like a luring siren.

"Hang on!" Nymeria screamed. Gen clung to Nymeria's hand with two of her own, sobbing as her leg dangled uselessly behind her. Nymeria looked between Gen and the edge, her fingers losing their grip already. All of the floating objects had started to fall into the vortex, the ceiling above them cracking and showering debris down upon both of them. Nymeria had to act now.

"You gotta live okay?" Nymeria called to Gen. "Don't live for anyone else apart from yourself."

Nymeria used the last of her strength to swing Gen upwards letting go of her hand when she saw Gen tumble onto the floor.

She was safe, that was all Nymeria wanted. Her fingers lost their grip on the broken tiles and she fell backwards. Gen leaned over the edge, hand outstretched reaching as far as she could, a word falling from her lips that was devoured by the wailing vortex. But Nymeria knew what that word had been and a peaceful smile crossed her lips.

As long as Gen, Halloran, and the survivors of Ghenna were safe, that was all that mattered.

The wind whistled past Nymeria and the wailing grew louder and louder as she fell further down, struggling to keep her eyes open. The earlier crescendo was nothing compared to the deafening roar of thousands if not millions of trapped souls in the river. Her body turned and twisted as the winds picked up, chunks of marble and stained glass falling past her and into the river. Nymeria's eyes widened as she looked down: below her were a thousand arms in various states of decay, some fresh, others rotten and a few just bone. Their hands reached for her, eager to tear into her flesh. Nymeria could have sworn she saw tufts of blonde hair underneath some of the gnarled fingers. Nymeria grimaced, this was going to hurt. Her vision blurred and her consciousness slowly faded, as everything went dark.

* * *

"You're not dying, you stupid tempestuous woman! Never." A familiar voice broke the dark and quiet. Before Nymeria could question it or open her eyes, white lightning flooded her vision and a sharp electric shock over her chest jolted her upright. Nymeria gasped for air, hand over heart and she rolled onto her front coughing and spluttering.

A hand on her shoulder harshly turned her onto her back again and a rough hand caressed her cheek.

"Nymeria?" Halloran's harsh voice was overtaken by an unusual concern. Nymeria opened her eyes. The rising morning sun surrounded Halloran's face in a heavenly halo. Even when covered head to toe in dust, grime and blood he was the most beautiful man she had ever seen. Her eyes darted around as she took a few heavy gasps of air. They were on a slab of road resting securely on the ground, a few feet away from a lightless sinkhole, now just a permanent wound on Ghenna.

Halloran rolled his neck and grunted, draconic wings dissipating in a flash of white magic. "Are you hurt?" His voice was barely above a whisper.

"Yeah, but alive. You?"

He nodded and Nymeria felt her breath catch in her throat.

Slowly, Nymeria pressed her forehead against his. Halloran flinched back at first, a flash of confusion in his eyes before eventually leaning into it. Nymeria felt the tension of the night leave her body as the morning sunlight grew brighter and warmer, casting them both in the glow of living to see another day. They had done it. They had won. Nymeria wrapped her arms around him tightly, her fingers digging into his ruined vest and shirt. She sighed in relief as she felt his arms wrap around her waist, holding her like she would slip through his fingers.

"We did it," he muttered. "We're all alive."

Nymeria sighed in relief again.

An excited shout broke the silence and the two pulled away, Halloran's hand remaining firm on her waist. Gen barrelled between the two, her arms wrapping tightly around Halloran and he smiled, chuckling warmly, wrapping one arm around her to hug her back. Nymeria grinned and ran a hand through Gen's hair, de-tangling a few already present knots.

"We're all okay," Nymeria barely whispered. Gen twisted in Halloran's hold and leapt out of his arms, knocking Nymeria onto her back, pain shooting up her thigh.

"Ow, ow. Easy on the hugs." Nymeria winced and Gen clambered off her. Halloran pulled away and stood up, straightening out his shirt and vest.

"Let's go home." He crouched down, lifting Nymeria, one arm underneath her knees and the other supporting her back.

"You don't have to carry me." Nymeria wished she could sound more indignant but she was so tired she was on the verge of falling back asleep.

"I know."

"So you'll put me down?" Nymeria shifted in his hold but his grip only tightened.

"No. You've been stabbed in the thigh, you can't put weight on that leg and I'm not waiting for you to hobble along." His tone was back to harsh arrogance, one that she didn't mind too much now.

"Halloran—"

"Harlo. You can call me Harlo," he said, his eyes focused ahead as they walked. Only now did Nymeria notice they were outside the city, smoke rising from Ghenna a few miles away, the cathedral no longer in sight.

"Alright, then. Harlo." Nymeria looked down at Gen who grinned impishly at her and Nymeria shook her head. "If Arwen sees, I won't hear the end of it. Put me down before we see him?"

Halloran chuckled. "Deal."

TO BE CONTINUED

31

Epilogue

"Where could he have gone?" Nymeria grunted, hobbling on her stitched leg. Despite the wound being healed, the pain still lingered. Nymeria followed a wide-eyed and panicked Eleanor around the back of the Aligihieri estate and towards the gardens. Nymeria tensed as they passed the grand doors. Numerous moving out boxes surrounded the foyer and a few windows were already being boarded up.

"You got some place sorted?" Nymeria asked and Eleanor nodded, fiddling with the rosary around her neck.

"An apartment in the city. It wasn't too hard to find somewhere." She chuckled but the sound was forced. "Also it's not too far from the Hospital. I'm helping out as a trainee nurse."

"Good." Nymeria nodded. "People need all the help they can get."

As they passed the bushes and the pool came into view, Nymeria paused and held her arm. She could almost feel the slicing fangs of Caliban tearing through her flesh.

"When I first got back," Eleanor started, walking to the edge of the pool and fiddling with her rosary more intently, "I thought the cement had dragged him down. That he would have just drowned at the bottom."

Nymeria walked to the edge of the pool and looked inside. The pool had been drained, and the statue removed, but there was no Caliban.

"Shit." Nymeria sighed. This was just another issue, another pain in the arse to deal with. She had been run ragged trying to fix up the city alongside Arwen. A loose and vengeful werewolf was just another issue in an already swirling shitstorm.

"Do you think he'll come back here?"

"Maybe. If he does, he won't be looking for you." Nymeria's lips pulled into a frown. From the bag over her shoulder, she pulled out Zai's tome. Now just an old empty paged leather-bound book with a blazing sun covered by a sword and shield.

"Do you think they'll come back?" Eleanor asked quietly.

"My sister doesn't like losing. I'm certain she will."

Nymeria looked to the skies. They had been much brighter than usual over the past few days and unlike most people who saw it as a sign of good fortune ahead, it filled Nymeria with dread. Because she could see what they couldn't, the golden city of Elysium sitting atop the clouds. It was finally visible again from Ghenna.

"Melantha will come and we'll hold out as long as we can." Nymeria rolled up her sleeve and looked at the scars on her arms. "But if we want to survive, we'll need to even the odds."

"How?"

"We will need an angel. One at full strength."

About the Author

Alex Ockenden is Welsh-English but has lived in the South of England all her life. She graduated from Oxford Brookes University in Digital Media Production with a specialisation in scriptwriting and later went on to do a masters in Digital Marketing at Exeter University. 'All The Gods Are Dead' is her first published novel, and book one in a trilogy. When she isn't writing Alex is baking, playing video games or walking her dog in the deep woods in search of witches huts and fae traps.

Also by Alex Ockenden

The Sequel for 'All The Gods Are Dead' and Book 2 in the 'Daughters of Mercury' trilogy is coming soon!

www.ingramcontent.com/pod-product-compliance
Lightning Source LLC
LaVergne TN
LVHW010051110826
845155LV00028B/281

* 9 7 8 1 9 1 9 4 5 4 4 0 5 *